# UNLEASHED

Leland's eyes immediately sought out the third panel on the opposite wall—the panel that provided the only entrance through the fake wall behind his desk—the panel that was . . . standing wide open.

"No," Leland gasped. His heart thumped savagely—painfully. "No!" he shouted, throwing his cane across the room in a futile reaction. "Not them!" he shouted. Tears came to his eyes as his point of focus shifted from one empty cage to the next. They were all gone. *She* was gone.

For over twenty years, Leland had been trying to find an answer. During that time, he'd faced one failure after another, but the drive that continued to surge from deep within had kept him going . . . had made him keep trying. Now, Leland wondered if he had anything left to continue.

He couldn't tell anyone they'd been taken. The animals he'd used for his personal experiments weren't registered laboratory specimens; they'd been obtained on the illegal market, bought from two backwoods mountain men he'd never seen in the full light of day. To admit to possessing such animals for experimentation could bring about a stiff fine or even a prison sentence.

But neither punishment would be as severe as having the name of Patton Pharmaceutical Laboratories defaced. Leland refused to allow that to happen.

# HAUTALA'S HORROR—HOLD ON TO YOUR HEAD!

**MOONDEATH** (1844-4, $3.95/$4.95)
Cooper Falls is a small, quiet New Hampshire town, the kind you'd miss if you blinked an eye. But when darkness falls and the full moon rises, an uneasy feeling filters through the air; an unnerving foreboding that causes the skin to prickle and the body to tense.

**NIGHT STONE** (3030-4, $4.50/$5.50)
Their new house was a place of darkness and shadows, but with her secret doll, Beth was no longer afraid. For as she stared into the eyes of the wooden doll, she heard it call to her and felt the force of its evil power. And she knew it would tell her what she had to do.

**MOON WALKER** (2598-X, $4.50/$5.50)
No one in Dyer, Maine ever questioned the strange disappearances that plagued their town. And they never discussed the eerie figures seen harvesting the potato fields by day . . . the slow, lumbering hulks with expressionless features and a blood-chilling deadness behind their eyes.

**LITTLE BROTHERS** (2276-X, $3.95/$4.95)
It has been five years since Kip saw his mother horribly murdered by a blur of "little brown things." But the "little brothers" are about to emerge once again from their underground lair. Only this time there will be no escape for the young boy who witnessed their last feast!

*Available wherever paperbacks are sold, or order direct from the Publisher. Send cover price plus 50¢ per copy for mailing and handling to Zebra Books, Dept. 4034, 475 Park Avenue South, New York, N.Y. 10016. Residents of New York and Tennessee must include sales tax. DO NOT SEND CASH. For a free Zebra/Pinnacle catalog please write to the above address.*

# DANGEROUS NATURE
## T.J. KIRBY

**ZEBRA BOOKS**
**KENSINGTON PUBLISHING CORP.**

ZEBRA BOOKS

are published by

Kensington Publishing Corp.
475 Park Avenue South
New York, NY 10016

Copyright © 1993 by T. J. Kirby

All rights reserved. No part of this book may be reproduced in any form or by any means without the prior written consent of the Publisher, excepting brief quotes used in reviews.

Zebra, and the Z logo are trademarks of Kensington Publishing Corp.

If you purchased this book without a cover you should be aware that this book is stolen property. It was reported as "unsold and destroyed" to the Publisher and neither the Author nor the Publisher has received any payment for this "stripped book."

First Printing: January, 1993

Printed in the United States of America

*To
Chink and Phyllis
for your
Continued Support
and to the
SHS Class of '66*

# Prologue

*Portland, Oregon*

Lesley Shumaker climbed onto the seat and leaned forward to look out across the parking lot. Off in the distance, the faint glow of streetlights drew her attention to an intersection, but the crossroad was too far away to distinguish anything more than subtle movement. In turn, she knew anyone at the crossroad would be too far away to be able to see her . . . or to see what she and her friends were doing. For the moment, distance and darkness were their allies.

Exhaling a long breath that verged upon being a sigh, Lesley slipped the hood of her sweatshirt off her head as she leaned back in the seat. She combed her fingers through her hair, freeing a cascade of auburn waves over her shoulders, then she looked down at the small cage cradled on her lap. A smile brightened her childish face as she touched the white fur sticking out through the wire mesh. "It won't be much longer," she whispered to the eight mice huddled inside the cage. "Soon, you'll be free."

Lesley heard a grating sound behind her and turned on the seat to look toward the back of the panel van. "Are you about finished?" she asked in a loud whisper. Her question was answered by a cacophony of meows, barks, squeaks, growls, whimpers, and thumps. "Shhh!" she reprimanded the animals, crowded into cages, packed together tightly in the back. "You're going to attract attention, then we'll all be in a world of hurt."

She heard the back doors close, and a few seconds later, the door to the driver's side opened. A hooded figure slid onto the seat behind the steering wheel.

"Let's get outta here," Lesley said as she straightened in her seat and took a firm hold of the mice's cage.

"We're as good as gone," Lesley's companion assured her with a nod of his head.

The key was already in the ignition; with a quick turn, the engine started. The van pulled away from the university's lab facility. It was followed closely by another van and a pickup truck, each filled to capacity with rescued cargo.

*Rochester, New York*

"Vonda, for Christ's sake, get outta the way!"

Vonda Bertram sidestepped to her left, but instead of getting out of the way, she bumped into someone else, almost causing him to drop the cages he was carrying. She quickly stepped back to her right and immediately came face to face with yet another person who didn't have the time or the patience to tolerate her misdirection.

"Vonda, get— Jon . . . Jon, can't you do something with her?"

Jon Gregory looked up from the wooden stocks where he was unstrapping rabbits and transferring them to transportation crates. He glanced at Vonda, and an understanding smile crossed his lips. He, too, had been overcome—overwhelmed—

with awe the first time he'd been a part of an animal rescue mission; he could readily identify with Vonda's bewilderment.

"I could use some help here," he said, nodding toward the rabbits to his right, trying to coax her out of the mainstream of traffic.

Vonda looked at Jon, then stepped toward him almost without realizing what she was doing. "I've read about it, and I've seen gruesome pictures of animal experimentation, but . . . but I never thought it really existed. Not like this, anyway." She looked down the long line of rabbits that were waiting to be released, then shifted her attention to the open lab beyond that housed dozens more animals in various stages of confinement. "How can people be so cruel to something so cute and harmless as a furry animal?"

"People like you encourage it."

"What!" The word exploded across Vonda's lips. "How could—"

Jon reached toward Vonda's face and gently ran a finger over her eyelid. "You want to look beautiful," he said, showing her the lilac-tinted eye shadow that had rubbed off on his fingertip, "and the cosmetic companies want to make sure you can look that way without suffering any side effects that might have a bearing on their sales and profits. They can't afford to manufacture a product that might cause an infection or turn out to be even a simple eye irritant, so some of them still test products extensively in places like this," he said, motioning with his head and sweeping his eyes around the lab in a quick survey.

"On poor helpless creatures like these," Vonda said as she slid her hand down the back of a rabbit Jon had yet to release. After stroking the soft brown fur for a few seconds, she asked, "But this *isn't* as bad as it gets, is it?" Again, she looked down the row of confined rabbits, then out over the rest of the lab.

"Having powders and creams and liquids and sprays poked in their eyes, ears, noses, and mouths really isn't as bad as it could be for them, is it?"

Jon shook his head. "Unfortunately, a place like this is just the bottom rung of the torture ladder. In a lot of testing labs, conditions are a helluva lot worse than they are in here."

"It's not right," Vonda protested, looking down at the rabbit she continued to stroke. "It's just not right to treat animals like they're not living . . . *feeling* creatures."

"That's why we're here," Jon reminded her. "That's why our organization was founded, and that's why you elected to join us—"

"We're all gonna be here *too* long unless you two get a move on," a stern voice said behind them. "I'd bet a year's pay a silent alarm has already alerted the cops we're here." He made a passing glance at his watch. "We've gotta be outta here and long gone in five minutes or less, or our asses'll be cooked."

"We'll make it," Vonda assured him as she began unstrapping the rabbit she'd been petting. "We'll have every last animal out of here in just a few more minutes." After she released him, Vonda lifted the rabbit to her chest and hugged it close. "This is going to be the best Easter you've ever had," she whispered into its long, slender ears. "In just a few more hours, we'll take you and all your friends here out in the country and set you . . . free."

*Minneapolis, Minnesota*

"Hey there, little fella." Penny Copenhaver slipped her hand through the cage's open door and offered her forefinger to the rhesus monkey strapped to the rack inside.

At first, the monkey's eyes widened with fear, and he tried to withdraw; he attempted to press his body back against the rack as much as his restraints would allow, trying to stay beyond her reach. But when Penny finally touched him and began to stroke the back of his paw, the monkey seemed to sense she had not come to harm him, and his body relaxed.

"It's going to be all right," Penny whispered. She continued to stroke the monkey's paw as her eyes shifted from the Medusa-like headdress of electrodes implanted in his brain . . . to the large patches of raw skin where his fur had been brutally burned away . . . to the unhealed incision on the front of his throat. His vocal cords had been severed to spare his tormentors the agony of his screams. "Before long, it'll *all* be over." Penny fought the lump growing in her throat and struggled to keep tears of compassion from brimming past her dark lashes, but her efforts to remain emotionally neutral failed.

The monkey studied Penny with his big brown eyes and watched the finger that continued to stroke the back of his paw. He liked the touch. It was the only touch he could ever remember, coming from a human, that hadn't been accompanied by pain.

He opened his mouth as if to tell her of his pleasure, but a wisp of soundless air was the only note to pass over his lips. Unable to communicate in any other way, the monkey wrapped his small paw around Penny's finger and squeezed it. Words could not have relayed his thoughts any more precisely.

"He's the last one."

Penny looked over her shoulder to see Lee Pedlow standing behind her. She glanced from his hazel eyes to the hypodermic needle in his hand.

"Couldn't we take this one with us?" she asked, looking again into Lee's eyes, then turning back to the monkey. "He seems to be so aware of everything—"

"You know we can't do that. You know as well as I do that the instant we would detach the electrodes, it would be the beginning of a slow and agonizing death for him. He'll be much better off if we stick to our regular procedure for this type of situation."

"I know you're right," Penny said, looking into the monkey's dark eyes as she continued to stroke his paw with her thumb.

*In this type of situation,* she thought. *Euthanasia . . . the act of causing death painlessly, so as to end suffering.* Webster had said it so eloquently.

"They won't be able to hurt you any more," Penny whispered. She saw the monkey's eyes shift from her to Lee Pedlow. She guessed it was watching Lee insert the hypodermic needle into one of the thin tubes that disappeared into the monkey's skull alongside the electrode probes. "They won't be able to hurt you any more," she repeated. The monkey's eyes returned to meet hers. "You won't have to suffer through any more of their horrifying experiments. Soon, you'll be free. . . ."

Penny swallowed hard. She continued to watch the monkey's dark eyes until the essence of life being transmitted there . . . vanished . . . and his paw loosened from around her finger.


*Key West, Florida*

Marsha Wycoff glanced at her watch, then looked across the moonlit water toward shore. "I don't like it. It's taking too long." She walked toward the bow of the boat, her eyes constantly scanning the rippling surface in the distance. She was looking for a sign—any sign—of an orange-painted snorkel tip that would indicate the divers had returned.

"I'm not worried yet," Stan Bellows said, glancing at his own watch, then again looking toward shore. "They're still well within the time frame." He joined Marsha at the bow. "I'd say we can give them at least another half hour or so before we should start to be concerned."

"But it's a military operation—"

"And we had some darn good inside information," Stan tried to assure her as he laid his hand on her shoulder and squeezed it gently. "Don't let yourself get worked up—"

"Look!" Marsha's arm jerked out in front of her as she pointed across the water. "Can you see it? Out there. Something's shimmering in the moonlight. Could it be—" Suddenly, the air was filled with the calls of bottlenose dolphins. "It's them! They made it!" Marsha smiled—laughed—as she watched the dolphins jump playfully and circle the boat, then she shifted her attention to the four divers who had surfaced some twenty yards away. "They made it," she whispered with a sigh of relief.

"None of us have made it yet," Stan cautioned as he lowered a rope ladder over the side and steadied it for the divers. "We still have to get everybody on board and get out of here without getting caught. The instant the Navy discovers their prize experimental dolphins are gone, all hell's going to break loose around here."

*Albuquerque, New Mexico*

Maurice Coy stood just inside the doorway, looking over the empty cages spread throughout the lab. All of the animals, once held captive there, had been removed and loaded onto trucks and vans; most were already being transported, on their way to freedom.

He nodded, and a smile of accomplishment brightened

his bearded face as he turned to leave. But something—someone—just barely visible through the lab office's partially open door, attracted his attention.

At first, he was apprehensive about a confrontation, but then he realized that whoever was in the office had to be someone from his own team. Whoever it was was wasting time clearing the area, and Maurice was none too happy that his orders to evacuate had not been strictly followed.

"What are you doing in here?" Maurice demanded as he yanked the office door open.

Carmen Hadley looked up from the notebook she held open in her hands but didn't appear to be startled by Maurice's abrupt entrance. "What's Duckett's disease?" she asked.

"I don't know," Maurice answered flatly.

"And what's cryp-tos-por-idium?" she asked, trying to sound out the scientific word she was reading from the notebook.

"I don't know," Maurice repeated.

Carmen was silent for a moment, then she closed the notebook and returned it to the desk where she'd found it. "Could we be making a mistake?"

"A mistake? How? By freeing laboratory animals that are being tortured? No way," Maurice stated adamantly, shaking his head. "Animal rights is the cause of the nineties, and we're getting in on the ground floor of it."

"But what if some of the animals we release into the wild have been infected with . . . with this Duckett's disease or . . . or this crypto-whatever-it-is or with something else that maybe there's no cure for yet. Have you—have *any* of us—ever really stopped to think about what could happen? What could happen if infected animals interact with the native wildlife?" Carmen paused as if to think, but it was mostly for the silent effect. "What could happen if an infected animal came in contact with people? Have you ever thought about that?"

"Sure . . . I've thought about it," Maurice said as he turned toward the office door and looked out into the lab. "I've thought about it off and on," he repeated as he tilted his head to look at Carmen over his shoulder, "and we just have to hope that something like that never happens. . . ."

# Friday

## (Day One)

*5:12 A.M.*

Leland Wagner reached for his cane as he leaned diagonally across the car seat and supported himself on his elbow. The position was awkward, but it allowed sufficient room for him to shift his artificial leg out from under the dash and swing it out the door.

A precisely tossed enemy hand grenade had robbed Leland of his left leg while he'd been a radio operator during the Korean conflict. Less than a month after he'd been shipped out—six months and seventeen days after his eighteenth birthday—he was flown back to the States where he underwent extensive surgery and rehabilitation. As soon as the stump of his leg healed, and he was ready to learn to walk again, his lost limb was replaced by a bulky wooden one. At the time, it was the best the government could offer.

For thirty-nine years, Leland had tolerated the ill-fitted extremity as if it were a badge to remind him of the past. Now, even though technology had improved and he could easily afford a more sophisticated prosthesis, he wouldn't even consider a new one. Inwardly, he sensed any change that might bring him comfort would also affect the tireless drive that surged from deep within him. Nothing was going to affect that drive; nothing was going to stop him from trudging on from one experiment to the next. He knew, sooner or later, he would find the end results he'd been searching for for almost twenty years. One of these days it would happen . . . as long as his motivation remained high.

Leland shifted his weight toward the seat's outer edge, grabbed the edges of the doorframe with both hands, pulled himself forward, and stood. He stepped away from the car, turned and closed the door, then nestled the hand-carved hickory cane under his arm as if it were a riding crop. He rarely used the cane unless he became fatigued; like the wooden leg, he kept it with him as a reminder.

Walking in a teetering gait, his weight shifting from his real leg to his wooden one and back again, Leland crossed the narrow parking lot, ascended the ramp beside the concrete stairs leading to the entrance walk, then turned onto the sidewalk itself. He was progressing along his route just as he did every morning, then, in sharp contrast to his daily routine, Leland slowed his pace. Fifteen feet from the front door, he stopped. Something didn't seem quite right.

He tilted his head back, his face angled upward, and his blue eyes began to scan almost methodically from left to right and back again. The amber glass panels fronting the three-story building in front of him reflected a predawn glow; the sun had yet to crest the horizon behind him. Subconsciously, he focused on the black letters, mounted above the entrance's arched canopy, that formed the words: PATTON PHARMACEUTICAL LABORATORIES.

Leland shifted his attention from the building to the dense stand of trees off to the right. He eyed the oaks, maples, pines, and firs curiously, then cocked his head at an angle . . . and listened. Nothing. Silence.

The silence. *That* was what had attracted his attention; *that* was what seemed to be so wrong on an otherwise typical morning.

Where were the morning songbirds that usually announced his arrival? An even more distressing concern came to him. Where were the sounds of the laboratory animals that daily heralded his approach?

Leland's eyes sought out the kennel runs barely visible beyond the back corner of the building. Where were— He saw one open door . . . two—

"No," Leland exhaled in a whispered plea. His attention returned to the front of the building, and his eyes shot toward the door . . . to the front door that stood barely ajar. "No!"

Leland's heart pounded out a half-dozen fierce beats, then it seemed to all but stop as he took his next step. Hurrying as fast as his wooden leg allowed, he half-hopped/half-skipped the rest of the way up the walk.

When he reached the entrance, Leland grabbed the door's handle and yanked it open. Two steps carried him into the narrow tiled entryway; a dozen more steps placed him beneath the archway to the carpeted lobby. The instant he saw the overturned furniture and spray-painted walls, he froze, realizing the reality of his feared speculation.

*MURDERER! BUTCHER! SCUM!*

The words, scrawled in red, all but jumped off the white walls at him. For effect, the paint had been applied much too heavily, causing it to run, resembling streamers and rivulets of blood dangling from the bottom of almost every letter.

Leland's eyes darted around the room, from the words on the walls to the overturned furniture to the security guard's vacant desk. "George?" Leland called as he walked into the heart of the lobby. He stopped to pick up a chair, and looked behind a sofa that had been stripped of its cushions. "George?" he repeated as he continued toward the desk George Beals normally occupied. Leland checked behind the desk and found no one.

After giving the lobby an additional quick survey, Leland turned toward the main hall that led to the ground-floor labs. These walls, too, had been spray-painted with red and—

Something thumped. Leland's heart skipped a beat in response.

He listened . . . waited. Something thumped again . . . and again. The sound seemed to be coming from somewhere further down the hall—

*Thump! . . . Thump! . . . Thump!* And it sounded as if someone was mumbling . . . as if someone was gagged and trying to speak.

"George?" Leland asked in a loud whisper as he took a couple of guarded steps toward the first door to his left. "George?" His summons was answered by three more quick thumps.

Leland grasped the knob firmly, hesitated, then turned it slowly and pulled the door open. The light from the hallway showered into the small closet, highlighting George Beals.

The night security guard lay on the floor on his side, his knees drawn up to his chest. His hands were tied behind him with white rope; the ends of the rope were wrapped around his ankles and secured there. Some type of cloth was wound around the lower part of his face; it worked as a gag to muffle any sound he tried to utter. George's gray eyes peeked over the top of the wide gag, looking up at Leland, relaying his impatience to be set free.

"What happened?" Leland asked as he lowered himself to the floor to assist George. Leland spoke the question, but he had a gut feeling he already knew the answer.

"Break-in," George answered after the gag was slipped down from his mouth.

"An animal rights group?" Leland speculated as he worked to loosen the rope holding George.

"That'd be my guess."

"Did you get a good look at any of them?" Leland asked anxiously. "If the police caught them, could you pick them out of a lineup?"

"No," George answered, impatiently trying to work his hands free. "They all had on hoods and masks."

"When did it happen?"

"Sometime around two. I'd just finished with my lunch break when . . ."

Leland didn't hear the rest of what George had to say. His attention turned to the labs . . . to the animals that might have been stolen . . . and to the projects that might have been interrupted or nullified. The projects. . . .

Using his cane for support, Leland pushed himself up to his feet and started down the long hall. Because he knew George was watching him, Leland stopped at the door to the first lab, pushed it open, and looked inside. He shook his head and pretended to contemplate the room with concern, but in all honesty, he barely noticed the spray-painted words *Nazi* and *Assassin* adorning the walls, nor did he take note of the expensive equipment that had been shattered on the floor. His thoughts were elsewhere, but Leland knew he had to convince George he was concerned about every aspect of the break-in.

"I'll call the police." George's voice rebounded off the hallway walls. Without even looking in George's direction, Leland nodded and acknowledged the comment with a halfhearted wave of his hand.

Leland continued to play the role of a concerned senior executive as he opened the doors to labs two, three, and four. He hesitated at each just long enough to appear interested as to what had occurred inside, then he walked on.

As he approached the end of the hall, Leland slipped his right hand into his front pants pocket and pulled out a circular key ring bearing four keys. When he came to the elevator beside the rear exit leading to the loading docks, he stopped, slipped the hexagonal-shaped key into its appropriate slot in the wall, then pressed the recessed button directly above it. Almost instantly, the doors to the elevator opened, and Leland stepped inside.

He pressed the numbered button for the third floor, then leaned against the side of the elevator's cab. Leland closed his eyes in apprehension; then, in frustration, he began to tap his cane against the shin of his wooden leg. "Let them be safe," he whispered in a heartfelt prayer. "Please, dear Lord, let them be safe."

The elevator's precision mechanism rocked him gently when it stopped on the third floor. Leland opened his eyes just as the doors began to slide apart; he stepped out into the hall even before they came to a stop on either side of the cab.

Leland walked past two doors on his right and one on his left. Whether the rooms there had been broken into or not didn't matter; their contents held no importance for him. He stopped in front of the second door on the left, hurriedly slipped the only gold key from his key ring into the lock, turned it, and opened the door to his office.

His eyes immediately sought out the third panel on the opposite wall—the panel that provided the only entrance through the fake wall behind his desk—the panel that was . . . standing wide open.

"No," Leland gasped. His heart thumped savagely—painfully—then it felt as if it sank to the bottom of his toes. "No!" he shouted, throwing his cane across the room in a futile reaction. "Not them!" he shouted. "Not them . . ." he pleaded helplessly. "Take any of the others, but not them! They were my life. She was my hope . . ."

Leland all but staggered to the leather chair behind his desk and slumped down into its soft cushions. "How could they have known?" he questioned in despair. Leland sat there for several moments in dumbfounded silence, then, pushing against the floor with his real foot, he slowly swiveled the chair around until it faced the open panel . . . and the secret room beyond.

Tears came to his eyes as his point of focus shifted from one empty cage to the next. They were all gone. *She* was gone.

For over twenty years, Leland had been trying to find an answer . . . for twenty long years. During that time, he'd faced one failure after another, but the drive that continued to surge from deep within had kept him going . . . had made him keep trying. Now, Leland wondered if he had anything left to continue.

"It would almost be like starting over," he muttered to himself in exasperation. "And you," he said, looking at the empty cage of the single animal he'd injected with his newest serum. "I wish I could have at least gotten a blood sample from you. You could have held the key." He continued to focus on the cage that had housed a brown and beige puppy with a white-tipped tail. "You could have been the one to make the difference. But now, I'll never know whether the serum—"

Serum. *Serums!* The old serums!

"Oh, dear God—" Leland took in a quick breath as he focused on the desktop-size refrigerator wedged beneath a shelf in the far corner of the small room. He'd never gotten around to throwing away the old serums from several of his bygone experiments, serums that should have been destroyed with the unfortunate animals that had suffered disastrously from their effects.

And just how long had some of the serums been in there? Two . . . three . . . four years or more? They had been dangerous enough when they were new; what effects might age have had on the formulas?

"Hopefully, that's one thing I won't have to worry about," Leland said, eyeing the refrigerator but not expending the energy to go see if, indeed, any of the old serums had been taken. "If they took any of the serum, surely they'll destroy it," he said confidently. "If they think, even in the remotest way, it had anything to do with animal experimentation, they'll destroy it. I know they will—"

The phone rang on the desk beside him. Leland turned slowly in his chair, eyed the phone as it rang three more times, then he answered it. "Yes."

"I've called the police, and they're on their way," the security guard said.

"Thank you, George."

"Is everything okay upstairs?"

Leland turned the chair back around and looked into the secret room. He swallowed hard, then said, "It appears they just wanted the lab animals."

"No damage upstairs then."

Leland continued to eye the empty cages as he said, "No . . . no damage." The words all but caught in his throat.

Leland couldn't tell George his animals had been taken; he couldn't tell anyone. The animals he'd used for his personal experiments weren't registered laboratory specimens; they'd been obtained on the illegal market, bought from two backwoods mountain men he'd never seen in the full light of day. To admit possessing such animals for experimentation could bring about a stiff fine or possibly even a prison sentence.

But neither punishment would be as severe as having the name of Patton Pharmaceutical Laboratories defaced. Leland refused to allow that to happen. Daniel Jerome Patton the Third had gone against his father's wishes in allowing Leland to proceed with his personal experiments, and Leland would never, knowingly, do anything to betray the trust of his benefactor—even though his benefactor had been dead now for over a year and a half.

"No damage," Leland repeated as he leaned forward in his chair and pulled the panel closed, putting an end to his eye's access to the empty cages. "Call me when the police arrive, and I'll come down to talk with them."

Leland returned the phone to its cradle and swiveled the chair around to face the heart of his office. His eyes drifted across the room to twin, black-painted aluminum stands, each supporting a twenty-nine-gallon aquarium. The container on the left was empty; the animal rights people had taken the lizards, chameleons, and annelids that had called the sand-bottomed terrarium home. The aquarium on the right still contained a host of starfish and sea cucumbers; it didn't appear as if anything had been disturbed. Evidently, whoever had invaded Leland's office hadn't come prepared for an aquatic transfer.

His attention shifted to a thick, well-worn, blue-covered notebook that lay atop one of the four-drawer filing cabinets lining the wall beside the hallway door. The notebook was barely visible because of the printout papers he'd laid on top of it the night before; if anyone didn't know of its existence, it would be difficult to locate. But Leland knew it was there; the notebook had been returned to the same spot every night for over twenty years.

"Maybe I'll give it a rest for a while," he said softly, his eyes focusing intently on the barely visible spine of the notebook. "My notes will always be there, and after all of this blows over in a few months, maybe I'll have the heart to try again." He leaned back in the chair, settled his elbows on the armrests, and tented his fingers together in front of him. "But I'll always be curious," he said, looking back at the starfish. "I'll always wonder just how this last one might have turned out."

## 5:17 A.M.

Barry Robbins twisted Milton Hawkins's right arm behind his back, then applied enough leverage to force the man to the ground. As he knelt and placed a knee firmly in the middle of his prisoner's back, Robbins was unaware Hawkins's bearded left cheek slid across—and then dug into—a liberal pile of rain-softened manure. Had he been aware of the fact, Robbins might have *accidentally* rubbed his prisoner's face back and forth across the ground several more times.

Robbins didn't dislike Hawkins personally; he barely knew the man. He did despise what the backwoods man from the Kentucky hills stood for.

During his fourteen years with Indiana's Dearborn County sheriff's department, Robbins had helped apprehend lawbreakers ranging from murderers and bank robbers to kidnappers and rapists. He'd come face to face with just about every classification of felon on record and, with the exception of cases involving child abuse and molestation, he'd been able to walk away from every case with his emotional status unscathed.

He had learned to deal with the injustices he saw man force upon his fellow man; for the most part, he could go to bed at night and not let the events of the day play havoc with his dreams. What Barry Robbins had not yet learned to master were the deep-down gut emotions that were yanked savagely to the surface every time he witnessed man's inhumane treatment of animals. On days like today, when he helped neighboring conservation officers apprehend poachers and illegal trappers, he could almost be assured of a restless night, tossing and turning in his sleep.

On days like today, he struggled with his own humanity. He struggled to keep himself from sinking to the same depths as the men he had come to arrest; he struggled to keep from giving *them* a taste of the cruelty they'd forced upon the captured animals. Sometimes, it was hard . . . hard to remember he had come there to help uphold the law.

Robbins closed his handcuffs around Hawkins's scrawny wrists. Unconsciously, he applied a little extra pressure to make sure the metal teeth caught one extra notch, tightening steel against bone. Unconsciously—or not—he failed to respond when Hawkins grunted in protest.

"Bastard scum," a young voice said. "They ought to be sentenced to the same kind of existence they've forced on those poor animals."

Robbins looked up to see Freddie Anderson towering above him. The raid this morning, to the mountain men's summer quarters, was the conservation deputy's first; the rookie, of less than three weeks, had yet to learn the elements of tact and public self-control. He still expressed his opinion much too freely and allowed his emotions to govern his common sense. Anderson reminded Robbins of himself when he had been a rookie and, if for no other reason than that, Robbins liked him.

"I doubt if the judge'll see it that way."

"Then somebody ought to rewrite the guidelines for sentencing. Let the punishment be determined by the crime," Anderson added adamantly.

"You won't get an argument out of me."

Robbins stood up, brushed leaves and dirt from his shirt and jeans, then looked down at Milton Hawkins and shook his head. The mountain man's faded flannel shirt and bib overalls were covered with filth; they reeked from a stench far greater than any animal would have tolerated in its natural environment.

Yes, deep down inside, Robbins could almost agree with Anderson. If he could have overlooked the fact that he was a law officer—if he could have had *his* way with the prisoner—

he might have split the man open from collarbone to crotch, pulled his guts out on the ground for the dogs to eat, then skinned the hide from the still-pulsing muscles and hung it on the side of the shack where Hawkins and his partner had already mounted twenty-seven illegally obtained pelts.

Yes, if he could have had his way, then . . . then . . . he wouldn't be any more rational than the young rookie standing beside him, and he would have been no better than the men he'd come to arrest.

"It looks like it's just the two of 'em up here with their families," Kevin McFall said as he stepped up behind Robbins and Anderson. A note of disappointment hung heavily on the veteran deputy's words. During his twenty-three years as a Kentucky conservation officer, he had longed for the ultimate *big bust*; it looked like he would have to wait awhile longer.

"What are we going to do about them?" Robbins asked, nodding toward the two women and nine children who had been corralled on the sloping porch of a rundown tar-paper shack not more than thirty feet away. He couldn't remember the last time he'd seen such a pitiful sight.

He focused on the group as a whole, then his eyes shifted from one face to the next . . . from sunken, hollow eyes . . . to tear-streaked dirty cheeks . . . to runny noses and crusted snot . . .

"Not a whole lot we can do with 'em," McFall answered.

. . . from tattered shirts . . . to patched jeans . . . to scabbed knees and callused feet . . . to holey socks and stringless shoes . . .

"The women . . . hell, they're innocent enough. Sure, they may know how their menfolk make a livin', but I'll lay odds they're not directly involved in it. That's not the mountain way. The womenfolk, it's their job to cook and wash and tend to the house and kids and all, and their menfolk, they bring home what little house-money they don't guzzle down in whiskey or stash away in some stronghold somewhere." McFall shook his head in sympathy. "It really amazes me how some of them mountain womenfolk get by."

. . . from torn, wornout, oversized dresses . . . to drooping panties . . . to diapers so filthy a dozen washings in concentrated bleach wouldn't even begin to brighten them to a dingy gray . . .

"And the kids there, they're all under age. Hell, you've heard the same old song and dance as often as I have. Welfare can't cut it. There ain't enough money or foster homes to even begin to handle the load we could haul down from outta these here mountains."

. . . from a sucked thumb . . . to a picked nose . . . to a dark-eyed, long-lashed little girl tightly clutching a hound dog's frayed rope leash . . . to a five-year-old boy with no front teeth, smiling and flipping him the bird—

"We can't get 'em now, but I'll bet in ten to fifteen years—at most—we'll have ever' one of them male young 'uns there all behind bars just like their pappies. Poachin' 'n' trappin' are a family business up here in the hills, and I'll lay odds ever' one of them young 'uns has already learned to set a snare. I'd even bet that even though neither one of them oldest boys there has seen thirteen, they both had a hand in skinnin' some of them pelts hangin' on the shed over yonder."

Robbins shook his head and looked at McFall in disbelief, but he knew the veteran officer could state the facts and make the predictions; Kevin McFall had had firsthand experience. The son of an Appalachian mountain man, he too had learned the "family business" by age thirteen. Had an outbreak of smallpox not swept through his family, killing his father, mother, one sister, and two brothers, he and his surviving sister would have never left the mountains to live with an aunt outside of Corbin, Kentucky, and today, he might be the one *doing* the illegal trapping instead of being the officer going after those who were.

"Let's go, Hawkins." McFall leaned over and grabbed the back of the prisoner's overalls and picked up a handful of flannel shirt in the process. With one smooth flex of his muscled arms, McFall lifted the lean man onto his feet and nudged him, none too gently, in the direction of his accomplice.

As they approached the fallen tree trunk where the deputies had cuffed the other trapper, Forrest Deem, McFall gave Hawkins a shove that sent him flailing. But the gangly man struggled to maintain his balance and somehow managed to turn around just as his legs scraped against the log's rough bark. Hawkins emitted a grunt as he sat down hard beside his partner.

"Now don't them two fellas there make one fi-i-i-i-ne lookin' pair," McFall drawled, intentionally overemphasizing the deep southern accent he normally attempted to subdue. "Why, they're just like Sprat and Fat," he quipped, glancing from Hawkins, who looked as if he could be suffering from malnutrition and rickets, to Deem, who definitely showed no signs of ever having missed a meal. Both men looked up at McFall and grinned spitefully, baring rotted teeth that were chipped and discolored from tobacco.

"You still got that same cook at the jail?" Deem asked in a lazy drawl. "I 'member the food there was mighty good—"

"McFall," someone called from behind them, "you better come over here and see what else we've found."

Kevin McFall turned around and looked at Larry Martlage, who was motioning for him from the edge of the woods. He glanced at Robbins and Anderson, then shook his head. "I can tell you right now, I'm not gonna like this—whatever it is." All traces of humor vanished from his voice; the words hung thickly, coated with dread. "Damn poachers," he swore as he started toward Martlage.

Freddie Anderson took off after McFall, following almost as closely as a shadow. Robbins hesitated until the two of them had a good four- to five-yard lead, then he followed. If whatever awaited them in the woods was something McFall wasn't going to like, then Robbins knew *he* would like it even less. In his line of work, he'd gotten used to seeing the human body ravaged, but he'd not yet become accustomed to seeing animals—

"Holy shit!" Anderson blurted out, his hand rising in a reflex action to cover his nose and mouth. Robbins stopped, still a good ten feet behind Anderson, beginning to pick up on the stench that had prompted the rookie's harsh reaction.

"Holding pens?" McFall asked as he continued toward Martlage.

*Holding pens.* The very thought sent a sickening tingle racing down Robbins's spine. Holding pens meant live—or at least *semi*-live—animals, animals that would be used as bait for training dogs to hunt or sold to unscrupulous entrepreneurs, their vital organs the prime ingredients for potions and elixirs that held no more magic than to fill the seller's pockets with money. At best, the animals would be sold to laboratories for experimentation.

Barry Robbins had only come across a half-dozen holding pens during his work with the Kentucky-based conservation officers. Those few contacts had led him quickly to believe that the animals being held in those pens would most assuredly have preferred death.

"Bastard scum," Anderson mumbled through his hand, loud enough for everyone to hear.

McFall stopped at the edge of the woods and made a sweeping glance along the row of makeshift cages that had been fashioned out of sticks and limbs and rotted boards, held together with string and wire and an occasional nail that protruded menacingly into the heart of the cage. Again, he shook his head in disgust. "Survivors?" he asked, almost wishing, for the animals' sakes, there were none.

"Maybe a third of them." Martlage paused. "It looks like some of them may have been here a pretty good while." McFall cocked his head to one side, the action silently asking what had prompted Martlage's speculation. "One of the cages down at the far end," he said, nodding in the direction. "There's a skinny ol' raccoon in it and what looks like the . . . the half-eaten remains of two or three little ones. My guess is, she turned cannibal on her own offspring just to survive—"

"When is it gonna end?" McFall questioned, again shaking his head.

"When we find out who's behind it," Freddie Anderson answered confidently as if his statement represented a totally new revelation that had never crossed the minds of his predecessors. "If we can find the buyers and lock them away, then there wouldn't be a market for the scumbags we've got here." Anderson turned on his heels and walked straight toward the log where the two prisoners sat. "Who's paying you?" he yelled at Forrest Deem as he approached. When he was close enough, the young officer grabbed the front of the trapper's flannel shirt and tried to pull him to his feet. "Who's paying you to trap live animals?" The shirt's worn fabric couldn't withstand Anderson's forceful yank, and in a matter of seconds, he held nothing more than torn strips of faded red and green flannel plaid.

Forrest Deem looked up at Anderson and flashed a grin of half-rotted teeth. Milton Hawkins chuckled beside him.

"You bastard scum ingrates." Anderson raised his arm, preparing to backhand Deem across the face, but McFall intervened, grabbing Anderson by the wrist.

"Get these two degenerates outta here before one of us does

somethin' that might put *us* behind bars instead of them," McFall ordered, nodding to a deputy standing a few feet away. "Anderson," he said, trying to bring a calmness to his voice as he turned the rookie toward him. "Granted, what we've seen here is bad, but you've gotta learn to control yourself. Goin' off half-cocked won't solve anything."

Freddie Anderson looked into McFall's weathered face. After a few seconds of silence, he nodded. "I know. It's just that this whole damn business of theirs sucks."

"That it does, my boy, that it does. But doin' what you were about to do won't make it any better. Truth is, it'd probably only make things worse."

"Guess I've got a lot to learn, don't I?" Anderson said sheepishly.

"You'll do just fine." McFall released the rookie's wrist, then touched him lightly on the shoulder. "Do you think you and a couple deputies can get those two back to town without killin' 'em?"

"Yes, sir."

"Then do it. Barry and me'll finish things up here."

Anderson nodded, then started toward the dirt path leading to the van where the deputies had taken the two prisoners. As McFall watched him walk away, he sidestepped closer to Robbins.

"Cocky little bastard," he said out of the side of his mouth. "Reminds me of another cocky bastard I met some ten to fifteen years ago."

"*That* cocky bastard turned out all right."

"That you did, my boy, that you did." McFall continued to watch Anderson until he turned onto the road and disappeared behind the trees. "And so will he."

McFall glanced toward Martlage, who still stood at the edge of the woods, then looked back at Robbins. "Do you think you can stand the stench long enough to help get those poor critters loaded onto the truck so we can take 'em to the compound?"

"I guess that's one of the reasons I came along."

"Then let's get at it." McFall and Robbins took several steps toward the woods, then McFall looked at Robbins and grinned. "Another reason you came along wouldn't have been to have an excuse to see Jackie, would it?"

"I don't need an excuse," Barry answered, returning McFall's grin, "but I kind of figured we might be making a trip to the compound before the morning was over."

"I thought so." McFall walked on a little farther, then asked, "So when are you gonna make an honest woman outta Jackie?"

Barry looked at him and smiled. "Just as soon as she'll let me."

*6:47 A.M.*

"No, I haven't changed my mind about going to the Governor's Ball with you." Jackie Mitchell finished scooping grain into the bucket she balanced on a shelf beside the feed barrel, then slid the barrel's lid in place. She picked up the bucket and turned to walk out of the feed barn, but Dan Patton stepped directly in front of her and blocked her exit.

She looked up into his emerald-green eyes, held his gaze for a moment, then stepped to the side, intending to go around him. He immediately countered her move, sidestepping in front of her. To add an additional barrier, he lifted his silver inlaid cane out to his side and let its tip come to rest on the shelf where she had balanced the feed bucket.

"I have a long day ahead of me, and I don't have time to play games," Jackie stated firmly, glancing at the cane and then looking at Dan directly.

"You don't want to play games with me anyway." An air of

arrogance flowed freely with his words. "You know I always win."

"Not always." Jackie glanced down at the hand-tooled leather boots Dan wore, made momentary eye contact with him, then quickly ducked under the cane before he had time to set up a new barricade.

"That's *not* very funny," Dan said blatantly.

He turned toward the barn's front door and watched Jackie as she walked away. Her shoulder-length brown hair bounced in rhythm with her steps. Her slender legs moved smoothly—effortlessly—beneath faded jeans, and her hips . . . Dan could almost sense his mouth water.

For almost twenty years, he'd wanted her. Twenty long years . . . Granted, there was no love lost between them, and maybe by now, it was no longer even lust. But the challenge still remained; *that* was what made her the top prize. Jacqueline Michelle Elrod Mitchell was the *only* woman Daniel Jerome Patton the Fourth had ever wanted to take to bed . . . who had refused him. And Dan was determined to have her—one way or another.

"You wouldn't treat me like this if I were a whole man," Dan called after her in a tone seeking sympathy.

Jackie hesitated, interrupting the rhythm of her walk, but she didn't stop. She'd endured this line of attack before; Dan had used those very same words so often, she wondered if he might not actually be starting to believe them himself.

But she didn't have the time—nor was she in the mood—to put up with his self-pitying banter now. Dan had better watch what he had to say. If he wasn't careful, Jackie knew she might expound upon all of the negative responses she had—at least up to this point—held in check in the name of compassion. But if Dan pushed her . . .

"If I had my legs, you'd go to the Governor's Ball with me," Dan continued in his pathetic tone. "You'd like me if—"

That did it; that was all she could stand. Jackie's blue eyes flashed as she stopped short, whirled around, and let go with a revelation for Dan Patton she'd been keeping to herself for far too long.

"I didn't like you even when you *had* your legs," she stated frankly. "I haven't liked you since I met you in grade school. I didn't like you in junior high or high school, and why I ever went out with you the few times I did, I'll never know—"

"*I* know why you went out with me," Dan said arrogantly. "Just like all the others, you liked the idea of my money."

"But, unlike the others, I matured and found out—at least in your case—that money can be a major indicator of decadence. And believe me, Dan, you're a prime candidate for the category."

Jackie paused to take in a breath. During the brief silence, she remembered the hot July evening, the summer after their graduation, when Dan had chased her through the park, pinned her to a picnic table, and would have raped her had two old ladies, walking their dogs, not come along.

"When you left to go out east to college," she continued, "I was one of the happiest people in the county. I was happy to be rid of you! I was happy not to have to worry about fighting you off any more. On top of that, I was overjoyed all those years you were away, and believe me, I was one of the most unhappy people in the county when you came back to take over your father's business."

"Oh, Jackie, my sweet . . ." Dan's voice softened, and his face took on a forlorn expression as he leaned on his cane and took a couple of slow and seemingly awkward steps toward her.

Jackie's eyes widened in disbelief, and her fury mounted. The very thought of Dan faking a lack of mobility stirred her ire deeper. She knew he'd mastered his custom-made, computerized prostheses less than six months after the accident that cost him both legs. She also knew that unless someone had failed to hear of his accident—and he was always eager to inform anyone of the grisly details—that person would have difficulty distinguishing Dan Patton's walk from a man with two normal, healthy legs.

And dancing . . . When he'd first started talking about going to the Governor's Ball, Dan had bragged to her as to how they would dominate the dance floor. And now—now he had the gall to try to play on her sympathy by faking—

"Stop it!" she shouted. "You're disgusting! Get out of here and leave me alone!"

"Mom? Mom, what's wrong? Are you okay?"

Jackie turned halfway toward the barn door just as her eleven-year-old son rounded the corner. When Kerk saw Dan standing a few feet beyond his mother, he pulled up short.

"Are you okay?" he repeated.

Jackie looked at Kerk and smiled . . . a smile that touched deep in her heart. At that moment, the boy looked so much like his father: compact and muscular . . . a square jaw . . . dark brown hair . . . and pale green eyes. Oh, how she missed Richard. Even after almost a year and a half, at times like these, she missed him even more.

"It's all right," Jackie answered. "I'm fine."

"What's *he* doing here?" Kerk asked in a tone clearly indicating his displeasure at Dan's presence.

"And just what are *you* doing here?" Dan countered childishly. "It's Friday. Shouldn't you be in school or something?"

"I'm on vacation. It's Good Friday . . . that's a religious holiday. But you probably don't know anything about something like that—"

"Kerk, that's enough," Jackie intervened. The boy had his father's spunk and temper as well. "Here," she said, handing him the feed bucket, "would you go feed the goats for me, please? We've got a lot of work to get done around here today."

Kerk took the bucket, then looked at Dan suspiciously. "Are you sure you're okay?" he asked, glancing at Jackie.

"I'm fine," she assured him. "Dan was just leaving."

"He better be—"

"That's enough of that kind of talk." A gentle squeeze to Kerk's shoulder helped emphasize her words. "Go on now and feed the goats for me. Okay?"

"Okay." Kerk eyed Dan once more, then turned and walked toward the barn door. As soon as he cleared the opening, he stopped, looked past the pond inside the oval drive, out across the pasture, and focused on the lane linking the compound to the distant road. A cloud of dust caught his attention. When he recognized the truck responsible for making the miniature whirlwind, a confident grin spread across his face.

"Good thing *he's* leaving," Kerk said, looking first to his mother and then to Dan. "Barry's coming," he said, a grin crossing his lips.

"Barry?" Jackie questioned, joining Kerk outside the barn. "I wonder what he's doing— Oh no," she said the instant she recognized the conservation department truck, "not more animals. We're full now. Where are we going to put any more?" Jackie shook her head, then started walking toward the right branch of the drive that led around the pond. "Kerk, go see if you can find Bruce, and tell him I think we're going to have a job on our hands."

Dan stepped up to the barn's doorway. He glanced at Kerk, running toward Bruce Cameron's house to his left, then focused on Jackie, walking along the drive toward the lane and the approaching truck.

She was ignoring him—totally ignoring him! She was all but treating him as if he didn't even exist.

"Bitch," Dan grumbled under his breath. "I'm not finished with you. One way or another, you're going to end up seeing things my way. One way or another...."

*6:50 A.M.*

"Yes." A bass voice answered the phone, its mellow tone rebounding off the office's picture-covered walls. Fifteen seconds of silence passed, then he added, "The book at the top of our reading list this month is the V. M. Thompson thriller, *Project GOD.*"

Recognizing the code words, a female voice responded, "This is Cardinal Three. They've been released."

"All of them?" he asked anxiously, scooting onto the edge of his chair.

"All but the domestics." There was a brief moment of silence, then she continued. "Most of them are being transported now. We should have them all in good homes in just a few days."

"Were there any complications?"

"None that I know of."

He hesitated and all but held his breath when he asked, "Were there any . . . sacrifices that needed to be made?"

"We didn't run across any unusual circumstances. The team was able to bring them all out alive."

He exhaled a sigh of relief, smiled, and nodded even though there was no one else in the room to share his happiness. "Good work. I'll see to it your report gets filed at headquarters. You and your team have done a commendable job."

"We're available whenever you need us. You know where to reach me."

"I'll keep in touch." He returned the phone to its cradle, then his eyes sought out a picture on the wall directly in front of him.

The photograph was dark; it had been taken in secret, without the benefit of a flash. But even though the images weren't sharp, it was easy to identify what had been taking place. The picture captured the workings of a laboratory . . . a laboratory where live animals were being used for experimentation.

"Maybe one of these days," he said, as he focused on the eyes of a shackled dog that appeared to be looking straight into the camera, "we'll be able to rescue all of you . . . before your time runs out."


*7:06 A.M.*

"You know it won't matter," Jackie said, looking over the animals in the back of the truck that ranged from squirrels, rabbits, weasels, and raccoons to a domestic dog and house cat. "I'll get ahold of Chuck Gillock at the paper and run a piece in the lost and found about those two," she said, glancing at Barry, then nodding at the dog and cat.

"Maybe I can get somebody to do that for you," Barry said as he slid a finger in between the bars of the transportation cage and scratched the cat just behind its ear.

"Who do you have in mind?"

"There's a new rookie in Kevin's department, and I think he might be willing to take the time to follow up on these animals."

"Another rookie, huh?" Jackie quipped, then she grinned and shook her head. "If you can get him to do it, fine. By the way things are piling up around here, I probably wouldn't get around to it for a few days anyway."

"Consider it done."

Jackie took a mental inventory of the twenty plus animals taken from the trapper's holding pens, then walked back to the front of the truck. "You're right," she said as she stopped beside the cab and looked at Kevin McFall. "I think this is the most you've ever brought out here at one time. But like I said before, you know it won't matter. One way or another, Bruce will find a place for them somewhere."

"Some of 'em may be too far gone to help," Kevin said as he crooked his arm out the driver's side window and leaned toward it. "If I'da known which ones didn't have a chance o' makin' it, I'da saved you all some time and effort and put 'em outta their misery up there on the mountain. But I know Bruce; he's got a way with critters. Sometimes I think he can almost bring 'em back from the dead. And just as sure as I'da put any of 'em outta their misery up there, sure as shootin', Bruce'd been able to save 'em. So I just left 'em be."

"You did the right thing," Jackie said, her words contradicting the shake of her head. "Bruce would probably get a bit peeved if he didn't have a chance to try to save even the most pathetic creature, but . . ." she hesitated.

"But what?"

"Oh, it's awful for me to even think it, let alone say it."

"Say what?"

She looked from Kevin to the animals in the back of the truck to Barry, standing beside her, and back to Kevin. "We're so overcrowded now the way it is, and donations always go down in the spring when it seems like too many other organizations are tapping the pot for contributions." Jackie shook her head again. "I don't know how much longer he can do it."

"What's he gone and done now?" Kevin asked.

"Has he done something else since he brought back those six mustangs from Nevada last week?" Barry added.

"Six wild horses isn't the half of it," Jackie said.

She hesitated, not knowing if she should burden Kevin and Barry with the financial problems facing the compound and farm. But if she couldn't confide in two of her closest friends, who else would she be able to talk to?

"Last week, he took out a second mortgage on the place," Jackie finally said, looking at Kevin and then Barry.

"I'm surprised anyone would give it to him," Barry said flatly.

"He said he went to talk to his old friend, Wayne Crist, at the bank. I guess he had to do quite a bit of finagling to pull it off, but somehow he did, and Crist approved it, so what's done is done." Jackie hesitated a moment, then looked again from Kevin to Barry. "What scares me now is whether we're going to be able to make the payments. He won't ask anything of people when they bring their animals out to him; most of his own money goes for the medicine he uses on their animals.

"The past few months, I've been giving him most of my check and part of Richard's pension check to help him make ends meet. I don't know where that's going to put us now that he's taken out this additional mortgage. And if something would happen, he doesn't have anything to fall back on. He's already pulled out just about everything he had put up for his retirement."

"I wouldn't fret about it too much," Kevin said. "Anywhere Bruce is involved, thing's always seem to have a way o' workin' itself out—"

A fiery-red Ferrari roared to life beside the feed barn. Jackie, Barry, and Kevin looked in its direction just as Dan Patton popped the clutch. The tires spun for a moment, churning up dirt, dust, and sod, then the deep tread grabbed hold of the ground. The car lunged forward, the back end fishtailing, coming close to swerving out of control.

The instant Barry recognized the vehicle, his jaw muscles tightened and his posture grew rigid. If he'd been an animal, the fur on his back would have been bristling the length of his spine. "What's *he* doing here?" Barry asked curtly.

"Nothing," Jackie said quickly, hoping to ward off any further reaction in regard to Dan Patton.

"He's not the type to drive all the way out here for nothing,"

Barry persisted as he watched the Ferrari speed around the far side of the pond, then turn onto the lane.

"I don't think I wanna be caught up in the middle o' all this," Kevin said half-jokingly as he lifted his foot from the brake and let the truck start to roll. "I think the safest thing for me to do is to find Bruce and help him unload these here animals wherever he wants 'em."

"Do you want me to go—" Jackie offered, but Kevin cut her short.

"Nope. Nope, I think I can find my own way. I think you oughta stay right here and smooth things over," he said, raising his eyebrows and nodding at Barry.

Jackie stepped back from the truck. Barry took a step backward as well, but his attention remained focused on the departing Ferrari.

After the truck passed by them, Jackie looked up at Barry, then glanced in the direction of the sports car. "Men," she stated with a hint of disgust, shaking her head. She turned and started toward the bucket Kerk had left sitting just outside the feed-barn door.

"What'd he want?" Barry persisted, following Jackie. "Why was he—" Barry was interrupted by a beeping from the pager on his belt. "I need to check in with the station."

Jackie stopped and looked back at Barry over her shoulder. She glanced at the pager, then nodded toward the concrete block building between the feed barn and the first of three livestock barns. "There's an extension in Bruce's office you can use." Without saying anything further, Jackie led the way.

While Barry talked to the desk sergeant at the county headquarters, Jackie leaned against the doorframe, arms crossed over her chest, eyeing Barry. She'd always thought him good-looking—tall, dark-haired, dark-eyed, muscular—and she did enjoy sharing his company. During the past year, they'd had countless good times together . . . the three of them. Kerk liked Barry. *She* liked Barry, and if he wasn't so damn pigheaded most of the time, she might be able to—

"Well, I'll be darned," Barry said as he returned the phone to its cradle. He looked at Jackie; she returned his gaze in silence, waiting for him to continue. "There was a break-in at the Patton laboratory out in the county last night."

Jackie straightened in the doorway, her interest aroused. "Were they after drugs?"

"Not by the sound of things," Barry said, shaking his head. "They just took the animals."

"An animal rights group?"

"That's the guess. Fleming said it looked like a pretty typical MO: empty cages and writing on the walls in red spray paint."

"I was due to make an animal check there this week."

"It doesn't look like you have to be in any hurry now."

"I guess not." Jackie looked from Barry out across the compound; three thin lines gradually worked their way onto her brow.

"That's not one of your everyday expressions," Barry said as he cocked his head to one side and eyed her. "What are you thinking about?"

"The lab."

"Patton's?" She nodded. "Do you think maybe your old buddy Daniel J. had something to do with it?" His eyes darted to the end of the drive where he'd last seen the Ferrari. "Do you think it was some sort of setup or something for the insurance?"

"No. By the way Dan was talking, I'd lay odds he doesn't even know the break-in's happened."

"What then?"

"I was just thinking about Wagner, the head man out there, and . . . and that strange little assistant of his. What's his name?" Jackie paused a moment to think. "Maxey? That sounds right. Warren . . . Warren Maxey. That's it."

"What about them?"

"I can't really pinpoint anything for sure, but I know one thing, every time I go into that place and have to be around those two for very long, I get the creeps."

"Evidently, their animals must check out, or you'd've turned them in by now . . ."

"Oh, their manifests always check out perfectly. It's something about them—personally—that gives me the willies."

"I don't know if I'd be able to recognize either one of them on sight or not. Say, if you're not too busy, why don't you go over there with me? You can introduce me to everybody and show me around the place."

"I've got too much work to do around here to take the time to go butting my nose into something that's none of my business."

"But it *is* your business. You're southeastern Indiana's animal welfare agent, and some of your animals are missing. It seems to me that you have a responsibility to check into it."

"But I've got too much to do here. We're going to be open for the whole weekend, and we're having an Easter-egg hunt out in the front meadow on Sunday. There are stalls to be cleaned, manes to be braided, decorations to put up, and heaven only knows what we're going to end up doing with that batch of strays you and Kevin just brought in."

"Not to worry; I've got it all figured out. I'll make you a trade. I'll help you around here this weekend, and you can take me on a tour of Patton's lab after we help Bruce and Kevin unload the animals. Is it a deal?"

Jackie looked into Barry's deepset dark eyes and couldn't think of a reason not to accept his proposition. "All right, but just remember *you* were the one to come up with this deal, and

*I'm* going to hold you to it for the entire weekend."

"No problem. I can hide Easter eggs like nobody's business."

"I was thinking more along the line of cleaning out stalls."


7:30 A.M.

Bruce Cameron sat on the straw-covered floor in the corner stall of the compound's northernmost barn. Corky lay on a blanket beside him. Bruce and his friend of nineteen years had come there to be alone.

"I've been telling folks for over thirty-five years that if they really love their animals, they'll love them enough to let them go," Bruce said with a crackle in his voice. He ran his hand slowly along the dog's side, feeling her fragile ribs beneath the soft brown and beige fur. "It never was easy telling other folks to do it," he said as he stroked Corky's head, "and I know it's going to be twice as hard to have to do it now myself." Corky reached for Bruce with a paw and whimpered as if to tell him she understood . . . and that it was all right. "I know, girl," he said, taking her paw gently in his hand and rubbing it with his thumb.

Corky lifted her head and looked up at him with clouded eyes. Maybe she saw his image, but Bruce doubted it. During the past few weeks, her eyes had deteriorated as quickly as the rest of her body.

"You've been a good dog, old Cork, and there won't ever be another one to take your place."

Bruce stroked Corky's head a few more times, then reached for the syringe he'd brought with him. He knew he had to put his dog to rest quickly, because if he hesitated—if he started thinking back about all the good times—he might prolong the dog's existence . . . and therefore its suffering.

"Just a pinprick, old girl," Bruce said in a soft voice as he ran his thumb along the dog's foreleg, coaxing a vein to stand up beneath the fur. "You've had shots before. This one won't be any different except..." a lump hardened in his throat, "... except that you'll..." He slipped the needle through the skin and into the vein.

Bruce hesitated. Memories flooded his mind.

He'd had no difficulty selecting Corky. She'd been the only brown and beige pup in a litter of seven, and her spirited playfulness and yippy bark immediately captured his attention. From the moment he'd taken her home and set her on the ground beside him, she'd followed him as closely as a shadow. She'd learned quickly and within but a few weeks had come to almost sense his every direction. They'd worked well together as a team... and they'd played. Oh, how they had played.

And she'd comforted him. The evening of his wife's funeral, after everyone had gone and the two of them were left alone, Corky had crawled up on the sofa beside him and laid her head on his lap. They'd cried together.

Her first and only litter... her many encounters with skunks and the tomato-juice baths afterward... the gentle way she mothered an orphan fawn... the open mouth that resembled a perpetual smile... the dark brown eyes that sought out his in trust and love. These were the things Bruce would remember about Corky... and that was the way it should be.

"Good-bye, old friend," he said as his thumb depressed the plunger. Tears gathered in his eyes; several brimmed over his lashes and trickled down his weathered cheeks. "Soon, you'll have peace," he said as he withdrew the needle and laid the syringe aside. "We'll meet again someday," he promised.

Bruce scooted closer to Corky, lifted her head onto his lap, and began running his hand the length of her side. He continued stroking the soft brown and beige fur even after her breaths stopped, and all signs of life ceased to exist.

Kerk stood in the doorway to the stall, motionless . . . silent. Tears clouded his young eyes as well.

He'd known this day had been coming and, all the while, he'd dreaded it. During the past few weeks, Corky's health had deteriorated rapidly; not a day had gone by that Bruce didn't mention yet another accident she'd had in the house.

Kerk remembered how Bruce had told him repeatedly, during the last couple of weeks, how animals should be allowed to die with the same dignity with which they'd lived. Kerk had always agreed; he sensed Bruce had been trying to convince himself.

"I've picked out a pretty place for you up on the hill at the edge of the woods," Bruce said as he lifted the dog's body off the floor and laid it gently in a cardboard box he'd lined with an old blanket. "You can keep an eye on us from up there and . . . and you won't be too far away for me to come visit."

As Kerk watched Bruce fold the edges of the blanket over Corky's body, he remembered his mother telling him of the compassion he'd inherited from his father's side of the family. Bruce was Kerk's father's uncle . . . well, in all reality, he wasn't a blood relative, but he might as well have been. He'd been a very close friend to Kerk's father's mother and, since Kerk's biological grandfather was never identified, Bruce had been brought into the family under the title of uncle. He was the only living relative—pseudo or otherwise—on Kerk's father's side of the family, and he was the only person who even came close to being a grandparent figure on either side of the family.

When the opportunity arose, Kerk bonded with Bruce as quickly as his father had before him. For the past year and a half, Kerk had relied upon Bruce as a father figure as well. They'd learned together . . . grown together. Bruce had taught him so many things his father had only had time to touch upon. Bruce presented himself to be more of a man than any other male Kerk had come to know. Now, as he watched Bruce shed tears over the loss of a beloved dog, Kerk knew that the aspects of the gentler side of life Bruce had told him about were indeed true. Grown men *could* cry; it *was* all right. Sadness and compassion were as much a part of being a man as were muscle and grit—

A horn honked. The muffled blare sounded distant; its source didn't appear to be very close. But the noise was enough to rescue Bruce from his train of thought and to remind Kerk why he'd come to the barn.

Bruce looked up and saw Kerk. A moment's silence passed when their eyes met, then Bruce asked, "Were you looking for me?"

Kerk's eyes shifted to the cardboard box. "Corky was a good dog," he said, looking back at Bruce.

"That she was, and that's how we'll always remember her." Bruce finished tucking in the edges of the blanket and slipped the box's fitted lid into place before returning his attention to Kerk. "Were you looking for me?" he asked again.

"Barry and Kevin brought in some animals they picked up this morning. Mom said to come find you because she didn't know where you'd want to put them."

"I don't know if *I've* even got an answer for that." Bruce picked up his brimmed straw hat, which was a mainstay of his wardrobe, put it on, then shifted onto his knees, stabilized one foot, and grabbed on to a rail beside him. Using his arm and shoulder muscles more than his legs, he pulled himself up to standing. "Getting up and down just isn't as easy as it used to be." Bruce walked out of the stall past Kerk, then hesitated and looked back at the boy. "Are you going to come help me find a place to put those new animals?"

Kerk glanced at the cardboard box, then looked up at Bruce

with his emerald-green eyes. "What about Corky?" he asked hesitantly.

"I'll see to her later. We've got the living to care about now."

Kerk glanced back at the box. "I'm going to miss her."

"We all will." Bruce took a couple of steps closer to Kerk and laid a hand on the boy's shoulder. "If you'd like to help me, we'll bury her later." Kerk nodded. "I think she'd like for you to be there."


7:55 A.M.

Warren Maxey stumbled into the kitchen, turned on the small television on the counter as he passed it, dropped a premeasured packet into the coffeemaker, picked up the water measuring cup, and carried it to the sink. Not yet fully awake, he followed his morning routine out of habit; he'd repeated the procedure so many times, he didn't have to think about it any more. Everything had become so instinctive, he didn't even need his thick glasses in order to be able to function.

As soon as the measuring cup was full, Warren returned to the coffeemaker and began filling the well. The television droned at a moderate volume in the background, then the newscaster expanded on a topic that captured Warren's attention.

"It appears that animal rights groups were out in full force last night. In the eastern half of the United States alone, more than one hundred and twenty-five labs were vandalized and their laboratory animals stolen. Once the tally comes in from the west coast, it's estimated that the count could rise to as high as three or four hundred.

"Locally, three break-ins had been reported as of seven-thirty this morning. WSHS reporter, Gail Senior, is on the scene at Patton Pharmaceutical Laboratories with an updated report. Gail."

Warren picked up his glasses from the narrow shelf beside the sink and put them on. He pulled a stool out from under the bar and sat down in front of the television, concentrating on the screen as an attractive dark-haired reporter began her segment by introducing his boss.

"I'm here at the Patton Pharmaceutical Laboratory, in rural Dearborn County, with executive scientist, Dr. Leland Wagner. As you can see," she said, motioning toward a spray-painted wall the cameraman obligingly brought into focus, "intruders left an explicit calling card. Dr. Wagner," she continued, returning her attention to him as the cameraman again centered them on the screen, "do you have any idea who broke into the building last night?"

"Everything seems to indicate it was an animal rights group," he answered calmly.

"I understand they took all of your lab animals."

"That's correct."

"Were you working on any specific projects or experiments the loss of these animals might jeopardize?"

Wagner cleared his throat then said, "Due to the highly competitive nature of our business, I'm not at liberty to divulge the nature of our experiments—"

"Thank you, Dr. Wagner," Gail Senior said as she turned toward the camera and brought the microphone directly in front of her.

"But," he said, grasping her wrist and pulling the microphone back in front of him, "I would like to make a plea to the people who have our animals." The veteran reporter tried to regain control of the microphone, but Wagner wouldn't relinquish even a fraction of the advantage he'd obtained over her. "Whatever experiments you have interrupted could be the very experiments that could result in a cure for the sickness or disease that might affect you or your loved ones in the future. By taking our animals, *you* could be the reason your parents . . . your spouse . . . your child . . . You could even be the reason *you* might die someday because the discovery of a cure was interrupted or completely negated by your actions."

For an instant, he thought of *his* animals that had been stolen and *his* experiment that had been interrupted. Over twenty years of work . . . For a moment, Dr. Leland Wagner lost control. "Give them back! Give us back our animals! All of them—"

The television screen went blank. In less than five seconds, the source of transmission returned to the main station where the news anchorman continued to highlight events that had taken place during the past twenty-four hours.

Warren stared at the television's small screen, dumbfounded, not hearing the next news story. He'd worked at the Patton laboratory for almost four years, and during that time, he'd never seen Leland Wagner represent himself in a manner other than one of a straight laced professional. Now, seeing Wagner in a lesser role made him wonder—

*Animals!*

Warren's eyes widened to the size of egg yolks as a burst of adrenaline shot through him. He stood up quickly from the stool, almost knocking it over, and turned toward the utility room and the house's back door. He started toward it but hesitated. "No one could possibly know—" Then he contemplated Wagner's atypical behavior a few moments before and knew—*knew*—someone had found—stolen—the animals from Wagner's secret lab. And if someone had been able to locate Wagner's animals, then someone might have been able to locate *his* animals as well. An uneasy tingling vibrated through Warren as he hurried toward the back door.

As he reached for the doorknob, Warren glanced down at

his T-shirt and boxer shorts. Following his morning routine, he'd been on his way to the shower, detouring through the kitchen only long enough to start the coffeepot; the newscaster's report concerning the break-ins had interrupted the ritual.

Looking at his underwear, Warren wondered if he should change. If not change, maybe he should, at least, put on a robe. But would it matter?

He looked out the door's double-pane window and focused on a prefabricated minibarn at the back edge of his yard. Could he make it out to the barn and back without being seen? Or would the neighbors be able to look out their windows and see him streaking across the backyard in his underwear?

Warren scanned the area on either side of the yard. Spring foliage was only beginning to fill in the branches on the sapling trees; they would provide him with little or no cover at all. But did he really need the trees to camouflage his movements? His house, like those on either side of him, was built on an angle to the others; each squarely faced the main circular drive out front. The very angles of the houses all but prohibited neighbors from seeing into each other's backyards.

And no one lived directly behind him. His property marked the edge of what his neighbors classified as civilized property. Just beyond the manicured backyards, a tangled woods rose like an untamed backdrop. It spread over five miles due east, then opened up to over three hundred and sixty acres of farmland that bordered Bruce Cameron's animal compound. There was no way that anyone in any direction could see him, and besides, at this time of day, his neighbors would be busy with their own morning activities and would have little time to be looking out their windows . . . watching for someone in his underwear.

Warren opened the exterior door. He stepped out onto the stoop, looked to his right and left, then ran across the backyard, urged on more by the morning chill than by his modesty.

When he reached the barn, he located the key above the casing, unlocked the door, and stepped inside. He turned on the power switch on the wall to his right and had to wait only a few seconds before the overhead fluorescent lights brightened the interior.

Warren quickly surveyed the cages on the shelves to his right, and a smile etched across his face. All of his animals were still there: four white mice and two rabbits that he'd marked on the inventory sheet at the lab as having died and been cremated in the incinerator, and two raccoons, two 'possums, three squirrels, and a weasel he'd bought from two scraggly mountain men he discovered had also sold Leland Wagner the majority of animals he used in his secret lab.

That day of discovery, a little more than three months ago, had been a milestone for Warren. In addition to learning his boss's secret for acquiring additional lab animals, he'd located the hidden lab and, over the course of the past several weeks, he'd been collecting blood serum samples from the vials in Wagner's refrigerator and injecting them into his own animals.

Even though he speculated as to their end results, Warren wasn't sure where Wagner's experiments were leading. Due to the secrecy of their very existence, he sensed the experiments might be more than simply important—he sensed they could be on the verge of a historical breakthrough. Warren wanted to be ready whenever that breakthrough came.

Warren had acclimated his animals to the serum he'd brought home from Wagner's lab, and within the past month, he'd begun collecting blood serum from them as well. The small refrigerator at the far end of the barn contained over ten vials of fresh serum, and Warren was adding to the supply almost daily. He was going to make sure he had all the serum he would need . . . even if, for the time being, he wasn't exactly certain what it could be used for.

*9:14 A.M.*

Alford Henry turned the wheel sharply and braked hard. The right front tire bounced up on the marble curb and off again before coming to a stop.

Going beyond the requirements of his job, he'd made the drive from downtown Cincinnati to the Patton family estate, secluded in the country just a few miles east of the Indiana border, in just a little over forty-five minutes. Henry was excited, and the news he had for Dan Patton wasn't something he'd wanted to trust to a phone call. Besides, he wanted to see the look on Dan's face when he received the news.

Henry stepped out of his car and hurried up the front walk. He ascended the twenty-four marble steps by twos and continued to walk quickly beneath the twenty-foot-wide entrance canopy that was supported by eight marble pillars. He stopped in front of the double-wide oak doors and rang the bell, anxious to be let inside.

Ten . . . fifteen . . . twenty seconds . . . The door opened, and a portly middle-aged, dark-eyed woman stepped into view.

"Is Mr. Patton here?" Henry asked as he pushed past the housekeeper and walked on into the foyer.

"You can't come barging in here," Vernita protested, grabbing for the sleeve of his suit coat and missing it. "Rusty," she called loudly. "Rusty—"

"I really don't think Mr. Patton will object to my being here," Henry said as he continued toward the opposite side of the foyer before stopping and turning back toward Vernita. "It's most important that I speak with him. Where is he?"

"Rusty," Vernita called again, glancing at the hallway

leading to the back of the house.

"Where is he?" Henry repeated. "I've come across something I know he'll be anxious to see," he said, patting the side of a briefcase he carried tucked under his arm.

"What's going on out here?" a husky voice echoed as a hulking figure stepped from the hallway into the foyer. Alford Henry turned with a start toward Rusty Snider, Dan Patton's formidable sandy-haired, green-eyed bodyguard.

"This man just came barging in like he owned the place," Vernita said, pointing an accusing finger at Henry. Snider took a moment to survey the intruder, then took a couple of steps toward him.

"Wait," Henry said, taking a step backward and holding out a hand in front of him as if to defend himself. "It's not what you think; I'm not an intruder. I work for Mr. Patton," he tried desperately to explain. "Take a good look at me," he said to Snider. "You know me. Mr. Patton hired me a few months ago to sort through all the boxes and files and stacks of papers his father had stored away in one of his Cincinnati office buildings. I've only just begun to scratch the surface of everything he kept down there, but I came across something this morning I'm sure Mr. Patton will want to see." Again, Henry patted the side of his briefcase. "Immediately," he added.

Snider continued to eye Alford Henry, and then he nodded. "I remember you." He looked at Vernita. "You did the right thing to call me, but it's all right. Go on about your business." He looked back at Henry. "Your name?"

"Alford Henry. Mr. Patton will know me—"

"Wait here, and I'll see if he's available."

"I'm sure he'd *make* time to see me if he knew—" Snider didn't hear him—or simply ignored him; he'd already disappeared down the hall.

Henry glanced at his watch, then began to teeter back and

forth from his heels to his toes. Several minutes passed, and he began drumming his fingers on the side of the briefcase. What was taking Dan Patton so long? If he only knew—

"Alford." Dan seemed to appear from out of nowhere, walking across the foyer toward him. "I'm sorry to have kept you waiting, but I was on the phone with the mayor." He stopped directly in front of Henry and looked down at the diminutive man. "Rusty says you're quite anxious to see me."

"Yes, sir." Henry leaned back against the wall and balanced the briefcase on his leg. He opened it, slipped his hand inside, and pulled out three envelopes. "I found these in one of your father's boxes that I've classified as random communication," he said as he handed Dan the envelopes. "I think all three will be of great interest to you."

"I really doubt if there was any big hurry for you to bring them all of the way out here," Dan said as he glanced at the top envelope. He noted the date penciled in the upper right corner—a date that had long since come and gone . . . just a few days before his father had died. Curious, Dan slipped the folded paper out of the envelope and took a moment to silently read the handwritten document.

Dan's jaw suddenly tightened. Every muscle in his face appeared to strain. His pulse rate increased; his blood pressure soared. The veins along his neck bulged beneath his skin as blood pumped forcefully through them.

Trying to maintain his composure, Dan refolded the paper and returned it to the envelope. "Did—" His voice broke. He swallowed and cleared his throat before attempting to speak again. "Did . . . did you show this to anyone else?"

"No, sir," Henry said crisply. "The information in that document is strictly family business, and it's my policy to keep family business within the family. I'm not a blabbermouth. I don't go around telling other people things about my clients. I've built my reputation—"

"And you can continue to build your reputation," Dan said as he began to tear the envelope and letter in half and then in half again, "if you forget about everything you read in this letter. You see, Alford, my father was a very sick man, and his mind played funny tricks on him. I wouldn't want it to get out that he lost all rational capacity right before he died because you see," Dan said, motioning with the torn envelope, "that is exactly what something like this would represent."

Henry looked at the torn pieces of paper curiously and watched as Dan dropped them into a floorstand ashtray at the corner near the hall. Old Mr. Patton hadn't been senile when he'd written that letter. Even though the date on the outside of the envelope had been fairly recent, the date below the personalized letterhead had been from twenty-five years ago—

"Let's hope these other envelopes contain more enlightening information," Dan said as he surveyed the second envelope.

"They're both from a Leland Wagner," Henry said, again looking at Dan. "I believe he still works for your company."

"Yes, he works at one of our smaller labs in Indiana," Dan acknowledged, eyeing the postmark from twenty years before. "And?" he asked, as he turned the envelope over and opened it.

Henry didn't answer. He watched in silence as Dan read the letter . . . and watched as Dan's face went ashen. He could have predicted the response.

"This . . . this is true?" Dan asked almost breathlessly as his eyes met Henry's.

"I've no reason to doubt its authenticity."

Dan swayed unsteadily, almost losing his balance. "Rusty," he called, reaching out to his side as if seeking support. "Rusty!"

"Yes, Mr. Patton." Rusty Snider had been standing just inside the hallway and was there in an instant, offering Dan a stabilizing arm.

"Have the car brought around front. I need to go to our lab in South Port, and I don't think I'm in the right frame of mind to drive there on my own." Dan took in a couple of deep breaths, then focused on Alford Henry. "You've done an outstanding job," Dan said as he turned and walked with the researcher across the foyer.

Rusty Snider watched them until they reached the front door, then he turned to go call for the car. As he stepped toward the hall, he glanced down at the floorstand ashtray and saw several torn pieces of paper. Curious, he picked them up and slipped them into his pocket. Later, he'd find time to put the pieces back together.


*9:40 A.M.*

"It could have been a lot worse," Dearborn County Sheriff Rex Joseph said. He stood just inside the lobby of Patton Pharmaceutical Laboratories, talking with Jackie and Barry. Since the lab was located in the county, outside the city limits of South Port, it fell within his jurisdiction; he'd been on his way to work when he'd intercepted the radio call. "I talked with Hickling just a few minutes before you got here. He said the college downtown got hit pretty bad. Besides losing all their animals, there was a lot of vandalism to the building and, to quote him, a ton of equipment has been shot to hell."

"How much damage was done here?" Barry asked, making a sweeping visual survey of the lobby.

"Not much. You see most of it," Joseph answered, nodding toward the overturned furniture and spray-painted walls. "It could have been a lot worse," he repeated.

"They probably only sent a splinter group out here," Barry speculated. "I imagine they were on a pretty tight schedule and couldn't spend any more time than it took to get the animals and leave a couple messages."

"If this is just a *little* damage, I'd hate to see what they would've done had they set their minds to it," Jackie said, looking over the lobby. "I presume no one was injured."

"Old George Beals was shaken up a bit. Dr. Wagner came in this morning and found him tied up in a closet, but he's okay." Joseph glanced at the painted walls. "It looks like it's just about the same thing here that's been reported happening all over the country. Seems like all they wanted was to take the animals," he said, looking at Jackie.

"Have you talked to Dr. Wagner about the animals?" she asked.

"They're gone," he answered, looking at her with a frown. "What more is there to ask him about?"

"For one thing, we need to find out if they were clean."

"Clean?" Joseph's frown deepened. "What difference does it make whether they were dirty or not?" he asked in all sincerity.

"Clean refers to their involvement in experiments," Jackie explained. "If an animal's clean, it hasn't been contaminated. Were the animals taken from here clean?"

"I didn't think to ask about that." Joseph paused. "And Wagner didn't volunteer any information one way or the other."

"Where is he?" Jackie looked across the lobby toward the hall leading to the labs. She'd been in the building several times and was familiar with its layout. "Is he down here in one of the labs or is he upstairs in his office? We need to verify whether the animals were clean or not, and if they're not, we have to find out what kind of contamination we may be facing."

"You don't think it could be anything serious, do you?" Joseph asked.

"We won't know until we talk with Dr. Wagner, but you

need to remember that this is a pharmaceutical laboratory." Jackie started across the lobby. Barry followed her; Rex Joseph fell in line behind him.

"What do they work on up here?" Barry asked, lengthening his steps to keep up with Jackie's fast pace.

"I would imagine most of the research is focused on some kind of drugs."

"Drugs? Like drugs to cure diseases?"

"Some of them."

"If they're working on cures, then it makes sense they've got the diseases up here too," he said with a note of apprehension. "These animals you're talking about, if they weren't clean, then they could be carriers."

"More than likely."

"And some of them could be serious."

"It's possible, but then again—"

"All the ID numbers are on the inventory sheet I gave you. Drew Coryell should be able to answer any other questions you might have." Leland Wagner stepped into the doorway of the first lab on their right. A county deputy was with him. When Wagner saw Jackie, he nodded in acknowledgment, then returned his attention to the deputy. "Is there anything else you need from me?"

"Not at the moment."

Rex Joseph joined the deputy, looked into the lab then glanced at Wagner. "When they finish dusting for prints—"

"I'll be around if you need me." Wagner cut Joseph short as he turned to Jackie. "I expected to see you sometime this week, but I didn't think it would be under these circumstances." He looked at Barry and nodded but said nothing.

"Did they take all of your animals?" Jackie asked, coming directly to the point.

"Yes." Wagner hesitated and cleared his throat. "They're all gone. I was just going over the list with the deputy."

"Were they clean?"

Wagner looked into Jackie's eyes, hesitated, and then answered, "Yes, they were ... clean. All of them," he emphasized a bit too brashly. He turned and looked down the hall at the painted walls. "If all they wanted was to free the animals, why did they have to do this?" He touched a red letter with his fingertip and momentarily studied the paint adhering to his skin. "Why—"

"I work here! Dr. Wagner ..." Wagner, Jackie and Barry looked toward the front door where a county deputy was detaining Warren Maxey. "Dr. Wagner," Warren called, "tell him I work here." Wagner made eye contact with the deputy and nodded. The deputy stepped aside and let Warren pass. "I heard about the break-in on the news," Warren said as he approached them. "Did they take all the animals?"

"They're all gone," Wagner repeated, an element of regret clinging to his words. "If you'll excuse me," he said, making quick eye contact with everyone in the small group, "I'm going up to my office." Before anyone could acknowledge his statement or produce a rebuttal, Leland Wagner turned and walked down the hall.

Jackie watched him for a moment, then directed her next question to Warren. "Were they clean?"

"Huh?" Warren looked at her through thick glasses, his irises and pupils magnified.

"Were all the animals here at the lab clean?"

Warren glanced down the hall to see Wagner step into the elevator, then he looked back at Jackie. "As far as I know, they were. We were short on numbers this week for some reason, and Dr. Wagner said to hold off until we had enough specimens to run a valid procedure. Another shipment's supposed to come in on Monday, so we weren't going to start anything new until after they arrived."

"You're sure?" The tone in Jackie's voice verged on accusing Warren of a lie.

"Y-y-yes." Warren glanced at Barry. The look in Warren's eyes came close to matching the look Barry had seen just that morning . . . in the eyes of cornered animals . . . that were being offered no means of escape. "Yes, I'm sure," Warren said a bit more confidently. After all, *he* didn't have anything to hide—at least nothing that could be directly connected to the lab.

"Jackie," a female voice called from the far side of the lobby, "you have a phone call. You can take it here at the desk."

Jackie glanced at Barry in question. "Who would be calling me here? Who even *knows* I'm here?" Barry shrugged his shoulders in answer to both questions, then walked with her to the reception desk.

Hollie Bass, Patton Laboratory's receptionist, secretary, all-around *girl Friday*, held her hand over the phone's mouthpiece and spoke to Jackie in a loud whisper. "It's the mayor."

"Who?" Jackie questioned, unsure she had heard Hollie correctly.

"The mayor. It's Mayor Fuller from South Port."

"I wonder what he wants?" Jackie said, glancing at Barry in question. Hollie handed her the phone, then watched Jackie intently. "Hello," Jackie said after a brief hesitation. She recalled the last time the mayor had contacted her; he'd wanted a political favor she hadn't been in a position to give. "Yes," she said, glancing from Hollie to Barry. "Monday?" Jackie shrugged her shoulders and arched her eyebrows in a synchronized gesture. "I think that can be arranged. Yes . . . I'll see you then. Good-bye." She handed the phone back to Hollie. "Thank you . . . I think."

"And?" Barry asked curiously. "What was that all about?"

"I have an appointment with the mayor on Monday."

"What for?"

"He didn't come right out and say, but I have a sneaky

feeling he wants something." Barry cocked his head to one side, knowing there was more. "He said it would take some work on my part," Jackie continued, "and I might have to make a few sacrifices, but when everything's finished, he said we'd have enough funds to support the compound for the next decade or maybe even longer—"

"Get the hell outta my way! I *own* the fucking place, and I can walk in and out of here any time I damn well please!" Dan Patton pushed his way past the deputy at the front door. When the young officer challenged him and shifted his hand toward his service revolver, Rusty Snider reacted in an instant, grabbing the deputy and twisting his arm behind his back in a hammerlock, pinning him—face forward—against the wall.

"Call off your hired help," Barry ordered as he walked toward Dan.

"I don't have time to fuck with you either," Dan yelled as he tried to push past Barry. "Where's Wagner—"

Almost as quickly as Snider had overpowered the deputy, Barry made a couple of unexpected moves that placed him behind Dan. In one smooth motion, he took control of Dan's left wrist and twisted it up toward the middle of his back; Barry then coiled an arm around Dan's throat, pressing it up under his chin and back against his windpipe.

"Now, call off your hired help," Barry repeated through clenched teeth. "I wouldn't want to have to arrest you for disturbing the peace . . . right here in your *own fucking place*," he added in a hoarse whisper only Dan could hear.

Dan looked at Barry out of the corner of his eye, his jaw set hard. "Let go of me, you son of a bitch." He twisted to the right and then to the left, trying to work free of the hold.

Barry tightened his arm against Dan's throat. "I could add resisting arrest—"

"Robbins!" Sheriff Joseph said forcefully as he stepped

out into the hall from the first lab. "What's going on out here?"

"We're just trying to do a little negotiating," Barry answered without loosening his grip. He nodded toward the front door where Snider still had the deputy pinned to the wall.

"Call off your man, Patton," the sheriff ordered.

"Call off . . . your trained . . . police dog," Dan choked past the pressure on his windpipe.

The sheriff's eyes met Barry's, then Rex Joseph motioned for his second-in-command to release his grip. Barry hesitated, then lowered his arm from Dan's throat and gave him a shove.

"I can sue you—" Dan threatened, rubbing his throat as he turned toward Barry.

"You're not going to sue anyone," Joseph said calmly. "Now, call off your man."

Dan looked from the sheriff to Barry and then to Jackie and Hollie, still standing at the reception desk. After a brief visual confrontation, he turned toward the entrance and nodded for Snider to release the deputy.

"Where's Wagner?" Dan demanded as he turned back toward the reception desk. "I want to see him now!" He glanced at Jackie, then at Hollie. "Where is he?"

"You don't have to concern yourself over the break-in," Hollie said in a soft voice. "Everything's under control—"

"I don't give a damn about the fucking break-in!" Dan shouted, his eyes widening, his temper flaring. "I want to see Wagner, and I want to see him now. Where is he?"

"I . . . I think he went upstairs to his office," Hollie answered timidly. "I can call him for you—"

"I'll find him." Dan took a couple of steps forward, came face to face with Rex Joseph, hesitated, then sidestepped around the sheriff. He would deal with all of them later. Right now, he had more important things on his mind.

*10:01 A.M.*

Jackie stopped a dozen feet from the front entrance. She turned back toward the building, concentrated briefly on the bold letters above the arched canopy, then scanned the rest of the exterior. The sun's stark glare reflected off the amber panels, attacking her blue eyes. She lifted a hand to her brow for shade and had to squint to counteract the glare, but that didn't prevent her from focusing on the set of windows on the third floor that belonged to Leland Wagner's office.

"What is it?" Barry asked, turning beside her. He looked at Jackie, looked up at the building, squinted, then lifted a hand to his brow as well, shading his eyes. "What are you looking for?" he asked as he glanced over the glass panels. "I don't see anything out of the ordinary."

"Something's going on." Jackie continued to stare at the windows to Wagner's office. "I can't put a finger on it, but . . . intuition . . . my woman's intuition tells me something's going on in there."

"I know one thing that's going on. Dan's going crazy," Barry said sarcastically. "Correction. Dan's already *gone* crazy."

Jackie lowered her hand and head and looked up at Barry from beneath arched eyebrows—the same way she looked at her son whenever he behaved foolishly. Barry felt himself being silently reprimanded.

"Dan may be a lot of things, but he's not crazy . . . not yet, anyway." Jackie took a few moments to ponder Dan's abrupt entrance into the building several minutes earlier. "But there was something more on his mind than just the break-in." She returned her attention to the third-floor windows. "I wonder . . ."

When Jackie didn't immediately complete the sentence, Barry nudged her verbally. "You wonder what?"

"I wonder just how truthful our good Dr. Wagner has been

with us." Barry stared at her, frowning. "I wonder if all of the animals taken in the break-in were really clean or . . . or whether something of importance *was* taken . . . something so important it—" Jackie cut her own sentence short. "Dan knows," she whispered.

"Dan knows what?"

"I don't know what it is," Jackie answered, pursing her lips as she looked at Barry, "but he knows something; something set him off in there a little while ago. In all the years I've known Dan, I've seen him make a fool of himself in just about every way known to man, but I've never seen him come so close to losing control . . . the way he did in there." She looked back at the third-story windows. "Dan and Wagner are up to something." Jackie was silent for several moments, then she looked at Barry and asked, "Didn't Wagner seem nervous to you when I asked him if the animals were clean?"

"I suppose so—"

"And that weasel Maxey," she said, a curl coming to her lips, "he was trying to cover up something as well."

"If you think something's wrong, let's go back in there and question them again. We've got the time now, and we might not have it later."

"It wouldn't do any good. If they lied to us before, they'd just lie to us again, and . . . and all I have is a hunch to go on anyway."

"How good is your hunch track record?"

"About sixty-forty. That's not enough for a substantial case, is it, Officer Robbins?" she asked, looking up at him.

"Maybe it's not good enough for a case right now, but it's enough to make sure we both keep our eyes open."


*10:26 A.M.*

The door to Wagner's office flew open and banged against

the filing cabinet behind it. Leland turned abruptly in his chair and looked up into Dan Patton's raging green eyes. For a moment, he sat motionless . . . as if frozen to his chair.

"Why?" Dan's voice cracked, the muscles to his vocal cords tense—strained.

Leland didn't answer; he couldn't. He didn't know what question Dan was asking.

"Why . . . why didn't you tell me?" Dan demanded.

"Tell you what?" Leland asked almost meekly.

"Starfish! Why didn't you tell me about the Starfish Project?"

Dan pulled back his right arm in a short backswing, then he threw something. Leland blinked reflexively as a large paper wad flew toward his face. The age-yellowed paper connected harmlessly with his chin and rebounded onto the top of his desk.

"Starfish," Dan repeated, walking on into the room.

Leland looked at Dan in silence, hesitated a few moments, then picked up the crumpled paper. He spread it open on the desk blotter and glanced at the letter he'd written to Dan's father over twenty years ago, requesting funds for his personal project. He didn't have to reread the letter to refresh his memory; every word had been branded into his mind the day it had been composed.

Leland looked up. His eyes met Dan's. Still, he said nothing.

"Why?" Dan asked again, the tone of his voice coming close to mimicking a pleading child. "Why didn't you tell me about the Starfish Project? You . . . surely you have to know how much it would mean to me— Why!" Dan shouted. His eyes widened in fury, and he brought both fists down hard on Leland's desk.

Leland looked up into Dan's angry green eyes, swallowed, then said—quite calmly, "There was nothing to tell."

"Nothing to tell?" Dan echoed. "I know you discovered something—"

"Yes, I discovered over a hundred formulas that didn't work," Leland replied brusquely. He took in a slow breath, leaned back in his chair, and tented his fingers in front of his chest, his eyes never wavering from Dan's. "Would you have wanted to know about all my failures?" He paused. "Would you have wanted to have your hopes lifted with each new batch of serum only to have all of those hopes shattered . . . dragged down into the depths of despair?" Leland paused again. "I protected you from all of that," he said as he leaned forward in his chair, "so don't come barging into my office—"

"But they *all* weren't failures," Dan said, his voice tense but surprisingly controlled, "at least not totally." He reached into his jacket's inner pocket, pulled out the third business-size envelope Alford Henry had given him, and tossed it on Leland's desk.

Leland glanced at the envelope . . . at the postmark . . . at the date . . . and guessed it contained the last letter he'd sent to Dan's father a few weeks before the senior Patton died.

Leland's throat tightened. A cold sweat oozed from his pores.

The letter was a fraud—a collection of lies. In an attempt to prevent a cutback in funds for his private experiments, Leland had fabricated a series of minor successes he'd described in the letter. He assured his benefactor he'd finally had a breakthrough, which, no doubt, would be the cornerstone for a whole new area of development for Patton Pharmaceuticals.

Leland had been grateful for Daniel Jerome Patton the Third's untimely death; he hadn't had to lie his way out of a corner the letter on the desk would have backed him into. But now, over a year and a half later, he was finding himself being backed into that very corner by the son. The son . . . the son who would pressure him until the truth about the Starfish

Project surfaced . . . and Leland Wagner lost his funding . . . and his job.

Leland couldn't let that happen. Somehow, he was going to have to lie his way out—

"The successes," Dan asked, "how successful were they?"

Leland looked up at Dan, glanced again at the envelope on the desk, then diverted his eyes across the room . . . in the direction of the aquarium . . . the aquarium he didn't really see.

What could he say? What lies could he come up with on the spur of the moment that would rescue him? What— His eyes focused.

*The aquarium!* It contained starfish and sea cucumbers—the only animals that hadn't been taken during the break-in.

*The break-in! That* was the answer. He would tell Dan the animals and all of his notes and records from the Starfish Project had been taken along with the others. Miraculously, Leland Wagner had found yet another way out.

"They were very successful," he said, looking up at Dan. "Unfortunately . . ." Leland swiveled his chair toward the wall behind him, reached over a stack of folders piled on a bookshelf to his right, and pressed a small lever that released the latch on the panel door. Solemnly, he pushed the door open to the secret room. "Unfortunately, the animal rights people were quite thorough in their search." Leland took in a deep breath and let it out in a convincing, heartfelt sigh.

Dan walked around the desk, stepped up to the panel door, and looked into the room . . . at the empty cages, their doors unlatched and open. "They . . . they were in here?" he asked. "The successes?" He reached to touch the corner of the nearest cage—the cage that had held Leland's prized beige and brown puppy.

"Yes, and they were . . . perfect," Leland boasted falsely, almost reverently.

"Tell me about them," Dan said in a near dreamlike state as he walked on into the room. He paused, then pushed an empty cage aside and sat down on the edge of the lab table. "Tell me about them," he repeated as his eyes met Leland's, "and tell me how long it's going to take to repeat the process."


Warren Maxey tilted his head back against the wall, and a grin stretched across his thin lips. For the past several minutes, he'd been standing outside the open door to Leland Wagner's office, listening to the explanation of the Starfish Project. Much to his gratification, the explanation had verified the speculation he'd been turning over in his mind since the day he'd discovered Wagner's secret lab.

As the grin broadened into a robust smile, Warren had to restrain himself; he fought to keep from exploding with a shout of joy. After all the years of being a virtual nobody at Patton Laboratory, he was now in a position where he could push for recognition—recognition he felt was long overdue.


"Why would it take so long?" Dan asked. "If the Starfish Project was working as perfectly as you say it was, why would it take another six to eight months to—"

"They took all my notes along with the animals," Leland said. "Without my notes to refer to, it's going to be like starting all over from the very beginning. Integral calculations need to be calibrated to match the exact structure—"

"But—"

"But nothing," Leland countered sharply. He looked at Dan, eyeing him almost as if to challenge him . . . backing *him* into a corner from which—most assuredly—he would attempt to buy his way out. "I've grown old, and I've gone beyond *my* need for the Starfish Project; as far as I'm concerned, it can vanish along with the stolen animals."

"No! *I* need it. Whatever it costs—"

"Then you have to let me continue with my work," Leland said bluntly. "If it takes another six months . . . eight months . . . ten months . . . a year—however long it takes to reestablish the formula, you'll have to let me take the time to do it. Eventually, I'll again have the project at the perfect state for . . . for application—"

"I'll see to it," Dan assured him. "Whatever you need—anything. Time, money—it's all yours."

Leland smiled smugly to himself, then he played the role, shaking his head and looking toward the empty cages. "Oh, if only my notes and animals hadn't been stolen . . ."

*Mine weren't*. Warren mouthed the words, but not a single sound crossed his lips.

Warren's smile broadened. Dr. Wagner's notes and animals had been stolen . . . but *his* were locked away safely in the small barn in his backyard . . . and his animals were all perfect specimens of the Starfish Project.


*2:38 P.M.*

Bruce Cameron tapped the dirt down on top of the mound with the back of a shovel, then stuck the blade into solid ground beside him. He crossed his arms and rested them on the shovel's handle, then let his eyes wander aimlessly over the land. "Sure is a perty view from up here," he said with a melancholy smile.

Kerk looked from the grave to Bruce, then made a sweeping survey of the shallow valley below and the woods bordering the farmland in the distance. Spring was beginning to touch the landscape, washing it in pale green and dotting it with a touch of color. Wild pampas grass was sprouting tufts of feathery plumage; a ballroom of daisies danced on the distant slope. Leaves were starting to dress winter's naked trees, weaving a curtain to obliterate man's encroachment on nature, hiding the vague outline of houses on the horizon.

"Yep, it sure is perty," Kerk mimicked with respect. "Corky'll be happy up here."

"She deserves to be happy. She was a good dog." Bruce pulled a red bandanna out of the front pocket of his bib overalls, wiped it across his brow, then touched it to the inner corner of each eye.

"That looks like Charlie down there," Kerk said, pointing toward the lane beyond the pond. "Is he delivering the ammonia for the fields?" he asked as he and Bruce watched a blue pickup truck, pulling a white trailer tank, drive past the livestock barns, then edge up close beside the equipment barn.

"That's Charlie," Bruce confirmed. "He's right on schedule, just like clockwork. And you, young man," Bruce said sternly, looking at Kerk, "you are not to go anywhere near that tank. Is that clear?"

"Yes, sir," Kerk answered sheepishly.

"Last spring, you were lucky you only got a few minor burns on your legs," Bruce reminded him. "You've got to remember you have to be doubly careful whenever you're around chemicals. You can never tell—"

"There come Bonnie and Alice," Kerk interrupted, not wanting to have a repeat of the safety lecture he'd heard at least a half-dozen times since his accident last spring. "They said they were going to come out and help get things set up for Sunday. I'd better go down—" Kerk stopped, turned back toward Bruce, then glanced at the grave. "Are we finished up here? I mean, have we . . . have we laid Corky to rest with the proper respect?"

An understanding smile pulled at the corners of Bruce's mouth, and he nodded. "Go on," he said. "Go on down and help Bonnie and Alice. See if you can remember everything your mother told you needed to be done today. I'll finish up here."

"You're sure?"

Bruce nodded again. "Go on." He glanced at the wooden cross he'd made in his wood shop; it still lay on the ground beside the grave. "I think, maybe, I'd like to be alone with Corky for a minute or two."

Kerk glanced at the grave, then looked up at Bruce. "It sure is a pretty place," he repeated. "Corky's going to like it up here." Kerk turned and walked away.

Bruce watched Kerk until the boy turned onto the tractor path at the edge of the field, then he knelt beside the grave, picked up the cross, and eased it into the soft dirt at the head of the mound. "You sure were a good dog," he said, taking off his straw hat and clutching it in front of his chest with both hands. "I'm going to miss you a lot, old girl. I'm—"

The shadow of a hawk glided across the grave. Bruce looked up just as the bird dipped its wing to circle overhead. A smile brightened his weathered face as he watched the hawk soar, then his attention returned to the grave.

"You can be like the hawk now, old Cork. Your spirit can fly free." Bruce looked back up at the sky and followed the flight of the majestic bird until it disappeared behind the treetops.


*3:49 P.M.*

Dan Patton slouched in the corner of an overstuffed leather sofa. Leaning against the padded arm, a half-empty tumbler—95 percent scotch whiskey, 5 percent soda—held loosely in his hand, he stared at the projection television screen mounted on the wall across the den. A field of snowy static stared back at him.

He took a hefty gulp, then his point of focus shifted to a gallery of ornately framed photographs clustered together on a pyramid of shelves behind a massive mahogany desk. The photographs—in both black-and-white and color—documented Daniel Jerome Patton the Fourth's growth and development; several of the pictures represented his halfhearted endeavors in a variety of sports.

In every photograph, his image was the central focal point. The part of each image that now commanded his attention was his legs. His legs—in the pictures—were both strong and healthy; they were both whole and complete. His legs . . . now . . . were both gone—

Dan gulped two more mouthfuls from the tumbler. His eyes darted back to the television screen, then they came to rest on the remote control lying on the coffee table in front of him.

He stared at the remote, focusing on the PLAY button. All he had to do was reach out and touch it—touch the PLAY button—then the cassette in the VCR would begin to roll, and the snowy static dominating the screen would be replaced by colorful pictures.

Just reach out and touch it . . .

Reach out and touch it—

Dan's fingers tightened around the glass; his hand shook. He downed two more hefty gulps before setting the tumbler on the coffee table, then, as he reached for the control, he hesitated . . . his hand hovered. Again, he focused on the PLAY button.

Reach out and touch it . . .

Reach out . . . touch it . . .

Touch it—*Touch it!*

Without thinking—without consciously willing his hand to move—Dan jabbed the PLAY button. Instantly, he jerked his hand back, responding as if the remote control had been white-hot.

His head turned; he looked across the room at the screen. His breath hung stagnant on the crest of his lips. Almost immediately, the snowy static was replaced by a colorful moving picture. A heavy sweat seeped from Dan's pores as he watched:

"Hi!" A young buxom blonde in a skimpy halter top winked and blew a kiss toward the camera. "I'm Marita, and this is my friend Devona," she said as she pulled a dark-haired girl in a string bikini into view beside her. "We're off the coast of sunny Puerto Rico, aboard the *Patton Princess*—that's a private yacht. We're here to help our dear friend, Dan Patton the Fourth, celebrate his inheritance. Actually," she giggled, "about fifty of Dan's *dearest* and *closest* friends are here to help him celebrate." The camera pulled back, and the picture took in a mass of swimsuit-clad men and women gathered on the deck of an elaborately equipped ship.

Dan jabbed at the remote control again and managed to press the FF button. As the picture raced across the screen at a staccato tempo, Dan sat motionless for several seconds, watching, then he reached for the tumbler of scotch and soda. He continued to watch the tape over the glass's rim as he gulped down two more mouthfuls.

It was coming: the part of the tape he hated . . . the part of the tape he *had* to see. It was getting closer: the part of the tape that had recorded the event that had changed his life forever . . . the event that had come all too close to taking his very life—

Dan jabbed the remote control again, pressing the PLAY button. The fast-forward action on the screen slowed to normal speed, and a chorus of laughter erupted from the stereo speakers in opposite corners of the den.

"Oh, Dan, you're such a tease," the buxom Marita said. She was on her knees on a deck lounge chair, snuggling close beside him.

The image of Dan Patton, enlarged beyond life-size on the television screen, looked at her and grinned. "You'll think 'a tease' after I get through with you." He reached behind her neck, released the small bow securing her halter top, and let the fabric slip from his hand. She giggled, and her ample breasts jiggled inches from his face.

"Do I excite you?" he asked, flicking one of her nipples with a finger.

"Sure you do," she said, giggling and leaning closer to him. "Anything you do excites me." Her breast brushed his cheek; her hardened nipple lingered at the corner of his lips. "Can I return the favor?" she asked in a voice suddenly breathy.

His tongue snaked out of the corner of his mouth and toyed with her nipple. She gasped with a quick breath.

"The invitation sounds appealing," he said.

"Then let's go down to your cabin and—"

"Down to my cabin?" He pulled back and looked at her as if stunned by her suggestion. "Why *go down* to my cabin? Why not just do it here?"

"Here?" She stared at him for a moment, then looked around at everyone watching them.

"Yes, here. I'm having *everything* I do today filmed," he said, pointing toward the camera, "so I'll always be able to remember this glorious day when I finally collected my inheritance. Boy"—he laughed—"I was beginning to wonder if my old man was ever going to kick off."

"That's an awful thing to say," Marita said with both surprise and revulsion.

"Don't let that bother you. Come on, lay down right here," he said, gesturing with his hand toward the lounge chair's extended leg rest. "The sun's just right and . . . and, Rusty"— he motioned to the cameraman—"move in close here so you can get a good angle—"

"Stop it!" Marita got up from the lounge and retied her halter top. "You're perverted."

He looked up at her with mock concern. "What? Don't I excite you anymore?" He couldn't contain himself any longer and broke into a hearty laugh. Everyone around him—except for Marita—joined in the laughter.

"You're ... you're *all* perverted!" she shouted. "And you—" she looked directly into the camera. "This is for you." She flipped the cameraman the bird, then turned around and walked away.

The camera closed in on Dan. He laughed, and lifted his champagne glass in a mock toast.

"Dan," someone off-camera said, "you've got to be the luckiest guy in the world. The ladies love you, you're good-looking, and ... now, you're rich. There's not a thing in the world you could possibly want."

The laugh eased out of Dan's face, and for an instant, he was somber. "There's just one more thing ..." Again, he lifted his glass to the camera. "To you, Jackie ... as soon as Richard's out of the way—"

"Dan!" A male voice shouted, drawing his attention. "Tell Rusty to bring the camera! Wally's hooked into a big one, and he's about to bring it in!" The screen went blank for ten seconds, then the picture resumed, focused on the yacht's lower fishing deck.

"Get back!" one of the crewmen ordered as he and three other muscled men in white strained to haul the big fish on board.

"Shark," someone whispered reverently in the background.

"I've never seen one that big."

"He could go sixteen to eighteen feet easy."

"I'd say he's more like over twenty." As comments by unseen bystanders emerged from the speakers, the picture on the screen focused on the crewmen bringing the shark on board . . . and on the shark itself.

Blood oozed from the side of its mouth where the steel-shank hook had been firmly set. Four additional wounds flanked its gleaming body where large hoisting hooks had been plunged into its flesh . . . and still remained. They too seeped a steady flow of blood that washed across the white tile deck.

The shark's massive body flailed and twisted. One hoisting hook tore free, ripping a large chunk of flesh from the fish's side. Blood spurted . . . pulsed forcefully. Frantically, the shark's gills opened and closed . . . opened and closed . . . again . . . and again in a useless effort to obtain oxygen from the thin air around him. Its black round eyes glistened, reflecting pain, terror, fear . . . and hate.

"What a glorious offering." Dan's image stepped onto the screen, bringing with him a short, stocky man. "To help celebrate my father's death—and the transfer of his money to me," he added in a tone no way touched by grief, "my good friend Wally, here, has brought pride to the *Patton Princess* by landing one of the largest sharks—"

As Dan turned and pointed to the shark, the big fish seemed to take the gesture as a cue. Flapping its tail—pushing itself away from the side of the boat—it slid across the blood-reddened deck . . . its cavernous mouth agape . . . razor-sharp teeth reflecting in the midday sun. Before anyone could react, the shark's mouth closed around Dan's legs.

Screams exploded from the speakers. Bright red blood spouted from the shark's mouth—

The camera was dropped, but it continued to record from its horizontal position on the deck, capturing images of feet slipping on the blood-slick tile . . . crewmen beating on the shark's head . . . gouging hoist hooks into its mouth, trying to pry its jaws apart . . . focusing on the shark's eyes—on its cold dark eyes that glistened with hate and revenge—

"No!" Dan threw the tumbler at the television. It broke, and what little scotch and soda remained in the glass dribbled down the screen and dripped on the carpet.

"No! No! No!" Dan closed his hands into tight fists and began beating on his thighs a few inches above his prostheses. "I shouldn't have to live like this. I shouldn't—" He began to sob. "Damn you, Wagner! You had it and let it get away. Damn you to hell—"

"Dan?" The door to the den opened abruptly; Rusty Snider stepped into the room. "Are you—" When Rusty saw the blood-ravaged picture that continued to play on the screen and the broken tumbler on the floor beneath it, he knew what had happened. The same scene had been repeated dozens of times before.

Rusty looked at Dan, huddled in the corner of the sofa, and shook his head in sympathy. "Why did you do it this time?" He walked to the coffee table, picked up the remote control, and turned off the television. "What made you want to watch it again?"

Dan looked up at him—green eyes looking into green eyes. He stared at Rusty as if seeing him for the first time, then Dan turned away. "Get out! Get out of here and leave me alone."

"If that's what you want," Rusty said as he returned the remote control to the coffee table. "I'll be right outside if you need me . . . if you want to talk."

Rusty walked to the door. He started to leave but stopped and looked back at Dan.

For almost twenty years, he'd been looking after Daniel Jerome Patton the Fourth. It had started when they'd both been in high school.

After Rusty's mother died, and no relatives could be found that would welcome the illegitimate child with open arms, Dan's father had taken him in on a business arrangement that benefited them both. In exchange for room, board, and spending money, Rusty's job was to take care of Dan—to be his bodyguard, so to speak.

The first few years were hell. Dan was a spoiled, arrogant brat, and he'd just as soon pick a fight as not, knowing Rusty would be there to take the brunt of it in his place. Thanks to Dan's misadventures, Rusty had more than his share of black eyes and bloody noses.

But as they grew older, Dan slowly matured, and the confrontations became fewer and farther between. Now, he rarely needed Rusty to defend him; he'd come to look upon Rusty as a friend. Within the past few years, their friendship had grown stronger. Sometimes it seemed they couldn't have been any closer, even if they had been brothers.

"I'll be right outside if you need me," Rusty repeated. He turned and closed the door behind him.


*5:03 P.M.*


Warren Maxey stepped out under the canopy, held the front door open for Leland Wagner, then fell into step beside his colleague. Neither spoke as they walked toward the steps and ramp leading to the parking lot; neither had spoken more than a few words to the other throughout the entire day.

When they reached the end of the walkway, Leland didn't break his stride as he turned onto the ramp and started down. Warren slowed his pace, then stopped at the top of the steps. When Leland finally noticed Warren wasn't staying abreast with him, he stopped, turned around, and looked back.

"I just remembered something I should have done today," Warren said, glancing back at the building, his eyes focusing on the front door. He hesitated, then looked back at Leland. "It'll only take me a few minutes, but if I don't do it right now while I'm thinking about it, I might forget about it altogether by Monday." Leland nodded, turned toward the parking lot, and continued down the ramp. "Have a good weekend," Warren called after him, "and Happy Easter." Leland motioned, raised a hand to his side in what might have been interpreted as a brief wave, but that was the extent of his response.

Without wasting any more time, Warren turned back toward the building and began walking. He thought to pace himself; he didn't want to walk too fast—or too slow; a medium stride was what he was aiming for. If Leland would happen to look back at him, Warren didn't want to present himself as being anxious—nor did he want to appear as if he were stalling.

Warren released a quick breath when he finally reached the front door and pushed it open. At last, he was beyond Leland's line of vision. Now, all he had to do was— His eyes darted to the reception desk on the right side of the lobby. To his relief, the area behind the counter was empty. He presumed Hollie Bass had already gone home.

Assured that no one was watching, Warren hurried across the lobby and continued on down the hall past the first two labs. He stopped in front of the third door, turned to face it, and glanced up and down the hallway as he reached into his pocket for his key ring.

He fumbled through the collection of keys on the ring and when he found the one for the lounge door, he slipped it into the lock. Moving smoothly through an oftentimes-repeated sequence, Warren opened the door quickly, stepped inside the room, closed the door behind him, and turned on the overhead light.

Directly in front of him, two fabric-upholstered sofas sat back to back in the middle of the spacious room. To the right, a round wooden table, flanked by four straight-backed chairs, filled most of the area between the sofas and a ceiling-to-floor bookshelf that spanned the length of the wall. To the left, a small gas stove, counter, and sink occupied the space beneath an upper set of kitchen cabinets. In the far left corner of the room, an old two-door refrigerator hummed loudly.

The room had originally been set up to be a lounge for the staff, but since most of the employees had a lab or office of their own, the only people to use the lounge with any regularity were the night watchman and custodial staff, and on occasion, Hollie Bass brought her lunch. Warren found it to be the perfect place where nothing was ever disturbed.

Warren sidestepped around the sofas and walked straight to the refrigerator. He opened the door and squatted down in front of it so he could reach a brown paper bag that had been pushed to the back of the bottom shelf. As soon as he had the bag firmly in hand, he opened it and pulled out a small wooden box.

A smile highlighted the pinched features of his face as he lifted the box's simple hook latch and opened the lid. Nestled inside, cradled on a soft bed of foam rubber, were two vials. Each vial was two-thirds full of a red-brown liquid.

"I thought you went home," a soft voice said behind him.

Startled, Warren turned awkwardly toward the hallway door. Still in a squat position, he lost his balance and fell, landing—half sitting—on his left calf and thigh. As he'd fought to maintain his balance, he'd lost his grip on the wooden box, and it had slipped from his hand. It now lay on the floor beside him—lid open—the vials fully exposed.

"Sorry," Hollie said as she walked across the room toward him. "I wasn't meaning to sneak up on you or anything. I brought a Jell-O salad in this morning to share with everyone, but with all the excitement today, we didn't take the time—" When she saw the vials in the box on the floor, Hollie cut her meaningless chitchat short. She studied the vials for a few moments, then looked Warren squarely in the eyes. "What's that?"

"N-n-nothing." Warren picked up the box, closed the lid, and put it back in the paper bag. He worked his way to his feet, closed the refrigerator door, and turned to face Hollie directly.

"They looked like . . . test tubes," Hollie said suspiciously.

"They . . . they are," Warren answered nervously as he sidestepped around her.

"What were they doing in the refrigerator in here?" she asked pointedly as her head slowly turned to follow his movement. "And where are you taking them . . ." Hollie's voice trailed off as the only logical answer she could think of crossed her mind. "Oh, Warren, how could you?"

"What?" Warren stopped short in his ill-designed escape and turned back toward Hollie. "How could I what?"

"How could you— How could you *betray* Dr. Wagner?"

"What?" Warren asked, totally confused.

"I've heard about people like you . . . and after all Dr. Wagner's done for you."

"What are you talking about?" Warren asked with outright sincerity. He was dumbfounded; Hollie's accusations had slipped past him completely.

"Espionage. You're taking samples of our new drugs to another company, and you're going to sell them—" Warren started laughing, cutting Hollie short. "I don't think there's a thing at all funny about it," she stated adamantly.

"Oh, Hollie . . ." Warren tried to control his laughter as he spoke, "Hollie, come over here." He sat down on the sofa facing the cabinets and gestured for her to join him. Hollie hesitated for several moments, then took a seat at the opposite end of the sofa. "Can I trust you to keep a secret?" he asked.

"It depends," Hollie answered bluntly. "I won't do anything to hurt Dr. Wagner—"

"And I wouldn't do anything to hurt Leland either." He paused. "I might have even come up with something that will help him." Hollie didn't comment; she eyed him skeptically.

"Okay." Warren adjusted himself on the sofa so he faced her directly. "Did you know Leland had a secret lab inside his office?"

"Why— How would I know?" Hollie asked defensively.

"You wouldn't, of course, but I found it by accident a few months ago and . . ."

Warren proceeded to tell Hollie about Leland's lab, about his own lab and animals, and how—in secret—he wanted to perfect Leland's experiment before telling Leland of his efforts. He told her the bare minimum he felt was needed to gain her trust, but he didn't expound upon the Starfish Project. There was no need for her to know.

5:37 P.M.

The phone rang two . . . three . . . four times. Denis Sweezy turned from the filing cabinet on the opposite side of his office and looked across the room. Five . . . six . . . seven rings. He wasn't expecting a phone call; everyone had checked in by nine o'clock that morning. Eight . . . nine . . . ten. The irritating rings echoed in the ceiling space above the room. Whoever it was . . . was persistent. Usually, not even a member of the group would let it ring more than five or six times . . . unless— Someone was in trouble.

A half-dozen strides carried Sweezy across his small office. The phone was on its twelfth ring when he answered. "Yes," he said as he sat down on the corner of his desk. A few seconds of silence passed, then he added, "The book at the top of our reading list this month is the V. M. Thompson thriller *Project GOD*."

"We missed some animals last night," a soft voice said in response.

"Where?"

"In a private lab out in the county. It shouldn't be too hard to find." The caller paused. "The new animals will be arriving on Monday at Patton's. A couple of extra people should be able to take care of the ones we missed previously as well."

"I'll contact our people and make sure enough are available to do the job."

"I'll call again Monday with details."

*6:28 P.M.*

Warren looked out the back-door window from the utility room. He drummed his fingers on the washer's lid, then glanced at the clock mounted above the kitchen door. He was fidgety; he was waiting for his neighbor, Randy Leonhardt, to go inside.

Leonhardt was the type of individual who, in an attempt to be friendly, could smother someone with backyard conversation and neighborly advice; at times, he could become downright nosey. At the moment, Warren wasn't in the mood to confront Leonhardt; he didn't want to take the time to be either neighborly or friendly.

Warren glanced at the small wooden box he'd brought home from the lab and set on the shelf above the washer. He was anxious to incorporate the new serum with the ones he already had and begin injections that evening.

He returned his attention to his neighbor's backyard. Randy Leonhardt was still sitting on a stool, tinkering with his garden tractor and, evidently, trying to explain the engine's workings to his ten-year-old son.

"Go inside, will you," Warren mumbled. He glanced at the small red barn on the back edge of his property, then looked back at Leonhardt. "Aren't you and your kid getting hungry? You've got to go inside and eat some—" At that moment,

Leonhardt's wife must have come to the patio door, because Leonhardt looked up from his garden tractor and nodded.

The boy ran to the house. Leonhardt took the time to put his tools back in the toolbox, then walked toward the house at a leisurely pace.

Anxious, Warren watched them intently. He pressed the side of his face against the door's window, straining to see whether Leonhardt went inside the house or not. But due to the houses' angular placement around the main circular drive, he couldn't see his neighbor's back door.

"They have to be going inside to eat," Warren said to himself, again glancing up at the clock on the wall. He waited impatiently for over a minute, watching his neighbor's backyard. When Leonhardt didn't return to his tractor, Warren guessed it was safe for him to venture outside without fear of being cornered.

Warren slipped the wooden box under his arm, stepped out onto the stoop, and scrutinized the backyards on both sides of his own. He saw no one.

Not wanting to waste another minute more, he hurried down the steps, picked up his pace as he crossed the yard, and didn't slow down until he rounded the corner of the small barn. Without hesitating, he reached above the door, located the key, unlocked the door, and went inside. Not until the door was closed behind him did he reach for the switch and turn on the overhead lights. His entrance was greeted by a chorus of growls, squeals, chirps, and chatters.

"And hello to you too," he said as his eyes swept over the cages on the shelves to his right.

Without any further delay, Warren went about his nightly routine, filling food and water bowls, then emptying litter pans from beneath the cages. After finishing his housekeeping chores, he went from cage to cage, drawing a small vial of blood from each animal. He placed the blood in a tabletop centrifuge for separation, then repeated his round of the cages, this time injecting a proportioned amount of the concentrated serum he'd brought home with him into each animal.

He'd followed the same procedure every night for over two months, speculating where the project might be leading. But today—after overhearing Leland explain the Starfish Project to Dan Patton—Warren's speculation had been verified. Tonight, he planned to take his experiment one step further.

"Which one of you would like to volunteer?" he asked, again looking over the wall of cages.

Only twice, since he'd gathered his menagerie together, had the barn been completely quiet. Tonight—following his question—marked the third time.

Warren took the time to look at them individually, from one animal to the next. In return, their small dark eyes focused on him in . . . what was it? Fear? Could they possibly have been aware of his intent—

"Come now, don't I have a volunteer?" he asked again. One of two white mice, together in a cage, moved; the other mouse squealed. "Very good, my laboratory friends," he said with a smile, his eyes homing in on the mice. "Of all the variety of specimens here, you know you're the ones best suited for the initial phase. How thoughtful of you to volunteer."

Warren picked up their cage and carried it to a worktable on the opposite side of the barn. He took a tray down from a storage cabinet beside the table and unfolded a white towel across it. Carrying the tray to yet another cabinet, he filled it with a variety of sponges, bandages, tape, and dressings. Lastly, he added several small-diameter rubber tubes and an assortment of scalpels.

Warren returned to the worktable and set the tray down beside the mice's cage. From a shelf just beyond the table, he retrieved a bottle of alcohol and a large ceramic tile. Lastly, he reached into his pocket and pulled out a tin of styptic powder, which he'd brought from his own medicine cabinet, and a circular piece of cardboard with a hole cut in its center.

"There, it looks like we have everything," he said as he reviewed a mental checklist to make sure he wasn't missing anything he might need. Warren stooped down beside the table and looked at the two mice on their own level. "Now, which one of you is going to have the honor?" he asked, looking at one mouse and then the other. The mice backed into opposite corners. "Come . . . come now, where is my brave volunteer who called out to me just a few minutes ago?"

Warren moved his hand toward the cage. The mouse closest to him tried to bite, but Warren retrieved his hand quickly, and the mouse's sharp teeth clamped down on the cage's wire.

"You're not going to be like that, are you?" Warren asked as he picked up a heavy glove from a shelf beneath the table and slipped it on his left hand. "Okay, it's been a long day, and I'm tired of messing around."

Warren opened the top door of the cage, reached in with his gloved hand, and cornered the mouse that had tried to bite him. The tiny animal squirmed and squealed as the leather glove wrapped around him. Its frightened companion backed into the opposite corner of the cage.

"Now just hold still, and it'll be over before you know it."

Warren held the mouse secure in his left hand. With his right hand, he slipped a piece of rubber tubing around the mouse's right front leg and pulled it tight. Working quickly, he held the mouse down on the ceramic tile, soaked its front leg with alcohol, then picked up one of the scalpels.

"This will only hurt for a minute or two."

Warren positioned the scalpel just above the joint to the mouse's right front foot. He laid his index finger across the back of the scalpel and began to apply a steady pressure. The scalpel was sharp; in an instant, it cut completely through skin and flesh and muscle and bone.

The mouse squeaked and squealed in agony. It tried to squirm, but Warren held it firmly against the tile. It tried to bite, but the heavy glove protected Warren's hand.

"Hold still," Warren said as he poured alcohol over the mouse's raw stub. Working quickly, he packed the wound with styptic powder, then bound it tightly with a dressing and then a bandage. When everything was secure, Warren released the rubber tubing from around the mouse's leg and watched the end of the white gauze for any signs of bleeding. When he saw no blood, Warren considered the operation a success.

"There, that wasn't too bad now, was it?" Warren talked to the mouse while he taped the circular piece of cardboard around the animal's neck. "And this will keep you from getting to your leg," he explained. "We wouldn't want you to chew the bandages off and get it infected but . . . but then, if you've *really* got inside of you what I *think* you've got inside of you, it wouldn't make any difference anyway."

After Warren was satisfied the mouse's collar was secure, he returned the mouse to its cage. The second mouse, leery of the strange contraption around its companion's neck, scurried to the opposite corner of the cage.

"You're not too sure of that, are you?" Warren asked the cowering mouse. "Or are you jealous?" He contemplated the situation for a moment, then Warren reached inside the cage and picked up the second mouse. "While we're at it, you might as well have one too," he said to the mouse as he placed it on the tile and poured alcohol over its left front leg. "It's probably a good idea to have two subjects anyway, and I can tell you apart as easy as right and left."

When Warren completed the procedure on the second mouse, he formed a makeshift collar for it out of a syringe-box lid, then returned the mouse to the cage. "You two take care of each other tonight," he said as he secured the spring-latch door.

Warren cleaned off the table, emptied the centrifuge, and placed the new batch of concentrated serum in the small refrigerator in the back corner of the barn. Just as he was about to leave, he stopped, surveyed all the animals in the cages on the shelves, then he focused on the two mice in the cage he'd left on the table.

"You two have a good night, and I'll be in bright and early in the morning to see how you're doing." A thrill of great expectation tingled through Warren as he turned off the lights and closed the door behind him.

# Saturday

## (Day Two)

*1:17 A.M.*

Jackie woke with a start. She lay motionless for several moments . . . listening, then she found the courage to sit upright in bed. Immediately, her eyes darted from one corner of the room to the next, trying to distinguish more than the shadows cast from the pole light outside her window. After a few uneasy moments, her eyes adjusted, and she was able to see that she was alone.

Still, her breaths came shallow, and a strange sensation tingled the length of her spine. What had awakened her so abruptly? What had—

Then she heard it . . . and was able to identify what had yanked her from her sleep. Kerk was shouting . . . crying out in his sleep.

Jackie tilted her head back and looked up at the ceiling; Kerk's room was directly above hers. She stared unknowingly at the darkened light fixture overhead, thinking . . . wondering. What had prompted Kerk to cry out? Unfortunately, she knew the answer: his nightmares. What she didn't know was what had caused the nightmare to return.

Kerk's nights had been relatively calm and secure for the past six months. What had brought on the regressive change?

Jackie thought for a moment—thought back over the events

of the past month . . . the past week . . . the past day— An obvious answer came to her: Dan had come to the compound that morning, and Kerk had confronted him.

Jackie scooted across the bed until she could lean back against the headboard. She slowly turned her head to look at the picture of Richard, Kerk, and herself on the nightstand, then she stretched to reach behind the frame and turned on a small lamp.

"If only you were still here," she whispered, leaning closer to the picture and propping herself up with her elbow. Jackie studied Richard's face for a few moments, then her attention settled on his green eyes . . . the green eyes that came so close to matching those of Dan Patton.

It had been the consensus of a handful of psychiatrists that those green eyes had been the founding core of Kerk's problems. They theorized, since Kerk and his father had been very close, anything that reminded Kerk of his father could trigger any number of unexpected behaviors; Kerk had subconsciously chosen nightmares.

But something specific had to be the catalyst for his dreams. The mere presence of green eyes, alone, hadn't been the sole source of his problems; if they had been, then he wouldn't have been able to look in the mirror at his own image or interact so openly with Bruce.

To help identify the element, the doctors compiled an extensive list of external stimuli they thought might contain the influencing factor. After weeks of discussion and counseling with Kerk, gradually, the list was shortened and the possibilities narrowed. The last item to remain was Dan Patton's intrusion into their lives.

It would have been difficult enough for Kerk to accept any man coming to see his mother only a couple of weeks after his father's death. But since Dan had green eyes—eyes almost identical to his father's—that had compounded the matter then . . . and, unfortunately, apparently still did.

"If only you were still here," Jackie repeated, again concentrating on Richard's smiling face in the picture. She blinked and felt tears gathering in the corners of her eyes. "If only they could find the man who shot you—"

Kerk cried out again. Jackie looked up at the ceiling, wondering if she should go upstairs and look in on him, but she knew it wouldn't do any good . . . for either one of them. Kerk was sound asleep, probably unaware he was even dreaming, and she . . . well, Jackie knew she didn't need any further reminder of what lay behind Kerk's nightmares.

Jackie looked at the picture again, smiled a lonely smile, then turned out the light. She slipped down in bed and pulled the sheet up close under her chin. It was going to be a long night for the both of them: Kirk fighting his nightmares, and Jackie fighting the loneliness of an empty bed.

# Sunday

## (Day Three)

*5:30 P.M.*

". . . and did you see Gladys Tabor?" Barry asked with a laugh. "She was dragging poor little Suzanne around all over the meadow, pointing out Easter eggs for her to pick up. I'm surprised she didn't yank the child's arm right out of its socket."

"I think mothers should be outlawed from Easter-egg hunts," Jackie added with a laugh. "The kids would have a lot of fun on their own; it's the adults who turn everything into a frenzied nightmare." With the mention of the word *nightmare*, Jackie's mood suddenly turned sullen.

"What's the matter?" Barry asked, immediately picking up on Jackie's mood change.

Jackie walked on a little farther, then stopped beside a fallen tree and sat down. "It's Kerk," she said after several thoughtful moments. "He had another one of his nightmares early Saturday morning."

"Was it bad?" Barry asked as he sat down beside her.

"Not as bad as they've been in the past, but since it'd been quite a while since he'd had one, I was hoping he might have outgrown them by now and they would be all over and done with."

"Why didn't you say something about it to me yesterday? I

was out here all day, and maybe I could have found some time to talk with him about it."

"I don't think talking would have helped. In all honesty, I don't think he even remembered having it. It just seemed so bad at the time."

Jackie looked out across the valley and let her mind wander. She was searching for peace and had yet to locate a place to find it.

"Was it because Dan was out here the other day?" Barry asked, visually following the outline of Jackie's profile.

"If what all the doctors had to say was true, I would imagine that's what prompted it," she answered, turning to look at Barry.

"You know there's a way to stop Dan from ever coming out here again," Barry said, a smile softening his face as he picked up her hand. "You know I love you, and you know I want to spend the rest of my life with you. All you have to do is say the word, and we'll get married, and I'll move out here."

"I know," Jackie exhaled in a whisper, looking into Barry's dark brown eyes. "You mean so much to me." Her hand rose to touch the crest of his square jaw.

Barry slid an arm around Jackie's waist and pulled her close to him. For an instant, they gazed into each other's eyes, then the distance between their lips grew shorter and shorter. "I love you," Barry whispered an instant before their lips touched.

Jackie closed her eyes. A warmth radiated along every nerve in her body. She slipped her arms around him and returned his kiss, feeling the desire to be held . . . to be touched . . . to be caressed. It had been too long since she had loved. Oh, Richard—

Jackie became instantly rigid. She pulled away from Barry and turned to again look out over the valley.

"What's the matter?" Barry asked, certain he already

knew the answer.

"I . . . I can't," Jackie answered, shaking her head. "It's not time yet."

"My God, Jackie," Barry said a bit too brusquely, "Richard's been dead for almost a year and a half—"

"Don't you think I know that!" she said, turning sharply toward him. "Don't you think I know how long he's been gone." Tears clouded her eyes, and she fought to keep them from brimming past her lashes. "I'm trying to get over him. I'm trying to make room in my life for you, but . . . but until they find the man who killed Richard, I don't think my soul will be at peace enough to love someone else—"

The branches rustled directly above them. They looked up to see a large hawk take off from its perch in the tree and soar out over the valley.

Neither spoke for several moments; they pretended to watch the majestic bird as it surveyed its territory from a vantage point high in the sky. Then, knowing their brief encounter had come to an end, Barry reopened their line of communication, as he had so often done in the past, by directing their attention to a neutral topic.

"Our tickets for tomorrow night's game are three rows up behind the backstop."

"Kerk will be happy to hear that," Jackie said, then she turned and again looked into Barry's eyes. "Thank you," she said softly.

Barry looked at her for a moment, then he shook his head and smiled. "It's all in a day's work," he said, slipping an arm around her shoulders and hugging her close. "It's a little hard on the ego, but this is a lot nicer than shoveling out horse stalls."

# Monday

# (Day Four)

6:45 A.M.

". . . and after we finally got the stalls cleaned out, I found a place to hide out where Jackie couldn't find me to give me more things to do. Fritz was a lifesaver. He let me ride along in the tractor cab with him while he sprayed ammonia on the fields. That took just about the rest of Saturday afternoon." Barry sat on the corner of Sheriff Joseph's desk as he recounted his weekend at the compound. "Then Sunday morning, we played Peter Rabbit and hid all sorts of candy and toys out in the front meadow for an Easter-egg hunt for the county home kids."

"Sounds like fun," Rex Joseph commented in passing.

"It sounds too much like work to me." Sergeant Terry Neville had stopped at the small table beside them to refill his coffee cup and had overheard the conversation. Not one to let an opportunity pass, he added his comment before walking on.

"Work . . . play, I don't suppose it really matters what Barry does as long as he has a chance to be with Jackie while he's doing it," Joseph quipped as he leaned back in his chair, laced his fingers together, and tucked his hands behind his head. "When are you going to make an honest woman out of that fine lady?" he prodded with a grin.

Barry eyed Rex, knowing, by the terminology he'd used, he'd been talking with Kevin McFall. "It's not me. She's the one who's dragging her feet," Barry answered. "She says it wouldn't be right yet."

"Yet? It's been a year and a half since Richard was killed. I'd say that's more than enough time for her to be a respectable widow."

"When was the last time *you* won an argument with a woman?"

"Point taken."

"Have you guys seen this?" Terry Neville asked as he walked toward them, a coffee cup in one hand and a folded newspaper in the other. "It says here," he said, gesturing with the paper, "that about a dozen elementary school kids down in Crowley, Louisiana, have come down with an unidentifiable virus. It says one of the kids found a white laboratory rat and had it in a shoebox, showing his friends. The boy, and every one of his friends, turned up sick in less than twenty-four hours. They're asking for information from anybody who was working with a new strain of virus who had their animals stolen Friday during the nationwide break-ins." Neville looked up from the paper. "That's awful to have something like that happen to kids."

"An unidentifiable virus would be awful to happen to anybody," Barry said. "I hope if somebody turned any animals loose around here, none of them had anything catching. I'd hate to think we'd have to face that on top of everything else that's already going on around here."

"That's something you might be able to check out," Joseph said as he straightened in his chair and picked up a piece of notepaper from his desk. "Have you ever heard of a man by the name of Denis Sweezy?" he asked, handing Barry the paper. Barry concentrated on the name for a moment, then shook his head. "We got a tip on him in reference to the local break-ins. It's not much, but I thought it might be something worth checking on."

Barry scanned the personal information the desk sergeant had scribbled on the notepaper. "So he's a philosophy professor at Bailey College, huh?" Joseph nodded. "I wonder who turned him in? A student unhappy over a grade?"

"Who knows. As you can see, the caller didn't leave his name."

"Think it could be a prank?"

"I'd say our chances are about fifty-fifty, but at least it's a lead, and right now, it's the only one we've got." Joseph thought for a moment, then added, "Come to think of it, it could be a pretty damn good lead. College professors are notorious for supporting causes. Why, just look at the trouble some of them caused during Vietnam—"

"What the hell?" Barry spouted in surprise.

Halfway across the station, he saw Milton Hawkins and Forrest Deem, the two mountain men he'd helped arrest Friday morning, walking toward the exit elevator with a man in a three-piece suit. Both men looked back at him, smug grins on their faces.

Barry was on his feet in an instant, all but ready to back up the ire he felt burning deep inside. "What are they doing here? And how did they get turned loose?"

"The same old reasons," Joseph explained, "time, space, and money. Kevin brought them up to us Friday afternoon because they didn't have any room down in their jail. Then when the circuit judge couldn't find an open date in his trial log for at least three months, he set their bail low enough so they could buy their way out."

"It's not right," Barry protested.

"Hell no, it's not right, but that's the way it is. And it's going to get a hell of a lot worse before it even looks like it might get better."

Barry watched the mountain men step into the elevator, then looked down at the paper in his hand. "When scum like that get away with what they do to animals, I can't help but question why we have to go after the people who set them free."

"We do it because we remember what side of the law we're on."

"Yeah . . . right." Barry folded the paper with Denis Sweezy's name on it and slipped it into his shirt pocket.

"You might want to get a move on if you're going over to the college. You'll probably have a better chance of finding Sweezy if you get to his office before classes start."

"Good old Bailey College, home of the Fighting Wildcats." Barry tilted his head and looked at Rex out of the corner of his eye. "I wonder if they ever kept one penned up in a cage. . . ."

*6:51 A.M.*

Warren stuck his head out the utility room's back door and glanced to the right, then to the left. When he saw no one in either of his neighbor's backyards, he stepped out onto the stoop. He hesitated and again looked to his right and left, then he descended the steps and began a fast walk toward the small barn.

During the past two days, Warren had made the same trip half a dozen times a day. As had been the case with each previous visit, he was anxious to see how the mice were progressing; he wondered if there would be any positive results.

It had been almost sixty hours since he'd amputated the mice's feet. How long would it take for the regeneration to begin . . . if the serum worked at all.

In spite of everything, Warren remained a realist. The possibility of failure continued to hang like a shadow in the back of his mind.

Warren retrieved the key from above the door, unlocked it, and stepped inside. He turned on the light, and his eyes immediately sought out the mice in the cage on top of the worktable.

"How are you two doing?" he asked as he walked toward the table and stooped down for a closer look inside the cage. "Do either of you have anything new to show me?" Both mice sat in the back corner of the cage, their bodies shaded by their cardboard collars. "I don't have a lot of time to spend with you this morning," Warren said as he picked up the glove from the shelf beneath the table and slipped it on his left hand. "Now don't be difficult."

Warren opened the cage and reached inside. For the past two days, both mice had tried to escape capture every time Warren put his hand inside the cage, but this morning, neither mouse moved; both sat surprisingly still. Neither even appeared to cower in response to his presence.

Warren picked up the mouse with the bandaged left front leg. After closing the cage door, he turned the mouse over in his hand and moved closer to the light. Using a small pair of scissors he'd left on the table the night before, he snipped the edges of the bandage, then carefully unwound it. Lifting the mouse even closer to the light, Warren scrutinized the animal's leg.

The blood vessels had sealed nicely with clotted blood. The raw end of the bone was still visible . . . but Warren thought its shape had changed from the day before. The end of the exposed bone no longer appeared blunt with sharp edges; it had taken on a rounded, smoother shape. And the muscle tissue . . . the flesh was still raw, but there was more of it—thicker, firmer . . . stronger.

Warren's heart thumped, and his hands began to shake. He took in a deep breath and closed his eyes.

Was his imagination running away with him? Was he

wishing hard enough—so hard—*too* hard—that his eyes were playing tricks on him as well?

Or was it possible? Was the regenerative process actually taking place right there in his own backyard?

"That's why you did two," Warren said nervously, "two, so you could double-check."

Warren's hand shook as he returned the mouse to its cage. His hand shook even more when he picked up the second mouse and began to cut away its bandages.

"This will tell me..." he whispered as he gently removed the dressing from the mouse's right front leg.

Warren focused on the stub of flesh and bone... and it suddenly appeared to change—*to grow*—right in front of his eyes!

"It's... it's working," he said in a choked whisper. "It's working!" he came close to shouting.

A shot of adrenaline jolted Warren. What would he do? What would be his next course of action?

He'd talk with Leland. He'd tell Leland everything, and together they could—

Together? Why *together?*

Warren suddenly questioned why *he* should have to share anything with anyone. After all, *he* was the one who'd completed the process right there in his own backyard. Why should Leland be in line for any of the credit? Leland had been stupid. If he had been smart, he wouldn't have lost his animals and—

"Patton." The word passed over Warren's lips as if it were sacred. *"He's* the one I need to talk to." He looked again at the mouse's front leg. "The two of you are so alike..." Warren turned his head, and his eyes sought out the small refrigerator in the far corner of the barn. "How much serum would it take? I'll need to calculate... for a man."

Warren carried the mouse with him as he walked to the

refrigerator and opened the door. He bent over so he could see the racks inside and counted ten and a half vials of serum.

"Proportionately . . ." A smile broadened across his face as his mind quickly estimated the calculations. "There's plenty. And with all of you here," he said, turning to face the wall of caged animals, "the supply of serum will be endless."

*7:48 A.M.*

A light-blue panel van, with the words SOUTH PORT HUMANE SOCIETY printed in dark blue on the side, came to a stop in front of the feed barn. The driver's door opened, and a tall, lanky woman, with dishwater-blond hair pulled back in a ponytail, got out. Almost in unison, the passenger's door opened, and a short, chubby woman with dark brown hair that looked to have been cut following the outline of a bowl placed over her head stepped out and walked around the front of the van. Both women wore light-blue jumpsuits with the humane-society logo printed in dark blue on the back.

"Bruce," the dishwater blonde called out, turning her head to take in the building housing Bruce's office, the feed barn, and the three livestock barns toward the north. "Bruce Cameron, if you're anywhere within shouting distance, come . . . on . . . down," she mimicked with a laugh. The dark-haired woman stood rigidly beside the van's front fender, watching her. "For heaven's sake, Bonnie, loosen up," the blonde said. "The way you're standin' there, you're gonna make Bruce think somethin's wrong with you."

"I'm nervous, Alice," Bonnie said, looking around the area as if she were a spy in fear of being caught. "I've never done anything like this before."

"Never done anything—" Alice said in rebuke. "Why, we bring animals out here to Bruce all the time to keep from having to put them to sleep."

"Regular animals, yes . . . but not *these* kind," Bonnie added in a whisper.

"These kind?" Alice mocked. "As far as I'm concerned, they're all just cuddly, adorable animals in need of a good home—"

"Alice?" Bruce questioned as he walked toward them from the feed barn. "Morning, Bonnie," he said, nodding as he stopped and glanced back and forth between the two. "What are you doing out here again today? After spending most of the day yesterday corralling kids, I figured neither one of you would show your face around this place for quite a while."

"We had so much fun on the Easter-egg hunt," Alice said, "we just couldn't wait to come back—" Two dogs started barking in the back of the van. They were immediately joined by a full canine chorus.

Bruce stood for a moment, pursing his lips, again looking back and forth between Alice and Bonnie. Before the chorus had a chance to die down, Bruce walked to the back of the van and opened the doors. He shook his head as at least a dozen dogs and cats announced his presence.

"So you just couldn't wait to come back, huh?" Bruce said sarcastically, looking at Alice. "And you had so much fun, I suppose, you just had to bring your friends here along."

"It's Monday, Bruce," Alice said in a somber tone as she stepped up beside him, "and you know what Monday means for us. When we're overcrowded, like we usually are at this time of year, any animal we've had in the kennel for over two weeks that hasn't been claimed or adopted . . . well, Monday's the day we put them to sleep, and you know I don't—"

"I know . . . I know," Bruce said, raising his hands in surrender. "Probably half the animals that go through here come from you one way or another."

"You're in a position where you can keep them longer than

we can, and you have a special knack for finding them good homes..."

"You don't have to lay it on so thick," Bruce said, looking directly at Alice. "You knew I'd take them in even before you started out here."

"You're such an old softie." Alice glanced at Bonnie and nodded, then stepped up close to the van beside Bruce. "There are thirteen of them. Where do you want me to help you put them?"

"I imagine we'll have to take them back to barn three until I can get things sorted out." Bruce made a quick survey of the animals, noting the coloring, size, and general breed of each. "You know, this might turn out to be pretty good timing after all. Damon Austin called me last week—"

"Damon Austin?" Alice asked, a twinge of excitement touching her voice. "You mean the animal trainer from Hollywood?"

"One and the same," Bruce answered with a nod. "We've worked together before and—"

A high-pitched yippy-bark came from behind them. Bruce and Alice turned to see Bonnie standing a few feet away. Cradled in Bonnie's arms was a brown and beige mixed-breed puppy that looked to be about six months old. The pup's ears were pricked alertly, its mouth was open in what appeared to be a smile, and its tongue lolled beyond the bounds of its lips, a collection of saliva getting ready to drip.

Bruce looked at the puppy and immediately thought of Corky . . . as she had been the day he'd first brought her home. The memory hurt . . . and hurt deeply.

"Kerk told us you lost your old friend," Alice said softly, laying a hand on Bruce's shoulder. "This little lady here, well . . . she sure could use someone to look after her."

"Maybe—" Bruce's voice broke. "Maybe Damon Austin can find some use for her." Bruce turned away and started toward the feed barn. "Pull on around to barn three, and we'll get you unloaded," he called over his shoulder.

"What about the puppy?" Bonnie asked as she stepped up beside Alice.

"Give him time," Alice said as she watched Bruce walk away. "Sooner or later, he'll come around. Like I said, he's an old softie."


*8:07 A.M.*

Barry's footsteps echoed in the empty hall. Walking down the long corridor brought back memories of his own school days. The building where he'd attended high school was very similar to the instructors' building at Edgar D. Bailey College.

The old wooden floors were uneven and creaky, darkened by decades of a buildup of oil and dirt. The walls were tiled four feet up from the floor, and rough, uneven plaster, painted a pale yellow, filled in the rest of the space to the twelve-foot ceiling. Large painted portraits of past presidents, professors, and benefactors adorned the drab walls, poorly highlighted by single-bulb ceiling fixtures spaced every eight to ten feet apart. The only difference Barry could distinguish between the two buildings was a lack of lockers built into the walls in this one and the glass in the rooms' doors. At his old high school, the glass had been clear so the principal could see easily into the rooms as he walked up and down the halls. Here, the windows were opaque, and each had been stenciled with the names of the room's occupying professor and his associates.

Barry followed the progression of numbers painted on the walls beside the doors, and stopped outside room 317. The names on the door's window read: Denis Sweezy, Professor, Associates: Charlene Kress, Ken Gerdt, Marcella Neff, and

Dana Shearin. He couldn't remember ever hearing of any of them.

Barry knocked on the door. When no one responded, he tried the knob. It turned easily.

"Hello," Barry said as he pushed the door open. "Is anyone here?" he asked as he looked around the door, then stepped on over the threshold. Still, he received no response.

Barry stood for a moment just inside the door and made a quick survey of the room. Directly ahead of him, a half-dozen antiquated wooden desks were arranged in unorganized fashion. Two threadbare sofas and a couple of easy chairs formed a makeshift conversation area beneath the windows to his left. To his right, a collection of mismatched shelves and filing cabinets stood behind a long wooden table flanked by eight straight-backed chairs. The room seemed typical for the setting . . . except for the pictures and posters hanging on the wall.

Cutesy posters of kittens and puppies and monkeys and bunnies were bordered by enlarged color photographs of cats and dogs and rabbits in various situations of confinement, depicting experimentation and torture. Next to the poster of a baby elephant wearing a circus hat were pictures of adult elephants, lying dead on their sides, their faces hacked and mutilated from where poachers had cut out their tusks. One section of a wall was covered with large colorful posters of the magnificent big cats . . . surrounded by black-market advertisements for coats and jackets and rugs made from the exquisite fur. There was even a pamphlet advertising a big-game safari—deep in the heart of Texas. For the right price, the desired game would be provided for the customer to hunt . . . and kill. Taxidermy fees were extra.

Scattered among the posters and photographs were poems, quotes, and simple verses, depicting the plight of animals. One short message held Barry's attention: *Extinction Is Forever*.

Last summer, when he, Jackie, and Kerk had gone to the zoo, he had bought a lapel button bearing those same three words. Now, looking at the pictures displayed around him, the meaning behind the words seemed more pronounced than before. Because of his love for animals—and after all of the cruelty he'd witnessed while helping the conservation officers—Barry knew it wouldn't take much to turn him into an animal rights activist . . . but he also knew he had to stay within the bounds of the law. *That* was where he differed from the people he had been sent to find.

Beyond the wooden desks, a makeshift partition had been erected fairly recently to separate the front part of the room from the back. Framing 2x4s spanned the distance from floor to ceiling, but the partition itself only reached the height afforded by a 4x8 sheet of pine paneling. Four feet of open space hovered above the partition.

Barry walked toward the windowed door in the partition that was located a panel's width from the right wall. As he neared the partition, a man's bass voice filtered over its top; when Barry stopped in front of the door, he could see a man in the next room, sitting on a desk, talking on the phone.

As the man turned to hang up, he glanced up and saw Barry. At first, he reacted with surprise, then the man nodded and held up a hand to indicate he would be finished shortly.

In that brief moment, Barry committed the man's description to memory. He was close to six feet four inches tall, weighed around one hundred and sixty pounds and looked to be in his mid to late thirties. His light brown hair was streaked with gray, thinning on top and receding at the temples. At one time, it had probably been styled in a layered cut, but it had since grown past his shoulders. He wore wire-rimmed glasses, tweed slacks that were too short for his long legs, an olive-green turtleneck sweater, and tennis shoes without socks. Barry immediately categorized the man who was now walking toward him; he would have fit perfectly in the late 1960s.

"What can I do for you, officer?" the man asked as he opened the door, his eyes moving quickly over Barry and his light brown uniform.

"I'm Barry Robbins from the sheriff's department. I'm looking for a man by the name of Denis Sweezy."

"Are you looking for him for anything in particular?" the man asked.

"I have a few questions I would like to ask him."

"In regards to what?"

Barry hesitated, then asked, "Are you Denis Sweezy?" The man hesitated as well, then he nodded. "Then why didn't you say so?"

"You just now asked." Sweezy walked past Barry and sat down on one of the sofas. "Won't you join me?"

Barry walked toward Sweezy but didn't sit down. "Do you have any knowledge or information pertaining to the animal thefts that took place here on campus and throughout the county last Thursday night and Friday morning?"

"Am I under arrest, officer?" Sweezy asked quite politely.

"No, I was hoping you might be able to give me some information."

"Animal thefts . . ." Sweezy tilted his head back slightly and appeared to scan the pictures on the wall across the room. "Let's see, I think I did read something about that in Saturday's paper." Sweezy shifted his head, and his dark eyes met Barry's directly. "Why did you come to me?"

"Procedure," Barry lied.

"Just because my associates and I show an open concern for animal welfare," Sweezy said, making a sweeping gesture of the room with his hand, "does that mean we're automatically the prime suspects?"

"Those are your words, not mine," Barry answered.

"Tell me, officer, what philosophy do you live by?"

"I don't know if I've ever tried to put it into words."

"I have, and my philosophy is quite simple. Live and let live."

"That sounds rather cliché for an educated man," Barry commented on the verge of a verbal challenge.

Sweezy scooted forward onto the edge of the sofa. "Would you rather it be 'Live and let die'?" Again he made a gesture with his arm to encompass the room.

Barry's eyes followed the movement and again he glanced at the morbid pictures on the wall. After a few moments, he looked back at Sweezy. "I'll send someone around in the next few days to take your statement." Barry turned and walked from the office.

Barry hadn't gotten the answers he'd been looking for. Maybe he hadn't asked the right questions. Maybe, deep inside, he had never intended to.

*10:12 A.M.*

Warren took only a few minutes to make a quick inspection of the animals that had been unloaded at the single-bay dock. Following the procedure he'd repeated dozens of times before, he signed the delivery receipt and tore off the yellow copy for the lab files. He located the truck driver at the edge of the blacktop drive, smoking a cigarette, and walked out to return the man's clipboard.

"Everything we ordered appears to be here," Warren said as he approached the driver.

"With any luck, maybe you'll be able to keep this batch a little longer than you kept the last one," the man said, multiple streams of smoke escaping between the gaps in his yellow teeth. "I read about your break-in in the paper. Wiped you clean out, did they?"

"They took every last animal," Warren answered with a nod. He turned and started walking toward the loading dock steps.

"You didn't lose nothin' important, did you?" the driver asked, ambling along behind Warren. "I mean, you weren't in the middle of any research that could cure cancer or nothing like that, were you?"

When Warren reached the top of the steps, he looked back at the driver and glanced at the man's cigarette. "Cure cancer? It's much easier to prevent cancer than it is to cure it." The driver picked up on Warren's implication, but it didn't faze him. He smiled broadly and took another long drag off his cigarette. "No, we didn't lose anything of great importance," Warren continued. "Fortunately, everything we were working on at the time can be duplicated."

Warern heard a shuffling noise off to the side of the loading dock. He turned his head toward the sound and barely had time to catch a glimpse of Leland as he turned away from the platform and reentered the main building via an automatic door.

Warren focused on the door as it closed, then he glanced at his watch. He wanted to talk to Leland; he *needed* to.

"I'm sure all of the new animals you brought will do just fine," Warren said abruptly, looking back at the driver. "Thank you for the delivery. I imagine it'll be a month to six weeks before we need to place another order. Thank you," he repeated unconsciously. "Have a good day and drive carefully." Warren turned away from the driver abruptly and walked hurriedly toward the automatic door that opened into the end of the laboratory hall opposite the front lobby.

As Warren stepped inside, he glanced to his left. The elevator motor was humming. He looked up at the numbers above the casing and watched as the lights behind the numbered panel seemed to jump from one digit to the next until the three remained lit. He presumed Leland was going to his office.

"I can do it," Warren muttered to himself, fisting his hands in self-determination. "All I have to do is keep my voice steady." He cleared his throat. "I lost a filling out of a tooth last night," he practiced, barely moving his lips. "I called my dentist this morning, and he said he'd try to squeeze me in sometime around noon . . ." Warren unclenched his fists and wiped his sweaty palms across his slacks. He was nervous; he wasn't in the habit of telling a lie. ". . . so if it's all right, I'll need to take an extended lunch hour." That was what he was going to tell Leland.

He lifted his hand, hesitated, then pushed the elevator's ground-floor call button. As he watched the numbers above the elevator door, Warren continued to rehearse, "I lost a filling . . ."


*10:52 A.M.*

"Bruce? Bruce, are you in here?"

Recognizing the voice of his farmhand's wife, Bruce responded automatically. "I'm in the back stall, Leah."

A few seconds passed, then a slender young woman, wearing blue jeans and a blue-checked flannel shirt, stepped up to the stall's Dutch door. "How are they doing?" she asked, watching Bruce as he examined one of the raccoons that had been rescued from the mountain men's holding pens.

"The vitamins and high-protein meal we mixed in with the dog food seem to have done their job on this one." Bruce lifted the raccoon up and down with both hands as if to check its weight. "By the way she feels, she should be ready to set loose by the end of the week," he said as he walked across the stall to return the animal to its cage. "I imagine she'll make it okay, but there are a couple . . ."

By the somber tone in his voice, Leah could sense the compassion Bruce felt for the animals. "You've done your best," she said, attempting to console him. Leah looked from Bruce to the shelves filled with cages at the end of the stall where the rescued animals were being temporarily housed. "Even if a few of them don't pull through, I think they all know you tried your best to help them."

A soft whimper drifted up beside Leah. She looked down into a pair of big brown eyes that were begging for attention. Leah glanced at Bruce and started to say something about the beige and brown puppy with a white-tipped tail, but she didn't. She already knew where he stood on the subject . . . even if she didn't agree with him.

"Kerk and I are going into town." As Leah spoke, an idea came to her. A mischievous grin puckered her rosy lips as she opened the bottom section of the Dutch door and used her foot to coax the puppy into the stall. "Can we pick up anything for you?"

"There's nothing I can think of I need at the moment."

"We probably won't be back until sometime this afternoon," Leah said as she pulled the door toward her.

"That's okay. More than likely, I'll be out here most of the day."

"There's a pot of chili on the stove if you get hungry after a while."

"I'll manage."

"Well," Leah eyed the puppy as it walked on into the stall and sat down not too far from Bruce, "I guess I'll see you when we get back." Not waiting for Bruce to reply, she closed the Dutch door and left.

When Bruce heard the latch mechanism click, he wondered why Leah had opened and then closed the door. Out of curiosity, he looked across the stall . . . and saw the puppy sitting a few feet from him.

"So it's you." Bruce glanced at the open space above the closed Dutch door, then looked back at the puppy. "So it's a conspiracy, is it?" The puppy stood up, yipped, and wagged its tail as if to answer. "And don't you think your being cute will make any difference as far as I'm concerned." The puppy yipped again and started to walk toward Bruce. "Stay there!" he said curtly. The puppy stopped abruptly, hesitated for a moment, then sat down again. She looked up at Bruce, tilted her head to the side, her tongue lolling out the side of her mouth, and wagged her tail. Bruce looked down into the puppy's big brown eyes for several seconds. His voice cracked when he finally said, "Good stay."

Bruce reached into a sack at the end of the examination table and pulled out a protein chew. "Now don't take this as meaning there's anything between us," he said as he tossed the chew to the puppy. "I just need something to help keep you busy so you'll stay outta my way and out from under my feet." Bruce turned back to the wall of cages, took out another malnourished animal, and carried it to the table. He continued with his examinations, but, occasionally, he glanced out of the corner of his eye and focused on the beige and brown puppy.


*11:00 A.M.*

The wind tugged at the hem of Jackie's skirt as she climbed the marble steps to the city building. When she reached the landing outside the front entrance, she turned back toward the street and looked up at the storm clouds gathering overhead. Someone was in store for a lot of rain.

She hoped the storm would pass north of the county. In her haste to drive into town, she had gone off and left several windows open in the house.

Jackie glanced at her watch. It was time—past time—to be in the mayor's office.

As she turned and reached for the door, a familiar question played again in her mind: What did the mayor want? His secretary hadn't been specific when they'd talked the previous Friday; she'd said only enough to entice Jackie to attend the quickly scheduled meeting. What little she could remember focused on the compound . . . and on enough money to make it financially stable.

"Jackie." Chuck Gillock from the *South Port Daily News* intercepted Jackie the moment she stepped inside the city building. "Jackie, fill me in. What's going on?"

Jackie looked at Chuck with a frown, then saw a half-dozen other reporters standing behind him, pushing their way closer to her. She scanned the group quickly and caught a glimpse of at least two television cameramen with logos on their equipment she recognized from the Louisville and Cincinnati areas.

She looked back at Chuck, making direct eye contact. "Maybe *you* can tell *me* what's going on here," she said. "I'm leveling with you, Chuck. I don't know anything, but by the looks of all these people, whatever it is, it's obvious the mayor wants plenty of press coverage—"

"Don't play games with me, Jackie," Chuck protested. "We've helped each other out too many times in the past to start holding back secrets now—"

"Ms. Mitchell." A short, petite woman in her mid-forties worked her way through the crowd of reporters as easily as if she'd been a six-foot-four, two-hundred-and-eighty-pound linebacker. "Hello, Ms. Mitchell, I'm Rebecca Welsh, the mayor's public-relations secretary," she said as she stopped directly in front of Jackie and extended her hand for an introductory handshake. "We've been waiting for you. Won't you please come with me." The woman turned sharply and started back through the crowd.

Jackie glanced at Chuck, raised her eyebrows and shrugged her shoulders to indicate she still had no idea as to what was going on, then turned to follow the woman. Chuck fell into close step behind Jackie; the rest of the reporters followed him.

When they reached the far side of the lobby, Rebecca Welsh stepped in front of a large, oak-paneled door and took hold of its knob. "In here, Ms. Mitchell," she said as she pushed the door open and motioned for Jackie to enter. "The mayor's expecting you."

Jackie made brief eye contact with her hostess, glanced at the armed guards on either side of the door, then walked into the room. Rebecca Welsh followed, securing the door behind them.

Jackie paused just inside the spacious conference hall. On the far side of the room, she saw two men leaning over a long table, looking at what appeared to be an unrolled set of blueprints.

She immediately recognized one of the men to be South Port's Mayor Arnold Fuller. The other man had his back to her, but his body build seemed familiar.

"Ms. Mitchell is here, Your Honor," Rebecca Welsh announced. She immediately turned her attention to Jackie. "May I get you anything? Coffee? Tea? A soft drink?"

"No, thank you—"

"Jackie," the mayor bellowed as he stepped out from behind the conference table and walked toward her. "It's been far too long since I've shared the pleasure of your company." He extended a plump hand, grasped hers, and squeezed it almost affectionately. "How nice of you to join us this morning."

"Thank you, Mayor Fuller, but I'm not sure why—"

"I think you're already acquainted with our benefactor . . ." As Mayor Fuller spoke, he turned toward the conference table and gestured to the man who took his cue to turn toward them,

". . . Daniel Patton."

In a reflex reaction, Jackie tensed and took in a quick breath. If the mayor noticed the change in her body posture, he was courteous enough not to react.

"Hello, Jackie," Dan said, an arrogant grin tightening his lips. "How nice of you to join us," he said, mimicking the mayor.

Jackie responded with a nod. For the moment, she didn't trust her voice to support a stable answer.

"Mr. Patton has offered to donate the land north of town to the city's zoological project and has agreed to a sizable monetary contribution as well," the mayor explained as he directed Jackie to the conference table. "He's even taken on the initial responsibility of contacting an architect with experience in the area," he added, gesturing toward the large blueprint spread out across the table. "What do you think of it?"

Jackie glanced at the blueprint but didn't take time to scrutinize it for details. "That's all very well and good," she said, returning her attention to the mayor, "but what does any of this have to do with me?"

"Since you're the area animal-welfare agent, Mr. Patton has asked that you work closely with him on the project."

Jackie shot a hard glance at Dan, which he acknowledged with a nod and a self-satisfied grin. "But the animals in a zoo," she said, looking again at the mayor, "are much more exotic than I have experience to—"

"As Mr. Patton explained to me, he feels you are more than qualified to assist in overseeing the multimillion-dollar project. In all honesty, I think you would feel proud that Mr. Patton has that kind of faith in you." The mayor hesitated, made sure Jackie was watching him as he looked at the blueprint, then extended a hand to lightly touch the edge of the paper. "For the past few years, you've heard me speak of my love for animals and of my hopes for building a zoo—a sanctuary, so to speak—for as many endangered species as we could support." He looked to Jackie, his soft brown puppy-eyes locking on hers. "That opportunity has arrived. We now have the land and the monetary backing."

"And your compound will benefit as well," Dan added.

Jackie turned her head sharply toward him. "What does any of this have to do with the compound?" she asked defensively.

"To compensate for the time you'll need to be away from the compound, Mr. Patton has offered to hire a couple of extra people to take over your responsibilities there, and . . ." The mayor paused, and a broad smile brightened his round face. ". . . and he'll establish a million-dollar trust fund to cover expenses the compound might incur in the future."

Jackie couldn't help but gasp. *One million dollars.* To Dan Patton, that amount of money was mere pocket change—a night on the town, jet-setting across the continent. But to Jackie—and to the compound—that amount of money was more than enough to solve their problems . . . *all* of their problems.

Jackie looked down at the blueprint—actually looked *through* it, because she didn't see even the barest of details. She was thinking . . . thinking about how she could get the money for the compound and yet not have to put up with Daniel Jerome Patton the Fourth any longer than was necessary.

Could she do it? Yes, she could. She *could* do it . . . and she would.

Jackie glanced at Dan, then focused on the mayor. "When do we begin?"

"Tonight," Dan answered for the mayor. Again, Jackie's head turned sharply toward him, her expression verging on one of anger. "I thought we could begin by discussing the preliminaries over dinner this evening."

Before Jackie could respond, the mayor added, "The sooner

we begin, the sooner we can break ground for the first building. You must forgive me," he said, again looking at Jackie with his puppy-eyes, "but I presumed you'd accept, and I've taken the liberty of contacting the governor's office. We have an appointment to meet with him on Friday . . ."

Jackie's eyes widened and moved quickly back and forth between the mayor and Dan. She had been railroaded into the situation—and she knew it—but at the moment, she could see no way to back out without putting the compound in jeopardy.

". . . and now, I believe the press is expecting us." The mayor gestured toward the door through which Jackie had entered. Rebecca Welsh stood next to it, poised with her hand hovering above the knob.

"Shall we." Jackie felt a hand touch the small of her back and turned with a start to look up into Dan's green eyes. He smiled at her, and the expression seemed to take on an almost sinister air. "Our public awaits."

Jackie took a couple of quick steps toward the mayor, then adjusted her path toward the door. She wondered just how long she could tolerate working with Dan . . . even if the future of the compound was at stake.


*1:03 P.M.*

Warren stood at the base of the marble steps, his head tilted back, his eyes wide, scanning the front of the Patton family mansion. To ward off the shadows accompanying the storm clouds overhead, automatic lights had already been activated; they glowed beneath the shrubbery bordering the steps and front walk. Additional miniature spotlights, camouflaged by exquisite lawn decorations and cascading birdbath fountains, were focused on the mansion, highlighting its elegant architecture.

Eight marble pillars graced the entrance of the three-story brick structure. Ivy scaled the front wall in random ramblings, its thickening spring foliage interrupted by six shuttered, double-paned windows on each level. A double-wide oak door, framed by Tiffany-panel stained glass, bisected the ground floor. A wide veranda skirted the front and curved around both corners; white wrought-iron latticework, standing nearly waist high, guarded white wicker furniture artistically arranged in conversational groupings beneath ornate ceiling fans. Flower boxes, at the base of each window, had been recently planted with budding pansies, petunias, and geraniums, lending a touch of color.

Warren had never seen a house so magnificent . . . and he had never felt so dwarfed. If the experiment taking place in his backyard barn turned out to be as successful as he hoped, maybe someday, he, too, would be able to afford more than a three-bedroom ranch house. Maybe someday, he might be able to afford a home as majestic as the one belonging to Dan Patton.

The sky brightened; thunder rumbled. Warren tilted his head back a little farther and glanced up at the charcoal-gray clouds rolling in overhead. A fat raindrop splattered on his left cheek, showering miniature droplets on his glasses. His head jerked in an automatic reflex. Another drop hit his forehead . . . then another hit his cheek . . . and another dampened his temple.

Warren glanced back at the house . . . at the steps above him . . . then at the step directly in front of him. He hesitated, took in a deep breath, then lifted his right foot.

Immediately, he felt his heartbeat multiply; he heard his pulse pound savagely in his ears. Even though the raindrops were cool and accompanied by a freshening breeze, Warren broke out in a sweat; his palms felt suddenly clammy. Warren was nervous; Warren was downright scared.

He'd only had occasion to speak with Dan Patton perhaps a half-dozen times during the four years he'd been at Patton Laboratories; each of those times had been nothing more than meaningless chitchat. Warren wondered if Dan Patton even remembered his name.

But his nervousness was caused by more than just the fact that he was about to face his employer; Warren was plagued with a sense of guilt. He was about to betray Leland. He was about to betray the man who'd given him his first job in research.

"And who was it who took all the credit for the VR-7 formula?" he uttered, trying to rationalize his betrayal. "I was the one who stabilized it. I was the one who should have been interviewed for the article in the journal—not Leland—not *Doctor* Leland Wagner . . . a master thief in his own right."

Warren glanced up at the house again, looked down at the step in front of him then set his foot firmly on the swirl-patterned stone. He was determined to—

A brilliant flash of lightning—bright enough to affect the electric eyes on the spotlights and make them flicker—made Warren freeze in his stance. An almost instantaneous clap of thunder vibrated the air around him, making Warren shudder. The silence that immediately followed came as a blessing.

The sound of a car engine broke into the silence, prompting Warren to turn on the steps. He looked beyond his own car, parked at the curb of the circular drive, to the mouth of the entry lane, canopied by century-old oak and maple trees.

A bright red sports car emerged from beneath the trees. It pulled to a stop and hesitated at the junction where the entrance lane, the front circular drive, and the drive leading around to the back of the house all connected.

"Mr. Patton?" Warren questioned himself as he tried to establish the identity of the man inside the car . . . who had evidently stopped to do the same with him. "Mr. Patton,"

Warren said a little louder when he made a positive identification. "Mr. Patton," he called out with a wave of his hand.

At almost the same instant, the charcoal-gray clouds overhead released the burden they'd been carrying for many miles, dropping a torrent of rain across the landscape. The red car didn't hesitate at the junction any longer. Dan revved the engine, then continued along the drive toward the back of the house.

"Mr. Patton, wait!" Warren waved frantically as he stepped off the marble steps, then he began to run across the yard toward the corner of the house, hoping to intercept the red car. When he rounded the corner of the veranda, he saw a garage at the back of the house; one of the five overhead doors was beginning to open. As he continued running along the side of the house, Warren saw the red sports car pull inside the garage. "Mr. Patton!" He waved. "Mr—"

Slipping on the wet grass, Warren fell. He tumbled down the gentle slope bridging the area between the front yard's upper elevation and the backyard's lower level. When he finally quit rolling, he was at the edge of the concrete entrance to the garage.

Shaken, Warren sat up and tried to regain what little composure he could salvage. He located his glasses a few feet back up the hill; because the grass was slippery, he had to crawl on his hands and knees to retrieve them. Fortunately, they were unbroken. His briefcase had slid on down the hill ahead of him and had stopped within a few feet of the open garage door.

When he finally found stable footing and began to work his way to his feet, Warren heard—and then saw—the garage door begin to close. "No! Mr. Patton! Wait!"

Warren ran across the drive, picked up his briefcase, and hurried on toward the garage. "Mr. Patton!" he called. The door was almost halfway down. "Mr. Patton, wait—"

Not knowing what other course to take, Warren set his briefcase on the ground beneath the closing door. When the bottom of the door contacted the briefcase, there was a sound indicating a motor was being stressed. After a few seconds, the garage door began to open again.

"Mr. Patton," Warren called out as he bent over to pick up his briefcase. When he was in a position to do so, he looked inside the garage. Rusty Snider stood opposite him, a gun aimed directly at his forehead.

"What do you want?" Snider asked gruffly.

"I . . . I came to see Mr. Patton." As the garage door continued to open, Warren followed it, straightening up quite slowly. Cautiously, he lifted his arms out to his sides to indicate he didn't pose a threat.

"Who are you?" Snider asked.

"I . . . I'm Warren Maxey. I work for Mr. Patton at the Patton Pharmaceutical Laboratories just north of South Port, Indiana."

Snider eyed Warren and his wet, disheveled appearance, then asked, "Do you have an appointment?"

"No, but I'm sure—"

"Then Mr. Patton doesn't want to see you. Go on, get," Snider said, motioning with the gun for Warren to leave by way of the drive. "You've got less than five minutes to get back in your car and get off the property or I'm declaring open hunting season on four-eyed geeks."

"But I'm sure Mr. Patton will want to speak with me," Warren insisted, showing more gumption than he thought he possessed.

Snider looked at his watch. "Four minutes and twenty-seven seconds."

"Tell him," Warren said, "tell him I . . . I have news about the . . . Starfish Project."

Almost before the words *Starfish Project* had crossed

Warren's lips, a door on the far side of the garage opened. Dan stepped out. "It's all right, Rusty," he said, motioning for Snider to leave, "I'll speak with him."

Dan waited for Snider to leave the area, then he crossed the garage and stopped in front of Warren. He studied the diminutive man briefly—suspiciously—then said, "I thought Wagner was working on the project alone."

"He was." Warren cleared his throat. "At least as far as *he* knew, he was." Dan cocked his head to one side and waited for Warren to continue.

"Unknown to Dr. Wagner, I . . . I appropriated a sample of his serum several weeks ago."

"*You* have the serum?" Dan questioned, a tingling of excitement racing through him.

"Yes."

"How much? How much do you have?"

"Almost a dozen vials."

"A dozen vials . . ." Dan repeated as he began to contemplate what change might lie ahead for his future.

"I thought we might be able to talk, Mr. Patton—"

"Yes . . . yes, we definitely have plenty to talk about, Mr. Manny."

"That's Maxey," Warren corrected, "Warren Maxey."

"Yes, Mr. Maxey, yes. Please, won't you come in." Dan slipped an arm around Warren's shoulders and directed him toward the door leading into the back kitchen. "Let's find some dry clothes for you to put on and some hot coffee to help take the chill off and then, when you're comfortable, you can tell me all about your experience with the Starfish Project."


*1:19 P.M.*

". . . and he had it all set up long before I got there. Who knows just how long he's been working on this. Days . . . weeks . . . maybe even months. He's . . . he's the most despicable man I've ever had the misfortune of meeting in my entire life." Jackie took in a deep breath, let it out forcefully, and leaned back in her chair. Unfortunately, the action did little to ease her frustration.

"You don't have to do this, you know," Barry said. "One way or another, we'll find the funds to keep the compound operating."

"No. I'm not going to let you become involved financially," Jackie stated adamantly, "so just erase any of this *we* business from your mental checkbook."

Barry looked at Jackie and shook his head, but he said nothing more. He knew she had already made up her mind and, as with a few other areas where they didn't always see eye-to-eye, he knew there was no use for him to argue; he knew nothing he could say would alter her decision. Jackie was as pigheaded as he had been throughout his entire life, and when the two of them met head-on, well . . . more times than not, he was the one to give in.

"So anyway, I stopped by to tell you I won't be able to go to the game tonight. But Kerk's still planning on going," she added quickly, leaning forward in her chair.

"Maybe I should go have a talk with Patton."

"It's none of your business," Jackie said a bit too brusquely, "so please just stay out of it."

"But it *is* my business. Breaking our date makes it my business."

"Oh, Barry, don't get started on it. Don't be an asshole like Dan. I don't think I could handle two of you at the moment." Jackie glanced at her watch and stood up. "I've got to be getting back to the compound. I've got a lot of things to get finished this afternoon before my big date tonight," she said sarcastically.

"Don't call it a date."

"You know I was only kidding."

"But I still don't like the sound of it."

"Men." Jackie looked at Barry and shook her head. "I've got to go. I may see you this evening when you come out to pick up Kerk, but if not, I'll talk to you sometime tomorrow." Jackie turned to walk away.

"Jackie." Barry took hold of her arm and turned her toward him. "I know I can't talk you out of this no matter how hard I'd try, but I do want you to know, I have a bad feeling about it."

Jackie looked up into his dark eyes and smiled. "I can take care of myself," she tried to assure him. "Between you and Richard, I think the two of you taught me everything a girl needs to know."

"Patton's a manipulator—"

"I know, and I know what I have to do to stay out of his reach. I've done it before. Trust me, I'll be all right. I'll play his silly game until he signs his name to the check for the compound, then I'll never have to put up with him again."

"Let's hope it turns out to be that easy."


*1:51 P.M.*

Dan paced back and forth across the den. Occasionally, he would pause at the window and look out, but he didn't take note of the rain nor, in reality, did he see anything else beyond the pane. The action was a mere gesture; he was trying to keep busy in order to pass the time. Again, he turned toward the heart of the room, and his eyes sought out the antique clock on the mantel. Less than two minutes had passed since he'd last noted the time.

He looked down at the scrap of paper he clutched tightly in his hand. The edges were crumpled, damp from the perspiration seeping into the palm of his hand. The paper's yellow tint had darkened, and the last few letters of the notation had begun to smear as his sweat combined with the ink and spread into the paper's fibers.

But even if the notation would disappear forever, Dan already had the information etched in his mind: *The Morthland Addition. 3 Alberta Court just off Handak Road. That* was Warren Maxey's home address; *that* was where the Starfish serum could be found.

Dan looked at the clock again. Time seemed to be standing still.

After Warren had told Dan about his success with the mice's regeneration, he invited Dan to meet with him at his home that evening. Dan had been ecstatic over the development, but so as not to show too much excitement—and give Warren the upper hand—he maintained a calm demeanor. He'd told Warren about his dinner engagement that evening and said he wouldn't be able to arrive until sometime between nine and ten. Warren had assured him he would be at home no matter what time Dan got there.

Now, as Dan stood in the den, staring at the clock whose hands appeared never to move, he wished he would have thrown caution aside and had Warren take him to the small barn's laboratory as soon as he'd learned of the mice's existence. Why had he tried to be so reserved? Why had he tried to put on the appearance that the serum's existence was so matter-of-fact?

Had he feared Warren might ask too high a price for the serum? Too high a price? Considering the vast fortune he'd received after his father's death, what was *too* high? Dan knew he would give away half of his fortune if it meant he could walk normally again . . . if it meant he could have his legs back.

Dan glanced at the paper in his hand, then started across the room. "I'm not going to wait for you, little man," he said as he approached the door. "I'm not going to wait until tonight for anything. I'm going to find your lab right now and see for myself just how well the Starfish serum has worked."

*2:04 P.M.*

Hollie Bass carried a folder of invoices tucked under her arm as she walked down the hall from the loading dock toward her desk. Warren had been in such a hurry to leave that morning, he'd neglected to turn in the invoices from the animal shipment.

It had taken Hollie over an hour to locate the folder, and only after she'd thought to attempt retracing Warren's steps had she been successful and found it. Now, she could finish her work for the day, and if all went well, she might get to leave early.

When Hollie passed the animal lab, she hesitated, then stopped and took a couple steps backward. Silently, she peered in through the open doorway.

Drew Coryell was on the far side of the lab, his back to her. He was printing identification numbers on white squares of cardboard and slipping them into the plastic sleeves attached to the doors of the animal cages. In addition to Hollie, over two dozen pair of tiny dark eyes were watching his movements.

Hollie's attention shifted from Drew to the cages, then from animal to animal. A compassionate frown creased her brow, and she shook her head ever so slightly. They were all so innocent . . .

Unidentified squeaks filtered down the hall from the lobby. Hollie turned toward the sound and saw Warren walking toward her. His hair was wet and disheveled, his clothes were damp and wrinkled, the rubber soles of his shoes half-gripped/half-slid across the floor, leaving black streaks on the tile.

"What happened to you?" she asked, eyeing him from head to toe and back again. A smirk pulled at the corners of Hollie's lips, threatening to break into a laugh that could have easily grown into a guffaw.

"I got caught out in the rain," Warren answered tersely. "Again!" As if his words were a cue, lightning brightened the windows, thunder boomed almost instantaneously, and the lights in the hallway flickered.

"That sounded too close," Hollie said, instinctively glancing up at the light fixtures. "I hope we don't lose power."

"There's nothing to worry about. Even if we do lose power, we wouldn't be without lights for more than a few minutes. The generator will kick on automatically and the reserve tank has plenty of gas. Drew checked it just last week."

"Generator or not, I still hate it when the lights go out. Even being in the dark for a little while reminds me of the spring when I was a sophomore in high school. An ice storm went through our area the end of March and tore down most of the power lines in the county. We were without electricity for ten days—"

"I know," Warren said impatiently. "You tell me that story every time the lights even start to flicker. I've got to go get out of these wet clothes." He started down the hall, but stopped and turned back at an angle to Hollie. "Did anything happen while I was gone I need to know about?"

"No."

"Okay." Warren nodded, then turned and walked away.

Hollie watched him until she was sure he was too far away to hear, then she added under her breath, "And there's not going to be anything happening the rest of the day you *need* to know about either."

Hollie glanced back into the animal lab, gripped the folder

beneath her arm, then started down the hall toward her desk. She had a phone call to make, and she wanted to make sure it went out before the storm started playing havoc with the telephone lines.

*2:48 P.M.*

Heavy clouds rumbled overhead, cloaking the sun and rendering the afternoon as dark as night. Torrents of rain assaulted the earth and were whipped into near-horizontal paths by outbursts of untamed wind. Hail peppered the ground, rebounding like a million miniature balls. The wind pulled at the trees, straining to overcome their foundations; occasionally, a limb succumbed and cracked.

Dan drove slowly through the housing addition on Handak Road, looking for Alberta Court. Hunched over the steering wheel, he strained to see through the rain sheeting across the windshield . . . persistent rain, defying the wiper's fastest speed.

His headlights did little to highlight the road and the junctions branching off it; only an occasional flash of lightning provided him with a brief glimpse at his surroundings. He was proceeding like a blind man—without the benefit of a lead dog or even a white-tipped cane to tap out his way.

Twice, since turning off the highway into the addition, Dan had thought about pulling over and stopping to wait for the storm to pass. But he was anxious to see Warren's miracle mice. Besides, he wanted to take advantage of the storm itself. The darkness would mask his activities from any prying eyes— if and when he ever found out just where it was he wanted to go—

A brilliant flash illuminated the area. Dan jerked back from the windshield in a reflex action and squinted against the brightness, but at the same time, he caught a brief glimpse of a street sign off to his left. His heartbeat multiplied in anticipation.

Progressing slowly, Dan edged the car in the direction of the sign and rolled down the window just enough so he could see over the rain-streaked glass. A second flash of lightning gave him enough light to pull up close to the sign and stop; a third flash allowed him to read the name: *Alberta Court*. Again, his heart thumped with anticipation.

Dan looked from the sign out through the windshield, its view all but obliterated by cascading rain. Warren had told him there was a house on either side of the entry lane and then five houses situated around the main circular court. Warren's house was numbered 3; his drive would be the second one on the right inside the circle.

Guided by his instincts, Dan lifted his foot from the brake and let the car roll forward for what he estimated was about ten feet. He then turned the wheel to the left and let the car continue to roll. Several seconds passed before he finally straightened the wheel and tapped the brake.

Dan thought he must be doing something right. He was making progress and, so far, he hadn't run into anything. But an uneasiness coursed through him, and he knew he would have felt more confident if he knew exactly where he was—

A spear of lightning tore across the sky. Dan saw something directly in front of him and jammed his foot down hard on the brake. The Ferrari came to an abrupt stop, the bumper just mere inches from a mailbox post. Without even thinking about his next course of action, Dan put the car in reverse, slowly backed up a few feet, then stopped and waited . . . waited.

Within a matter of moments, a series of jagged lightning bolts ravaged the sky, lighting the area with a strobe effect. Dan took advantage of the brightness, adjusted the car's direction, then turned into the next driveway on his right. He continued to let the car roll and finally stopped when his headlights reflected back at him off a white aluminum garage door.

Dan leaned forward in his seat and looked up through the windshield. A smile slowly spread across his lips when he located a large, black-painted 3 mounted just above the garage door, a few inches below the eaves.

Immediately, Dan shifted into park, turned off the lights and ignition. He pulled the hood of his rain gear up over his head, reached for his flashlight and cane, and grasped the door handle. Without hesitating, he stepped out into the rain and started toward the corner of the garage.

When he reached the back corner of the house, Dan paused beneath an overhang that offered minimal protection from the rain. He scanned the backyard, looking—

Another flash of lightning highlighted the area. During that brief instant, Dan caught a glimpse of the small red barn on the far side of the yard.

Without waiting for additional lightning to highlight his way, Dan started across the yard. Rain pelted his face, stinging like a swarm of bees; wind whipped the tail of his rain jacket up around his chest. His hood blew off. Hurrying across the wet grass, he slipped and would have fallen several times had he not jabbed his cane into the soft ground and used it for support. Fighting the onslaught of nature, he worked his way to the front of the small barn.

Dan tried the door. It was locked.

He considered looking for a window to break, then he thought of a possible—simpler—solution. He lifted his left hand and ran it lightly across the top of the doorframe. Almost immediately, he located a nail protruding from the wood . . . and on that nail . . . was a key.

Dan chuckled as he retrieved the key and slid it into the

door's lock. With one turn of his wrist, he was inside the small barn.

Lightning flashed and thunder bellowed as Dan closed the door behind him. A chorus of chatters and squeals erupted off to his right. Dan didn't know whether the protest was due to the cacophony outside or to his entrance; he really didn't care.

Dan pointed the flashlight toward the floor, turned it on, then slowly lifted it. He scanned the cages on the shelves to his right, looking for the white mice Warren had boasted about. The mice weren't housed among the raccoons, weasels, and squirrels.

Turning to his left, Dan let the beam play across a cabinet . . . a set of shelves . . . a series of hooks mounted randomly on the wall . . . a worktable—a worktable with a wire mesh cage on top of it.

Dan took a step toward the table and cage. His heart thumped with excitement when the flashlight's beam reflected off two sets of dark eyes.

"Hello, there," he whispered, as he bent down over the cage. "Are you the two special mice I've come all the way out here to see?" Dan tilted the cage up on its back corner, hoping the angle would prompt one of the mice to move so he could see its legs beneath the cardboard collar, but neither mouse cooperated.

Dan settled the cage back on the table, then turned to his right and scanned the shelves. He was looking for some kind of probe. Unable to find anything suitable, he opened the cabinet to the right of the shelves. Immediately, he located two small-diameter dowels.

"Let's see if you'll give me a look at your legs now," Dan said as he returned to the cage.

Dan laid the flashlight on the worktable, aiming its beam directly toward the mice. Working deliberately, he slipped the dowels in between the cage's wires and used them to corner one of the mice. The animal squeaked at being bothered, but it didn't put up much of a struggle in protest.

Using the dowels, Dan maneuvered the mouse onto its back feet. Hunching down, so he could look beneath the cardboard collar, he saw where the left front paw had been severed... and where the pink leg bud was beginning to regrow.

Dan's heart pounded more severely than it had when he'd first heard of the project. In spite of a chill that had been brought on by the rain, sweat dotted his forehead and clung to his upper lip. An unusual warmth radiated through him.

"Starfish," he whispered. "It's possible. It *is* possible," Dan said as he slid the dowels out of the cage and laid them on the worktable, "and it's all mine," he added as a self-confident smile crossed his face. "Mine."

He glanced at his watch and considered his schedule for the rest of the day. The afternoon would drag by as he waited for it to pass, then dinner with Jackie... Jackie... and a return visit here tonight to talk with Warren and possibly—just maybe—he might be able to talk Warren out of some of the serum.

"It won't be long," Dan said as he retrieved the flashlight and walked to the door.

He picked up the cane he'd left propped beside the door, hit first one of his artificial legs, and then the other. "No, it won't be long," he repeated with a confident smile. "Then, Jackie, my dear, there won't be any more excuses, and you will be mine as well."


*5:07 P.M.*

"Cardinal One, come in, Cardinal One," a muffled voice called.

"Cardinal One here."

"This is Cardinal Three. We've got a problem."

"Hold on, Cardinal Three." Dale Congleton slid across the wet bed of pine needles beneath the tree where they had taken shelter and handed the field phone to his team leader. "It's Cardinal Three. They've got trouble."

"Did he say what it was?" Gary Bell asked, looking through the binoculars at their target a few seconds longer before reaching for the phone.

"Whatever it is, it can't be much worse than getting drowned out here like we are," Congleton said as he handed Bell the phone. "I've never seen rain like this."

"Cardinal One here," Bell said into the mouthpiece, "what's your problem, Cardinal Three?"

"We've got a flat tire. It looks like we picked up a nail somewhere along the way."

"You do have a spare with you."

"I think so."

"Then how long will it take for repairs?"

"I'd guess fifteen . . . maybe twenty minutes." Bell looked at his watch—

"Hey," Congleton said, nudging Bell's arm, "there go some more leaving the area."

"Hold on, Cardinal Three." Bell again looked through the binoculars and focused on the entrance of the building the team had been watching for the past twenty minutes. "Three more men and . . . her. Is that the last of them?"

"According to the tally sheet, that should be all," Congleton answered.

"And is that him?"

"He fits the description."

Gary Bell glanced at his watch, then returned his attention to the field phone. "Make your repairs and get to your assigned location as soon as you can. Set up a watch on the target but don't act immediately. The subject's getting ready to leave now. Wait until after he gets home and settled in, then proceed with caution at your own discretion."

"Check. Cardinal Three out."

"Look, she's going back in like she said she would."

Bell and Congleton shifted onto their knees and watched as Hollie Bass walked back inside the Patton laboratory building. "Get ready," Bell said, glancing at the three people huddled beneath the tree to his right. "When she comes back out, that'll be our signal the building's clear. We'll only have about a half hour to get in and out before the night watchman arrives . . . and we don't want to have to tie him up like we did the last time."


5:52 P.M.

". . . and I don't like him coming out here bothering you." Kerk stood in the doorway to Jackie's room, watching her put on the diamond and sapphire earrings his father had given her the last Christmas they'd spent together.

"Believe me, I don't think much of Dan either. Our dinner this evening is strictly business. If the future of the compound wasn't hanging in the balance, I wouldn't be going out with him at all." Jackie paused to admire her earrings in the mirror.

"If it doesn't mean anything to you, then why are you getting so dressed up?" Kerk asked as he touched the sleeve of her blue silk dress. "Why don't you just wear blue jeans or something really ratty and embarrass the hell outta him. If you'd give him a really hard time, maybe then he'd leave you alone."

"I've already given him a *really hard time*," she mimicked, "several hard times, in fact, and you can see how much good it's done. And if I'd try to do something just to embarrass him, more than likely, it would also embarrass the hell out of me,"

Jackie countered, then she paused, looked at Kerk, and tilted her head to the side in question. "Does Bruce let you get away using language like that when I'm not here?"

"No." Kerk hung his head sheepishly. "Not unless the situation calls for it—and this situation sure as hell calls for it," he added quickly, again looking her in the eye.

"I think not," Jackie said in her stern motherly voice. She picked up her purse and shawl from the chair beside the dresser and walked out into the hall leading to the living room. "Are you ready?" she asked Kerk as he walked beside her.

"All *I* need are blue jeans and a sweatshirt," he said, holding his arms out to his side and turning in a small circle to model the clothes he was wearing. "Unlike some people, I don't need to get gussied up to go out. I'm just going to a ballgame."

"And what about a jacket?" Kerk didn't respond. "You know it's too early in the season to go without one."

"But it's warm out."

"It might be warm now, but it will be downright chilly by nine o'clock tonight."

"But—"

"I don't want you to take the chance of catching a cold. You know if you pick one up this late in the season, it'll probably hang on clear through to summer, and neither one of us wants that. So go upstairs and get your denim jacket."

Jackie and Kerk looked at each other for several seconds, then Kerk grinned, shook his head, and turned toward the stairs at the opposite end of the living room. "One of these days, I'll win in our stare-down."

"Not until you're thirty-five and living on your own you won't," she countered with a smile. Jackie watched Kerk until he disappeared up the stairwell then glanced at the portrait of Richard, Kerk, and herself hanging on the wall at the foot of the stairs. "Like father, like son," she whispered as she visually compared the two male faces in the photograph: their angular jaws... their brown hair... their green eyes... "Stubborn and bull-headed... oh, if only you were still here," she whispered as she focused on Richard's face... on Richard's eyes, "and if only Dan's eyes were another color. So many problems could have been avoided—"

A knock rattled the front door; Jackie gasped silently as she turned toward it with a start. Holding her breath, clutching her purse close to her as if it were a shield, she stared at the door's window, focusing on the masculine silhouette shadowed across the curtains. The time had arrived she'd been dreading all afternoon. Dan was here; he'd come to pick her up for their dinner meeting. There was no turning back now.

"Just a minute," she called, but Jackie still didn't move. She continued to stare at the window for several more seconds before encouraging herself to answer the door. "It's for the compound," she whispered. "I can put up with Dan for the evening if it means security for the compound. I can. I can do it."

Jackie hesitated a few seconds longer, then walked across the room. She took in a deep breath and reached for the door.

"Good evening," she said quite pleasantly as she pulled the door open. To her surprise, it wasn't Dan who was standing opposite the screen door; Barry had arrived early to pick up Kerk.

Barry hesitated a moment, eyed Jackie from head to toe, then let go with a complimentary wolf-whistle as he opened the door and stepped inside. "You look lovely," he said in a soft voice. Smiling, he again looked her over from head to foot. "Very lovely." Without giving her an opportunity to object, Barry slipped his arm around Jackie's waist, pulled her close to him, and kissed her. "Remind me, after this is all over, that I need to take you someplace nice for dinner."

"After all of this is over, I'll *need* to go someplace nice," she said, looking up into his eyes.

"You know you don't have to go tonight—"

"Don't start in with it," Jackie said, stepping away from him. "I've worked all day to build up my courage, and I don't need any distractions that will help tear it down." She glanced at her watch, then looked out the front door and down the lane toward the road. "Where is he, anyway?"

"Are you in that much of a hurry to be with Dan?"

"I'm in *no* hurry to be with Dan, but the quicker we get this evening over and done with, the sooner I can start to forget it."

*6:11 P.M.*

Warren unlocked the barn's door, stepped inside, and turned on the overhead light. Without even thinking about what he was doing, he turned to his left and walked to the worktable.

"How are you two doing this evening?" he asked the mice as he automatically picked up the glove from beneath the table and slipped it on his left hand.

As Warren reached for the cage, he noticed two wooden dowels lying on the table beside it. Curious, he picked them up and studied them, not remembering having gotten them out of the cabinet for any reason.

"Where did you come from?" he asked more of himself than of the inanimate objects. After pondering the situation, Warren glanced at the door, then saw the large puddle of water on the floor just inside the door, which he hadn't noticed when he'd first walked in. "It was locked," he reassured himself, again focusing on the door, "unless . . ."

"Somebody's been in here," he said, looking back at the mice, "and if you could talk, I bet you could tell me who it was." Warren again pondered the dowels, glanced at the caged animals on the opposite wall, then returned his attention to the mice. "And whoever it was, it looks like he was just interested in you two." He looked from the mice to the dowels and back again. "I wonder how much he saw." Warren again turned to look at the animals on the far wall. "And I wonder if he knows *all* of you are special as well.

"No matter. There's nothing any of you can show him for the time being." Warren turned back to the mice. "You two are the only ones sprouting . . ." he laughed at his spontaneous choice of words, ". . . sprouting any evidence of my success, and I'm not going to make the mistake of leaving you out here any longer. I won't take the chance that ruined Leland Wagner; I don't want anyone stepping in on my discovery and stealing you. Tonight, you two are going inside the house with me."

Warren decided he would wait until later to examine the mice's legs. He took off the glove, replaced it on the shelf beneath the table, and began to quickly go through his nightly routine of feeding and watering the animals and scooping out their litter boxes. When he finished with his chores, he tucked the mice's cage beneath his arm, locked the barn door behind him, and started toward the house. He was unaware his movements were being watched by a half-dozen pairs of eyes peeking out from beneath the tangled brush at the edge of the woods.


*6:15 P.M.*

No one waved good-bye. Everyone on the porch watched in silence as the limousine pulled away from the front of the house and drove off down the lane. Even when Jackie turned and glanced out the back window, no one reacted with a response. By the expression on her face, she looked like an orphaned child who was being taken away to a home where she didn't want to go.

"I hate that man," Kerk said with a grumble, his eyes following the limousine as it turned onto the main road.

"Hate's a mighty powerful word," Bruce said, looking down at the boy standing on the porch beside him.

"I don't know, there's just something about him that gives me the creeps." Kerk shuddered. "It's almost spooky."

"Try not to let it bother you," Barry said, laying a hand on Kerk's shoulder. "It'll all be over before we know it," he added, hoping to leave the topic of Dan Patton behind.

"I bet that's not soon enough for Mom—and how can you just stand there and let her go off with him?" Kerk asked bluntly, looking up at Barry. "I thought you and Mom had a thing going. How can you let her go out with another guy? I know I wouldn't let her go if she was my girlfriend."

"I wouldn't classify the dinner meeting your mother's having tonight as *going out*," Barry tried to explain. "Besides, haven't you learned yet that when your mother makes up her mind to do something, nothing or no one is going to change it."

Kerk looked up at Barry and grinned. "She doesn't let you win very often, either, does she?"

Barry looked at Kerk and chuckled. "Nope. She's one hardheaded lady for sure. That's one reason I'm not worried about her," he said, looking after the car, trying to convince himself as much as anyone. "She's the kind of person who can handle herself in just about any situation." Barry looked back at Kerk. "Are you ready to go?"

"The game got rained out, didn't it?"

"Yep."

"Then, where are we going?"

"Between you, me, and Cincinnati, I think we ought to be able to find something to do." Barry looked beyond Kerk to Bruce. "Are you sure you don't want to come with us? You might be able to think of some more exciting places to go than we can come up with."

"Thanks for the offer, but I think I'll stay put for the evening. The swing, here, needs some exercise, and I've got the paper to finish reading— Say, did you see where someplace out in Nebraska, they found several dead laboratory-type animals in some old lady's basement?"

"Seems like I heard something about it up at the station."

"That, and those kids gettin' sick down in Louisiana, makes for kind of a scary situation. Did they ever find out anything about the animals that were taken from around here?"

"Nothing's turned up yet," Barry answered, shaking his head.

"I sure hope none of the animals from Patton's were contaminated with anything."

"Dr. Wagner said they were all clean."

"I sure hope he's not the kind of fella to lie—"

"Hey, remember me? I'm ready, let's go," Kerk said impatiently as he started down the porch steps.

"Wait a minute, young man. Don't forget your jacket," Bruce reminded him.

Kerk stopped halfway down the steps, exhaled a heavy sigh, then gave Bruce a you've-been-talking-to-Mom look. Without arguing, he walked back up the steps, went to the front door, reached inside, and took his denim jacket off the coat rack. "*Now* I'm ready. Okay?"

Bruce grinned and nodded. "Okay."

"You're sure you won't come along with us?" Barry asked again as he stepped down from the porch.

"I'm positive. Thanks anyway," Bruce said. "Now you two go on and enjoy yourselves."

"Enjoy a quiet evening," Barry said with a wave. "We shouldn't be back too late."

"Have a good time." Bruce pulled a pipe out of his front bib pocket and stuck it in the corner of his mouth. As he walked toward the porch swing, he pulled a tobacco pouch from his hip pocket and unrolled the top. Settling down in the corner of the swing, he began packing his pipe as he watched Barry and Kerk get into Barry's jeep and drive off down the lane.

"No sir," Bruce said to himself, "if ever'body took off, there wouldn't be nobody left around here to do the chores, and it's a damn sight, they're not gonna get done on their own." Bruce chuckled to himself. "But when I was young, chores weren't the most important thing on my mind neither."

When his pipe was packed, Bruce reached into his bib pocket for a match. Finding none there, he stood and slipped his hand into his hip pocket. He was all but certain he'd stuffed a couple extra books of matches into that pocket with his tobacco pouch, but all he could feel was a bandanna handkerchief.

Still certain there was at least one matchbook hiding somewhere in that pocket, Bruce grabbed hold of the bandanna and yanked it out. Verifying his speculation, a book of matches came flying out of the pocket as well and landed on the porch near his feet. "I knew I put some in there somewhere," he mumbled. "I may be getting old, but I haven't lost my memory yet . . . at least not all of it."

Bruce sat down on the swing and leaned over to pick up the matchbook. Just as he was about to grasp it, something furry stuck its head out between his legs and yipped. In a reflex action, Bruce jerked his hand back.

"What the hell—"

The beige and brown puppy yipped again, then she pranced out from beneath the swing and sat down on the porch facing Bruce. She cocked her head to one side and stared up at Bruce with large brown eyes; her beige tail with a white tip swept back and forth across the porch floor like a tireless metronome. Receiving no immediate response, the puppy yipped again, then left her mouth partially open, the expression coming close to resembling a silly grin.

"It's not gonna do ya any good. I don't want another dog, and I don't want ya around. So go on and get."

Bruce leaned over to pick up the book of matches, but before he made contact, the puppy stood up, ran to the matches, picked them up in her teeth, and backed up a few steps before sitting down again. "What the?" The puppy woofed, the sound muffled by the matchbook in her mouth; her beige tail wagged back and forth in double-time. "Give those here." Bruce leaned toward the puppy, reaching for the matchbook in her mouth. The puppy eluded Bruce's hand, sidestepped, and sat down again.

"I'm not in the mood to play games," Bruce said gruffly as he stood and stepped toward the pup. Elusively, the puppy darted to the side, then ran down the steps onto the walk. "Come back here, you little—" Bruce called as he walked down the steps after her.

The puppy thought this game of Keep Away was fun, and she continued to dodge left and then right, always keeping a half step or two away from Bruce. As if to make sure the human wouldn't lose interest in the game, twice the puppy dropped the matchbook, barked, then picked it up again a split second before Bruce could bend over and grab it. To add to the merriment, the puppy circled Bruce two or three times and darted in close to him as if playing tag. Each time, Bruce grabbed for the puppy and missed.

"Okay, enough," Bruce finally conceded, exhaling a heavy breath as he sat down on the porch steps. "I'm too old to play puppy games." He still held the bandanna in his hand and used it to wipe the sweat from his brow and from the sweatband inside his straw hat. Bruce leaned back against the porch post, began fanning himself with his hat's wide brim, and looked at the puppy. "Okay, if they mean that much to you, they're yours. I've got plenty more in a box at home."

The puppy looked at Bruce, dropped the matchbook on the

ground, then looked at Bruce again. When Bruce made no attempt to go after the matches, the puppy sat down, yipped, and looked at him soulfully.

"Nope, the game's over." Bruce wiped his forehead again, then replaced his hat and stuffed the bandanna into his hip pocket. "And I guess I don't really need this anymore either." He slipped the pipe back into the bib pocket, stem down, then leaned back against the porch, propping himself on his elbows. "So now that the game's over," he said, looking at the puppy, "what are you gonna do?"

The puppy barked. Bruce didn't respond. The puppy barked again and wagged her tail. Still, Bruce provided no answer. As if defeated, the puppy whimpered, pawed at the matchbook on the ground, then picked it up with her teeth.

She walked toward Bruce, climbed the steps, and sat down on the porch close to him. She hesitated, as if waiting for a reaction. When she received none, she dropped the matchbook near Bruce's elbow and laid down on the porch, resting her head on her outstretched paws, looking up at him with sad brown eyes.

"Well, thank you . . . I guess." Bruce picked up the matches, pulled his pipe from his bib pocket, and lit it. As he puffed the tobacco to an amber glow, he felt something press against his leg. He looked down. The puppy had moved down onto the step beside him and was inching her way closer to him. When she finally settled, she laid her head on top of Bruce's leg.

"What's this?" Bruce asked in a surprisingly mellow tone. The puppy didn't whimper, yip, or bark; she just looked up at him with large, brown, soulful eyes.

"No . . . don't do that." Bruce turned his head sharply. Trying to ignore the puppy, he looked away—looked out across the pond, looked beyond the goats in the front pasture. He puffed heavily on his pipe, trying to drive away the memories those big brown eyes had pulled from the back of his mind.

The puppy edged closer. She lifted a paw and laid it on Bruce's leg.

Continuing to look out across the compound, Bruce let his hand slip down his leg . . . and slid it toward the puppy. When he felt her furred side, he hesitated, then slowly—gradually—he let his hand settle on the puppy's back. With a light and tender touch, he began stroking the soft beige and brown fur.

"Nobody can take . . . Corky's place, you know," Bruce said after several minutes, a break coming to his voice. The puppy nudged her cold nose beneath Bruce's hand; her wet tongue licked Bruce's fingers. "But . . . but I guess it's good for everybody to have . . . a dog."

Bruce reached into his back pocket, pulled out the bandanna, wiped his eyes, and blew his nose, then stood up. "Well, we're not gettin' any work done just sittin' around here."

Bruce walked down the steps and halfway across the walk, then hesitated and looked back over his shoulder. "You comin'?" he asked, looking into the puppy's brown eyes. "You comin' with me . . . Little Cork . . ."


*6:42 P.M.*

"Cardinal One. Come in, Cardinal One."

Gary Bell leaned across the van's seat to pick up the field phone from the floor. "Cardinal One here," he said into the mouthpiece. "Go ahead."

"This is Cardinal Three."

"What's your target status, Cardinal Three?"

"We scored a bull's-eye."

Bell nodded, and a smile of accomplishment spread across his face. "Good job, Cardinal Three. Proceed with distribution at your own discretion."

"And your target, Cardinal One?"

"We scored a bull's-eye as well."

"Good job. Are we still to rendezvous as scheduled?"

"As scheduled. Cardinal One over and out."

*7:22 P.M.*

Jackie said nothing when Dan ordered their meal without consulting her; she really didn't care, and she wasn't about to confront him on even a minor point that might prolong the time they would have to spend together. She was just going through the motions. As far as she was concerned, she could make a meal out of soup and crackers if it meant putting an end to their so-called business dinner.

But dinner was not quick; Dan had planned it to be a gala affair, served in seven elaborate courses. He'd made a point, while they were being seated, to command the waiter as to his personal preference on dining procedures. With an air of pompous grandeur, he called the chef to the table, giving strict instructions as to how the pheasant was to be prepared and to what exact temperature the wine was to be chilled.

Each word leaving Dan's mouth was bold and demanding. He could be heard by everyone around the room, and everyone responded just as he'd hoped they would, making him the center of their attention. Dan loved it; Jackie was embarrassed by it. With each passing second, she wished more and more that she had stayed at home, but that decision would have been of no benefit to the compound. The compound . . . *that* was the reason she had agreed to be subjected to an evening with Daniel Jerome Patton the Fourth.

The compound. Jackie kept reminding herself what might lie ahead for the compound if she didn't find a way to cope with their financial demands. *That* was the only aspect that kept her in her seat . . . and kept her from getting up and walking out of the restaurant.

After the chef and waiter left the table, and the people around them returned their attention to their own meals, Jackie decided to approach the topic that —for her— was the sole focus of the entire evening. "What exactly is it you want me to do?" she asked, sitting back in her chair and looking across the table at Dan.

Dan smiled at her all-knowingly, folded his hands, and braced them on the edge of the table as he leaned toward her ever so slightly. "Always look as lovely as you do this evening," he answered in a low voice. Slowly, his emerald-green eyes moved over her, taking in every feature of her face . . . her neck . . . her shoulders . . . her breasts . . . When Dan's eyes returned to meet hers, they spoke openly of his inner desires; there wasn't any question as to the thoughts being guarded by their emerald-green sparkle. "Yes . . . lovely."

Jackie felt violated. Dan was raping her mentally, and there was little she could do to defend herself. Mustering all of her strength, she bit the inside of her lower lip to keep from blurting out a reply that would, no doubt, jeopardize funding for the compound.

"What do you want me to do?" Jackie repeated, surprised by her self-control and at how smoothly the words seemed to slide over her lips. Yes, she kept reminding herself, she was definitely going to make it through the evening. "You've already selected an architect, and there are over a dozen good curators in Cincinnati and Indianapolis—or even in St. Louis—who would jump at the chance to help set up a new zoo. I still don't understand what you want *me* to do."

"I want you to be there whenever I need you," Dan answered. An almost sinister grin twitched at the corners of his mouth, then his lips parted, and his tongue slowly skimmed along the edges of his pearl-white teeth. "Be there whenever I ... *want* you."

"You're disgusting," Jackie said. The skin along her nose puckered, and her lips curled in response to Dan's suggestive statement.

"I may be disgusting, but then, I can afford to be."

Jackie diverted her eyes to something on the far side of the room ... something she didn't actually see. How long could she continue in this battle of wits? She was beginning to wonder if she had the stamina to keep up with—to continue to counter—every move Dan threw at her. But she had to. The compound was at stake.

"Things would be different if I had my legs," Dan said in a sorrowful tone.

Jackie's eyes snapped into contact with Dan's. "Don't start that," she said through clenched teeth.

Dan chuckled. "I'll start anything I damn well please, and you know there's nothing you can do about it."

Dan slid his hand across the brocade tablecloth toward her. Before he could touch her, Jackie withdrew her hand to her lap.

"What price do you charge to hold hands in public for all the world to see?" Dan asked as he turned his hand palm up and motioned with his fingers for hers. "Whatever it is, you know I can afford it."

"I'm not a prostitute," Jackie whispered curtly, her eyes glaring with the rage that was burning deep within her. "You can't buy me—"

"We all prostitute ourselves for something at one time or another," Dan countered as he leaned back in his chair and eyed her with an arrogant air. "For you, my dear, the price may be high, but I think a three-hundred-and-sixty-acre farm with an adjoining animal compound just might be your asking price."

"My agreeing to work with you is based on the compound. It has nothing to do with the farm. The farm was bought and paid for a long time ago."

"Are you sure?" Dan said. Jackie eyed Dan curiously as he slipped a hand inside his suit jacket's inner pocket and pulled out a yellowed business-size envelope. "I've been holding on to this little item for quite some time," he said as he laid the envelope on the place mat in front of Jackie.

"What is it?" she asked, looking at the envelope, not sure whether she wanted to touch it or not.

"Apparently, Bruce Cameron and my father made an agreement, concerning the property, before either you or I were born."

"What kind of an agreement?" Jackie asked with a note of apprehension.

"It's nothing elaborate. It's only a couple of paragraphs; go ahead and read it for yourself," he said, nodding toward the envelope. "There's no secret about it. One of these days, it will be open for public scrutiny."

Jackie hesitated, then picked up the envelope, opened it, and withdrew a sheet of paper almost as yellowed as the envelope. Carefully, she unfolded the paper and read the handwritten agreement, concerning a personal loan between Bruce Cameron and the senior Daniel Jerome Patton, which had been signed by both on a date almost thirty-five years ago.

When she finished reading the agreement, Jackie looked at Dan apprehensively. "This can't be legally binding."

"Oh, but it is."

"But it wasn't witnessed and notarized—"

"According to my lawyer—who, by the way, has done extensive research into the matter—it's a perfectly legal document." Dan leaned back in his chair and smiled arrogantly. "And payment is long overdue," he added with a twitch to his smile. "Being the sole heir of the deceased participant, I have a perfectly legal right to demand payment or . . . to take possession of the property. By all rights, the farm *and* compound—to help cover past-due interest and expenses—are both legally mine."

Jackie slumped back in her chair; she felt as if someone had reached inside her and yanked out her heart. She glanced at the paper again—reread the paragraphs—then refolded the letter and slipped it back into the envelope. She slid it across the table to Dan.

"So what is it you want me to do?" she asked reluctantly, purposely avoiding Dan's eyes.

"For starters, the Governor's Ball is coming up in the very near future and, as I have made my wishes known before, I would like for you to accompany me to the affair."

Jackie hesitated, then gave in to Dan's request. "All right, I'll go to the ball with you. But before this little deal of ours goes one step further," she added, looking him directly in the eye, "we're going to make an agreement of our own." Dan nodded, the arrogant smile still dominating his face. "When all of this is over, the compound *and* the farm will be written off as free and clear." Dan nodded again. "And I want that in writing."

"I'll have my lawyer get to work on the papers tomorrow. Is there anything else?"

"Stay away from my home. It bothers Kerk for you to come out there."

"Very well, I can send Rusty to pick you up, or we can set up an agreeable location to meet. Is there anything else?"

Jackie stalled for as long as she could before answering, "There's nothing more I can think of."

"Very well then, it's all settled." Dan leaned closer to the table and extended his hand to Jackie.

Jackie stared at Dan's hand for several seconds, then slowly—unwillingly—she slid hers up beside his. A feeling of defeat poured through her; she felt absolutely powerless.

Dan's smile broadened as he slid his hand over on top of hers. Jackie tensed when he touched her, and she started to withdraw her hand, but Dan grasped it firmly. "I told you, everyone will prostitute herself for something," he whispered, his green eyes homing in on hers.

Jackie looked at Dan directly, and she set her jaw firmly before speaking. "Holding hands will be the extent of it. I still have no intentions of ever going to bed with you."

"We'll see."


*7:41 P.M.*

Warren wrung out the sponge mop and made one last swipe over the gold-speckled linoleum in the corner of the basement. His cleanup job was almost finished.

The electricity had gone off sometime during the storm and when it had come back on, the automatic switch on the sump pump had failed to engage. When Warren had gone to the basement, looking for a pair of gloves to use with the mice, he'd been met with over six inches of standing water. It had taken him only a few minutes to get the pump's motor running, but it had taken over an hour to pump the water out of the basement. For the past several minutes, he'd been trying to clean up the silt and mud the receding water had left behind. It had been quite a mess; he felt fortunate he kept nothing of any great value stored in the basement.

"That's good enough," he said, hanging the mop head over a couple of nails hammered into the floor joist beside the stairs. "I've got to remember to pick up a new relay switch for the pump," he told himself as he dumped a bucket of muddy water into the sink beside an old wringer washer. He glanced at his watch. "I'd better get dinner out of the way before—"

A shrill squeal knifed through the open stairwell leading down from the utility room.

"What the?" Taken by surprise, Warren took a couple hesitant steps toward the stairwell. "What's going on up there?" he called out, looking up the stairs, knowing damn-good-and-well he'd jump right out of his skin if he received an answer.

Another high-pitched shriek splintered the air.

"What—" Then Warren thought he knew what might be causing the ruckus.

Taking the steps by twos, he ran upstairs, hurried through the utility room, and turned the corner into the kitchen. Immediately, his eyes darted across the room to the counter— to the counter where he'd placed the mice's cage—to the pale yellow counter and the wall behind it... that was splattered with blotches of bright red blood. The mice were fighting.

"Stop it!" Warren shouted at the mice. Inside the cage, the squealing, tumbling mass of blood-splattered fur ignored his command.

"I've got to separate them," he said to himself.

Warren remembered an old wire bird cage he'd stored in the basement. Hurrying as fast as he could, he ran back downstairs, retrieved the cage, and returned to the kitchen.

"Hey!" Warren shouted. He hit the side of the mice's cage with the flat of his hand as he leaned over to look at them. "What's gotten into you two?" As if to reply, one of the mice momentarily broke free from the fight and snapped at Warren's hand. Had Warren not reacted instinctively and jerked his hand away, the mouse's front teeth would have sunk into his finger. Instead, the blood-lathered incisors clamped down on the cage's wire mesh, then the mouse returned his attention to the fight.

For a moment, Warren continued to stare at the wire mesh. Was it just his imagination... or had the mouse's teeth seemed longer than normal? And had the mouse, itself, seemed *bigger?*

"No," Warren whispered, shaking his head, "it just looked that way . . ."

Another shriek shattered the kitchen's silence. The more aggressive mouse bit into his cagemate's neck and wouldn't let go. The weaker mouse fell over onto its side, succumbing to the choke hold and apparently accepting its fate.

"Stop it!" Warren shouted, again hitting the side of the cage with his hand.

The aggressive mouse released its hold on its cagemate and turned squarely toward Warren. Their eyes met. For a brief moment, Warren had the feeling he was being challenged.

"I've got to get you out of there," Warren said out loud to the mouse as if to reassure himself of his human supremacy.

Warren reached toward the cage. The mouse bared its teeth. And yes—*Yes!* Those teeth *were* longer—bigger! The mouse itself was bigger. It had grown!

Warren glanced around the kitchen, saw an oven mitt hanging from a magnetic hook on the stove, grabbed the mitt, and slipped it on. "This isn't as heavy as my gloves in the barn, but it'll have to do for now."

He again reached for the cage; again the mouse defied the intrusion. This time, Warren didn't pull back. He opened the cage door, reached inside, and grabbed the aggressive mouse.

As he picked up the mouse and carried it to the bird cage on the kitchen table, Warren could feel the pressure of the mouse's teeth as it tried to bite through the oven mitt. "What's gotten into you?" he asked, continuing his one-sided conversation. "You've never acted like this before. I thought you two were friends." The mouse's small, dark eyes again met Warren's, and again, Warren had the feeling he was being challenged. "Well, I can guarantee you one thing, with an attitude like that, you're not going to make very many friends."

Warren turned the mouse over and looked at the stub of the animal's foreleg where the foot had been amputated. The pink-skinned leg bud that had prompted his excitement that morning had almost doubled in size.

"It's working... it's working," Warren repeated in a singsong manner. He put the mouse inside the bird cage and closed the door. "I just hope you haven't done any irreversible damage to your buddy over there." Warren took a couple of steps toward the wounded mouse, then stopped and smiled to himself. "But then, if the Starfish formula works, I suppose *nothing* is irreversible."


*7:53 P.M.*

"You're free now. Go on and get outta here." Jim Cox clapped his hands together as an incentive for the raccoons to leave their transport cage. Neither of the pudgy animals budged; they looked up at him through the bars, trembling. "The rest of them took off so fast," Cox said, looking to his companions. "I've never seen two animals so stubborn about reclaiming their freedom," he added.

"Maybe they're too afraid to move," Janice Doty said.

"Maybe they've never had the chance to know what they're missing," Becky Haines added as she stepped up beside Cox and looked down at the raccoons. "Most animals only appreciate freedom when they've had it and then had it taken away."

"Well, these two are going to have to learn to appreciate it in a pretty big hurry." Cox lifted the back end of the cage and began to shake it gently. Gradually, the raccoons slid across the floor toward the open door and, eventually, slipped out onto the ground. "Go on now. Scoot," he said, rattling the cage in hopes of scaring the raccoons off.

"Go on," Becky echoed. "Get."

The raccoons looked up at them, looked at each other, then sat up on their back legs and nosed the air around them . . . picking up the human scent they would always remember. One raccoon chattered; the other answered. In unison, they dropped down on all fours and scampered off into the woods.

"That's the last of them," Cox said as he closed the door to the transport cage and picked it up.

"I wish they could be the last animals we'd ever have to rescue," Becky said, eyeing the break in the underbrush where the raccoons had disappeared.

"Maybe someday . . ." Cox glanced at his watch as he started toward the van. "We'd better get a move on. Rendezvous is scheduled in a little over an hour, and we've still got a good thirty miles of hills to maneuver to get back on time."

"At least we didn't have to take these as far away as Frank and Claudia had to take the domestics," Janice said.

"Yeah, we had the lucky draw on this one. Since all of ours were wild, we could just let some of them out in the woods along the way and turn the rest of them loose out here in the park."

"I wonder if they'll find any relatives?" Becky asked as she again looked in the direction where the raccoons had scampered off.

"I bet it won't take them too long to get acquainted. Come on, we don't want to be late for the rendezvous."


*9:27 P.M.*

"I'll call you," Dan said as he leaned back from the window

and scooted back on the plush seat.

Jackie didn't respond; she watched in silence as the automatic, smoke-tinted window rose to conceal Dan's face. Standing at the edge of the drive, she continued to focus on the limousine as it pulled away slowly and drove down the lane. Something didn't seem right to her.

During the course of the evening, Dan's behavior had changed. He'd started out as a boisterous, self-centered, arrogant individual, seeming—at times—to push Jackie . . . to attempt to dominate her. But as time passed and the evening wore on, Dan seemed to mellow. With each dinner course, he appeared to lose his need for external attention, and instead of him focusing on Jackie, Dan's watch became the object he referred to frequently.

Jackie hadn't minded that Dan became preoccupied elsewhere; in fact, she actually enjoyed it. She'd been able to enjoy her flaming dessert and after-dinner cocktail in relative peace.

Dan had surprised her even more when he instructed the driver to bring them straight back to her house. Jackie was relieved when their dinner meeting came to an abrupt end, but at the same time, she was more than a little bit puzzled by it.

"At least round one is over," she said beneath her breath as she turned toward the house. Jackie was halfway to the porch steps before she looked up. Immediately, she saw Bruce sitting on the porch swing, highlighted by the soft yellow porch lights.

"How was your evening?" Bruce asked as she climbed the steps and walked toward him.

"I survived," Jackie answered. She draped her shawl over her shoulders, sat down beside him, and took in a slow, deep breath. "Ah, the air smells so clean after a rain." Bruce grunted in reply and puffed on his pipe. "I take it Kerk and Barry aren't back yet or you wouldn't be sitting out here by yourself."

"It looks like they're making more of an evening of it than you did." Bruce took another long drag off his pipe, then exhaled slowly, watching the smoke as it drifted up toward the ceiling. "I didn't expect you home this early," he added.

"I didn't expect to *be* home this early."

"What happened?" Bruce chuckled. "Did you kick him in the balls like I suggested?"

"No," Jackie answered with a laugh, "but you know, I'm not exactly sure what did happen. One minute Dan was being his typical obnoxious self, and the next minute, he was bringing me home."

Home. Jackie thought of the old farmhouse where she and Richard had spent eleven happy years together. She thought of the compound . . . and of the farm. Then she thought about what Dan had said, about the property being his, and about the loan Bruce had taken from Dan's father those many years ago.

"Dan showed me a letter at dinner that took me totally off guard," Jackie said, turning her head slightly toward Bruce. "It was the agreement you signed with his father when you borrowed money from him to buy this farm."

"You needn't concern yourself with that."

Jackie turned directly toward Bruce. "But Dan said since you hadn't paid off the loan, legally, everything out here belongs to him."

"If push comes to shove, I have the papers to prove otherwise."

"I don't understand." When Bruce didn't respond to her statement, Jackie tried to prod a little deeper. "What kind of agreement did you have with Dan's father?"

"A gentlemen's agreement," Bruce paused, "and I'll leave it at that." He looked at Jackie, and by the expression on his face, she knew she had come to the end of her questions on the subject.

Jackie sat back in the swing and pulled the ends of the shawl up across her chest. Bruce was so stubborn—so close-mouthed; he was exactly like someone else she had loved.

Richard had been just like Bruce. Yes, *just* like him—right down to his green eyes... and the love they shared for Richard's mother. Just like him... Richard had always wondered if Bruce might be his father, but he'd never asked... and his mother had never told him. It was a secret she took to the grave with her.

They sat for a few moments in silence, Bruce puffing on his pipe, Jackie looking out over the pond and pasture, mentally catching a ride on the backs of fireflies darting in and out of the darkness.

"When are you and Barry going to get together?" Bruce asked without any forewarning. "The boy needs a father," he added bluntly.

Jackie shifted uneasily on the swing. "I'm not ready yet."

"It's been a year and a half since Richard died. You've served your time in mourning, and it's time you got on with your life. You're too fine of a woman not to be matched up with a good man, and in my opinion, Barry's a damn good man." Bruce hesitated a moment. "You do like him, don't you?"

"Yes, I like him," she answered hesitantly, "it's... it's just that I'm not ready yet."

"You're not ready for another man? Or you're just not ready for another cop?" Jackie glanced at Bruce but didn't say anything. "The percentage of policemen killed on duty is very small. Just because Richard was shot doesn't mean Barry will be—"

"I know... I know," she repeated in a softer voice. Jackie paused for a moment, trying to collect the thoughts that had been bouncing around inside her head for the last year and a half. "I can't let go of Richard... not just yet. I can't put him to rest until I know who killed him."

"His own department has practically given up on that—"

"But I haven't," Jackie said adamantly. "Sometime . . . somewhere, I'll find out who it was who killed Richard, and . . . and then I'll be able to put him to rest without feeling like I deserted him."

Bruce reached toward Jackie and placed his hand on top of hers. "I hope it's not a long and lonely life for you."

Bruce's movement disturbed the ball of fur curled up on the swing between them. The puppy whimpered, yawned, and stretched, pushing against Jackie's leg.

"And just what do we have here?" Jackie asked, happy to change the topic. She scratched the puppy's chin and rubbed her rotund belly. "Have you two finally become friends?" she asked, looking at Bruce.

"I guess she finally persuaded me," he answered, reaching to rub the puppy as well.

"I'm glad. I was getting worried about you. Nobody needs to be alone."

Bruce looked at Jackie, then cupped her chin in his hand and lifted her face so he could look directly into her eyes. "Nobody needs to be alone," he repeated, "and neither do you."


*9:44 P.M.*


The two young raccoons huddled beneath a tangle of briars, their dark eyes wide, their ears pricked forward. Their heartbeats had slowed, approaching normal, but an occasional tremor still pulsed through their muscles, prompting them to shiver . . . to tremble. They were still frightened.

Their noses twitched. The scent of humans was fading—it no longer crowded in around them like it had just before they'd been set free—but it was still there. It lingered . . . in the air . . . on the grass . . . on their fur where the humans had touched them. Human scent. When would they be able to escape from it? Maybe the rain would wash it away. The rain . . .

They listened. Thunder rumbled in the distance, but only an occasional raindrop disturbed the leafy canopy overhead. The storm had passed. Mother Nature was settling in for a calm and peaceful night.

Cautiously, the young raccoons stepped out from beneath the briars. Looking up, they peered through branches coming to life with spring foliage and saw a half moon partially guarded by retreating clouds. Their noses twitched as they took in deep breaths . . . again . . . and again. For the most part, the air smelled fresh and clean, but a faint human scent still lingered.

They chattered back and forth, as if engaged in conversation, then looked in both directions along the narrow path bordering the briar patch. They had come into the woods, following the path to their right; to return in that direction would, no doubt, lead them back to the humans and to the cages that had held them in confinement for the past several months. If logic held any merit, the path to their left should take them deeper into the woods—away from the humans . . . and the cages. For the two raccoons, there was really no choice as to which way they should go.

The male raccoon glanced up at the moon, chattered a few syllables, then turned to his left and began walking along the path. The female watched him, hesitated a few moments, then followed along behind. Together, they waddled along the path in a roly-poly raccoon gait, chattering to one another and stopping every now and then to nibble on tender young roots and berries or to forage for grubs nesting in the hollow of a fallen, rotted tree. Their journey from man's world back into the wilderness was so pleasant and inviting, they all but forgot about the human scent that still lingered—

Something snapped.

*PAIN!* The male raccoon cried out. He yeowled and screeched and squealed and bawled. *PAIN!* Excruciating *PAIN* knifed through his left front paw and radiated like lightning bolts up his leg, into his shoulder, and all along the nerves to his spine.

He tumbled to the ground and rolled, trying to pull away from the *PAIN*, but the steel teeth on the spring-loaded trap wouldn't yield to his frenzy. With every move, the razor-sharp edges bit deeper and deeper into the young raccoon's fur and muscle and bone.

The female stood frozen at the edge of the path, her eyes wide with fear . . . watching her tortured companion. She was helpless.

After several minutes of useless struggling, the young male lay spent, still a prisoner of the trap. He cried out in agony as he eyed the sharp teeth, wet with blood, glistening in the moonlight. The sharp edges had come within a half inch of meeting—of closing completely; beyond the steel teeth lay his limp, near-severed paw.

Free. He wanted to be free.

Again, the young raccoon began to roll and pull—*PAIN!* Again, he lay still, looking at the trap and his captured paw . . . at his captured front paw. There was no mental question or debate; his instincts told him what had to be done.

The raccoon slid forward on his belly and propped his upper body up with his right front paw. He glanced at his companion, chattered out a message, then looked back at his captive paw. Without hesitating an instant longer, he lowered his head and began to gnaw on the remaining strands of sinew and bone that connected him to the useless paw on the other side of the steel trap's teeth.

*10:03 P.M.*

Warren sat at the kitchen table, eating the last of the dinner that had taken him almost an hour to prepare. He hadn't intended on eating so late, but in addition to the water in the basement, there had been a phone call from his mother in Greenwood and a return call made to his brother in Salem. In spite of everything else that had complicated his life, Warren's family still came first.

Then there were the mice. Every time Warren would be about to begin his meal, he would glance at the mice in their cages. After only a few moments, he would become intrigued and interrupt whatever he was doing and sit down for a few minutes to look at the mice—to study them—and write down a few more comments in the notebook he'd been keeping since the very first day he'd brought home a vial half filled with serum.

Tonight, the aggressive mouse looked bigger; in fact, Warren suspected it had grown during the past few hours. And the wounded mouse . . . well, evidently its wounds weren't as serious as Warren had first thought. Within the past hour, it had begun scurrying around its cage, sniffing and smelling, seeming to search for its cagemate that had been abruptly taken away. But Warren wondered why he was so amazed by— or why he even questioned—the mouse's speedy recovery; after all, it *was* a product of the Starfish Project.

"I don't think I'm going to leave you in that bird cage overnight," Warren said to the aggressive mouse, eyeing the rodent's temporary home. "It's cheap, and the wire gauge isn't as sturdy as my regular cages. If you'd get in the mood to do some chewing after a while, you could gnaw your way out, and I could end up with a mouse loose in the house. And since I don't know exactly what you might be capable of, I don't think it would be a good idea to take any chances. I'd hate to wake up in the middle of the night with you perched on my chest and those ugly teeth of yours only a few inches away from my face." Warren cleared the dishes off the table, set them in the sink, then started toward the back door. "Do you think you can behave yourselves while I go out to the lab for another cage—"

The front doorbell rang.

Warren glanced at the clock. "Patton," he said in a whisper. He took a couple of steps toward the living room archway, then stopped and looked back at the mice. "I don't think it would be a good idea for him to see you just yet," Warren said as he crossed the kitchen and picked up the cages. "The spare bedroom would be a good place for you," he added as he entered the living room and turned toward the hall to his left.

The front doorbell rang again . . . and again.

"Just a minute," Warren called out as he set the cages on the floor just inside the bedroom. "I'm coming," he shouted in response to the third ring. "Give me a second," he muttered mostly to himself as he crossed the living room, heading for the front door. "There's no use to be in such a big hurry. Nothing's going to happen tonight."

The instant Warren turned the deadbolt lock, the door flew open. He jumped—was pushed—back in surprise when Rusty Snider muscled his way into the room. Warren's heart suddenly rose to pound in his throat.

Snider took a moment to look around Warren's living room. When he was satisfied that everything was secure, he positioned himself beside the front door and nodded. Dan Patton then stepped calmly into the room.

"Mr. . . . . Mr. Patton," Warren stammered, trying to regain his composure. "I—"

"Where's the serum?" Dan demanded, foregoing any pleasantries. He looked at Warren with eyes as cold as steel.

"The serum—"

"The Starfish serum. I want it, and I want it now!" Dan

pushed past Warren and walked to the center of the living room. After taking a quick survey of his surroundings, he turned back sharply toward Warren. "Do you have it hidden in here somewhere, or is it out back in your lab?"

"My lab—" Warren started to question, then he remembered the dowel rods he'd found on the table beside the mice's cage. "It was you. You were in my lab—"

"Hell, *anybody* could get into your lab. It amazes me. With all the scientific degrees you've got tacked on behind your name, it sure looks like you'd be smarter than to leave a key hanging above the damn door. Now, where is it?" Dan asked abruptly.

"The serum's out in the lab, but—"

"No buts—no nothing. I want it, and I want it now. Is that clear?"

"Yes, but—"

"No yes-buts either," Dan shouted as he stepped toward Warren and grabbed him by the front of his shirt. "You weren't lying to me—you weren't leading me on this afternoon, were you?"

"No, but—"

"The serum from the Starfish Project can do everything you said, can't it?"

"I . . . I think so—"

"Then I want it, and I want it now!" Dan lifted Warren up by his shirt until he was standing on his tiptoes. "Listen to me, little man," he shouted in Warren's face, "I'm not used to having to ask for something more than once. I'm in a position where I can buy you a thousand times over, so when I say I want something, I mean I want it *now!*"

Warren squirmed and tried to pull himself free, but Dan held firmly to the front of his shirt. "All right . . . all right, you can have it," Warren finally said. When Dan released him, Warren fussed with the front of his shirt as if the action of straightening his crumpled clothes would somehow rub off and rescue his dignity.

"Now, where is it?" Dan demanded.

"I told you, it's out in the lab—"

"I know it's out in the lab, but where? Show me." Dan grabbed Warren by the arm and forcefully ushered him through the living room toward the kitchen. "How do we get out there from here? Through this way?" Once in the kitchen, Dan continued toward the utility room. "Is this the right way?" Before Warren could comment on either question, they were standing on the back stoop, looking out over the yard toward the small red barn.

Dan hesitated, and in his excitement, his grip tightened on Warren's thin wrist. "I'm this close—*this close*—and I can almost *feel* it." He took two steps down to the ground, pulling Warren with him. "Hurry. Hurry!" Practically dragging Warren behind him, Dan moved across the rain-softened backyard as fast as his legs would carry him.

When they rounded the corner of the small barn, Dan stopped abruptly and jerked Warren around in front of him. "The door," Dan said almost fearfully, "it's open."

"What?" Warren questioned in surprise.

"With something as important as the serum out here, how could you have been so stupid not to have shut the door."

"But I *did* shut the door." Warren yanked his arm free, used a hand to ease the barn door the rest of the way open, stepped inside, and turned on the power switch. As the flourescent lights began to flutter overhead—even before they were at full illumination—Warren could see that all of the cages were empty . . . their doors hanging open on their hinges. "No!" he cried out as he stepped in front of the wall of cages, looking at each and every one of them, touching them, as if the action would reverse the theft.

"What is it?" Dan asked, following Warren into the barn.

"What happened?"

"They're gone. They're all gone."

"What's gone?"

"Someone broke in and took all the animals I've been using for Starfish."

Dan glanced at the empty cages and was overtaken by a surge of panic. "The serum! Where's the serum?" he shouted, grabbing Warren by the arm and yanking him around. "Where's the serum?"

"In the refrigerator," Warren answered, pulling his arm free and motioning toward the far corner of the barn. "It's in there."

"Get it. Get it and show me how to take it."

"You can't be serious."

"I've never been more serious about anything in my life."

For a moment, Warren just stood there, staring up at Dan. How could anybody be so foolhardy—so desperate—as to demand something that hadn't been proven safe . . . that might not even be compatible to the human organism? Granted, he had been the one to approach Dan with the idea that—someday—the Starfish Project *might* benefit man, but the real reason he had gone to see Dan was to ask for funding for his own research. He was sick and tired of never getting any credit . . . sick and tired of being Leland Wagner's—

"Now!" Dan grabbed Warren and shoved him toward the refrigerator. Warren stumbled, barely managing to maintain his balance. "Give me the serum, and show me how to take it."

Warren turned around and looked Dan directly in the eye. "You're crazy if you try this."

"I may be crazy, but at least I'll be whole. Now do it. Get the serum and show me how to take it."

Warren hesitated, shook his head, then walked to the cabinet beside the worktable. He took out a pad of paper, a pencil, and a box of disposable syringes and returned to the refrigerator. He hesitated again, glanced at Dan, then opened the refrigerator and took out a rack containing six serum vials. "How much do you weigh?" Warren asked as he set the rack on a nearby stool.

"What difference does it make?"

"To date, my largest specimen has been a thirty-three-pound raccoon. I need to know your weight in order to calibrate the exact dosage that should be used."

"I weigh around two twenty, now get on with it."

Dan watched impatiently while Warren figured his calculations. When he finished, Warren picked up a syringe and began filling it from a vial. When the syringe was almost two-thirds full, he held it out in front of him and pressed the plunger until a few drops of serum squirted from the needle's tip.

"Take off your jacket and roll up your shirt sleeve." Dan followed the instructions without question, then held his bared upper arm out toward Warren. "This is your last chance to change your mind—"

"I'm not going to change my mind. Do it!"

Warren glanced at Rusty Snider, who was standing in the barn's doorway. Snider remained stone-faced; no sign of communication—pro or con—passed between them.

Warren didn't take time to sterilize the area with alcohol; he jabbed the needle into Dan's left tricep and depressed the plunger without hesitating. After all of the serum was pushed out of the syringe, he pulled the needle free and tossed it in the trash can beside the refrigerator.

"How much and how often?" Dan asked as he rolled his shirt sleeve down and slipped on his jacket.

"So I can monitor you, you'd better come back here and let me—"

"I'll do it." Dan picked up the box of syringes and rack of

serum vials. "How much and how often?" he asked again impatiently.

Warren looked at Dan but knew there was no use for him to protest. "I'll write it down," he said. He wrote the dosage on a piece of notepaper, then handed it to Dan. "I was injecting the animals once every twenty-four hours. I would recommend you follow the same timetable . . . oh, and make sure you get it in a muscle. Your thigh or abdominal area would probably be the easiest for you to reach."

Dan nodded, cradled the rack in his arm, and started across the barn. When he reached the door, he stopped and looked back at Warren. "How long will it take?"

Warren shook his head. "I haven't the faintest idea."

"If you don't think this will be enough to do the job," Dan said, nodding at the six vials of serum, "you better get busy and make up some more." He glanced at the empty cages. "And don't go telling people you had your animals stolen. I don't want anybody else to know about this." Dan turned and stepped out of the barn. Rusty Snider followed.

Warren continued to stare at the vacant doorway and mouthed a reply he knew Dan couldn't hear. "I don't want anybody to know about it either . . . especially if something goes wrong."

# Tuesday

## (Day Five)

*8:01 A.M.*

Barry looked at the names stenciled on the glass, hesitated for a moment, and then he knocked. The opaque pane rattled loosely in the door's frame, the vibration the only response to his summons.

He grasped the crystalline doorknob and twisted. It turned easily in his hand.

"Hello," Barry called as he opened the door and took a step inside. Receiving no reply, he continued across the outer room toward the half-wall partition and the door to Denis Sweezy's inner office. "Is anyone here?" he asked, peering in at an empty desk. The room was vacant.

Barry glanced at his watch, then mumbled to himself as he walked back across the room toward the hallway door. "I found him here about this time yesterday and figured I could do it again. I guess philosophy professors just don't keep regular hours like normal people," he added with a hint of sarcasm.

As he neared the door, Barry heard voices coming from out in the hall. Hoping one of the voices belonged to Denis Sweezy, Barry stepped back, bumped into the corner of a wooden table, and decided to sit on its edge and wait.

". . . and I can see there would be no reasonable doubt if the logistics were adequately explained—Oh!" A young girl with long straight blond hair, dressed in blue jeans and a jacket, stopped the instant she stepped inside the office. Her eyes widened, and she gasped in surprise when she saw Barry, in his brown uniform, perched on the corner of the table, looking at her.

"What is it, Wanetah?" Denis Sweezy asked as he peeked around the door. When he saw Barry, a smile came to Sweezy's face, and the middle-aged professor walked on into the room. "Why, it's Sergeant . . . Roberts, I believe."

"That's Robbins," Barry countered, "*Deputy* Robbins."

"Ah yes, Deputy Robbins from the sheriff's department."

"I'll talk to you later, professor," the young blond said, then she turned abruptly and stepped back out in the hall.

"There's no need for you to go—" but before Sweezy could convince his young colleague to stay, she was gone. "Well then, Deputy Robbins," Sweezy said casually as he walked to the well-worn sofa and sat down, "what can I do for you today?"

"There was another break-in in the area last night," Barry said, shifting on the edge of the table so he could look at Sweezy head-on.

"A break-in? What sort of break-in this time?"

"Someone stole a new shipment of laboratory animals from Patton Pharmaceutical."

"My . . . my," Sweezy said in a patronizing tone, "with two break-ins taking place so close together, you'd think the higher-ups at Patton Pharmaceutical would get the idea that people might prefer they not experiment on innocent animals."

Barry stood from the table, walked to a chair directly opposite Sweezy, placed his hands on the chair's back, and leaned toward Sweezy. "What do you know about it?" he asked, looking Sweezy directly in the eye.

"Me?" Sweezy lifted a hand to his forehead as if to dramatize his ability to think, then he made a broad circular gesture with his arm as he continued. "This entire scenario seems strangely familiar. Didn't you ask me a similar question about . . ." he glanced at the clock on the wall above the hallway door, ". . . just about twenty-four hours ago?"

"And I'm still waiting for an answer to both questions," Barry said, continuing to look Sweezy directly in the eye.

Sweezy looked back at him in silence. They stared at each other for almost a minute, then Barry straightened, turned, and walked halfway across the room.

"All right," Barry said, adding his own touch of drama, "let's take a hypothetical situation, shall we?" He turned back toward Sweezy. "Hypothetically, *if* you were involved with a break-in, what would you do with the animals once you had them?"

Sweezy looked at Barry for several seconds before deciding whether he wanted to play along. "Hypothetically," he began, scooting forward onto the edge of the sofa's cushions and resting his elbows on his knees, "*if* I was involved with any such operation as you have described, I believe I would try to make sure every domestic animal that was rescued from captivity would be provided with a safe and loving home."

"Is it hard to find that many homes?" Barry asked quickly.

"Not as hard as you'd think—" Sweezy cut himself short, looked away, then shifted uneasily on the sofa.

A smile of confidence crossed Barry's lips; he'd made a dent in Sweezy's hard shell. "What about the other animals?" he asked. Sweezy glanced at him but didn't answer. "What about the nondomestics, you know, the rats and mice and guinea pigs people wouldn't readily welcome into their homes. What would you do—hypothetically—if *somehow* you came across a substantial number of them?"

Sweezy hesitated, then said, "I would imagine they would be let go."

"Just . . . let go? What exactly do you mean by 'let go'?"

"Let them go in the wild. I would imagine someone would take them out to the woods or to the state park." He eyed Barry. "That's not very far from here, you know."

Barry nodded but didn't say anything. He paused for several moments, letting the time work as a point of emphasis on his behalf, then he again looked Sweezy directly in the eye and asked, "Did you ever stop and think about what might happen if even one of the animals set loose in the wild was contaminated?"

It was now Sweezy's turn to pause before speaking, and he played upon a lengthy silence before answering. "I would say—hypothetically, of course—that any organization dealing with the type of animals you're referring to would have to have an inside source to verify which of the animals were clean and which ones were contaminated."

"And what would happen to the animals known to be contaminated?" Barry asked with sincere interest.

"I would imagine that, most likely, they would be humanely destroyed."

"But let's say a group of contaminated animals were mistakenly released. What do you think would happen then?"

"I'd say everybody would be on their own." A smile tugged at the corners of Sweezy's thin lips. "After all, that's more of a chance than the animals ever had."

*8:32 P.M.*

Dan fidgeted nervously as he paced back and forth across the den. Frequently, he stopped at the bay window and looked out, glancing, unseeingly, at the lengthening shadows spread by the aged trees guarding the front lane. Each time he turned back toward the heart of the room, his eyes immediately sought out the rack of serum vials sitting on the desk a few feet away. After staring at the vials for several seconds—thinking of the miracles contained within—he would look at the clock over the mantel. Rarely had more than five minutes lapsed since his last check; time seemed to be standing still.

Twenty-four hours. Warren had told him to wait twenty-four hours before making the next injection, but . . . but—

"It's close enough."

Dan walked to the chair behind the desk and sat down. He slid the rack of vials closer to him and concentrated on it, setting the red-amber color of the serum in his mind, etching a place for it in his memory. The hope for his future—as a whole man—was contained in those six glass vials.

His focus shifted from the vials to the box of syringes on the desk beside the rack. Did he have the fortitude? Could he do it? Could he fill one of the syringes with serum and then stick the needle into his . . . into his . . . what? Where would the injection site be? His thigh? His belly? Dan lifted a hand to his midriff and cupped it against the flesh. Just a pinprick, he thought, surely it couldn't hurt too badly . . . could it?

Slowly, Dan reached across the desk. He watched his hand as if it were disconnected from him; he watched as it approached and then hovered above the box of syringes . . . trembling . . . shaking. His future hung in the balance.

Powered by a sudden surge of adrenaline, Dan quickly opened the box, took out a syringe, and filled it from a vial. Leaning back in the chair, he pulled up his shirt and pinched a layer of flesh between his thumb and forefinger. Hesitating, he looked at his belly . . . at the syringe . . . at his belly . . . at the—

Dan jabbed the needle deep into his flesh. He winced in an instinctive reaction, but the discomfort wasn't near what he'd expected. "It's just a pinprick," he said with a chuckle as he pressed the plunger. Fascinated, he concentrated on the syringe until it was empty, then he pulled the needle out.

A contented smile crossed Dan's lips as he leaned back in the chair and closed his eyes. Tomorrow, giving himself the next injection would be much easier... and the day after that... and the day after that... as long as it didn't take too long.

# Wednesday

(Day Six)

6:12 A.M.

Loretta Dunn stood at the kitchen window, looking out across a small valley. The view was priceless, but that was the extent of her wealth. Born in the hills outside Gnaw Bone, Tennessee, she'd married young and moved with her husband to the hills of southeastern Indiana. She'd traded one life of poverty for another, and there was little hope she would ever know anything else.

Even though she was poor, Loretta was a proud woman. She kept her house clean and clothes washed, kept food on her family's table, tended a garden and raised chickens, ducks, and geese to sell at the farmer's market down on the river. She earned her way; she didn't believe in handouts.

She was a religious woman who thanked God every day for the bounty He'd bestowed upon her and she knew, in His ultimate wisdom, that everything He'd made had a purpose. She guessed there was even a purpose for her drunken husband . . . even though she had yet to figure it out.

Loretta was a big woman, standing almost six foot tall and weighing close to two hundred and thirty pounds. Hoeing in her garden and chopping wood for the cookstove had padded her frame with muscle; she was well equipped to take care of herself. No one ever challenged her . . . except, on occasion, her husband, and then, that rare confrontation came only after he'd had too much to drink.

"Loretta, ya got any money hid away in the cookie jar fer me?" her husband asked as he stepped into the doorway from the bedroom and leaned against the frame for support.

Danford Dunn was as lean as his wife was sturdy and, unlike Loretta, he didn't hold much purpose for God or anyone else he couldn't hit up for a loan he had no intentions to repay. He didn't mind working—as long as he didn't have to work too hard. And he wasn't bothered by the fact that during an average month, Loretta always made more money than he. What he did mind—and downright detested—were the ideas she had about keeping her money to herself.

"I ain't got no money fer yer soul-damnin' boozin'," Loretta answered without even looking at him. She gritted her teeth to keep from saying anything more and continued to wash the dishes and stack them on the drainer beside the sink.

"Oh, Loretta, don't ya have just a couple dollars fer yer ole honey boy?" Even before Danford touched her, Loretta could tell he'd crossed the kitchen and was coming toward her. She could smell his whiskey-stale breath.

"Ya get ya a job and hold it down, and ya can spend the money on whatever ya want," she said as she turned to face him, "but ya ain't gettin' none o' my chicken money fer yer booze."

"Oh, Loretta—"

"The good Lord didn't give me none o' them there chickens ta tend and raise just ta sell 'em ta buy ya hell-fire's whiskey. The devil's, sure enough, gone and latched onta yer soul, Danford Dunn, and only by shunnin' that evil whiskey and turnin' ta the Lord are ya ever gonna have a chance o' livin' out eternity in a place not ragin' in sin."

"Don't preach at me, Loretta, hell, it's only Wednesday—"

A terrified squawk penetrated the cabin's thin walls.

"Sounds like somethin's botherin' my chickens," Loretta said, glancing at the window overlooking the yard. "Market's comin' up next Saturday, and I can't afford ta miss takin' even one." Loretta sidestepped Danford and headed for the door. "Are you gonna come help me?" she called back over her shoulder. "'Cause if I ain't got no chicken ta sell, yer gonna be eatin' mush again fer ever' meal until I do."

"I'm comin'," Danford drawled, "but I gotta get my shoes on first."

Loretta stepped out on the porch as the screen door closed behind her. She picked up the hoe hanging over the railing, and hurried on down the steps. "Get away from my ducks and chickens," she hollered as she ran across the grass-bare yard toward the chicken coop. Her call was answered by a cacophony of squawks, quacks, and honks.

As she neared the sparsely fenced poultry yard, Loretta could make out a lifeless carcass on the ground ahead of her, its white feathers bathed in blood. Beyond the carcass, she saw a variety of maimed fowl flopping in the dirt. One chicken was minus a leg; one had a broken leg. One duck had a gash in its neck and was bleeding severely; Loretta doubted it would last for very long. A second duck looked to have had half of its beak bitten off.

A drawn-out honk drew her attention to the coop. "Get away from my prize goose," Loretta shouted as she ran across the yard, waving the hoe in front of her.

Just as Loretta reached for the coop's door, a large weasel slipped out from beneath a loose board. It hesitated long enough to look up at her, then it started for the nearby woods. "Oh no ya don't," Loretta shouted, bringing the hoe down in a quick chopping action.

The hoe's sharp blade slid down the weasel's back, cut into its tail and sliced through its right back thigh. The animal squealed in agony as it rolled away from the hoe blade, then it got up and scurried away on three legs, disappearing into the woods beneath a low-growing bush.

"And don't ya come back ever again," Loretta shouted after it, "or I'll chop off yer other leg too."

"Anythin' I can do?"

Loretta turned her head sharply to see Danford standing at the edge of the chicken yard, leaning against a wobbly fence post. "I sure hope ya like mush," she said as she shook her head, then Loretta went to tend to her wounded fowl.

7:30 A.M.

". . . and like I said before, I recommend you stay on the marked trails the whole time you're in the park," the ranger emphasized, eyeing the two teenagers standing outside the information booth.

"I know where I'm going," Corbie Wasson said, a bit too cockily. "I've been hiking in these hills since I was a kid, and I know every trail like it was my own backyard."

"Make sure you stay on the marked trails," the ranger repeated, handing the boy a map of the park, "and make sure to build all campfires only in the designated areas, and douse them before leaving the area."

"Yeah, sure." Corbie grabbed the map and stuffed it in his hip pocket. "Let's go, Ragina," he said, turning away from the ranger and taking hold of the girl's arm beside him. "I know what I'm doing," he said as he led her away. "I've been hiking in here a hundred times before."

The ranger watched the two teenagers head off into the woods, backpacks shifting, improperly secured, telltale camping gear bulging at the seams. "There goes trouble," he said to himself, shaking his head. "I hope nobody gets hurt on their little misadventure."

*6:13 P.M.*

Warren paused at the counter to turn on the television, then walked on through the kitchen to the utility room. He'd been running late that morning and hadn't had time to look at the mice any longer than it had taken for him to set their cages on top of the washer and dryer next to the window. Now, he wanted to move them back to the kitchen where the light was better and where he could examine them at his leisure.

Following a habit he'd quickly developed, Warren pulled on a pair of heavy leather gloves before picking up the cages by the makeshift wire handles he'd attached to the top bars. He wondered if he was being a bit too cautious, but each time he questioned wearing the gloves to pick up the cages, he remembered how the aggressive mouse had tried to bite through the oven mitt . . . and he wondered what might have happened if it had. Those teeth were damn sharp. Even though there was little likelihood of either mouse being able to reach his hand now, Warren wasn't about to take any chances.

"And how are you two this evening?" he asked as he picked up first one cage and then the other, lifting them, momentarily, to eye level and taking a quick peek at each mouse. As if to respond to Warren's question, the aggressive mouse bit the cage, its long yellow teeth wrapping completely around the wire mesh. The other mouse cowered and huddled in the far corner of its cage. It looked as if it were trying to put as much distance as it could between itself and its onetime—long ago—companion.

"At first glance, you don't look any different," Warren said in passing as he carried the mice into the kitchen, "maybe you're a little bigger—"

". . . and . . . and it's just plain weird. That's the best word I can come up with—weird."

Warren stopped in front of the television, balanced the

197

cages on the counter's edge, and focused on the camera's view of a town street littered with blanket-covered bodies. The commentator's voice continued in the background.

"Just plain weird . . . that's how UPS driver Jack Hoffman described the small town of Elbo, North Carolina, when he drove down Main Street for a routine delivery and pickup a little after one o'clock this afternoon."

The picture shifted to a closeup of the UPS driver. "It looked like something that could have come right out of a science fiction movie," he said. "I'd never seen anything like it before, and I hope I never see anything like it again. Bodies were lying on the sidewalk everywhere. It looked like they'd just been walking down the street and *ZAP*, they collapsed right where they were standing."

"Collapsed right where they were standing," the commentator repeated. The camera made another slow sweep of the street, then came in close on the reporter. "Authorities have been on the scene now since a little before three o'clock this afternoon, but no one has yet to even speculate on what might have killed the twenty-three people and the half-dozen domestic animals who were unfortunate enough to be walking down Main Street when this unexplained catastrophe hit." He paused for emphasis and turned slightly to look over his shoulder at the street in Elbo, North Carolina. "Maybe Jack Hoffman is correct. Maybe this is a scene out of a science fiction movie . . . and we're all going to have to wait until the credits roll by at the end before we uncover the answer.

"This is Jeff Harrell with WKBD On-The-Spot news."

"That is weird," Warren said, shaking his head. He picked up the cages, walked on across the kitchen, and set them down on the table. "I bet it would be really interesting to investigate a situation like that," Warren thought aloud. "There are all sorts of things that could have caused the deaths of those people, but to be able to isolate the factors and say what it was for sure . . . wow, that'd be one heck of a job." His thoughts returned to reality, and he looked back at the mice. "Oh well, that would be interesting I'm sure, but I imagine it's a lot less nerve-wracking to work with mice than it would be to have to do autopsies on all those people. Now," he said, settling down on a kitchen chair, "let's have a closer look at you two."

Warren opened the door to the aggressive mouse's cage and slipped his hand inside. The animal resisted being caught. It eluded Warren's hand twice, then backed into the corner and bared its teeth to defend itself. When Warren's hand moved too close, the mouse bit into a gloved finger. Its teeth clamped down hard, then it began to shake its head like a dog, as if the action would break the intruder's spine and render it helpless. The mouse fought viciously, but Warren was finally able to wrap his free fingers around its back and grasp it in a firm hold.

"I'm not going to hurt you," Warren said as he lifted the mouse out of its cage and held it up in front of the light. "I won't even have you out of your cage for very long. All I want to do is have a look at your leg."

Warren tilted the mouse back in his hand so that its belly was exposed and its legs pointed upward. Even though the mouse protested, flailing its legs and trying to squirm free, Warren could see its right front leg fairly well. The pink leg bud appeared to have grown over half an inch long, and four tiny appendages were beginning to emerge from its rounded end.

"Toes . . ." Warren whispered breathlessly. A thrill of excitement coursed through him, making him shiver. "It's working," he whispered, then he shivered again. "And if it works as well on Dan Patton . . ." Warren closed his eyes and tilted his head back toward the ceiling. Even in his wildest dreams, he couldn't begin to imagine where such success might lead. "And when you die," Warren said as he looked back at the mouse, "I'm going to have you stuffed so I can set you on a shelf in my office." He squeezed the mouse gently, as if to hug it, then returned it to its cage.

After Warren made a few notes in his journal in regards to the aggressive mouse's progress, he shifted his attention to the second mouse. "And are the same good things happening to you?" he asked. The submissive mouse peered up at him with tiny round eyes; it didn't attempt to resist capture when Warren reached inside its cage.

"Let's see," Warren said with great anticipation as he turned the mouse over onto its back. "How's—" When Warren saw the animal's left front leg, his breath lodged in his throat.

The pink leg bud had grown to about a half inch in length and at the end of the leg bud were tiny appendages . . . appendages that were gnarled and deformed . . . appendages resembling neither hand nor paw—nor even a claw—that had ever graced an animal on the face of the earth.

"What's . . . what's gone wrong?" Warren breathed in a choked whisper.

He held the mouse closer to the light and studied the misshapen paw. Curious to see its underside, he touched it, attempting to turn it palm up—

The animal shrieked in a high-pitched squeal. It began to squirm, and if Warren hadn't been quick to react, he would have dropped the mouse.

And that was when he saw it.

A bulbous, tumorlike mass was protruding from the mouse's neck, originating from the site where the aggressive mouse had bitten it during their fight a few days before. The tissue was pink, similar to that of the leg bud, but the shape was . . . was—it was bizarre, a strange mass that wasn't even supposed to be there—not on the mouse's neck!

"What's going on?" Warren asked as he looked from the

mouse in his hand to the mouse in the cage on the table.

Then—slowly—he looked across the kitchen and out the back window of the utility room toward the small red barn on the far side of his yard.

"Oh, my God." The words crossed Warren's lips in a whisper. He had just thought of Dan Patton.


7:37 P.M.

Dan turned off the jets in the Jacuzzi and reached for his tumbler of scotch and soda. He took two quick gulps and, as the water's agitation began to subside, he focused on the stumps of his legs. Looking at his thighs through the rippling water, a shot of frenzied adrenaline shot through him when he thought they appeared distorted. Only after he touched the stumps and cupped his hands over their rounded ends was he assured they hadn't changed. They hadn't changed. Damn!

For the past two days, Dan had subjected himself to injections of serum, but nothing had happened. Nothing.

Already, he was becoming frustrated and disheartened. How long was it going to take?

"Just once every twenty-four hours can't be nearly enough," he speculated. "I'm over a hundred times bigger than most of the animals Maxey was working with, so why isn't my dosage a hundred times bigger than what he was giving them?" Dan took another gulp from the tumbler and again focused on his legs. Drawing upon his limited knowledge, he tried to consider the factors that might be influencing the serum's inability to work any more quickly than it had. He came up with no immediate answers.

"And why should I have to inject it into a muscle?" he questioned, knowing no one was going to contradict him. "Doesn't it make sense that it should go directly into the bloodstream? That way it would get into my system quicker . . . much quicker. And if I'd double the dosage . . . *twice* a day . . ." Dan took another gulp from his glass, then leaned his head back against the padding bordering the hot tub and closed his eyes. "Twice as much . . . twice as often . . . and directly into the bloodstream. Then maybe things will start to happen."

# Thursday

## (Day Seven)

*6:54 P.M.*

Warren stood beside the kitchen table, looking down at the mice's cages, hesitating to lift the bath towel he'd placed over them before leaving for work that morning. He was a little unnerved; he was afraid of what he might find.

The new developments, he'd discovered that morning, had been bad enough to stomach. Overnight, the bulbous growth on the mouse's neck had almost doubled in size, and its paw—claw—had become even more grotesque and disfigured. In addition to the submissive mouse's deformity, the aggressive mouse's developing paw had taken a turn of its own. The smooth pink skin that had grown out of the amputation site had darkened and thickened, turning leathery . . . scaly. It had verged upon looking reptilian.

Dreading what additional new developments might have taken place during the past twelve hours, Warren reached for the towel. When his fingertips touched the edge of the soft terry cloth, he hesitated, then he grasped a handful of the plush material and pulled the towel away. His fears were immediately realized.

The submissive mouse lay on its side, weighed down by a pulsating mass of tumorous tissue protruding from the front of its neck. The deformed left leg stuck out at an awkward angle from its body, so overgrown in length and structure that it would never be useful for walking or even minor support. The mouse looked up at Warren through the wire mesh, and Warren thought he detected a plea for mercy in the animal's dark round eyes.

Warren then looked at the aggressive mouse's cage. A sneer of disgust immediately curled his lips. The severely deformed reptilian leg lay on the floor of the cage, severed from the mouse's body.

"What did you do?" Warren asked the mouse, his tone of voice relaying his amazement at what had happened. "Did you go and bite off your leg just to get rid of it?" As if the mouse understood the question, it hissed and bit at the wire mesh in reply. "And did it work out well for you?" Warren asked as he squatted down beside the table so he could look directly into the cage. "Is a better one growing back in its place?"

The mouse turned squarely toward Warren, hissed again as if to reply, then rose to a defensive posture, standing on its hind legs. Immediately, Warren saw the outcome of the gnawed paw. Dried blood caked the mouse's belly fur, chest, and unaltered left front leg, but it couldn't hide a triple appendage that was sprouting from the stump where the reptilian paw had been chewed off.

"Good God in heaven," Warren gasped.

The mouse shrieked and lunged at the side of the cage, hitting it head-on. Warren acted instinctively and tried to move back, but he lost his balance and fell to the floor. Righting himself, he scooted across the kitchen until his back was pressed against the cabinets. For several moments, he sat there in silence, watching the aggressive mouse as it again began to chew on its new—unwanted—appendage.

"What went wrong?" Warren finally asked himself. "I didn't change the serum, and I heard Dr. Wagner tell Dan Patton it worked perfectly." He glanced at the phone on the wall and contemplated calling Wagner, explaining everything he'd done and asking what might have gone wrong. But—

"No. I'm not going to bring him in to this." Warren chuckled uneasily. "Hell, I can't even tell him what I've done, without taking the chance of going to jail. All he'd have to do would be press charges—"

He turned his head sharply back toward the aggressive mouse and watched as it continued to chew on its regenerating leg. "And what's going to happen to Dan Patton?" He looked back at the phone and knew there was at least one phone call he needed to make—*had* to make.

Warren shifted his legs beneath him, then reached for the cabinet for support to help him stand. As he pressed down with his hands to lift himself up, pain shot through his wrist and traveled up his forearm.

Warren gasped with a quick breath, then he looked down at his aching wrist. A blue-yellow bruise marked the skin and distinctly formed the impression of fingers on his lower forearm. He contemplated the bruise for only a moment, then he remembered how he'd received it. Dan Patton had grabbed him savagely a few days before, had all but dragged him out to the barn and forced him to turn over the serum. He had *forced* him—

Warren rubbed his wrist gently as his attention returned to the phone. An almost evil grin came to his lips.

"You wanted it so badly . . . so now you've got it. Besides, it wouldn't do me a bit of good to call you. It's already started . . . and there's nothing either one of us can do to change what's going to happen." Warren laughed. "You wanted it so damn bad, and now you've got it. No amount of money in the world is going to buy your way out of the mess you've gotten yourself into." Warren laughed again. "I only wish I could be around to see what's going to happen to Mister High and Mighty, Daniel Jerome Patton the Fourth."

# Friday

## (Day Eight)

*6:07 A.M.*

Corbie Wasson and Ragina Browning snuggled together inside their double sleeping bag. The morning was cool, and the air was brisk; neither wanted to venture out of the warmth offered by the thick fluffy down.

"Somebody's gonna have to get the fire going," Corbie whispered as he nibbled at the lobe of Ragina's ear.

"That's the man's job," Ragina said, pulling away from him and slipping down deeper into the sleeping bag.

"I thought you were a liberated woman," he countered, locating her ribs and tickling her.

"I'm only liberated when it's to my advantage." Ragina giggled and tried to tickle him in retaliation, but she was outmatched in both size and strength.

"An advantage?" Corbie rolled over on top of Ragina, straddled her, and pinned her hands to the ground beside her head. "Now who has the advantage?" he asked as he leaned forward and flicked the end of her nose with his tongue. "Huh?" He flicked again . . . and again. "Who?"

"I . . . still . . . have the advantage," Ragina persisted, rolling her head back and forth from side to side, trying to keep out of reach of his tongue.

"And how's that?"

Ragina lay still for several seconds, looking up at Corbie with her big brown eyes, then she lifted her head, extended her tongue, and used its moist tip to slowly outline Corbie's lips. "Because I don't play fair," she whispered. "That's why I'll always have the advantage."

"At times like this," Corbie whispered as he lowered himself down on top of her, "who cares."

Ragina giggled, and slipped her arms around him, pulling him toward her. "We don't really need a fire to keep warm, do we? I think we can both come up with something a lot nicer—"

A loud cry—sounding like the combination of a howl, a bark, and a squeal—tore through the woods around them.

Startled, Corbie flipped the edge of the sleeping bag back from his head and peeked out toward the trees. Ragina brought her head up close to his. "What was that?" she asked, a tremor shaking her voice.

"I . . . don't know." Corbie tried to act brave, but his voice shook as well. Quickly, he scanned the perimeter of the small clearing where they'd set up camp.

"There's nothing *real* wild out here, is there?" Ragina asked apprehensively, looking to him for the answer she hoped to hear. "I mean, there aren't any bears or anything—"

The cry echoed through the trees . . . again . . . and again. It was sounding clearer . . . closer.

"I . . . I don't know." Corbie continued to scan the perimeter as he grabbed their bundled clothes and shoved them inside the sleeping bag. "Get dressed." An urgency came with his words.

"You didn't answer me," Ragina said as she contorted her body so she could pull on the blue jeans she now wished didn't cling to her like a second skin. "Are there any dangerous animals out here?"

"I've heard . . . they're more afraid of us . . . than we are of them," Corbie answered as he too squirmed inside the sleeping

212

bag, attempting to put on his clothes.

"The hell they are—"

Another wild cry shattered the air. Underbrush, less than six feet from the sleeping bag, began to rustle and shake.

Ragina screamed. Corbie pulled the corner of the sleeping bag up over his head and pressed a palm over Ragina's mouth as he rolled on top of her. "Be quiet," he whispered, "and don't move. If we don't do anything to attract their attention, maybe whatever it is will go away and leave us alone."

Growls, barks, and hisses sliced through the air. A squeal . . . a screech . . . a cry—the underbrush shook savagely, then two animals rolled out of the woods, locked together in fierce combat. Tumbling over each other—attacking and retreating—they bumped into the foot of the sleeping bag three or four times before moving on across the clearing.

Curious as to what was going on, Corbie lifted the edge of the sleeping bag and peeked out from under it. He saw two massive-sized raccoons, their gray/black fur matted with blood, a frothy drool lathering their mouths, and . . . and one of the raccoons— No, that was impossible! Corbie shook his head and blinked several times, but still couldn't believe what he saw. One of the raccoons had what appeared to be a giant eagle-type claw where its left front leg should have been.

"What's wrong with that raccoon?" Ragina whispered, looking out from beneath Corbie's arm.

"I don't know. It looks like it's deformed or something. I've never seen anything like it—not even at the fair's freak show."

They watched the pair tumble and roll for several seconds, then Ragina whispered, "I never knew raccoons grew to be *that* big."

"Me either." Corbie concentrated on the animals for a few moments more. "Those things look almost as big as my Uncle Verne's prize sow, Rosie."

A stillness suddenly enveloped the clearing. The two raccoons stopped fighting and stood up on their hind legs. They nosed the air, their nostrils twitching, as if seeking out an unknown scent. Then—in unison, as if they'd rehearsed the move—both turned their heads slowly toward Corbie and Ragina and looked the humans directly in the eye.

For several silent moments, the four were locked in a visual standoff, then one raccoon hissed; the other cried out. Ragina screamed; Corbie shouted. The two raccoons resumed their fighting with each other and tumbled off into the underbrush on the far side of the clearing.

"Let's get the hell outta here," Corbie said as he crawled out of the sleeping bag. He sat down on the ground only long enough to grab his boots and yank them on, then he scrambled to his feet.

Ragina had crawled only halfway out of the sleeping bag when Corbie grabbed her by the arms and pulled her to her feet. Taking hold of her hand, he ran—all but dragging her behind him—toward the narrow path they'd followed into the clearing.

"What about our camping gear?" Ragina asked, looking back at the disheveled sleeping bags and the pots that still sat on the rocks at the rim of their cooking pit.

"Forget it," Corbie said, jerking on her arm to keep her close beside him. "I want to get out of here now. I want to be long gone from this place just in case those two monster raccoons change their minds and decide to come back."

*6:15 A.M.*

"Sure looks like it's gonna turn out to be a mighty fine morning," Bruce said, leaning forward in his seat and looking up through the truck's windshield. He sat on the passenger's side; Fritz Webb, his only full-time farmhand, drove and Kerk and Little Cork sat in the middle, squeezed in between them. "There's not a cloud in the sky, and I don't remember the forecast calling for any. With the weather on our side, we ought to be able to get in a full day's work without any interruptions."

Fritz glanced at Kerk, then looked at Bruce and grinned. "None of us'll be able to put in a full day's work wrestlin' them chain saws around," he said with a chuckle. "We're all too outta shape. I'd say we'll be lucky to stick with it 'til noon."

"You're such a pessimist," Bruce countered.

"I'm a realist, and you oughta be too. We've sat on our butts all winter, not doin' anything much more physical than carryin' feed bags and movin' bales of hay from one stack to another. You can't expect us to go from doing next to nothin' to cuttin' down trees without anticipatin' any consequences." Fritz glanced at the drive, then looked back at Bruce out of the corner of his eye. "Even if we do manage to stick with it past noon, we're gonna be sore as hell tomorrow. We'll all be lucky if we can even get outta bed in the morning."

"I don't wanna work too hard today and get all worn out," Kerk said, looking from Fritz to Bruce. "I'm going fishing with Allen and his dad in the morning, and I don't wanna be too sore to reel in the big ones."

"I don't think you have to worry. I've never known a boy your age to work *too* hard," Bruce assured him.

One of the truck's back tires sank into a mud hole. The seat springs squeaked; the doors creaked. The tailpipe on the old red Chevy rattled, and the muffler backfired.

"Somebody oughta spend some time and money fixin' up this old relic," Fritz said as he eased the truck out of the hole. Bruce shot him a glance out of the corner of his eye, but he didn't say a word. Fritz had already heard his excuses a dozen times before; there wasn't enough money to fix the truck.

As they drove past the equipment barn at the north end of the drive and headed for the tractor path bordering the edge of the field, Bruce caught a glimpse of the white ammonia tank parked near the back of the building. A frown furrowed his brow as he turned in the seat and focused on the tank as they continued along the tractor path toward the woods. "When did Norwood say he'd be back to pick up that tank?" he asked, looking at Fritz.

"I think he said Monday or Tuesday."

"Why's it gonna take him so long to get back for it? It's already been out here a week, and I don't like havin' it just sittin' around." Bruce focused on Kerk. "Some people don't know enough to leave things alone when they don't know anything about it." Kerk looked up at Bruce and rolled his eyes, then returned his attention to Little Cork.

"I think Charlie and Velda went someplace down south this week. It's her spring break from school, and they figured this would be the only time they'd have to take a vacation until after the crops come in this fall. After that, it'd be time for Velda to go back to school again."

"I just don't like it sittin' around," Bruce said again, continuing to eye the tank.

"It can't hurt anything," Fritz tried to assure him. "It's practically empty, and it's parked back there out of the way. It's in the shade most of the day, so there's not gonna be any chance for the pressure to build up—"

"You stay away from it," Bruce said sternly, putting a hand on Kerk's leg and squeezing it to get his attention. "I don't want you to get burned like you did last year. You were lucky—"

"I know . . . I know," Kerk said, squirming as much as he could in the confined space, trying to free himself from Bruce's grip. "You've told me at least a hundred times how lucky I was," he added, a bit sarcastically.

"And I'll tell you a hundred more times if that's what it takes to get it branded into that thick skull of yours, young man. Anhydrous ammonia is nothing to mess with. Chemicals can burn—"

"Can I run one of the chain saws?" Kerk asked, interrupting Bruce in hopes of changing the subject.

Bruce looked at Kerk for a few silent moments, then exhaled heavily and smiled. "It's just that I care about what happens to you."

"I know you do . . . and I'm glad you do," Kerk said, returning the smile. "But believe me, I've learned my lesson. I'm not going to get within twenty feet of an ammonia tank ever again. Now, can I run one of the chain saws sometime today?" he asked again.

"We'll have to see." Bruce straightened around on the seat and focused on the dense section of woods where they were heading. "We'll just have to wait and see. Your mother wouldn't be very happy with me if I brought you up here and let you cut your leg off."


*6:18 A.M.*


"And just where do ya think yer goin'?" Loretta Dunn watched her husband as he crossed the room to the front door. She followed him out onto the porch but stopped just short of the steps. "I asked ya where ya was goin'," Loretta said, settling into a wide stance, her fisted hands perched on her broad hips.

"Inta town."

"What ya goin' inta town fer? Ya ain't got no money ta spend unless ya— Danford Dunn! Did ya go and swipe the church money I've been savin' back in my panty drawer?"

"Oh, Loretta—"

"If I find ya've gone and got the church money outta my panty drawer, I'll turn ya over my knee just like ya was a young'un and tan your sorrowful hide."

"Oh, Loretta, ya know I wouldn't ever go an' do such a thing. I might take a peep in yer panty drawer ever' once in a while, but I'd fer sure never go stealin' from yer church money. Me an' the Lord, we ain't on the bestest terms anyhow, and I sure wouldn't want ta go and get Him any more pissed off at me than He already is."

"If ya didn't steal the church money, then where did ya get money in the first place? Did ya go an' get a job I don't know nothin' about?"

"I ain't got no job. I went and sold me a couple o' pelts to that city peddler man down by the river. Okay?"

"Well, if it's truly yer money ya got from yer trappin', then I suppose it's okay. But if I go an' find out ya been snitchin' from my church money, I'll pluck ya as hairless as I'm gonna do that chicken we'll be havin' fer supper. You will be back fer supper." Danford looked Loretta directly in the eye, then, without saying a word, he turned away from her and started walking toward the dirt path leading to the gravel lane that connected to the black-top road that eventually led into town. "Ya better be back. The preacher's comin' here fer dinner tonight, then we can all go up ta the church fer prayer meetin'." Danford didn't reply; he just kept walking. "The good Lord's the only one who knows how much prayin' it's gonna take ta save yer soul—and don't ya come back here drunk, neither. Do ya hear me?" Danford didn't answer . . . he just kept on walking.

Loretta watched him until he disappeared beyond the trees at the base of the hill. She shook her head, then walked down the steps and around the house to check on the pot of water she'd set to boil over an open fire. "Why I ever let myself get hooked up with that man I'll never know," she mumbled as she picked up a rag and lifted the lid to the black, cast-iron kettle. "A fine sweet-talker he was fer sure, but them perty words shoulda choked that lyin' man and made him gag." When Loretta saw the water was on the verge of boiling, she returned the heavy lid, then picked up an old broom handle she'd propped against a tree a few feet away. "No sir, it wouldn't take much fer me ta dip him in that boilin' water a half-dozen times and pluck him clean naked just like a chicken. Might even snatch me a handful o' his tool too," she added with a giggle. "It ain't never gone an' done me a whole lot o' good just hangin' 'round where it is.

"Here, chick . . . chick . . . chick. Here, chick." Loretta reached into the front pocket of her brightly-colored apron and pulled out a handful of corn. She tossed the kernels into the chicken yard, then stepped over the short fence. "Here, chick. Come on, chick . . . chick." A half-dozen hens answered her call and began pecking at the corn on the ground.

Loretta eyed the brood, trying to pick out the chicken that looked to be the best for frying. When she finally made her selection, she grabbed the hen by the neck and carried it outside the chicken yard.

"Squawk all ya wanna 'cause it ain't gonna make no difference one way or t'other," she said to the hen as she maneuvered it into the position she wanted. When Loretta finally had both of the chicken's legs secured in one hand, she let go of its neck. "Are ya ready fer the ride o' yer life?" she asked as she let her arm drop to her side. Loretta looked down at the chicken hanging from her hand. "This is gonna be the last thing ya ever remember. Here ya go."

Keeping her shoulder as the center of the arch, Loretta began to swing the chicken around . . . and around . . . and around in giant vertical circles. With each revolution, the chicken's squawks grew weaker and weaker; by the end of the tenth circle, the hen was making no noise at all.

"Sounds like yer ready fer the killin'."

Loretta laid the chicken's head on the ground. Its eyes stared blankly—glazed in stunned bewilderment—as she laid the old broomstick across its neck. It squirmed a little when she stepped on the stick on either side of its head, then Loretta leaned her weight back . . . and pulled.

The chicken's body ripped free from its head. Blood spouted—pulsed—from the headless neck as the hen's heart continued to pump. The muscles began to spasm.

Loretta tossed the hen's body onto the grass and watched it tumble and flop until the last muscle impulses ceased, and it finally came to rest. "It probably wouldn't hurt ta get another one," she said as she turned back to the chicken yard. "I wanna make sure there're enough giblets fer gravy and dumplin's, and we can always eat leftovers fer the rest of the week.

"Here, chick . . . chick. Here, chick." A couple of ducks waddled out of the coop to join the brood, but Loretta didn't give them any more than a passing glance. She was looking for another good hen, one with enough fat to give substance to her gravy—

"Ouch!" Loretta kicked in a reflex action, but the pain didn't go away. She looked down to see a duck biting—holding on to—her leg. "Let go o' me, ya crazy!" she said as she bent over and swatted the animal. The duck released its hold, backed up a couple of steps, shook its head, then opened its mouth and emitted a strange quack, exposing uneven rows of oddly shaped, blood-dappled *teeth*.

"What in the name of our Lord Jesus Christ—" Loretta stared at the duck in disbelief, then took a moment to identify it. The duck was one of the fowls that had been attacked and bitten by the weasel a few days before. "What in the name of all's holy happened ta ya?" As if to reply to her question, the duck released another strange-sounding quack . . . then it charged.

"No! Get away!" Loretta took a couple of steps backward, then she turned and started to run. But something flew up from the ground in front of her, startling her and halting her retreat. It was something *like* a chicken... only it *wasn't* a chicken. It had a large pincher-claw where one wing should have been, and one of its legs looked as if it could have belonged to a lizard. The pincher clamped down hard onto the side of Loretta's face.

"No! Get away! Get away from me!" Loretta grabbed the chicken-thing and pulled it off her. The pincher held fast and ripped a chunk of flesh out of her cheek and pulled the skin loose from the muscle halfway down her jaw.

"Help!" Loretta cried out as she started to step over the fence. "Help—"

The duck with teeth bit into the back of her leg, tripping her. Loretta lost her balance and fell. One of the metal rods, used to hold up the fence, skewered her thigh as she went down. The chicken-thing jumped on top of her, grabbing a pincherful of breast-flesh, ripping it open.

"Help!" Loretta flailed her arms frantically, trying desperately to free herself from her unearthly attackers. "Help—"

The word caught in Loretta's throat when she saw a big black-brown weasel sitting up on its haunches at the edge of the chicken yard. But it wasn't a weasel, at least not a weasel... totally. Its tail and right back leg were deformed into a hideous mass of flesh and fur and bone and claws ... claws... wicked-looking claws. Together, its tail and leg looked like the medieval spiked balls used for torture—

The weasel's dark eyes locked on Loretta's. Slowly, the animal settled down on its forelegs and took a step toward her.

"No!" Loretta cried out. She sensed the weasel's hate; she knew it had come back to seek revenge for her maiming it with a hoe.

"Go away!" Loretta tried to move—tried to turn away—but

the steel rod through her thigh held her firmly to the ground, and the duck and chicken-thing were on top of her . . . biting . . . chewing.

Her eyes again locked with the weasel's. "No!" Loretta screamed as the animal charged. She lifted her arms in a meager attempt to protect her throat, but she knew her actions were useless.

*9:11 A.M.*

". . . and they ran over us, growling and fighting and . . . and . . ." Corbie Wasson was so excited, telling the park ranger his exaggerated tale about the two raccoons, the words left his mouth almost faster than his brain could think to make up more. ". . . and if we hadn't been huddled down inside our sleeping bags for protection, they would have torn us apart for sure."

Carl Briner looked from Corbie to Ragina Browning and back again, then shook his head. He'd been a conservation officer for twenty-six years; for the past eleven, he'd been the head ranger at the Whitewater Valley State Park. He thought he'd heard every story imaginable that could come out of the hills, but the one the two teenagers seated in front of him had just relayed was one that would match—no, it was one that would *outshine*—any he'd ever heard in the past. "Giant raccoons," he said, eyeing the two skeptically.

"Yes, sir," Corbie answered crisply, sitting forward on the edge of his chair.

"The size of pigs, you say."

"Yes, sir. Full-grown porkers—the kind that win first prize at the fair."

Briner studied the two teenagers a few moments longer, then he leaned back in his chair and tented his fingers together above his rotund abdomen. "And just how big was the joint you two were smoking before you saw these giant raccoons?"

"We weren't doin' no drugs," Corbie protested, taking on a defensive air.

"Honest," Ragina added in a petite voice. "We . . . we did take a pint of cherry vodka up there with us, but that was all. We didn't have anything stronger. Honest," she repeated. "The raccoons were for real. They were big and real, and they had this icky, foamy white stuff dripping out of their mouths."

"White stuff?" Briner shifted forward in his seat, his questioning taking on a new interest. "Did you say they were foaming at the mouth?"

"Yeah," Corbie answered, "all over the place. I ain't never seen nothing that was mad before, but those two raccoons sure looked like they could've been. Do you think they could have had rabies or something? If they did, we were mighty lucky they didn't bite us."

*Rabies.* The mere mention of the word sent an icy shiver racing down Carl Briner's spine.

It had been years since a case of rabies had been reported in the area. In light conversation, Briner and the other rangers considered the possibility that the disease might have all but died out. It wasn't beyond comprehension; after all, people rarely heard of new cases of polio and smallpox anymore. If they were lucky, maybe rabies was following the same course . . .

An unsettling thought crept forward from the back of Briner's mind. In response, he leaned over in his chair and retrieved the paper from the wastebasket, spread it out across his desk, and began turning the pages slowly. He scanned every column; he was looking for an article he'd read with his morning coffee.

"What are you doing?" Corbie asked curiously, watching Briner and wondering why he was no longer the center of the ranger's attention. "Don't you believe me? Don't you believe what I said about the raccoons?"

Briner ignored Corbie's inquiry. He continued turning the pages slowly and scanning them for the article— "Here it is."

"Here's what?" Corbie asked.

After Briner finished rereading the article, he turned the paper around on his desk and pointed to it. "Here. Read this. Read about what was found out in Boleen, Oklahoma, yesterday."

Corbie read the article, then looked at Briner wide-eyed and fearful. "Do you think that's what could have happened here? Could . . . could those giant raccoons have been experimental animals the animal rights people let loose in the park? Could Ragina and me . . . could we have been exposed to some kind of disease?"

"Who's to say. But if that is the case, I'd say rabies would have been the least of our problems. Come on," Briner said as he stood and put on his Smokey the Bear hat, "I'm taking you two into town to the hospital."


*10:52 A.M.*


Bruce bit lightly on the tip of his tongue and concentrated on the cutting line as he guided the chain saw through a thick branch. So far, the morning had been productive. He and Fritz had downed two good-sized maple trees, and they were in the process of cutting off the limbs, making their way to the trunk.

A shadow fell across the cutting line. Bruce glanced up and saw Fritz standing on the opposite side of the tree. Bruce frowned in question. Fritz tried to shout an explanation, but the noise from the saw overrode him, then he tried to pantomime a message. Bruce shook his head. Unable to understand, he turned off the saw, took off his hat, and removed his ear protectors.

"What's up?" he asked. "Is something wrong?"

"The chain broke on my saw," Fritz answered. "Kerk said he wants to go down to the house with me, while I fix it, so he can say good-bye to his mother. Do you want to take a break and go with us?"

Bruce glanced down the length of the tree on the ground in front of him, then looked at the three major branches still waiting to be cut from the trunk. "I need to get this finished. If I stop now, I may never get started again."

"You've been at it pretty hard all morning. You could use a rest."

"I can rest when I get my work finished. It's for sure it's not gonna get done on its own."

Fritz glanced at the branches remaining on the trunk, looked back at Bruce, and shook his head. "It won't get done if you overdo it all at once, either."

"I know how far I can push it before I need to stop. Go on back to the house and fix your saw."

"The links came apart on the chain. Depending on what parts I can scrounge, I'm not sure how long it'll take to fix."

"You don't need to be in any hurry on my account. I'll still be here whenever you get back."

"We may take some time out to eat a bite of lunch."

"If you think about it, bring me back a sandwich, and I'll be happy."

Fritz hesitated for a minute, then said, "Dag-gone it, Bruce, can't you get it through that thick skull of yours that I'm trying to talk you into going back to the house with us?"

"Why?"

"First of all, you need to rest, and second, I don't think it's a good idea for you to be up here all by yourself running a chain saw. What if something would happen?"

"Nothing's going to happen."

"You don't know that—"

"I do know that if you keep standing there jawin' all day, we won't get anything more done—either one of us. Now, if you're gonna go fix that chain, go fix it. And bring me a couple sandwiches and some of Leah's homemade brownies when you come back." Without any further debate, Bruce slipped the ear protectors back in place, put on his hat, grabbed the saw's start-rope, and gave it a firm pull. The small engine started without a sputter, and he returned to sawing the thick branch.

Fritz watched him for a few moments, then shook his head and turned and walked away. He didn't like leaving Bruce alone in the woods, but, then, he knew there wasn't any use to argue.

*11:13 A.M.*

Rusty Snider pulled the limousine to a stop in front of Jackie's house so that the back door was in precise alignment with the walk to the front porch. After turning off the engine, he reached for the door handle and started to get out, but Dan stopped him. "No use wasting your energy standing outside." Rusty looked at Dan via the rearview mirror. "Knowing Jackie, she's going to make us wait for a few minutes." Dan glanced at the house and at the window, where he thought he saw a figure step out of view. "When she finally does decide to make an appearance, you'll have plenty of time to get out and open the door for her."

Rusty nodded. He continued to look at Dan in the mirror. "I thought you promised her you wouldn't come out here anymore . . . because of the boy."

"With these tinted windows, he can't see me, and she won't know I'm here until she gets in." Dan chuckled. "And then it'll be too late."

Rusty hesitated, then asked, "Do you think this debt angle

on the farm and compound will finally get you what you've been after all these years?"

Dan focused on Rusty's mirrored eyes. "If it doesn't, I'm about at the end of my options."

Rusty studied Dan's eyes for a moment, then said, "You know, for as long as we've been together, I don't remember you ever working so hard for anything."

"You've never seen me come face to face with anything else I had such a hard time getting. Usually I can buy—"

A loud backfire drew their attention to the far side of the drive. A couple of seconds passed, then an old red truck drove out from behind the last barn.

"And that little shit isn't helping matters any," Dan said with a scowl, focusing on Kerk in the truck's front seat.

"He's just reacting like any kid would, trying to look out for his mother," Rusty said, watching the truck as it approached.

"If he keeps getting in my way, I'll have to think about having him taken care of just like I did his fa—" Dan's words stopped abruptly.

An elongated groan rose from the back seat, prompting Rusty to look in the rearview mirror. He saw Dan's face, contorted in pain. A louder groan escaped Dan's drawn lips, then he doubled over onto the seat.

"What's the matter?" Rusty asked as he turned in his seat and braced himself with a knee. "What's wrong?"

Dan didn't answer—he couldn't. His jaw was clenched.

He began to shake, and then he shivered violently, as if he were trapped in severe cold. He threw his head back against the seat; his eyes rolled up into their sockets until only the whites were visible. The muscles in his jaw suddenly slackened, and his teeth began to chatter. Unconsciously, Dan bit the soft skin on the inside of his lips; a trickle of blood mingled with the frothy saliva that began to ooze out of the corner of his mouth.

"Dan?" Rusty asked apprehensively as he reached over the

seat toward Dan. "Dan, what's the matter?"

The instant Rusty's hand touched Dan's leg, Dan's mouth stretched open wide, and he emitted a muffled cry. Instinctively—almost fearfully—Dan turned on the seat and pulled away from Rusty, drawing his knees up to his chest and appearing as if he were trying to squeeze himself into the corner of the car between the seat and the side door.

"Dan . . ." Rusty touched Dan's knee.

Dan cried out, producing a sound that verged upon being nonhuman. He opened his mouth again, this time pulling his lips back from his teeth. He hissed, he growled. He extended a hand toward Rusty, his fingers arched in a clawed position. He—

Dan blinked once . . . twice. His facial muscles relaxed, and his eyes returned to their normal position.

He sat for a moment in silence, focusing on Rusty's concerned expression, then his eyes slowly trailed down to his artificial legs that were contorted on the seat beside him. "What happened?" Dan asked hesitantly as the muscles in his thighs regained control of the prostheses and returned his feet to the floor.

"I don't know for sure," Rusty answered, a bit unnerved. "I was hoping you could tell me."

Dan slid his tongue along the inside of his mouth, then lifted a hand to touch the corner of his lip. A red-tinged froth clung to his fingertips when he pulled them away; a gelatinous streamer stretched between his fingers and lips, then snapped like a rubber band, falling limply onto his chin. Dan wiped the streamer away with the back of his hand.

"What happened?" Dan asked again, looking at Rusty. He wiped a hand across his forehead and withdrew a palm glistening with sweat.

"For a moment, you . . . you reminded me of a cornered animal," Rusty tried to explain. "It . . . it was like *you* weren't even there—"

"O-o-o-h-h-h." Dan threw his head back against the seat and groaned; his legs again drew up close to his chest.

"Dan," Rusty called out, "Dan, what is it?"

"My . . . my legs." Dan slipped his hands in between his chest and thighs and tried to push his legs down. "I . . . can't on my own. Help . . . me."

Rusty turned completely around in his seat. He grasped Dan's legs just above the knees and pushed them back down on the seat. "What's happening with your legs?" he asked. "Why are they doing that?"

Dan looked into Rusty's green eyes, and a grin crept slowly across his face. "You know why—we *both* know why. It's working." Dan's face contorted again. He threw his head back and released another agonizing groan. "It's work—ing," he said between clenched teeth. A few seconds passed, then he began to laugh . . . laugh almost maniacally as he pushed himself upright in the seat. "I can feel it. It's working." He began massaging his thighs. "I can feel it! It's working!"

A terrifying uneasiness crept over Rusty as he watched Dan slump forward on the seat, massaging his thighs. "Something's not right, Dan. Maybe I should take you home—"

"No!" Dan looked up sharply, his emerald eyes locking on Rusty's. "I can handle it," he said, forcing control into his voice. "We're going to the governor's office just like we planned and"—a sinister grin crept onto his lips—"and before you know it, I'll have Jackie right where I want her."


*11:28 A.M.*

Warren opened the front door and all but ran through the living room to the kitchen. He was in a hurry; he didn't have time to waste; he didn't even hesitate long enough to remove the key from the lock.

It was close to a fifty-minute drive between the lab, on the north side of the county, and his house in the Morthland addition—fifty minutes . . . and *that* was when the traffic flow was with him. Normally, he didn't mind the drive, except when he was in a hurry. Today, Warren was in a hurry.

He was on his lunch hour, which, more than likely, would come closer to being two hours today. Even though a conference had taken Leland Wagner out of the lab for the day—and, therefore, Warren could take all the time he wanted for his lunch break—Warren still felt as if he were under his employer's watchful eye. Sometimes, he knew he was just too damn conscientious.

The instant he stepped through the kitchen archway, Warren's eyes homed in on the covered cages sitting on the cabinet across the room. He stopped and listened, unconsciously holding his breath so the noise of his own respiration wouldn't mask even the faintest sound.

To his disappointment, there were no squeaks or squawks or squeals or cries to greet him. Everything was quiet . . . too quiet. No senseless mouse chatter rose to fill the void.

"Are you still with us?" he asked almost apprehensively as he walked across the kitchen, then reached for the towel.

Warren had been troubled all morning. The brief examination he'd given the mice before leaving for work had prompted several areas of concern. Both mice had continued to grow and, since their breathing appeared to be labored, he wondered if their internal organs were growing at the same rate and in proportion to the rest of their bodies. He wondered if their hearts and lungs were capable of keeping up the pace that was being demanded of them?

In addition to their general overall growth, their deformities had taken on an accelerated spirit of their own. The tissue mass on the submissive mouse's neck almost equaled the size of its body. The legs—that was what Warren still called the bizarre appendages emerging from the amputation sites—on both mice had continued to overdevelop. When they attempted to move, the mice could do little more than drag the massive caricature of muscle, skin, and bone behind them.

"Up until a couple of days ago, I was anxious to see every new development you two had to show me, but now..." Warren clutched the edge of the towel in his hand, hesitated—actually stalled for time, hoping, if he waited long enough, something positive might happen—then, he finally lifted it. The instant he pulled the towel away from the cages, a putrid stench assaulted his nose.

Warren gasped and jerked back away from the cages. He turned his head to the side and tried to take in fresh air, but the foul odor had spread quickly through the kitchen, and there was no fresh air left to be had.

After taking a few moments to adjust, Warren looked back at the mice. Immediately, he saw the source of the disagreeable odor.

Massive sores had erupted—had actually *erupted* from the inside out—all over the mice's bodies. A greenish-yellow pus seeped from the sores and crusted at their perimeters. Along their abdomens, the open sores exposed internal organs; spaghettilike strands of small intestines had been pushed out onto the cage floor. Near their hind quarters, pus, combined with feces and urine, oozed from unexplainable orifices. Lying motionless—all but encased in their own excrement—the mice squeaked weakly and looked up at Warren with pleading... haunted eyes.

"What's gone wrong?" Warren whispered in self-question. "What did I do? Where did I make a mistake?" The grandfather clock in the living room chimed once, marking the half hour. Warren glanced at his watch, looked back at the mice, then threw the towel back over the cages. "You two are coming back to the lab with me. I've got blood tests to run, tissue samples to take, and a half-dozen other things to check on, and I can do it a lot easier back at the lab than I can do it here."

*11:41 A.M.*

Bruce shut down the chain saw and set it on the ground beside the downed tree. He took off his hat and ear protectors, slid his safety glasses down around his neck, then pulled a red bandanna from the front pocket of his coveralls and wiped his forehead and the sweatband inside his hat. He turned and sat down, then looked out over the valley and watched a lone hawk circle lazily over its domain.

He needed the rest. His muscles were tired and, even though the day was cool, he'd worked up a sweat wrestling the saw . . . and there was still a long way to go before the tree could be cut and split, ready to stack for next winter's firewood.

Bruce took in a slow, deep breath, appreciating the freshness filling the air around him. He looked from the valley to the fallen hickory tree beneath him to the ancient, mammoth oaks towering overhead. Some of those trees had probably been growing for well over a century. He thought it sad that most of them would probably fall victim to a chain saw within the next couple of decades.

A high-pitched whine attracted Bruce's attention. He shifted on the tree and looked around the area. "Cork? Little Cork?" he called. "Where'd ya go?" Bruce turned almost completely around before he finally located the beige-and-brown puppy. She was digging frantically at a hole in the ground. "What ya got there, Little Cork?" The dog stopped digging long enough to look up at Bruce and bark, then her attention returned to the hole that was steadily growing in diameter. "Ground squirrels," Bruce said to himself with a chuckle.

As he turned back around, Bruce's eyes trailed along the branches that still needed to be removed from the old hickory's trunk. "Ground squirrels," he repeated, glancing again at Little Cork. "Wish I had the time to play around, but . . ." Bruce stuffed the bandanna back in his pocket, pulled his safety glasses up over his eyes, put his ear protectors and hat back in place, then stood and turned toward the tree. "Let's get it over and done with so when Fritz and Kerk get back, they can go to work and I can take a long rest over lunch."

Bruce picked up the saw and set it on the tree. He took a firm hold of the saw handle and the start-rope and, with one quick pull, brought the engine back to life. Out of habit, he pressed the engage button and watched the chain race around the outer edge of the frame.

"Well, let's get at it," he said to himself as he carried the saw to the nearest limb.

Bruce revved the engine, then lowered the saw to the limb. Instantly, the chain's jagged teeth began gouging out chunks of bark and wood, showering Bruce, and a good-sized area around him, with hickory chips.

He'd never liked cutting hickory. The wood was hard and oftentimes stubborn . . . and the tree in front of him was proving to be no different. Even though he was working on a limb no bigger around than his thigh, Bruce had to put his weight behind his work to force the chain saw deeper . . . and deeper into the cutting crevice.

Something scampered past the tree, marginally entering Bruce's field of vision. He looked up to see Little Cork chasing a ground squirrel . . . cornering it . . . then letting it slip free . . . to chase it again. Bruce chuckled to himself, amused by the puppy's antics—

The chain saw ate through the bottom of the limb—

The force Bruce was exerting on the saw continued to carry it downward—

The revolving steel teeth bit and sliced and gouged . . . tore through denim . . . and muscle . . . flesh—

A cry of agony burst from Bruce's lips as he dropped the chain saw and grabbed his lower left thigh. He turned around, leaned against the tree trunk, then looked down at the jagged wound. Fear washed through him as blood pumped out of him. It was bad—deep—and Bruce knew he was in trouble.

Keeping the heel of one hand pressed against the wound, he reached into his front pocket and pulled out his bandanna. He tucked one edge beneath his chin and spread the rest of the fabric open across his chest. Starting at the nearest corner, he began rolling the bandanna into a makeshift bandage.

Bruce suddenly yawned, and he began to feel lightheaded. In an attempt to keep from falling, he slid down the side of the tree trunk and sat on the ground. If he passed out now, he wouldn't fall far; he would only topple over onto his side.

Working as quickly as he could, he wrapped the rolled bandanna around his leg just above the wound and tied it as tight as he could pull. He picked up a sturdy stick, tied the ends of the bandanna around it, then began to turn the stick in a slow clockwise rotation. Gradually, the makeshift tourniquet slowed the blood flow to the wound.

Bruce didn't have the strength to tie the tourniquet in place; the best he could do was hold it. He leaned his head back against the tree trunk and closed his eyes. He felt tired—exhausted. He didn't know whether the condition was fostered by physical fatigue or by a loss of blood—

Something nudged his leg.

Bruce opened his eyes to a slit and lifted his head slightly. Through blurred vision, he could see Little Cork licking the cut on his leg.

"Get away." Bruce's actions were slow and not too well

coordinated, but he managed to pick up a handful of wood chips and throw them at the dog. "I'm not gonna be a meal for any freeloading mutt." He picked up another handful of chips . . . and lost his balance . . . toppling over onto his side. "Go away," he muttered as darkness began to close in around him. "Go . . . away." Bruce thought he could still feel the dog nudging his leg, but he didn't have the strength to drive it away.


*12:02 P.M.*

Milton Hawkins gathered a mouthful of saliva and spit, then he swiped the back of his hand haphazardly across his mouth. Part of the tobacco drool clung to his hand; most of it slid past his lips to cling to the hairs of his scraggly beard. In another couple of minutes, he'd spit again; then, following an unconscious habit, he'd repeat the process.

"If the comin' summer's as lean as the spring, it's gonna be a mighty poor year." Forrest Deem knelt a couple of yards away from Hawkins and carefully sprinkled a handful of fresh leaves over the spring trap he'd just finished setting.

"Maybe next time, we can git a few more dollars outta that doctor man down in the city. I heared on the radio he got all his animals stole."

"Maybe. Could be that puny four-eyed man might be needin' some more too." Deem stood, picked up the half-dozen steel traps that were lying on the ground near his feet, and slung them over his shoulder. "Didja check the traps in line by the park?" Hawkins grunted, then spit. "Anything up there?"

"Just this here." Hawkins wiped his hand over his mouth, then slipped it into the breast pocket of his old flannel shirt. He pulled out a partially decomposed paw and held it out for Deem to see.

"What is it?"

"Looks like 'coon ta me," Hawkins said, turning the paw over in the palm of his hand.

"Went and chewed it right off, huh?" Deem said in passing, glancing at the paw briefly. "Too bad," he added, shaking his head as he began walking, following an animal trail.

"Why's that?"

"If he hadn't gone and chewed his paw off an' got loose, we coulda had us another 'coon pelt ta sell."

"Sure woulda been nice. They're still worth a buck or two." Hawkins laughed. "Them city folk, they sure git a kick outta wearin' a coonskin hat and pretendin' they're Dan'l Boone."

The two mountain men followed the animal trail through the woods for several minutes before Deem broke the silence with an elongated, "Pheew! The wind musta just shifted an' put me downsmell o' you. You sure stink, Milt." Deem stopped, shook his head, then turned to the side in search of fresh air. "You smell rotten."

Hawkins spit and wiped his hand over his mouth then said, "Can't be me. Them po-lice, they made me take a shower when they put us in jail. 'Member?"

"That was a week ago."

Hawkins lifted his arms and sniffed first one armpit and then the other. "Nope," he said, shaking his head, "ain't me. They stink, but they don't smell rotten. Must be somethin' else 'round . . ." He stuck his nose up in the air and began sniffing like a wild animal. "But you're right, somethin' sure does stink." He looked around the area for several moments, then asked, "Say, don't we have a couple more traps set not too far on up here?"

Deem eyed the area as well, checking his bearings, then nodded. "I think we left them maybe twenty . . . thirty feet beyond that thicket up there."

"Bet we got us a dead'n." Hawkins nosed the air again then puckered his face into a frown. "Yep, by the smell o' things,

I bet we got us a dead'n so bloated, he's ripe and ready ta pop."

Deem looked beyond the thicket and frowned. "Shouldn't have. I woulda swore we set live traps out here."

Hawkins looked toward the thicket as well. After a brief hesitation, he spit and said, "Live . . . dead . . . ain't no never mind. We ain't ever gonna know nothin' by just standin' here. Let's go see what we got."

The two men left the animal trail and worked their way through the tangled underbrush. When they reached the edge of the next small clearing, they stopped and Deem once again checked the trees around him to verify his location. "Unless I'm turned completely bass-ackwards, they should be set just on the other side o' that tree yonder," he said, pointing to a towering hickory as he continued to walk toward it.

"Phew!" Hawkins drew in a shallow breath and coughed. "Whatever it is, it's dead all right. Stinks bad enough ta gag a maggot." He pulled a dirty handkerchief from the hip pocket of his overalls and opened it over his mouth and nose. "I ain't never smelt anythin' this bad ever in my life. Why don't we just go and leave it?"

"Mosta these here traps along this line are perty new. Do ya wanna spend another six to eight hours makin' one to replace it?"

"I'm willin'—"

"Yeah, sure you're willin' 'cause you—" Deem stopped short, his attention drawn to a wire cage trap a few feet beyond the tree . . . and to the swollen furred mass contained within. "Good God Almighty," he stammered as he took a couple of guarded steps closer to the trap.

"What . . . what is it?" Hawkins asked as he stopped and focused on the cage. He became so mesmerized by the misshapen animal, he unconsciously lowered the handkerchief from his face and didn't even react when he breathed in the thick, pungent air rising around him.

"Looks like there're two of 'em in there," Deem said as he leaned over the trap to have a closer look. "Fur looks like it could be a rabbit and maybe a 'possum— What the—" He stepped back with a start.

"What's the matter?"

"I don't believe it. They can't be—"

"They can't be what?"

"They can't be . . . growin', but they are. They're growin' . . . growin' right outta their skins!"

"You been in the corn mash this mornin', Forrest?"

"Come 'ere and take a look fer yourself if ya don't believe me." Deem motioned for Hawkins to join him. "Along the belly . . . look there along the belly"—he pointed—"the skin's split and the meat and guts are pushin' their way out."

"That's bloat. They're dead, and that's bloat."

"Ain't never seen bloat work like that before—"

Suddenly, the animal in the cage closest to them rolled over onto its side . . . and exploded. A potpourri of fur, flesh, blood, and pus flew out between the trap's bars, splattering the trees and ground . . . and the legs and feet of the two men witnessing the animal's bizarre demise. A concentrated stench erupted from the carcass as well.

"That ain't bloat," Deem said, watching a piece of pus-covered flesh bubble and curl on top of his boot. "There's somethin' powerful wrong with them animals," he said as he kicked the flesh from his foot, "and I sure hope we ain't got us some kind o' sickness goin' through these here woods, 'cause if we do, it could spread on across the river and get down in our prime huntin' ground."

"Think maybe it's rabies?"

"That ain't no rabies like I ever seed." Deem looked from one piece of the exploded animal's carcass to another . . . and another. "I got me a funny feelin', Milt," he said as he looked at his partner. "I got me a feelin' the people 'round these parts are gonna wish it was somethin' as simple as rabies."


*12:16 P.M.*

Bruce Cameron slowly rolled his head across a pillow of wood chips. A muffled groan escaped his lips. Only half conscious of his surroundings, he tried to open his eyes.

The noonday sun, filtering down through the canopy of leaves, met his gaze. He squinted. His eyelids fluttered briefly, then closed again. The bright assault only added to his discomfort—

But wait. He didn't really feel all that bad. In fact—after having a chain saw slice halfway through his leg—he didn't feel bad at all.

The fact that he *didn't* feel that bad made him wonder. Could he be— Was he . . . dead? Had he died and gone to . . . was it heaven?

Bruce slowly opened his eyes again. The light—the *bright* light met his eyes. He'd heard that when people died, they saw a bright light . . . a bright light that seemed to call to them—

A fly buzzed around Bruce's face and then landed on his cheek. Bruce swatted at it and missed. The fly flew away—

*Flies?* Did heaven have flies?

Bruce blinked several times, then squinted to block out the sunlight so he could focus on the leafy branches overhead . . . on the scrub grass . . . on the hickory tree trunk on the ground beside him. He wasn't dead; he was at the edge of the woods, on the hill overlooking the compound.

A smile spread across Bruce's lips, and he tingled with relief. He never thought he'd fear the day he would die; he felt at peace with his maker. But dag-gone, he still had a lot more living he wanted to do, and he wasn't ready to give it up quite yet—

He remembered what happened.

Bruce lifted his head and looked across his chest toward his left leg. The bandanna he'd wrapped around his thigh had slipped off during his lapse of consciousness; it lay on the ground beside him. The ripped denim, bordering the hole in the leg of his overalls, was wet and darkened with blood. The wound that had—

A puzzled frown knitted Bruce's brow. The wound . . . the massive cut to his leg . . .

Bruce pushed himself up to his elbows, then shifted so he could lean back against the tree trunk. He looked at the wound, and not believing what he was seeing, he leaned forward and scrutinized the flesh . . . flesh that—but a few minutes before—had been savagely ripped open by the chain saw. What *should* have been a gaping—life-threatening—wound was instead a minor laceration that looked as if it was already beginning to heal.

"It can't be," Bruce said, shaking his head. "There has to be an explanation. Hallucinations. I'm hallucinating," he whispered, then he hesitantly reached toward the wound. "I've lost so much blood, I'm out of my mind, and I'm seeing things that can't actually be."

Gingerly, he touched the skin at the outer edges of the cut. He expected a bone-jolting pain to bolt through him like lightning, but instead, a dull ache was the only answer to his touch.

Bruce shook his head in bewilderment as he leaned back against the tree. "Did I overreact? Did I panic and think I was injured far worse than I really was when . . . when all that happened was some insignificant cut?"

Then his eyes homed in on the blood on his hands . . . on his pant leg . . . and on the wood chips scattered beneath his left thigh. By all indications, he *had* lost more blood than the laceration on his leg could account for. But how? What could have— Then, he remembered.

"Cork?" he called almost hesitantly, looking around him. "Little Cork," he called with more certainty, "where are you? Come here, girl." Bruce sat silently for a few moments, then he heard a whimper rise from the far side of the tree. "It's all right. Come here, girl. Little Cork, come here." The whimpering subsided. Bruce heard a rustling sound—paws shuffling through wood chips—then he saw a beige-and-brown head peek cautiously around the cut end of the hickory tree.

"Little Cork, come here, girl." Bruce patted a hand against his right thigh and motioned for the dog. "Come on. It's all right."

The young pup wagged its tail vigorously, the white tip blurred in the action. She barked in response to Bruce's words, then trotted across the short distance between them and sat down beside him. Immediately, she began working her nose beneath Bruce's arm and nuzzling up closer to his side. She barked again and looked up at him with anxious eyes.

"I want you to be the first to know I don't really believe what I'm thinkin'."

Bruce ruffled Little Cork's ears, then gently lifted her head in his hands. Making a quick survey of the animal, he immediately spotted patches of dried blood around her mouth, beneath her chin, down her chest, and along one side. After finding what he had expected—but still didn't believe—he cupped her head in his hands and looked directly into her dark brown eyes.

"You're some kind of special dog, aren't you?" Little Cork barked and wagged her tail as if to reply.

"I thought so." Bruce slid his hand over the dog's head, then took a moment to look inside each of her ears. "I don't see any tattoos," he said, a smile brightening his face, "which means no one can lay claim on you without going through a lot of hassle." He continued to pet the dog, talking to it as freely as if it could understand. "I bet you came from somebody's lab that was broken into a few days ago. And I'll bet you're a part of some special project that not too many people know about. 'Cause if you weren't a secret, there'd be scores of people out looking for you and there'd be lost-and-found ads in the paper and on TV. But they're not; nobody's looking for you—at least not so as anybody would know about it. So I just bet you're something somebody wants to keep real secret." Bruce's smile broadened, and he ran his hand the length of the puppy's back. "And you know, we're gonna do just that. We're gonna keep your little secret all to ourselves. We're not gonna tell anybody what happened between us up here today." Bruce glanced at the wound on his left thigh . . . that already appeared to have gotten smaller since the last time he'd looked at it. "But you know something, I don't think anybody would believe us anyway. Nobody'd ever believe a dog could just lick a wound and make it heal almost in front of your eyes."

*12:44 P.M.*

"Look this way, Governor," a photographer urged as he lifted his camera, ready to take a picture.

Governor Gerald Marling stepped in behind Jackie's chair, placed a hand on her shoulder and one on Dan's, then leaned down between them. He pulled them together toward him, until their heads almost touched, and looked up at the camera. "Smile," he whispered, then he flashed the toothy smile that had helped win over voters during the past two elections.

"Over here, Governor," another photographer urged.

"Just one more," still another requested.

After the flashes faded, a reporter asked, "When did you say construction was going to begin on the first habitat?"

The governor straightened his posture, smiled and nodded at Jackie and Dan, then turned to the architectural drawing of the zoo, mounted on a large easel behind him, he'd unveiled earlier. After posing for additional pictures with the South Port mayor, the governor repeated the timetable that would, if kept on schedule, allow the first wildlife habitat to be fully operational within a year of the coming fall.

While Governor Marling and Mayor Fuller were basking in the limelight proffered by Dan's contribution to the zoo, Jackie sat none too patiently, waiting for the hoopla to pass . . . waiting for an opportunity to leave. The entire ordeal had been a strain. She'd endured the ride into town with Dan, repeatedly smiled—convincingly—for all the photographers and reporters, and had tolerated being squeezed between Dan, the governor, and the mayor for the majority of the catered affair. Now, as the questions were winding down and members of the press were starting to leave, there was hope that she, too, might soon be set free.

Without any pompous fanfare, Mayor Fuller suddenly sat down in the chair beside Jackie and leaned in close to her so he could speak in a whisper. "The governor has an idea that might help bring in a few more donations for your animal compound."

Jackie focused on the mayor intently. She was always eager to hear about new and innovative ways to collect donations; at the moment, she was probably more attentive than she might have been even a few days ago. If she could find a way to finance the compound, then she could pay off Dan and never be indebted to him again. In addition to a financial settlement, she would also be able to negate the other obligations he had forced upon her. She would never have to attend another function with him again . . . or even tolerate his presence.

"The governor thinks it would be a good idea for you to

attend the ball next week." At the mention of the Governor's Ball, Jackie tensed, but she tried not to let her agitation show. "A lot of influential—wealthy—people will be attending, and it will give you an opportunity to talk with them and solicit their support. You know, of course, all it would take would be for you to get a handful of prominent people behind you, and you wouldn't have to worry about financial matters ever again. Do you think you could arrange your schedule so you could attend?"

"I imagine I could—"

"Good. I'm sure the governor will be more than pleased to know you'll be attending." The mayor patted Jackie's hand, then slid his chair back from the table. "I need to go do a little PR work with the press before they get away," he said, looking around the room. He stood up in an instant and immediately began mingling with the reporters.

Jackie watched the mayor for a few moments, then she sensed *she* was being watched. Responding to her instincts, she turned her head slowly, and her eyes eventually came in contact with Dan's.

He was sitting in a chair just a few feet away, his arms crossed over his chest, smiling smugly. Dan nodded. Jackie nodded stiffly in response, but that was where their communication ended. She feared that if she opened her mouth, something might come out she would live to regret—

Without warning, the smile melted from Dan's face. It was immediately replaced by a grimace of pain. His eyes widened; his breaths came in short gasps. He wrapped his arms around himself and began to tremble.

"Dan," Jackie asked in a low voice, looking at him with concern, "are you all right?"

Dan didn't answer. His eyes grew wider until they looked as if they might pop out of his head, then, suddenly, they rolled up in their sockets, exposing only bloodshot white. He grabbed at his stomach savagely, then threw his head back until his neck was braced over the chair.

"Dan?" Jackie asked again, shifting on her chair closer to him. "What's wrong? Is there something I can do to help—"

A primitive cry exploded from deep within Dan's throat and raked across his lips.

Everyone in the room silenced their chatter and turned their attention to Dan.

"Out! Get everyone out of here!" Throughout the luncheon and press conference, Rusty Snider had stood like an invisible shadow against the back wall. Now, he was shouting commands and even giving orders to the governor's security guards. They obeyed him immediately—without question—and began ushering people to the nearest exits.

"Dan—" Jackie reached for Dan just as he started to slide out of his chair. Rusty ran up beside her, and together they eased Dan down on the floor. "What's the matter with him?" she asked, looking at Rusty, an uncertainty tinting her eyes. "Is there anything I can do to help?"

"Just get out and leave us alone."

"A doctor—"

"Get out! All of you, get out," Rusty said, looking up at the governor and mayor who had moved in close behind Jackie. "Just give him a few minutes alone, and everything will be all right."

Jackie looked from Rusty to Dan, then took the governor's hand as he helped her up from the floor. "I didn't know," the governor said, as he walked beside her toward the door. "I didn't know epilepsy ran in the Patton family."

Jackie hesitated at the door and looked back at Dan. During all the years she had known him, she'd never heard the condition mentioned either . . . and she wondered if that was what was really affecting him now.

Rusty looked after them until they left the room. After the

exit door closed, he returned his attention to Dan. "What have you gone and done to yourself?" he whispered, shaking his head. He watched Dan tremble and shake; he watched Dan's muscles jerk beyond control. "Whatever it is, is it worth it? Is it worth all this?"

Almost as suddenly as the attack had begun, it lessened in severity and finally stopped. Dan lay motionless on the floor for several moments, then he rolled his head slowly back and forth over the carpet before finally opening his eyes. Confused, he looked up into Rusty's worried face. "What happened?" he asked in a hoarse whisper.

"The same thing that happened in the car a few hours ago, only this time, it lasted longer, and it was worse."

"I passed out," Dan said as he lifted his hands to rub his temples. "I— Holy shit! What am I doing down here on the floor?" he asked with a start when he realized where he was. "Did I make a fool of myself?" Rusty didn't answer. Dan pushed himself up on his elbows; Rusty took a hold of his arm and helped him sit up. "Where is everybody? Where did they go?" he asked nervously, looking around the vacant room. "I did. I did make a total ass of myself—" His words were cut short by a series of sharp stabbing pains that coursed through his legs and seemed to explode from the tips of his stumps.

"Dan," Rusty said apprehensively, "what's the matter—"

"My legs—my legs!" Dan shouted in a pleading cry. "Stop it!" In an attempt to drive the pain away, he began beating on his thighs with his fists. "Stop the pain! Oh . . . the . . . pain!"

"What can I do—"

"The pain! Pain! Stop the pain—" Dan gasped, then he took in a slow, deep breath and looked at Rusty, puzzled. "The pain . . ."

"What can I do to help you?"

"Nothing." Rusty looked at him in question. "It's . . . it's gone. It's gone . . . and—"

246

Moving almost in a frenzy, Dan pulled up his left pant leg. When the hem exposed the buckle to his prosthesis, he unbuckled it and yanked off the artificial limb. The stump of his leg immediately became his point of focus.

"Look." Dan grabbed Rusty's arm in excitement and pointed to the stump. "Look! Can you see it!—can you see it!"

Rusty leaned closer and looked at the end of Dan's leg. "It's . . . it's changed," he whispered in astonishment.

"Yes, it's changed. It's growing! The serum's working just like Maxey said it would. I'm going to have my legs back. My legs!"

"Don't get too excited too soon. Don't expect—"

"The serum. I used the last of what I had this morning." Dan grabbed the lapels of Rusty's jacket and pulled him close. "I need more serum. You've got to take me to Maxey's house. I need more serum, and I need it now."


*12:49 P.M.*


Danford Dunn stumbled up the lane, tripped over an exposed tree root, teetered on the brink of a deep rut, then fell. He lay motionless—face down—for several moments, then he hoisted himself up on his hands and knees. Swaying, he crawled to the edge of the lane where he found a sapling strong enough to support his weight while he pulled himself back up to his feet.

Even though it was only a little past noon, Danford had already consumed enough alcohol to sedate him well into the next day. The preacher was coming for dinner, and being drunk was the only way he could tolerate the outspoken holy man who was hell-bent on saving every sinner's soul.

Danford stopped at the edge of the clearing a few feet from the cabin's porch. He leaned against an old oak tree and eyed the homestead he'd carved out of the woods, on the edge of Haggerty Ridge, some thirty years ago. The cabin was drafty but sturdy, built on a foundation of river rock he and Loretta had hauled up the mountain in a mule-drawn cart. The roof needed a new coat of tar and maybe an extra layer of black paper, but for the most part, it looked to be in pretty good shape. It had made it through the winter and, no doubt, it would survive through many more.

His eyes drifted left across a knoll to the chicken coop Loretta had built from scrap, and to the yard that had only a makeshift fence of secondhand wire and— A patch of brightly-colored fabric attracted Danford's attention.

It looked like it could be one of Loretta's aprons; Loretta liked brightly-colored aprons. She made them from remnants she picked up at church and hand-fashioned into miniature works of art. She liked bright colors; she liked to add a touch of gaiety to her otherwise drab world.

But what would one of Loretta's aprons be doing out by the chicken yard? Danford glanced at the clothesline; it was bare, but Loretta could have hung a single apron out to dry and the wind could have carried it away . . . but Danford doubted if that was what had happened. Loretta was economical. Had she drawn a pan of water to wash an apron, she would have also used it to wash socks and underwear as well. But nothing else was hanging on the line, and the wind . . . well, there wasn't any, and there hadn't been a breeze all morning that could have wrestled the clothes free from the snap pins on the line.

Danford could think of only one way the apron could have gotten out to the chicken yard. Loretta had to have been wearing it and—

"Lo-retta?" he called, a note of uncertainty clinging to the word. Uneasiness suddenly sobered him. "Loretta!" he shouted, starting toward the patch of brightly-colored fabric. He stumbled over a root, fell to his hands and knees . . . and continued in a crawl. "Lo-ret-ta," he wailed—

A sinister growl struck out at him from the underbrush not a dozen feet away. Danford froze on his hands and knees, then slowly turned his head toward the dense thicket. A glistening pair of dark eyes met his gaze. Danford's heart thumped savagely, and it felt as if it leaped up into his throat.

"G-get away." Danford looked around for something to throw, but nothing was within his immediate reach. "Get away!" His shout was answered by a louder growl . . . and then a snarl . . . and then a hiss. "Get away—"

The animal took a couple of steps forward and eased out from beneath the underbrush. Danford stared at it in disbelief.

It could have been a rabbit or a squirrel . . . but it wasn't. It could have been a badger or a groundhog . . . but it wasn't. It could have been a cat or a dog . . . but it wasn't any of those, either. It was no singular animal; it looked to be a grotesque combination of the half-dozen Danford had thought of . . . and more.

Whatever the creature, its lips suddenly pulled back from spikelike teeth, and it growled again. Its eyes remained locked with Danford's as it dropped its hind legs down low to the ground. There were no secrets about its actions; it was preparing to spring.

"Go . . . 'way . . ." The words didn't leave Danford's lips as either a shout or a command but rather as a helpless plea emitted by a terrified child.

The animal's forehead furrowed; its eyes narrowed to tiny slits—

"Lo-ret-ta." Danford scrambled to his feet, stumbled, but retained his balance, then he felt something pull on his pant leg. "Lo-ret-ta!" He yanked his leg forward, pulling it free, and started running toward the brightly-colored fabric. But again he tripped . . . stumbled . . . and this time he fell.

Danford reached out in front of him and tried to catch

himself. His left hand came down on something squishy, furry, and soft, and it slid out from under him. He landed hard on his chest, knocking the air out of him ... coming face to face with the pointed snout of the dead animal he'd inadvertently overturned.

A hideous smell rose from the decaying carcass. Danford pulled back from it in disgust, then saw the greenish yellow pus clinging to its fur ... and to his hand that had slid across the animal's remains.

"What's goin' on—*yeeoow!*"

A savage pain tore through Danford's left calf. He rolled over and kicked, but the spike-toothed animal sank its uneven teeth deeper into his leg and held on, refusing to give up its hold.

"Lo-ret-ta!"

Danford shook his left leg frantically, then kicked the animal with his right foot. Still, the creature clung to its prey, its tiny dark eyes meeting Danford's in a deadly gaze.

"What are you?" he screamed. "Where did you come from—"

A growl ... a howl ... a hiss.

Danford turned his head sharply and again looked toward the nearby underbrush. Now, almost a dozen pairs of glistening dark eyes stared back at him ... and like an army following a command, the creatures behind the eyes all stepped out in the open.

Danford's eyes darted from one to the next. A cat ... a 'possum ... a rabbit ... a dog ... a raccoon. They were all animals he knew, and yet, they were all animals he could barely recognize. Each was grotesquely malformed—misshapen—an unearthly combination of creatures never meant to be.

"Go away!" he shouted. Frantic, Danford looked around for something—anything—he might be able to use to protect himself. A small branch lay on the ground some six feet away.

It wasn't much, but—

Danford rolled over and reached for the branch. As if his movement had been a signal, the creatures from the underbrush charged. They were on him in an instant, scratching . . . nipping . . . biting . . . gnawing.

Danford flung his arms desperately, trying to drive them off, but his actions were to no avail. He didn't even maintain control long enough to reach the branch. His cries—screams—echoed throughout the chicken yard, but eventually, the sounds faded, captured by the new spring foliage rustling gently overhead.


*1:21 P.M.*

Jackie looked up from her seat in the back of the limousine at the young man who had taken on the role as her escort. He nodded, she smiled, then she took his proffered hand and pulled on it slightly as she stepped out onto the sidewalk.

"On behalf of the governor," he said, with a broad campaign-poster smile, "please allow me to extend my apologies for having to cut the luncheon short today."

Jackie glanced at the official name tag on his lapel—*Ellis Motley    Capital Security*—then met his gaze. "Mr. Motley, please assure the governor, I understand the situation completely," she said, returning a smile not nearly as broad as his. "Thank you for bringing me here. I hope it didn't take you out of your way."

"It was no bother at all. Would you like for me to accompany you inside?" he asked as he released her hand and stepped to the side, opening an unobstructed path to the city/county building.

Jackie looked past him to the front door of the building that housed both the city police and the county sheriff's departments. After a brief hesitation, she let her eyes travel up the three stories of the building's front, anticipating her destination.

"I think I can make it all right from here," she said, glancing back at Ellis Motley. "Thank you again for the ride across town."

"The pleasure was indeed mine." He paused, then added, "Any time I can be of service, please don't hesitate to contact me. I can be reached through the governor's office."

"Yes, thank you. Good-bye."

Jackie smiled to herself as she walked toward the marble steps leading up to the building's front entrance. No matter how often she had been involved—or might be involved in the future—with official events, she knew she would never get used to the pomp and circumstance surrounding political affairs. She was a down-home, country-bred girl, raised on truth and straightforwardness, and anything else always seemed fake—

Rex Joseph pushed open the door just as she reached for the handle. "Jackie," he said with a note of surprise, "what brings you into our fair city in the middle of the day?" he asked, stepping to the side and holding the door open for her.

"In all honesty, I came here looking for a ride home," she answered, not wanting to expound on the luncheon or the reason for its abrupt end. "Is Barry still here?"

"I think he's around somewhere. We haven't had a very busy morning, so I imagine he's upstairs, trying to catch up on some paperwork for the FOP. Do you know where his desk is?"

"On the third floor, isn't it?"

Joseph nodded. "If he's not there, ask around, and sooner or later, you'll find somebody who can point you in the right direction. I'd take you up myself, but I've got to run. Mary just called and wants me to stop by the house. Something about one of the grandkids falling out of a swing."

"I hope it's nothing serious."

"If it's going to be anything serious, it'll be Mary having a fit." He chuckled. "She can't stand to see any of them even get a scratch." Joseph shook his head. "I don't know how she survived our three—and believe me, every one of them had more than an occasional scratch . . . Well, got to go. I'll talk with you sometime later."

Joseph lifted a hand, touched the brim of his hat, nodded, then turned and hurried down the steps. Jackie watched him until he got into his squad car and sped away, then she grinned to herself and turned and walked into the building.

She glanced around the massive foyer as she walked toward the elevators in the back left corner of the room. In the past, she'd seen a variety of activities taking place at the front desks of both the city police and the county sheriff's department, but today, everything was quiet. No one loitered; there wasn't even a rambling of idle chatter.

Jackie waited for the elevator doors to open, then stepped inside an empty car. The ride from the first floor to the third was quick. In a matter of seconds, the doors opened to a huge room housing the main office of the county sheriff's department. A few desks directly opposite the elevator were occupied, but other than that, the activity there was no different from the first-floor foyer; everything was quiet. Sheriff Joseph had been correct when he'd said they hadn't had a very busy morning.

"He's over there in the back." Jackie glanced in the direction of the voice and saw Joyce Wilhite, Sheriff Joseph's secretary, pointing toward the back part of the room. Jackie nodded at Joyce and smiled, then looked down the narrow aisle in front of her that separated a multitude of desks, almost equally, on either side of the room.

Way in the back, sitting at the last desk on the left with his back against the wall, was Barry. He looked busy—at least he was occupied—shuffling through a stack of papers. He was unaware of Jackie's approach.

"Rough life," Jackie said teasingly as she stepped up to the desk.

"It's a tough job, but somebody's got to do it." Barry had used the line so often, he responded without even thinking about what he was saying. When he looked up and saw Jackie standing next to him, a frown creased his brow. Puzzled, he leaned back in his chair, cocked his head to one side, and looked up at her out of the corner of his eye. "It's not that I'm not happy to see you, but what are you doing here?"

"I came to bum a ride home . . . that is, if you're not too busy to take me," she added with a mockish grin, glancing around the room.

"What happened?" Barry asked curiously. "I thought you and Dan— Dan didn't try anything, did he?" he added abruptly.

"No, it's much more bizarre than that."

"What happened?" Barry asked, leaning forward in his chair.

"Are you busy?" Jackie asked, nodding at the stack of papers on the desk in front of him.

"It's nothing I can't finish later."

"Then how would you like to take a pleasant little drive out in the country, and while you're taking me home, I'll fill you in on what went on at the governor's luncheon."


*1:45 P.M.*

Hollie Bass stood just a few feet away from the open panel door behind Leland Wagner's desk. Looking into the secret room—scanning the empty cages—she smiled. One week ago, those cages had been filled with over a dozen innocent animals . . . animals that were all now free. Hollie felt proud that she had been involved with restoring their freedom, even if it had only been in a small way.

A sharp sound echoed in the hallway behind her. Hollie's heart thumped, and she turned with a start to focus on the hall door.

What was it? *Who* was out there?

Dr. Wagner was scheduled to be gone all day to a conference, and he had said he doubted if he'd return to the office before going home. Hollie glanced at the clock above the hallway door. But even if he'd changed his mind and decided to come in to the lab, it was too early in the day for him to be returning. But . . . but what if it *was* him?

What could she tell him? What excuse could she use for being in his office? What— Hollie glanced around the room in desperation and then looked at Wagner's desk. *Phone messages.* The thought came to her almost at the same instant she focused on the telephone.

Hollie thought for only a moment, then she picked up a pen and scribbled the names of two colleagues who had called the lab that morning. Even though Dr. Wagner didn't approve of anyone being in his office during his absence, if it *was* him out in the hall, maybe Hollie could justify her presence with the alibi of delivering phone messages—

Another sound split the silence. Hollie's eyes again shot toward the door. She expected to see Dr. Wagner step into the room, but no one was there. She waited a few seconds . . . still, no one entered the room. A frown slowly etched across Hollie's brow. If it wasn't Dr. Wagner out in the hallway, then someone else was on the third floor—and Hollie was curious to find out who it was.

Walking on her tiptoes, Hollie crossed the room. She stopped at the door, took in a deep breath, then cautiously peeked around the doorframe and looked out into the hall. No one was standing there to return her glance.

Puzzled, Hollie stepped out into the hall, looked to her left and then to her right. She eyed the three doors further down the hall, hesitated, then began walking toward them. If she remembered correctly, she thought the first two doors opened into unoccupied offices, but the third door— She just couldn't remember. She hadn't ventured down the hallway since she'd first been hired over a year ago. There had been no need; no one had ever summoned her there.

As Hollie neared the third door, she could see that it was ajar. She stopped for a moment, took in another deep breath, then continued on cautiously. Who was in the room behind the third door? Should she call security? Should she—

Hollie sidestepped up close to the wall, then leaned forward just far enough so she could look inside the room. She saw a man dressed in a lab coat, but since his back was to her and he was standing hunched over a lab table, she couldn't readily identify him.

On the floor beside the man she saw a blood-splattered towel. The towel was partially spread open; it covered a tray containing some type of fleshy, furry mass Hollie couldn't readily identify. Perhaps, when the tray had fallen from the table onto the tiled floor, *that* had been the sound that had attracted her attention.

The man turned. Hollie immediately recognized his profile.

"Warren?" she questioned, stepping out into the doorway now that she knew she had nothing to fear.

Warren cried out meekly and gasped in surprise as he turned toward her. The expression on his face startled Hollie, and it prompted her to take a step backward in retreat. The expression unnerved her and yet, she couldn't describe it, but she knew it was more than just one of surprise. It relayed dismay, frustration . . . and fear.

"Is . . . is something wrong?" Hollie asked hesitantly, glancing from Warren to the partially concealed furry mass on the tray on the floor. "Did you do an experiment," she asked, looking back at him, "and have something go wrong?"

"Wrong?" Warren's eyes widened and he began to shake his head. "Everything's gone wrong. It's . . . it's as close to a tragedy as I've ever come in my entire life." He looked down at the tray on the floor and concentrated on the legs of the mouse that were sticking out from beneath the towel. "A tragedy . . . but at least now, I think I know why they died." His voice trembled. "I think I finally figured out what killed them." He looked back at Hollie.

"What was it?" she asked barely above a whisper, eyeing the creature on the tray as she took a couple of steps toward it. "What kind of animal were you experimenting with?"

"A mouse."

"*That* was a mouse?" Hollie questioned in disbelief, taking a couple more steps toward it. "What . . . what happened to it?"

"I just have a theory right now, but I'm sure a few more tests will back it up." Warren paused. "But in all honesty, I'm almost afraid to run any more tests. I really don't think I *want* to verify my theory."

"What happened to it?" Hollie asked again as she leaned over to have a closer look at the mouse.

"I don't want to run any more tests, but I should . . . I *have* to." Warren returned his attention to the test tubes and microscope on the lab table beside him. "If I can't verify it, maybe Dr. Wagner can find something in his notes that would apply." He was speaking to himself now, totally ignoring Hollie's presence. "Maybe he can find an antidote—"

"Warren!" Hollie said forcefully, placing her hand on his arm. Warren again turned toward her with a start, and their eyes met. "What happened to it?" she asked in a calmer voice. "What happened to the mouse?"

"A tragedy," he finally answered, "a very unfortunate experimental tragedy." Warren scooped the mouse up off the floor, laid it beside its companion on the table, then wrapped both mice together in a towel. Holding the bundle in one hand, he slipped his notebook under that arm and used his other hand to direct Hollie toward the door. "I'm tired. I have a few things I need to finish downstairs, and then I'm going to go home for the rest of the day. If Leland happens to come back to the lab and wonder where I am, tell him I went home sick or something."

"Are you going to tell me what happened to the mouse?" Hollie persisted as she walked beside him down the hall.

Warren looked at her but didn't answer. For the moment, his theory was too scary—even for him—and he didn't have the strength to put it into words. He wondered if he ever would.

But of one thing, he *was* sure. As soon as he got home, he was going out to the barn and destroy every last vial of the serum. *That* would be the easy part. Confronting Dan Patton wouldn't be quite so easy.


*2:14 P.M.*

"I'd suspected it all along, but when the mayor told me the governor wanted Dan and me to go to the ball together, I knew for sure the whole thing had been a setup from day one." Jackie leaned her head back against the seat, closed her eyes, and exhaled a heavy sigh. "I wonder how much Dan's contributing to the governor's favorite cause to get him to play along."

"So, are you going to go?" Barry asked, glancing at Jackie.

"I don't think I have a choice . . . not if I have any hopes of saving the compound," she added. "I really think he'd take it away just to be spiteful." The dappled rays of the early afternoon sun, coming in through the side window, formed dancing shadows on the inside of Jackie's eyelids. She watched them in silence for several moments, then said, "So you've never heard anything about Dan having epilepsy either."

"Not that I remember."

"You know, it was really strange." Jackie sat up in the seat, glanced at Barry, then focused out the windshield, trying to picture in her mind the events that had taken place at the luncheon. "He was just sitting there, talking like any normal person, and then all of a sudden—" Something ran out of the woods onto the road. "Look out!" Jackie shouted, instinctively reaching for the dash to brace herself for an impact.

Reacting on sheer reflexes, Barry braked and turned the wheel hard to the left, trying to avoid hitting the animal. The car swerved; the back end started to fishtail. He lifted his foot off the brake for an instant, then began pumping the pedal. As he turned the wheel back to the right, he brought the car under control.

In a split second, the incident was over, and the animal was gone. Barry straightened the car out on the road, then pulled off onto the shoulder and stopped.

"Did you see that?" he asked, turning sharply in his seat to stare at the spot where the animal had reentered the woods on the opposite side of the road.

"I saw . . . something," Jackie answered uncertainly, turning almost completely around in her seat to look out the back window, "but I'm not exactly sure what it was."

"Do you think it could have been a ground hog?"

"Maybe . . ." Jackie shook her head. "But I doubt it. It was too big for a ground hog. It looked more the size of a . . . half-grown bear." Then she looked at Barry in question. "Was it just me . . . or did you see it too?"

"Did I see what?" he asked, looking at Jackie as if she could verify something he, himself, hadn't been sure of.

"It went by so fast, I couldn't tell for sure, but it looked like it had a . . . a *beak*."

Barry continued to look at her, his eyebrows knitting his forehead into a frown. "A beak, you say?" Jackie nodded. "I didn't see a beak . . ." he hesitated, "but it might make sense," he added with his own note of uncertainty.

"What might make sense?" Jackie returned Barry's confused look. "Why would it make any sense whatsoever for a furred animal to have a beak? We're on the wrong continent to be seeing a platypus—"

"I know, but a beak would make about as much sense as what I thought I saw." Jackie looked at Barry in question, waiting for an explanation. "I know it doesn't make any more sense than a beak would, but I thought I saw a small winglike projection growing out of its side."

"A wing?" Jackie looked toward the woods where the animal had disappeared. "A furred animal with a beak and a wing . . ." she said, barely louder than a whisper.

As if identical thoughts crossed their minds at the same instant, their eyes locked and they verbalized speculations in unison. "The break-ins."

"The stolen laboratory animals."

"But everyone we talked to told us all the animals taken were clean," Jackie said.

"Obviously, somebody lied."

"Or maybe it was brought in here from someplace else and let go in the woods."

"I doubt it. Whatever it was," Barry said, remembering his last conversation with Denis Sweezy, "it looked more wild than domestic. Whoever had it probably thought it could fit in with the wildlife out here and didn't drive any farther than they had to before setting it loose."

"And the closest laboratory around here that was broken into is . . ."

"Patton Pharmaceutical."

"... and Dr. Leland Wagner," Jackie added in a disgusted tone. "I told you I've had a funny feeling about him."

"Then I think our dear doctor has some more questions to answer. Are you in a hurry to get home?"

"If that animal was anything even *close* to what we thought we saw, I'm in a hurry to find out what's going on around here—"

"Two. Dearborn County." A voice from the police radio broke into their conversation.

"Robbins here," Barry answered into the microphone.

"Two and passenger dispatched to the Danford Dunn residence up on Haggerty Ridge."

"Two *and* passenger?" Barry questioned, glancing at Jackie, shrugging his shoulders and raising his eyebrows in question.

"Don't give me any lip, Barry," the female radio operator retorted. "I'm just passing on the request for personnel. Something's going on up on Haggerty Ridge, and since there're animals involved, the sheriff told me to send you and Mrs. Mitchell up there."

"Animals?"

"That's what I said."

Jackie leaned across the seat and spoke into the microphone. "Do you have any idea what's happened?"

"I didn't receive any details other than they found a couple of dead animals with numbers tattooed inside their ears."

"Numbers?" Barry questioned.

"Lab animals," Jackie speculated. She turned in the seat and looked out the back window at the woods where the strange-looking animal had disappeared. "Haggerty Ridge," she said, glancing at Barry. "That's clear over on the other side of the county."

"On the *far* side. And there are more hills and valleys than flat land between here and there."

"Then if what I'm thinking actually happened, somebody

must have done a lot of driving the night they let those animals loose."

"Or maybe there was more than one driver in the area."

"Let's hope that's not the case," Jackie said. "If there was more than one driver, then that probably means they were turning loose animals from several different places . . . and I'd hate to think we were talking about more than one lab that wasn't being honest with us about whether their animals were clean or not."

*2:27 P.M.*

"Someone's going to see us," Rusty Snider said, glancing toward the windows in Warren Maxey's neighbor's house. During his brief survey, he lagged behind, and then had to lengthen his strides to catch up with Dan.

"At this time of day, I'd lay odds, nobody's at home in this entire housing addition," Dan said in reply. "This is the kind of place where people buy in way over their heads, then the husband and wife both have to work full-time just to even come close to making ends meet." They rounded the back corner of Warren's house, then angled diagonally across the yard toward the small barn. "But even if somebody would see us, who cares? As long as we look like we know what we're doing . . ." Dan shot Rusty a glance out of the corner of his eye. "Even if we *don't* look like we know what we're doing, nobody's going to stop me. I'm already in this thing too far to let anybody get in my way." He glanced at the bulge beneath Rusty's left arm, knowing full well a .357 Magnum was holstered there beneath Rusty's jacket. "And *you* won't let anybody get in my way either, will you?" he asked, meeting Rusty's green eyes. Rusty hesitated, then took in a breath as if to speak, but Dan cut him short. "No, I didn't think you would."

Dan slowed his pace, then stopped opposite the barn's door. He reached above the frame and slid his fingers along the horizontal surface. He found the nail, but he wasn't able to locate the key. "It's not . . . here," he said with a break in his voice.

"What are you looking for?" Rusty asked, watching Dan as he reached above the door with both hands.

"The key!" Dan shouted. After a futile search, he stepped back and knotted his fists in frustration. "See if you can find it!" he demanded.

Rusty reached above the doorframe and slid his hand from left to right along the upper edge. "There's nothing up there," he said, looking at Dan and shaking his head.

"Not there. Not there!" Dan repeated with increased volume.

He lifted his fists in front of him and shook them viciously, then his eyes widened, and an inner madness seemed to explode from just beneath the surface. Without calculating his actions, he took a couple of steps backward, then charged the door, shouldering his weight against it. The weathered half-inch plywood splintered without too much resistance. Dan stumbled into the heart of the small lab.

Driven by rage, he picked up an empty cage and threw it . . . then another . . . and another. He bumped into a stool . . . and threw it. He—

As quickly as the frenzy had erupted, it subsided. Dan stood in the center of the room . . . panting.

"Are you all right?" Rusty asked hesitantly, stepping over the splintered door into the barn.

"I'm going to be perfect before too much longer." Dan focused on the small refrigerator on the far side of the lab, took in a deep breath, and walked directly toward it. Without hesitating, he opened the door, pulled out a rack containing four full vials of serum and one vial half full. He carried the rack to the worktable, set it down, and turned on the overhead light. "A needle," Dan mumbled as he took off his suit jacket and began rolling up his left shirt sleeve. "I need a needle." He looked at the shelves on the wall in front of him, then scanned the worktable. Nothing. "I need a needle!" he shouted.

"Dan, don't you think you're pushing this—"

"I want a needle!" Dan began rummaging through boxes on the shelves to his left, throwing unwanted items haphazardly off to the side. When he didn't find what he was looking for, he swept everything off the shelf with one quick swing of his arm. "There have to be some needles in here." He opened the doors to the cabinet to the right of the worktable. A blue box, labeled *Sterile Syringes*, stood out against the cabinet's white background.

Dan grabbed the box, set it down on the worktable, and took out a single syringe wrapped in clear cellophane. "Find me something elastic," he told Rusty, then Dan hurriedly ripped into the corner of the syringe's wrapping with his teeth.

"What?" Rusty asked in uncertainty.

"Anything," Dan said, "anything," he repeated, looking around the room. "There"—he pointed—"on the wall there, that tubing. Is it stretchy?"

Rusty picked up the coil of surgical tubing from a hook at the far end of the worktable. Holding on to one end, he pulled on a section of the tubing and immediately found elastic resistance. "It'll stretch a little," he answered.

"Cut me off a piece a couple of feet long."

While Rusty found a knife and cut the tubing, Dan filled the syringe with as much serum as it would hold and then laid it on the table. Both finished their tasks within a few seconds of each other.

"Let me have it," Dan said, extending a hand to Rusty, palm up.

Rusty glanced from Dan's eyes to Dan's hand to the section

of surgical tubing he held in his own hand. He knew what was about to take place, and he wondered—

"I said, let me have it!" Dan demanded. Impatient with Rusty's slow response, he yanked the piece of tubing out of Rusty's hand.

Working with the speed of an addict long overdue for a fix, Dan wrapped the tubing around his upper left arm and pulled it tight with his teeth. He focused on the vein just inside his elbow—on the vein that was already marked with telltale bruises and puncture marks from previous injections—thumped it a couple of times with his forefinger and watched it swell. A smile of triumph tightened his lips.

"Now," Dan said as he reached for the filled syringe, "in just a few seconds, I'll have the essence of re-creation pulsing through my veins."

"Dan, are you sure you should—"

Before Rusty could finish his caution, Dan plunged the needle into his vein and pushed down on the syringe's plunger, forcing the serum out of the calibrated cylinder. When he was finished, he pulled out the needle, untied the tubing, and leaned against the worktable. Dan released a sigh as he closed his eyes and let his head drop back. He thought he could actually feel the cool serum working its way through his bloodstream.

"Again," Dan whispered as if he were in a dream.

"What did you say?" Rusty asked, watching him closely.

"I said again," Dan repeated louder, lifting his head and looking at Rusty. "I want it again." He took another syringe out of the blue box and filled it with the remaining serum from the vial that had begun as only half full. He looked across the top of the worktable, searching for the tubing, then located it on the floor near his feet. When Dan bent over to pick up the tubing, he swayed and had to support himself with a hand on the table.

"Are you okay?" Rusty asked, stepping in close to Dan and taking a firm hold of his arm.

"I'm going to be just fine after another injection," Dan said as he straightened beside the table.

"Don't do it. I don't think you need any more—"

"Think? Nobody keeps you around to think!" Dan shouted as he pulled his arm free. "You're kept around for the muscles on your arms—not for the muscle between your ears." Without any further hesitation, Dan repeated the procedure and injected another syringeful of serum directly into his bloodstream. When he finished, he again leaned against the table, closed his eyes, and smiled.

"The more, the better," he whispered. "That's the way it will always be." For several silent moments, Dan just stood there, his head tilted back, his eyes closed, and a smile on his face.

"Make sure we have all the vials out of the refrigerator," Dan finally said in a dreamy tone. "We're going to have to tell our good friend, Warren, we're in need of an additional supply." He laughed; the sound vibrated with a maniacal tone. "Soon, I'll have my legs back . . . then won't Jackie be surprised," he said, not following a single thought pattern but picking up on any fragment passing through his mind. "Did you get all the vials?" Dan lifted his head and opened his eyes to narrow slits to see Rusty taking a rack of six vials out of the refrigerator. "When I get my legs back . . . Is that all that's in there?" Rusty looked at Dan and nodded. ". . . I'll get her back too. Don't leave these," he said, motioning to the rack on the worktable. "We're going to have to find something to do with Barry." Dan rolled his head back and let it circle loosely over his shoulders. ". . . and that brat kid of hers." He laughed again. "It may not be as easy as before . . ."

Dan lifted his arms up over his head, as if reaching for the ceiling, then lowered one hand in front of his face and studied it. "Oh look," he said, pointing to the back of his hand, "I cut my hand . . . when I broke down the door. Oh, look. Look!" he said, taking a couple of unstable steps toward Rusty. "Look at it, it's already starting to heal—" A grimace overtook Dan's face. He grabbed for his stomach and doubled over in pain.

"Dan?" Rusty reached for Dan and caught him just before he fell. "Dan, what's wrong?"

"N-n-nothing's wrong," Dan gasped. "The . . . the serum's just starting to . . . work. That's all. Take . . . take me home, and I'll be . . . all right."

Rusty gathered Dan up in his arms and carried him back to the car. He would take Dan home and watch over him like he'd done in the past, but Rusty doubted—this time—if everything would be all right.


*3:44 P.M.*

Terry Neville, from the sheriff's department, met Jackie and Barry at the road at the base of the hill. "I've been with the department for over seven years," he said, walking with them up the lane to the Dunns', "and I've never seen anything like it."

"Can you speculate on what might have happened?" Barry asked.

"There's no speculation to it. It's plain and simple: the animals killed them. They bit those people over a hundred times—until they bled to death—and then, they chewed on the bodies until—for some unknown reason—the animals died themselves. Funny." Neville shook his head. "Well, maybe funny isn't the right word to use in a case like this. Strange would be more like it."

"What's so strange?"

"Some of the animals—that is, the ones I got close enough to see— I'll tell you one thing, they sure did stink. And that was funny too. I've never been around animals that stunk as bad as that unless they'd been dead for a while, but these animals couldn't have been dead long enough to smell as bad as they did. Why, the flies hadn't even begun to swarm yet, and Phil"—Neville sneered and wrinkled his nose—"Phil said he found a couple that were still twitching . . . that is, whatever parts of them were still left in one piece."

"In one piece?" Jackie questioned.

"Yeah, that was what I started to tell you before I got sidetracked on the smell. Some of the animals look like they . . . well, I can't think of a better word for it than to say they *exploded*." Neville used his hands in broad gestures to dramatize his words. "It looked like they just kept getting bigger . . . and bigger . . . and bigger until their skins couldn't hold their insides anymore and they just popped open. They exploded, plain and simple."

Barry looked at Jackie, a frown dominating his face. "Any ideas on what might cause something like that to happen?"

Jackie shook her head. "I doubt if anybody could put a finger on it without running some lab tests."

"I imagine Doc Calvin's going to have a heyday with this one when he gets around to it. Who found the Dunns?" Barry asked, looking back at Neville.

"Vaughn Simon. He's the preacher from the little church farther up on the ridge. He and his wife came down to the Dunns' for a visit before dinner, and they found them both out in the yard."

"Is he still up here so we can have a talk with him?"

"No. The Dunns don't have a phone, so Simon had to go back to his house to call it in. He and his wife are still there as far as I know. I think Fred Anderson went over to get a statement from them—"

"Geez!" Barry pulled up short at the edge of the clearing marking the Dunns' yard. He coughed forcefully and tried to limit his breaths to shallow gasps, but still, he felt as if he was going to gag.

"The smell gets worse the farther in you go," Neville warned, making a face of his own in disgust.

"Then let's get in and get out of here in a hurry."

Neville led the way, showing them first the remains of Danford Dunn and then those of his wife, Loretta. At the far edge of the clearing, he pointed out what looked like the remains of a brown and white rabbit. It had a tattooed number clearly visible inside its right ear. Once they made a complete survey of the scene, Jackie took a few minutes to take a closer look at a couple of the animals, then they left the clearing.

"Any ideas now?" Barry asked as they walked down the lane.

Jackie looked up at him and shook her head. "But I will be interested in seeing the lab reports on the animals . . . and I did write down the tattoo numbers so I can check them against the files at the office. If Wagner or anyone at Bailey College lied to us about their animals being contaminated, we'll be able to pin them down in a hurry." They walked on for several yards, then Jackie shook her head again and said, "You know, it just doesn't make sense to me about the animals . . . their condition, that is." Barry looked at her but didn't verbally question. He knew she would tell him what she was thinking whether he asked or not. "Logic tells me that for an animal to have as much pus in its body as those did back there, they would have had to have had some kind of serious infection for quite some time. But none of those animals looked like they'd been sick."

"How can you tell?"

"For one thing, they weren't skinny. The herbivores were plump, and it didn't look like the carnivores had had any trouble finding prey in the woods. They were just as fat. And another thing, I couldn't find any wounds or open sores, on the animals I took a quick look at, that would have been the prime source for an infection." She shook her head again in bewilderment. "No, for something as massive as took place in those animals, I'd almost have to say their metabolism had gone berserk and their bodies were mass-producing white blood cells for some other reason."

"For some other reason?" Jackie looked at Barry and nodded. "Some other reason like . . . an experiment?" Jackie nodded again. "I think we need to take a detour on the way back to the compound. It might prove to be beneficial if we stop by Patton Laboratory and have a word or two with Dr. Leland Wagner."

*4:22 P.M.*

Warren turned the key, pushed the door open, and hurried across the kitchen toward the living room. He'd heard the phone ringing as he'd stepped out of the car in the garage; so far, it had rung over a half-dozen times. He wondered if whoever was calling had the patience to wait through one more ring—

"Hello," he answered breathlessly, even before he had the phone to his mouth.

There was a brief silence, then someone said, " Mr. Maxey?"

"Yes," Warren answered a bit hesitantly as he sat down on the edge of the sofa. No one ever called him *Mr.* Maxey unless it was a salesman or someone taking a survey. Ordinarily, Warren didn't mind answering questions for a survey, but he hated to talk with salesmen.

"Mr. Maxey, I'm Rusty Snider. You may not remember me, but I work for Dan Patton. We met in a rather strange sort of way several days ago when you came out to the house to see Dan."

A shiver inched down Warren's spine, and he inhaled with a noiseless gasp. Several seconds ticked off the grandfather clock in the hallway before he responded. "Yes . . . yes, I remember. What can I do for you?"

"It's Dan." Rusty hesitated. He was as unsure of himself as he was of Warren. "I . . . I think he's sick. Well, he's not *sick* exactly, but he's . . . well, he's taken a large dose of the serum you gave him— Oh hell, you're going to find out sooner or later. Dan and I broke into the lab at your home this afternoon, and we took the rest of the serum you had stored out there in the refrigerator." Warren gasped louder this time and almost dropped the phone. "He's been injecting himself with extremely high doses of serum more often than I think is wise. For the past couple of days, he's had bouts with severe abdominal pain, and he's been shaking and chilling and . . . and there have even been times when he's blacked out, and he doesn't know what he's doing." Rusty paused, then said, "I'm worried about him, Mr. Maxey. I'm afraid something might be wrong, and I was wondering if there's anything I can do for him? Is there some kind of antidote I can get from you that would reverse the effects of the serum?" Warren didn't respond. "Mr. Maxey? Are you still there?" Warren's grip on the phone loosened, and it slipped out of his hand onto the sofa's cushion. "Mr. Maxey? Mr. Maxey . . ."

Warren sat in silence, staring out the front window, not seeing anything beyond the pane . . . just staring. What had he done? Dear God in heaven! What had he done?

Slowly, his eyes settled on the towel-wrapped bundle he still clutched in one hand. The mice. They were fortunate. They were dead.

*5:03 P.M.*

Jackie and Barry stopped at the top of the parking-lot steps and looked toward the entrance of Patton Pharmaceutical Laboratories. The sun was setting far to the west, but a lingering hint of its presence touched the amber glass fronting the building, making it appear as if the building were on fire.

Barry glanced at his watch. "Do you think anybody'll still be here?"

"Aw, the pleasures of a nine-to-five job," Jackie said sarcastically. "I don't think either one of us would know how to act if we had one."

As they started along the walk toward the entrance canopy, the front door opened and someone came out. "Who's that?" Barry asked.

"Hollie Bass, the combined receptionist and all-around girl Friday. You saw her when we were here the other day."

"Do you think she'd know anything about the animals?"

"Who's to say? Hollie," Jackie called out as they approached each other, "is Dr. Wagner still here?" she asked as she stopped opposite Hollie in front of the entrance.

"He hasn't been here all day," Hollie answered. "He's been gone to a conference in Indianapolis."

"Is Warren Maxey here by any chance?"

"No," Hollie answered, shaking her head. "He wasn't feeling well this afternoon and decided to go home early."

"Is there anyone else left in the building?" Barry asked, a bit frustrated.

"Just George Beals, the night watchman." Hollie looked at Barry, then directed her question to Jackie. "Is something the matter? Maybe I can help."

Jackie glanced at Barry then said, "The animals that were taken during the break-in last week . . ." She paused.

"Yes." Hollie prodded, "What about them?"

"Were they all clean?"

"As far as I know. They'd only been here a few days, so I doubt if—" Hollie tilted her head to the side and looked at Jackie out of the corner of her eye. "I thought you asked all of these questions during your investigation."

"We did," Barry answered, "but something new has surfaced, and we were wanting to retrace a few steps."

"Something new?" Hollie asked curiously. "And you think it might have something to do with our animals?"

"When do you think we might be able to talk with Dr. Wagner?" Barry asked, sidestepping her question.

"As late in the day as it is now, I doubt if he comes back to the lab until Monday."

"Was the conference in Indianapolis to last all day?"

"As far as I know."

"When do you think we might be able to reach him at home?"

Hollie glanced at her watch. "Oh, probably just about any time now, I guess. Most all-day conferences really don't last all day; they usually come to a close between three and four unless there's a dinner speaker, and I don't remember making a reservation for him for dinner. I could go back in and call his home for you," she offered.

"We'd appreciate it if you would. It might save us an out-of-the-way drive."

As they walked into the building, Jackie asked, "Did you say Warren went home sick?"

"I think it was a headache or something," Hollie answered evasively. "What's new concerning the break-ins you're looking into?" she countered with her own question.

"Just a few discrepancies here and there," Barry answered vaguely.

"Concerning the stolen animals?" Hollie asked almost too abruptly.

273

"It could be." Barry eyed her, noting her reaction. "Did you remember something you might have missed telling us about before?"

"No. No, I don't remember anything. I'll go make that phone call for you and be back in a few minutes." Hollie turned sharply to her right and walked across the lobby to the reception desk, leaving Barry and Jackie standing just inside the entrance.

"She knows something she's not telling us," Barry said softly as he watched Hollie out of the corner of his eye.

"That wouldn't surprise me." Jackie paused. "The way things have been popping up from out of nowhere, I have a feeling nothing's going to surprise me by the time all of this is over."

As Hollie dialed the number for Leland Wagner's home and then listened to the phone ring, she made plans for a detour on her own way home. It wasn't much out of her way to swing past Warren's house, and she was quite sure he would be interested in knowing that the authorities had been asking questions about . . . well, she would just call them *his* animals.

5:09 P.M.

Sweat pumped from Dan's pores, bathing him in a warm dampness that was quickly followed by an icy chill. His breaths were quick and shallow. Blood surged through his veins; his pulse pounded loudly in his ears. As he released the temporary tourniquet from his upper arm, he thought he could feel the serum cells actually attach themselves to his own blood cells and then speed off to various parts of his body, seeking a defect in need of repair.

After all the serum was pushed out of the syringe, he pulled the needle from his arm and watched in mystified amazement as the tiny puncture wound closed in front of his eyes and became crowned by a knob of scar tissue. To Dan, that was proof enough the serum was working; even the tiniest flaws—the tiniest imperfections throughout his body—were being repaired.

Dan dropped the syringe on the bathroom counter, then lifted his head so he could look into the mirror above the sink. Hollow, sunken eyes stared back at him. Ringed with dark flesh and mapped with gorged vessels, their surrealistic state conjured up visions of destruction and death instead of re-creation and life.

During the past two and a half hours, Dan had pursued the philosophy *The more the better*. At half-hour intervals, he'd injected half a vial of serum directly into his bloodstream; at that rate, he'd receive the final dose in just a few more hours.

"More." Dan focused on his mouth in the mirror, mesmerized by the way his lips moved as they formed the words he spoke. He watched his lips. He watched a streamer of saliva slip past its bounds and slither down his chin . . . to dangle and then stick to his shirt. "I . . . more. I need . . . tell Maxey . . . more." For the moment, Dan's speech was following the same broken thought patterns that were ricocheting back and forth across his brain.

Fascinated—and, at the same time, trying to make some kind of connection between the movements of his lips and the sounds coming from his mouth—Dan reached toward the mirror to touch his reflected lips. As his hand moved into his line of vision, he noticed something different . . . something strange. The wound on the back of his hand—the wound he'd gotten that afternoon when he'd broken into Warren Maxey's lab—had healed . . . had healed—not just as a mass of scarred flesh—but as a jumbled collection of irregularly shaped . . . *scales!* And the scales had spread far beyond the boundary of the wound. The entire back of his hand . . . was beginning to look *reptilian*—

A stabbing—fire hot—pain ripped through Dan's stomach. He screamed in agony, then dropped to his knees, clutching his abdomen so savagely his fingers became almost instantly numb. He fell over onto his side, striking his head hard against the tiled floor. Coiling into the fetal position, Dan began to shake violently.

With each heartbeat, intense pain tore through his body. In response to the pain, an arm jerked out from his side and recoiled fiercely . . . an arm . . . then a leg. His back arched into an impossible contortion, throwing his head back to nearly touch the base of his spine. He turned and twisted. Muscles strained; ligaments stretched; tendons tore—

Then, as quickly as it had attacked, the pain was gone.

Dan was totally exhausted. He lay motionless on the bathroom floor.

"Dan?" Rusty knocked anxiously on the door. "Dan, what's going on in there? Are you all right?" He tried to turn the doorknob. It was locked. "Dan!" Rusty pounded on the door with his fist.

"I'm . . . okay," Dan finally managed to say barely loud enough for Rusty to hear.

"Dan, what happened? What's going on?" Receiving no answer, Rusty asked, "You didn't take any more of that serum, did you?"

"Go away," Dan said a little louder. Using his arms for support, he pushed himself up into a sitting position, then dragged himself across the floor so he could lean against the wall.

"Dan—"

"I said, go away!" Dan shouted. "Go away and leave me alone! Go someplace else, and mind your own goddamn business and leave—" Another savage pain attacked him, but this time it bypassed his upper body and drove directly into his legs.

"No!" he screamed. "N-o-o-o! Not again!" Dan fisted his hands and began beating on his thighs. Maybe . . . just maybe he could beat the pain away—

"Dan!" Rusty shouted, again rattling the doorknob to no avail. "What's going on in there? Let me in!"

Dan hit his thighs once . . . twice . . . three times— Each time he struck his legs, the tissue reacted with an instantaneous response. Any place he hit—hurt—bruised—immediately began to heal . . . to regenerate . . . to grow.

Overtaken by fear—not believing his eyes—Dan watched his jeans as they began to stretch . . . and strain . . . then finally rip open at the fabric's weakest grain. A multiplying mass of uncontrolled tissue erupted through the torn denim.

"No!" he shouted. "Go away!" Dan tried to slide away from the monstrous extremities, but his back was already pushed firmly against the wall; he was as far away as he could go . . . and besides, there was no way he could avoid them; they were attached. "Go away!" he shouted in desperation.

"Dan! What's happening?"

The elastic straps holding Dan's prostheses in place stretched to their limits—beyond their limits—then they finally gave way to the strain and snapped. Once the stumps of his legs were freed, they began to grow, fingering out in primitive appendages. Dan was terrified by the runaway regeneraton, but he was also amazed . . . watching his legs grow.

"Dan!" Rusty finally shouldered the door and attacked it with all of his weight; it opened under the strain of the first contact. "Dan, what—" When Rusty saw the disheveled mass of flesh sitting on the floor in front of him, the words lodged in the back of his throat. He was repulsed; he had to fight with his inner self to keep from turning away.

Dan looked up at Rusty with bloodshot eyes, peering out from sunken sockets that had been pushed off-center of his misshapen skull. Confusion shadowed his face. "What happened?" Dan asked with the innocence of a child. He held his scaly hand out to Rusty as if his old friend could touch it and make it well again.

"Oh, Dan . . ." Rusty muttered. All strength ebbed out of him, and he sunk down on the toilet facing Dan. "What have you gone and done to yourself?"

Dan looked from Rusty . . . to his hands . . . and then to his legs. His legs . . .

His left leg was split. From the knee down, he had two calves and two feet that looked remarkably human . . . except for the blotches of heavy hair—fur—and patches of silvery-green iridescent scales. The growth on his right leg had remained a singular appendage, but its circumference was more than twice the normal size . . . and it was longer—almost six inches longer—than his left leg. A misshapen, webbed foot lay on the floor at an awkward angle from the right ankle. Dan's legs were grotesque, but at least for the moment, all growth and regeneration seemed to have stopped.

"What have *I* done?" Dan asked as if he were totally free from blame. "Don't you mean, 'What has *Maxey* done to me?'" He cocked his awkwardly shaped head to one side and looked up at Rusty with green eyes, their pupils beginning to narrow to vertical slits. "I'll tell you what he did. He lied to me. He told me his serum would make everything all right again. He said I'd have my legs back. Well," Dan said, gesturing toward his grotesque legs with his reptilian hand, "do you call *this* all right?"

"You took too much—"

"It shouldn't have mattered." Dan reached for the edge of the counter and took hold of it with both hands. Straining, he pulled himself up and stood for a moment, trying to balance. "It shouldn't have mattered."

"But it did—"

"But it shouldn't have. Don't you see"—he turned to face Rusty—"Maxey lied to me. It's his fault things turned out the way they did, and I'm going to get even with him for it."

"What are you going to do?" Rusty asked, standing to face Dan, fearing he knew the answer.

"I'm going to get even. I'm going to go get him for what he's done to me." Dan took a shaky step toward Rusty, then stopped and looked down at his legs. "I guess I can't fault him for everything," he said with a maniacal laugh. "He *did* give me back my legs." Abruptly, Dan lifted an arm and swung at Rusty, knocking him backward against the wall. "Stay out of my way, and don't try to stop me."


*5:47 P.M.*

Barry rang the front doorbell to Leland Wagner's modest brick ranch home, then looked at Jackie. "I expected the head scientist for Patton Laboratories to have a more elaborate house than this," he said in a low voice as he made a sweeping glance of the exterior.

"I would imagine his portfolio more than makes up for a lack of a fancy home."

The front door opened. Leland made eye contact with Barry and nodded, then he looked at Jackie, but he hesitated a few seconds more before speaking. "Is . . . is something wrong?" he asked with apparent concern.

"Are you *expecting* something to be wrong?" Barry countered, a bit brusquely. He guessed that, all along, Dr. Leland Wagner had known contaminated animals had been taken during the break-ins and, fearing he was about to be confronted about them, Wagner was coming close to losing control.

"My wife . . . and daughter," Leland added with a tremble in his voice. "They flew out this morning to visit relatives in California." He swallowed hard and took in a deep breath before continuing, "No, I'm not really *expecting* anything to be wrong, but when I looked out the window and saw a police car, I . . . well, I guess my mind ran away with itself. Are they all right?" he asked. "My wife and daughter?"

"We're not here about your family," Jackie answered softly, remembering her own torment when she'd received news of Richard's unexpected death. "We would like to ask you a few more questions about the animals that were taken from the lab during the break-ins."

"There's nothing more to say about them," Leland said flatly as he turned away from the door.

Jackie glanced at Barry. What were they going to do if Leland didn't cooperate with them?

Barry didn't appear to care whether Leland was going to be cooperative or not. He grasped the knob on the screen door, opened it, and ushered Jackie inside. "I think there *is* more to be said about them," Barry countered as the door closed behind him. "We've found several animals in various locations throughout the county, and some of them have lab numbers—*your* lab numbers—tattooed in their ears." Barry was stretching the truth; as of yet, they hadn't learned exactly whose lab the numbered animals had come from, but since he was already pushing his luck, he thought he might as well go all the way.

"That's to be expected," Leland said defensively, turning squarely toward them. "All of the animals that were stolen from the lab were marked with one of our ID numbers."

"But you told us all of your animals were clean."

"They were," Leland persisted.

"Then how come some of them are growing beaks . . . and wings . . . and extra legs . . . and are exploding from an overproduction of their own white blood cells?" Barry knew he was now pushing his limited knowledge of the subject to the ultimate limit, but he felt it was the only way to get a reaction out of Wagner. "Some of the ones we've come across so far have looked like creatures out of a John Carpenter nightmare."

"Creatures from a nightmare?" Leland questioned. A look of total confusion enveloped his face. "What are you talking about? You've got to be mistaken." His eyes shifted from Barry to Jackie and back again. "My animals couldn't—" Then, as if a forgotten revelation suddenly surfaced from a far corner of Leland's mind, his face went blank. His skin turned ashen.

"Dr. Wagner?" Jackie asked, taking a step toward him. "Are you all right?" She touched his arm with her hand. When he didn't respond, she led him to the sofa and urged him to sit down. "What's the matter? Please, tell us the truth about your animals."

After several silent moments, Leland turned his head toward Jackie and looked at her—looked deep into her eyes—then he stared out across the room as if he were looking into another time . . . into another dimension. "Not so very long ago," he began slowly, "the strange animals you speak of *could* have been found outside a nightmare. At one time, they . . . they *were* real . . . so very real."

"I thought so," Barry said, looking down at Leland as if he were a father towering over an errant child.

"But no more." Leland glanced at Jackie, then looked up at Barry, his eyes begging to be believed. "They're gone. They're all gone now. They were destroyed—*I* destroyed them—over a year ago. They were all cremated at the lab. I saw to it personally."

"Are you sure you destroyed all of them?" Barry asked skeptically.

"Most certainly. I—" Leland hesitated. "It was a personal experiment," he confessed, "known only to me. I had total control over everything, and I was the only one responsible. I assure you—you must believe me when I tell you—they were all destroyed . . . all of them."

"Is there any way that even one of the animals could have gotten loose?" Jackie asked. "Could one have slipped out and run away into the woods behind the lab and . . . and mated with a compatible species in the wild—"

"No," Leland stated adamantly. "None of the animals were ever out of their cages unless I was in direct contact with them. None of them ever escaped. I know it. And I know they were all destroyed. I made a note on each and every one of them. It's all written down in my journal in my office at the lab."

"What about tissue samples . . . or blood serum?" Jackie asked. "Could they have been misplaced . . . misidentified . . . or misused?"

"No! Never—" Then Leland gasped, and that same ashen shade of gray returned to his face.

"What?" Barry asked, responding quickly to Leland's reaction. "What is it? What are you thinking about?" When Leland didn't answer immediately, Barry added, "There is something else, isn't there?"

"No," Leland said, shaking his head.

"Yes," Barry countered, "there *is* something else. You just thought about something else concerning your animals. Now, what is it? Tell us!"

Leland was silent for a few more moments, then he said, "Maybe . . . I suppose it's possible, but no—"

"What's possible?" Barry demanded.

Leland glanced at Barry and then to Jackie. "But no one from an animal rights group would even consider injecting an animal with . . . with a serum they know nothing about. Would they?"

"A serum?" Jackie asked. "Was some kind of serum taken from your lab?"

"It's possible, but I can't be sure . . . not without going into the lab and checking. Then . . ." he hesitated, "I'm not sure whether I could tell or not anyway. It's been so long since I even took the time to look over the vials."

"What would you be checking for? What was the serum from?"

"The old experiments," he answered in a partial lie. Then Leland looked up at Barry. "But even if someone was foolish enough to take it . . . and then inject it into an animal, it would take weeks—maybe even months—for it to have any effect unless . . . unless—"

"Unless what?" Barry asked.

"Unless it was administered in massive doses."

"What would a massive dose do?"

"Speed up the effects, of course. And . . ."

"And what?" Barry asked impatiently, almost shouting.

"Since most of the serum was old, who's to say how age might have affected it. Oh," Leland said soulfully, "I should have destroyed the serum along with the animals." He paused. "It's kind of strange, but I had that very same thought the morning I discovered the first break-in."

"But I agree with you," Jackie said after a few moments of thought. "No animal rights activist would ever consider injecting an unknown serum into an animal. If anything, they would see that the serum was destroyed."

"So what kind of degenerate *would* consider injecting an animal with an unknown serum?" Barry asked. "Other than a scientist," he added. His attempt at sarcasm was poor, but it registered with all of them.

"Would Warren Maxey be capable of doing something like that?" Jackie asked, looking at Leland directly.

"Who's to say?" Leland answered with a shrug of his shoulders.

"Did Maxey know where you kept the serum?" Barry asked.

"No, no one did . . ." Leland hesitated, ". . . at least, I didn't think anyone knew. But then, if no one else knew where it was, how did they know where to look to find my animals—"

"Where does this Maxey live?" Barry asked.

"Somewhere up in the hills south of the lab. I think it's in the . . . the Morthland Addition," Leland answered. "That sounds right. The Morthland Addition."

"Do you have his street address?"

"I think I have it written down in a book in the den."

"Would you get it for us, please?" Leland nodded, and walked from the living room into an adjacent hall.

Barry glanced at his watch, then focused on Jackie. "It's dinnertime. With any luck, we should be able to catch Maxey at home." He studied Jackie for a moment, then asked, "You said you had a strange feeling about him. Do you think he'd try something like this?"

"I don't know."

"Aren't scientists supposed to work under some kind of code of ethics like doctors do?" Jackie didn't answer verbally, but by the look in her eyes, Barry sensed she doubted if scientists followed any code—ethical or otherwise. Barry shook his head. "You know, Denis Sweezy's animal rights group is looking more and more inviting by the minute—"

"I was right," Leland said as he walked back into the room. "Warren lives up in the Morthland Addition at number three Alberta Court. I've written it down here for you," he added, handing Barry a slip of paper.

"Thank you for your help," Jackie said as she stood up from the sofa.

Leland walked Barry and Jackie to the door and watched as they drove away. Learning about the deformed animals had troubled him, but what bothered him more was the possibility of Warren's involvement. Had his protégé betrayed him? Had

Warren taken off on a tangent of his own?

Then a positive thought crossed Leland's mind. If Warren knew about the secret room in his office and about the serum, could he also know the whereabouts of the stolen animals? Could Warren know where to find the beige and brown dog?

Leland turned abruptly and walked across the living room toward the kitchen—toward the door in the utility room that opened into the garage. If Warren did know something about the missing animals, Leland wanted to be there when he was questioned . . . and to hear all of the answers for himself.

*6:04 P.M.*

Dan was having trouble driving. His hands had changed in physical structure to such an extent that grasping the steering wheel was awkward. His palms looked as if they were swollen or padded with extra layers of fat. The excess tissue all but prevented him from touching his fingertips with his thumb. The scaly, snakelike skin had continued to spread over the back of his right hand; it was stiff and unyielding, further limiting his flexibility. But even if Dan could have closed his fingers into a tight grip, he wouldn't have done so. His fingernails—claws—had grown so long that if he could have made a fist, he would have gored his own hand.

The appendages protruding below his knees had, at least for the moment, stopped growing. Even though the driver's seat was pushed back as far as it would go, his three lower legs were squeezed tightly into the sports car's compact compartment that had been intended to accommodate only two. His webbed right foot spanned the gas pedal, the brake, and the clutch.

Dan had to tilt his enlarged head to the side in order to see out the windshield. He propped himself up, leaning against the passenger's seat, and sat across the driver's seat at an angle. In his awkward position, pain periodically inched up his spine from its base. No matter how hard he tried, Dan couldn't adjust himself to a comfortable position. He was beginning to wonder if he was sprouting a tail.

In a regular-size car, shifting gears would have been hampered by his awkward shape and size; squeezed into the confines of the sports car, it was next to impossible. Once Dan had the car moving forward in first gear, he hadn't tried to shift into anything higher. The transmission whined and squealed, objecting as speed increased, but he didn't seem concerned for the welfare of his car. Somehow, he knew it really wouldn't matter.

As Dan leaned with the car as it cornered a curve, he caught a glimpse of himself in the rearview mirror. A tingle of revulsion made him shiver.

Five . . . ten . . . fifteen . . . twenty seconds passed before he found the nerve to look into the mirror again . . . to actually *look* at his hideous reflection. Emerald-green eyes stared back at him, their cat-slit pupils widened to capture the twilight's fading glow. He looked at his reflection for several seconds in silence, then a pool of salty tears began to gather at the rim of his drooping eyelids.

"Why?" he asked in a whisper. The simple question rose from the depths of his soul.

"Why!" he shouted. Dan leaned his head back, as far as the confined space would allow, and screamed . . . *screamed* . . . drawing from the heritage of time that dated back to . . . before the dawn of man.

"Why?" he whispered as he again looked into the eyes reflected back at him in the mirror. He stared into those eyes—gazed into the depths of their emerald-green essence—not knowing what lay beyond.

The pools of tears grew and clouded his vision. Gradually, they overflowed their boundaries to slip past stubby lashes, to trickle and shimmer over parched, leathery skin. He lifted a deformed hand to wipe them away—

Something darted out onto the road. Dan's vision was blurred; he couldn't see; nothing was clear.

Acting on instinct, he turned the steering wheel hard to the right. He tried to lift his right leg—tried to control the webbed foot long enough to hit the brake—but he couldn't plant it firmly, and it slipped . . . slipped off the brake and onto the accelerator.

The car bounced across the berm and became airborne. It soared for an instant, then brushed past a pine tree, a fir, and a maple sapling. A branch from a sturdy, age-old oak caught its left front fender, tilting it, sending it into a spiral, nose down toward Mother Earth, then it rolled . . . and rolled . . . and rolled.

When the red Ferrari finally came to rest at the bottom of the hill, an ominous silence engulfed the woods. It was as if, for a mere moment, time had stopped.

Stopped.

A primal scream rose from the twisted wreckage. Using the animal strength growing within him, Dan pushed against the dented metal . . . bent it . . . tore it . . . freed himself from a prison no mortal would have been able to conquer. He crawled out of the wreckage onto the ground and lay there for a moment. A hundred unassociated messages raced across his mind in unorganized sequence. He could make so sense of them; *they* had no sense.

He tried to concentrate—tried to remember what had happened, where he had been and where he was going. Going . . . going. Finally, he remembered.

Awkwardly, Dan worked his way to his feet and grabbed hold of a branch to help maintain his balance. He looked up through the trees at the twilight sky, then glanced back up the hill to the road behind him. He remembered where he was going, and he remembered how to get there.

Dan looked back at the wrecked car, then glanced toward the heart of the woods. He sensed a kindred with the woods; it seemed to call to him . . . in an ancient language long ago forgotten.

Dan took a step . . . a second . . . a third. To compensate for his longer right leg, he bent his right knee and tried to push off only with the toes of his left feet. It was awkward at first, but he soon figured out a gait that would utilize his right foot and two left feet efficiently: step left, step right, step left, hop right.

Left . . . right . . . left . . . hop.

Left . . . right . . . left . . . hop.

Mastering the footwork, he increased his speed until . . . at last . . . he ran. Dan ran . . . and ran . . . and ran on legs the dawn of time had forged for him . . . on legs that time should have forgotten.

*6:26 P.M.*

Hollie Bass knocked on Warren's front door for the third time. Impatient at not receiving an answer, she stepped in front of the picture window, shaded her eyes against the reflection of the setting sun, and looked inside. She saw nothing more than unoccupied living-room furniture.

"Where are you?" she asked more mentally than verbally. Returning to the driveway, Hollie stopped in front of the garage and stood on her tiptoes so she could look in the windows bordering the door's upper panel. She saw Warren's car parked inside. "Where are you?" she repeated with more emphasis. Still, she couldn't think of an answer.

Hollie stood in the driveway for several moments, glancing from the garage to the front door of Warren's house and back again. Where could he be?

Turning toward the street, she scanned the driveways of the houses spaced around Alberta Court. All of the drives were vacant; there were no signs of life. Apparently, Warren hadn't gone visiting.

"Where—" As she turned to look back at the house, a thought came to Hollie. She grinned sheepishly, chided herself, and immediately shook her head in self-reproach, wondering why it had taken so long for her to figure out Warren's whereabouts. "His lab," she said to herself as she started toward the near corner of the house. "He has to be in his lab."

The instant Hollie entered the backyard, she saw the small barn sitting just this side of the woods. Without breaking her stride, she walked directly toward it.

When she rounded the barn's corner, Hollie saw the broken entry door and stopped. Immediately, her heartbeat multiplied in uncertainty, then, one cautious step at a time, she inched her way forward until she could peek around the doorframe and look inside.

The interior of the barn was a shambles. Overturned stools leaned precariously against one another; cages had been scattered, smashed, and thrown against the walls. Medical supplies littered the floor; debris from the shattered door covered the area directly in front of her.

Hollie inched forward another cautious step . . . two. Then, looking past the mess beyond the door, she saw Warren standing at a worktable on the far side of the barn, his back to her.

"What happened?" Hollie asked as she gingerly stepped over the debris, working her way toward him.

Taken by surprise, Warren cried out as he turned toward the barn's entrance. When he recognized Hollie, he gulped a quick breath of air, then leaned back against the table and laid his hand over his heart as if to ease an attack.

"This place is a mess," she said, looking around the barn as she took a few more steps inside. "What happened?" she asked again, focusing on Warren.

"Someone broke in," he answered curtly.

"I can see that," Hollie answered matter-of-factly. "And you don't have to snap my head off," she countered. "*I* didn't do it."

"I'm . . . sorry," Warren said, after taking in a couple of slow, deep breaths, "it's just that you took me by surprise." He picked up the pen he'd dropped and turned back toward the worktable. He hesitated for a moment, then looked over his shoulder at Hollie and frowned. "What are you doing here, anyway?"

"Jackie Mitchell and Deputy Robbins stopped by the lab this afternoon after you left."

"And," he prompted, turning toward her, "what did they want?"

"They were asking more questions about the animals that were taken during the break-ins." Warren looked at Hollie in silence, waiting for her to continue. "Something new seems to have come up, and they wanted to talk about it with you or Dr. Wagner."

"Did they say what it was?" Hollie shook her head negatively in response. Warren hesitated, as if to ponder the situation for a few moments, then he turned back to the table.

"I thought you might want to know they were looking for you. I thought it might have something to do with *your* animals," Hollie emphasized. She continued to pick her way through the debris, moving closer to him. "Did you find out what killed them?" she asked as she stopped beside Warren and looked at the notebook open on the table in front of him. She glanced at the last few lines he'd written, but the combination of technical terminology and his scribbled handwriting prevented her from understanding anything she saw.

"I think they . . . killed themselves," he answered as he closed the notebook.

"What?" Hollie questioned in disbelief. "How could that have happened?"

"I ran a few more tests after I got home this afternoon," Warren said as he turned and sat down on a stool. Unlike their brief exchange earlier in the day, he now seemed unusually calm and a bit more willing to talk about what he had done. "And I think I verified my theory." Hollie continued to look questioningly at him. "I was wanting to make sure all of my notes were in order so I could take them in to Dr. Wagner on Monday," he said, gesturing toward the notebook. "I need to tell him about everything I did with the serum I took from his personal lab, and I need to ask him if he can help me find an antidote for it. I need to find an antidote," he said with a note of urgency. "I really need to find one."

"Wait a minute," Hollie said, shaking her head and holding up her hands in front of her as if to stop traffic, "back up. What do you mean, 'they killed themselves'?"

Warren thought for a few moments, trying to select words Hollie could comprehend that at the same time would explain the complex process on an understandable level. "You know how the white blood cells work in the body to fight off infection and foreign substances." Hollie nodded just enough to relay her vague understanding. "And you know that it's this factor that can make transplanting organs difficult because of the rejection factor." Hollie didn't shake her head or nod it; she just looked at Warren with a growing frown. "How can I explain it?" Warren took a couple of moments to collect his thoughts, then began, "Since a transplanted organ is a foreign substance introduced into the body, the white blood cells will work to destroy it unless they're counteracted by some type of antirejection drug. Are you with me?" he asked. Hollie nodded slightly, but her brow was still wrinkled by a frown. "Now, consider for the moment that the foreign substance that's introduced into the body has a regenerative factor . . . that is, it can reproduce on its own. So, let's say that for every foreign cell that's destroyed by the body's white blood cells, two . . . three . . . or more of those foreign cells are regenerated—reproduced—in its place. Once this process begins, it snowballs. The foreign cells keep regenerating to compensate for the ones the white blood cells destroy, and the white blood cells keep multiplying to try to keep up with the additional foreign cells. It's really quite a fascinating phenomenon if you stop to think about it. Are you starting to understand how it works?"

"And that's how your animals killed themselves?" Hollie asked.

"Basically, yes. The bounds of the body can be contorted only so far before they will finally give."

"Give?"

"Give . . . rupture." Warren hesitated, then reached for the towel-covered tray near the back of the worktable. "These two unfortunate creatures used to be ordinary, everyday laboratory mice," he said as he lifted a corner of the towel.

Hollie glanced at the two masses of disorganized flesh, then gasped in disgust. "Mice?" she questioned in disbelief. Barely able to control her gag reflex, she looked at the animals a few seconds longer, then turned away. "They . . . in some places, they look more like lizards than they look like mice. What caused that? Why are parts of their bodies so leathery-looking and covered with scales?"

"That, I don't know for sure."

"But knowing you, I'm sure you've *guessed* at a reason."

Warren looked at the mice for several silent moments, then he picked up one of the reptilian-clawed paws and stroked it gently with his thumb. "A guess . . . I'd guess it's linked to the chromosomal history of the original serum. I'd guess the regenerative process begins at the dawn of evolution . . . and has yet to work its way up to the developmental stages of the common mouse," he said, looking at Hollie. "Let alone to man," he added softly as an afterthought.

"What about those bulbous masses of flesh?" Hollie asked. "And that big one there on his neck," she said, pointing to the submissive mouse. Apparently, Warren's reference to man appeared to have escaped her.

Warren studied the mouse briefly and thought for a moment. "A guess . . . no, a theory," he answered in speculation. "Before I separated them, those two mice fought quite a bit. I didn't keep a detailed record like I should have, but if my memory serves me correctly, I'd say that every one of those masses is at the site of an injury. I do know that the mass on his neck is right where he was pretty severely bitten. I *do* remember when that one happened. That was what prompted me to separate them."

Warren again concentrated on the mice for a few more moments before continuing. "Imagine . . . can you even begin to consider the possibilities? Any place the body is injured, the regenerative cells are going to go into high gear to replace whatever tissue has been damaged. Combine those efforts with the efforts of the body's own white blood cells to keep pace with the foreign cells, and . . ."

"And sooner or later, the body can't take it anymore," Hollie said, beginning to understand the process.

"That's right." Warren covered the mice with the towel and turned on the stool toward Hollie. "Now do you understand how the animals killed themselves?"

"I think so. Their insides grew too big for their bodies, and they finally . . . just blew up."

Warren nodded. That wasn't exactly how he would have stated it, but at least he felt Hollie had a grasp on the concept.

"So if that's the case—if they're going to blow up and end up dying anyway—why are you so worried about finding an antidote for the serum?" Hollie asked.

"Another theory," Warren answered. "If the animals don't die fairly quickly after they *blow up*, to use your terminology, the regenerative process just might act fast enough to heal them. I've even considered the possibility that it could make them bigger . . . and stronger."

"I didn't think about that."

"And something else bothers me," Warren said, glancing at the cages scattered on the floor and then at the shelves on the wall where they had once sat. "All of the animals that were taken from here had been injected with the regenerative serum." He looked at Hollie. "If they were turned loose in the wild and then they fought with other animals, there's a very good possibility that the regenerative cells could be transferred from one animal to another through a bite. If enough of the cells could travel from the saliva into the bloodstream, the whole process could begin anew in the animal that was bitten."

"That's kind of spooky," Hollie said, feeling a shiver slither down her spine. "Those mice are so much bigger than normal," she said, glancing at the tray. "Could you imagine what it would be like if a ground hog or a raccoon— Oh, my gosh," Hollie gasped, her eyes growing wide. Warren nodded; he knew what she was thinking. "What if one of your animals bit . . . a man."

"I know. *That's* why we need to find an antidote for the serum."

"I don't think you should wait until Monday," Hollie stressed. "I think you should take the mice and your notebook over to Dr. Wagner's right now so the two of you can start working on an antidote—"

A shadow suddenly loomed over them. Warren and Hollie both turned with a start and looked toward the doorway.

A man-creature, towering over seven feet tall, stood there,

staring at them with cat-slit, emerald-green eyes. Its head, disfigured and enlarged on one side, was streaked with rivulets of dried blood; a massive mouth and nose were pushed well off-center of its face. Its skin bore blotches of leathery, reptilian scales and patches of heavy animal fur. Its bare chest was broad and muscled, still carrying human characteristics. Its arms were elongated; its hands were puffy and clawed.

Remnants of blue jeans hung ripped and ragged from a narrow, belted waist. Its hips flared; its muscled thighs rippled with animalistic strength; its penis stood erect, indicative of its excitement. It stood on two—three—legs, each bearing full witness to the evolution of its species . . . that had not yet progressed to the time of man.

Flies swarmed around it, filling the air with a menacing drone. A yellow pus and pungent stench oozed freely from its gaping pores.

The man-creature tilted its head back and opened its cavernous mouth. A prehistoric wail exploded from the saber-toothed orifice to echo off the walls of the small storage barn. When it finished its cry, it lowered its head, focused its cat eyes on Warren, then lifted a heavy arm and pointed a clawed finger at him.

"Y-o-u d-i-d t-h-i-s t-o m-e!" it said with great difficulty, its fleshy lips catching on the edges of its jagged teeth . . . tearing . . . ripping . . . and immediately healing, regenerating into even fleshier pulp.

"Oh my God," Hollie gasped. "That . . . that voice. It . . . it sounds like . . . Dan Patton!"

"You did it to yourself," Warren countered, ignoring Hollie. "Rusty Snider called me. He told me you were taking too much of the serum too often. What could I do to stop you?"

"Y-o-u l-i-e-d t-o m-e! Y-o-u l-i-e-d a-n-d n-o-w y-o-u d-i-e!" With an effortless sweep of his arm, Dan pushed aside the overturned stools and cages between them and took a step toward Warren.

Hollie screamed. Warren picked up the stool he'd been sitting on and held it out in front of him in a meager show of defense.

"Go get help!" Warren shouted to Hollie as she began sidestepping toward the outer wall. "Hurry! Get somebody to help me!" But even as he watched Hollie slip out the door, Warren wondered what kind of help anyone could be. In Dan Patton's condition, was there any way to stop him?

*6:38 P.M.*

"This is it," Jackie said, leaning forward in her seat and pointing at a street sign a few feet to the left of the car. "Alberta Court." She glanced at the paper she was holding that contained Warren's address. "He lives at number three."

"That must be it over there," Barry said, pointing across the dash, "the second driveway off the circle. There's a car in the drive; it looks like he already has company."

"Maybe we shouldn't bother him now," Jackie said, settling back in her seat.

"We're already here, and what we have to talk to him about won't take long."

Barry pulled the car up next to the curb and stopped in front of Warren's house. As he reached to open the door, he glanced in the rearview mirror.

"What's *he* doing here," Barry asked as he watched a car ease up behind them and stop.

"Who's doing what?" Jackie asked, turning in her seat to look out the back window.

"Wagner." Barry and Jackie looked at each other in question, then they got out of the car and met at the end of

Warren's driveway.

"I hope you don't mind if I join you," Leland said as he walked toward them. Barry gave him a questioning glance. "I suppose if Warren *has* gone and done something . . . how shall I say it? If he's done something *stupid*, maybe I might be able to help."

"Or, maybe you came over here to make sure he wouldn't tell us something *you* didn't want us to know," Barry said in an accusing tone.

"Deputy Robbins, I can assure you—"

"Help! Somebody help!"

All three whirled around to look up the driveway toward the house. Hollie Bass came running around the corner of the garage and stopped the instant she saw them.

"Help!" she shouted, waving frantically for them to join her. "Out back! He's after Warren! He's going to kill him! Please, help!"

Drawing his revolver, Barry sprinted up the drive. "Stay there," he called over his shoulder. Ignoring the order, Jackie and Leland followed him as far as the corner of the house.

"What's going on?" Jackie yelled, grabbing hold of Hollie's arm. "Who's back there? Who's after Warren?"

Hollie was speechless with fear.

"Hollie!" Jackie shook her. "Who's after Warren?" Still no answer. "Hollie—"

A gunshot echoed from behind the house.

Jackie glanced in the direction of the sound, then looked back at Hollie. "Who's after Warren?" she asked for the third time.

Hollie looked at Jackie, stammered a few times, swallowed, then said, "Dan . . . Dan Patton—"

A second shot rang out . . . a third.

Jackie's eyes looked from Hollie to Leland, then she started around the corner of the garage. "He's . . . he's changed," Hollie screamed after her. Jackie hesitated, looking back. "He's not . . . he's not *human* anymore." Jackie glanced at Leland, then took off running.

Rounding the back corner of the house, Jackie saw the small barn on the far side of the yard. Noises . . . noises indicative of a scuffle—of a fight—were coming from its direction. Without breaking stride, she continued across the yard and slowed only after she turned the corner and saw the jagged opening where the barn door had once stood.

She heard a scream. It sounded like Warren. She heard a cry . . . a howl . . . a wail. It sounded like . . . like *nothing* she had ever heard before.

Leaving caution behind, Jackie stepped up to the opening. It took a moment for her eyes to adjust to the dimness inside, then she saw it—

Her breath caught in her throat; a cold sweat oozed from her pores. Not since she had been a child—when she used to watch horror movies about prehistoric monsters—had she seen such a grotesque creature. Then, she had pulled the blankets up over her head to protect herself—to make the creatures go away. Now . . . now, what could she do?

"Get back."

Jackie looked to her right. Barry stood just inside the barn's shell, his back pressed against the wall, his gun leveled at the creature.

"I heard shots," Jackie said.

"I fired at it three times. Hell! I *hit* it three times! Point blank! But it just kept on going like nothing happened."

"Where's Warren?" Jackie asked, squinting, trying to see further into the barn.

"He's under the table and shelving built into the far wall. That . . . that *thing*—whatever it is—can't bend over far enough to get at him, so it's ripping the place apart."

"No! Noooo," Warren screamed. "Let go of me! Let go! Noooo . . ."

Jackie stepped out into the middle of the doorway. Rays from the setting sun cast her elongated shadow over the creature on the far side of the barn.

"Dan," Jackie shouted, "leave him alone."

"What are you doing?" Barry asked with a start. "Get back here," he ordered, grabbing her by the arm.

Jackie yanked her arm free and took a couple more steps toward the heart of the barn. "Dan," she called again. "Dan! Stop it!"

A howl filled the confines of the small barn. Almost defiantly, Dan turned his massive head to look over his deformed shoulder, then he swiveled to face her.

The sunlight glared in his delicate cat eyes. He lifted a hand to shade them, angling his head. Even though he couldn't look at her directly, Dan knew the voice that had called his name.

"J-a-c-k-i-e," his bass voice bellowed. Blood-tinged saliva hung in streamers from his jagged teeth and lips. The stench of decay hung on his every breath. "H-a-v-e y-o-u c-o-m-e t-o m-e n-o-w t-h-a-t I h-a-v-e l-e-g-s?" Dan looked down at his lower body—at his *three* legs—and then he laughed . . . laughed a laugh voiced only by the insane. "I'-v-e w-a-i-t-e-d a l-o-n-g t-i-m-e f-o-r y-o-u, J-a-c-k-i-e." He shifted out of the sunlight so he could look her directly in the eyes. "A-n-d t-h-e t-i-m-e h-a-s c-o-m-e f-o-r y-o-u t-o b-e m-i-n-e." Dan took a step toward Jackie.

"Stay away from her!" Barry shouted as he stepped up beside Jackie, his revolver leveled toward Dan.

Dan looked at Barry—glanced at the gun—then laughed, the acrid scent of his breath washing over them. "Y-o-u c-a-n'-t k-i-l-l m-e, b-u-t y-o-u . . . y-o-u w-i-l-l b-e a-s e-a-s-y t-o d-e-s-t-r-o-y a-s h-e-r f-i-r-s-t l-o-v-e-r w-a-s." Jackie looked at Dan in question. Again, their eyes met. "Y-e-s, m-y d-e-a-r-e-s-t

J-a-c-k-i-e, i-t w-a-s m-e. I h-a-d y-o-u-r b-e-l-o-v-e-d R-i-c-h-a-r-d k-i-l-l-e-d." Dan laughed. "I w-a-s n-e-v-e-r m-y b-r-o-t-h-e-r'-s k-e-e-p-e-r." Those eyes—there was something about those emerald-green eyes—

Dan took another step toward Jackie.

Barry fired. The bullet grazed Dan's left shoulder; blood, bone shards, and muscle tissue splattered from the impact.

Dan looked at his shoulder and laughed. In a matter of seconds, the bleeding stopped, and the wound began to heal. "N-o o-n-e c-a-n s-t-o-p m-e." He took another step toward Jackie . . . and another. With each of Dan's steps, Barry fired again . . . and again. Each time, the results were the same; in a matter of moments, the gunshot wound healed in front of their eyes, leaving an unorganized mass of scar tissue in its place.

"N-o-w y-o-u a-r-e m-i-n-e."

Barry raised the sight of his gun, held it steady and fired once . . . twice. The first bullet grazed Dan's forehead; the second bullet sank deep into Dan's left eye.

A howl of agony burst across Dan's lips. Instinctively, he lifted a clawed hand to cover the wounded eye . . . to protect it from any further harm.

Barry shot again. The bullet bounced off the bony ridge protruding above Dan's right eye.

Knowing a weakness had been discovered, Dan turned away. He quickly looked around the interior of the barn, then glanced down at Warren, whom he'd been able to pull only halfway out from under the table. All of it could wait until later; for the moment, he had to focus on his own self-preservation.

"I'm n-o-t f-i-n-i-s-h-e-d w-i-t-h y-o-u . . . b-i-t-c-h." Dan glanced at Jackie, then ran off to her right. He hurdled the overturned stools and scattered cages, then he ran headfirst into the barn's north wall. The half-inch plywood gave way without resistance. Dan broke through. Leaving a howl in his wake, Dan ran off into the woods.

Jackie ran over to the hole in the wall and looked out, but she saw no trace of Dan; he had already disappeared, hidden by the trees. "He looked like a living nightmare," she said when she felt Barry's presence beside her. "What happened to him?"

"He went one step too far." Barry looked out toward the woods. "It's too late to do anything tonight, but tomorrow, I'm going to round up every man I can who'll help me go after him."

"Do you think you'll be able to find him?"

"I can only hope so."

"And if you find him, do you think you'll be able to capture him?"

Barry hesitated. "I truly doubt it. I just hope we found a weakness that'll give us a chance to kill him—"

"He bit me. He bit me! No! No! I don't want to die! Don't want to explode!"

Jackie and Barry turned toward the heart of the barn. They weren't exactly sure what Warren was shouting, and for the moment, they wondered if they really wanted to know.

*11:43 P.M.*

Dan lay face down on a bed of last year's fallen leaves. After fleeing from Warren's backyard lab, he'd collapsed just a few yards into the woods. Sleep had been forced upon him.

His metabolism had run rampant. Every ounce of energy had been drained from his body, and he'd needed time to rest . . . time to regenerate . . . to rejuvenate. He'd had no choice but to give in to the heavy veil of sleep that swept over him.

Now, he teetered on the brink of consciousness. He wanted

to wake up, yet he clung to the peace that cloaked his slumber. In his dreams, he was a man . . . a man of flesh and blood . . . a man who could walk and run and jump. He was a *MAN* . . . a *WHOLE* man, and he knew that once he left his dreams, he would also leave that image behind.

Dan rolled over onto his side, then settled on his back. Even though he was more awake than asleep, he still fought consciousness—fought the return to reality . . . fought coming face to face with the unearthly creature he had become.

Funny, his head didn't hurt anymore. After being shot—after having a bullet embedded in his eye socket—he wondered why it didn't hurt. It should hurt; by all rights, it *should* hurt. Unless . . . maybe . . .

Dan lifted a hand and touched the left side of his forehead. He touched his temple, then he touched his cheekbone. The leathery skin covering the pads of his fingers and the side of his face wasn't sensitive to touch; he couldn't tell the extent of the damage . . . nor the extent of the repair. He only knew it didn't hurt anymore.

He wondered. If the regenerative process had worked on his injured eye as dramatically as it had worked on the rest of his body, he wondered just how extensive the repairs might be. Had his eye been merely replaced? Or had a mass of scar tissue healed over the socket . . . covering it . . . leaving him a hideous cyclops? Dan wondered about the possibilities, and then he wondered if it would really matter. Did anything really matter anymore . . .

Dan opened his eyes.

Taken by surprise, he cried out in a deep bass voice and scrambled onto his hands and knees. Frightened, he crawled under a nearby bush, trying to hide from *them*, seeking cover and protection from *them*.

Too many things were around him. Too many things were coming after him. Too many things—

Dan blinked. He blinked again and again, then he hesitantly tilted his head from one side to the other. He looked around the area at the grass . . . at the flowers . . . at the leaves . . . at the multitude of insects and ants crawling up the bark on a nearby tree. There were hundreds—thousands of them. Everywhere!

He blinked again . . . and again, then a smile of understanding came to his twisted face. His injured eye had healed—healed tenfold—healed ten times tenfold. Instead of having a single vision eye, he now possessed a flylike, multifaceted eye that could pick up each and every detail hundreds of yards away. And, like his distant lizard cousins, the massive eye could swivel in its socket. He could see as easily behind him as he could see in front.

The advantage was totally his. Nothing—and no one—could sneak up on him from any direction.

Dan crawled out from beneath the bush and stood. He stretched like an animal awakened from a long sleep, then he looked through the trees toward the small barn in Warren's backyard and at the north wall he'd burst through a few hours before.

The last time he saw Jackie, she'd been standing there at the hole in the wall, looking out at him. He had seen her, but she hadn't seen him.

Emotion overtook him. He didn't know whether it was hate or jealousy or love; he didn't care. What he did know was that Jackie was the reason for everything that had happened to him. If she would have only accepted him the way he had been, then he wouldn't have gone and done something foolish—something foolish that turned him into a freak.

*She* was the reason. And if she wouldn't accept him now—

Dan turned and looked from the barn toward the heart of the woods. If he remembered correctly, somewhere out there . . . beyond the woods . . . past acres of open fields . . . many many miles away, was the animal compound and Bruce Cameron's farm . . . and the house where Jackie lived. Dan's directions were vague, but he had an inner feeling that he'd be able to find exactly where he wanted to go. Maybe his animal instincts would lead the way . . . after they led him to a meal that would satisfy the empty pain in his stomach.


*11:55 P.M.*

*"Take care of your mother, son," Richard said as he laid his hand on Kerk's shoulder and squeezed it gently."*

*"You can count on me, Daddy," a young Kerk answered, looking up at his father and smiling. "Nothing will ever happen to Mommy as long as I'm around to protect her," he said, puffing out his small chest with pride.*

*"That's my boy." Richard stooped down beside Kerk, gathered him in his arms and hugged him close. "I can always count on you."*

*"You can count on me." Kerk returned the hug, then pulled back to look at Richard's face. But instead of seeing his father, Kerk was looking into the vacant face of a dark, hooded figure with oversized emerald-green eyes.*

*Kerk screamed and tried to pull away, but the figure's skeletony arms encircled him. "No!" Kerk shouted. He wiggled and squirmed . . . twisted and turned. "No! No—" Something was wrapping around him and pulling tighter and tighter—*

Kerk's eyes shot open. His heart was pounding; his breaths came in rapid pants. Sweat bathed his face, pasting his hair to his forehead.

For a moment, he just lay there, staring into the dark, adjusting to the fact that he had returned to reality. When, at last, he tried to move, Kerk discovered his range of motion was limited.

Curious, he lifted his head and looked toward the foot of the bed. His sheet and bedspread were both wrapped snugly around him.

Logic quickly explained his predicament. While trying to escape from the stranger in his dream, he had, inadvertently, turned and twisted his way into a bedspread cocoon.

Embarrassed, Kerk worked his way free from the entanglement. He swung his legs over the edge of the bed and gazed across the room out the window. The pole light was right outside, and all he had to do to look at the bulb directly was adjust his position a little to the left.

He always sought out the light after being awakened by a dream . . . even after a dream he couldn't remember clearly. The light seemed to offer hope; he took its brightness as an indication that everything was going to be okay . . . even though he doubted if it actually would be. The light was too simple a symbol to alleviate all of his problems.

Kerk scooted to the edge of the bed and stood up. He walked to the window and looked out . . . looked past the light towards the woods in the distance. All of the dreams he was able to remember bothered him, but the one from which he'd just awakened troubled him more than any other he'd had for a long, long time. His father had been in this dream.

His father hadn't appeared in any of his dreams since late last summer, and Kerk wondered about—was almost scared by—Richard's reappearance now. The psychiatrists had told his mother that Richard's gradual disappearance from Kerk's dreams was a good sign. Supposedly, it meant he was facing up to his father's death and accepting it as reality.

So, if the disappearance of his father from his dreams was a good sign, then what might a reappearance mean?

Kerk glanced at the light a few feet from the window, then looked back across the open field at the woods.

*Take care of your mother, son.*

Kerk turned sharply toward the heart of the room. He

searched in every corner—tried to look behind each shadow, but he knew no one was there. The voice had come from inside his mind.

"You can count on me," Kerk whispered, replying just as he had in his dream. He looked toward the family picture sitting on the nightstand beside his bed. The lighting in the room was near nonexistent, but he knew the picture by heart and visualized it in his mind. "You can count on me," Kerk repeated, looking at the part of the photograph where he knew his father's image was located. "But why am I going to have to take care of Mom?" he asked.

In response, an icy shiver raced down Kerk's spine, making the hair on his arms stand on end. Kerk looked back at the light and then at the woods; he sensed he had just received a warning.

# Saturday

## (Day Nine)

*12:12 A.M.*

Dan crouched beside the carcass, guarding his kill the same as any wild animal protecting its prey. His breaths came shallow and quick; his heart pounded rapidly. The thrill of the hunt still vibrated through him.

The scent . . . the taste—blood . . . thick . . . warm . . . satisfying blood.

The young buck had put up a fight; it had even gored Dan at the onset of the confrontation. But the wound had been superficial and had begun to heal almost as quickly as it had been inflicted. At best, it served as a catalyst to evoke Dan's ire.

In spite of his malformed legs, Dan had been able to outmaneuver the deer. He'd grabbed the animal's antlers and used them for leverage, twisting the buck's neck around until its body gave in to the force. Unable to resist, it fell on its side like a calf taken down at a rodeo.

The instant Dan commanded the upper hand, he pounced on top of the deer. The increased weight from his developing muscle mass broke the animal's ribs and sent splintered bone deep into its lungs. The buck's frantic cries echoed through the forest, and it only ceased to struggle when Dan's saber-toothed bite sank deep into its neck, crushing the vocal cords and severing the arteries on either side of the throat.

For several long seconds afterward, Dan didn't move; he held the pose: teeth gripping, securely embedded in solid flesh. Blood gushed from the buck's ruptured arteries, flowing beyond Dan's lips ... into his mouth ... and over his taste buds. The taste was ... was pleasant ... was downright enjoyable. He didn't remember tasting anything that seemed so much ... *alive*.

His senses were honed.

The coppery-sweet scent of blood rose to fill his nostrils. He'd never known a smell so acute ... so intense. It was as if every molecule of air had been saturated with the aroma ... and that aroma then jam-packed into every crevice and cavity inside his head. Everything was so intense. Everything was beyond the scope of a mere mortal human.

A wiry red fox scampered out of the underbrush. Startled at coming face to face with a creature foreign to its habitat, the animal froze in its stance and stared at Dan.

Dan's eyes locked with the fox's. Even though the small animal didn't pose a threat, Dan gripped his prey tighter and curled his lips back from massive teeth. A growl rose from deep within his throat. It was a warning to the intruder—a warning he had the power to stand behind.

The red fox held its ground for only a moment, and then he thought it best to retreat. He barked, as if to tell Dan he was leaving of his own free will and not because he'd been intimidated, then he turned sharply and scurried back into the underbrush.

Dan watched the opening in the bushes where the fox had disappeared. He concentrated on the area for several minutes, but when the fox didn't return to challenge him for his prey, Dan loosened his grip on the deer and settled down on his haunches to consume his prey.

He was ravenous. His metabolism was running rampant. Every cell seemed to be crying out for nourishment, and he needed to replenish his source of energy so they could continue to grow and multiply.

Using the claws that had grown from the ends of his fingers, Dan sliced open the buck's belly. A steamy mist rose from the opening when the warm entrails were touched by the cool midnight air. The aroma was enticing.

Dan reached inside the abdominal cavity and pulled the viscera out onto the ground. An inner instinct told him to go for the liver and the heart and cautioned him about rupturing the intestines so as not to contaminate the meat.

He ate his fill—gorged himself on the nutritious venison—then Dan settled back against a tree and closed his eyes. Again, he needed rest. His body needed the time to take the food supply and turn it into energy for his hungry cells. Energy . . . for his cells.

Dan drifted in and out of consciousness . . . in and out of a dreamlike state. In his dreams, he fantasized he and Jackie were together . . . together . . . caressing . . . embracing. After all the years of denial, at last, she was his . . . his.

Jackie . . . so soft . . . so fresh. Dan gathered her in his arms . . . pulled her close to him. His hands—his *human* hands—glided over her naked body . . . touching . . . feeling . . . probing into crevices all warm and inviting . . . inviting.

Dan snuggled against her neck . . . smelled her freshness . . . gently nibbled at the flesh near the crest of her shoulder. He needed her; he wanted her. His longings were strong, and his passion grew.

Dan's breaths became shallow and rapid; his heart pounded savagely. His heartbeat multiplied tenfold. He needed her . . . *wanted* her—wanted the only bitch who had ever denied him satisfaction—

Dan grabbed Jackie and held her tightly as he rolled over on top of her. Now, she was his. No matter what she did to avoid his advances, he was going to have her. He was going to have her NOW.

But Jackie didn't fight him; she didn't try to pull away. With but the merest touch of his hand, she opened herself up to him and let him enter . . . enter.

Deep inside . . . inside of her, he grew . . . pulsed and surged. He cupped her round hips in his hands and urged her closer to him. He guided her—pulled and released her—until their rhythm became as one . . . one. Together. They were together, rising on an uplifting torrent . . . soaring beyond any realm capable of mere mortal man.

Together . . . they were approaching the zenith. Together . . . they would crest the peak—

Dan cried out in ecstasy. The roar of his deep bass voice echoed through the treetops and rebounded back, startling him as much as it did the woodland creatures around him.

Reluctantly, Dan opened his eyes, leaving his dream world behind and reentering the world of reality. He—

Wait— What had happened? Where was he?

He was no longer leaning against the tree. He was lying on his stomach—his legs splayed—and there was something beneath him . . . something soft and furry beneath him. What—

Bracing his talon-tipped hands against the ground, Dan pushed himself up. As his upper body pulled away from . . . the deer carcass, Dan looked farther down his body . . . toward his groin. He was repulsed by what he saw.

His blood-gorged, scale-rimmed penis was firmly embedded between the buck's back legs. In his dream state, he had made love to Jackie. In reality, he had screwed the deer.

"N-o-o-o-o!" Dan bellowed as he pushed himself away from the carcass. Throughout his life, he'd participated in a variety of disgusting activities, but he had never stooped so low as to engage in bestiality—and with a *dead*, disemboweled animal—

"It's your fault!" Dan shouted, his thoughts focusing on Jackie. "If it wasn't for you, none of this would be happening—*none* of it!" He looked at the carcass and had to fight his urges to keep from throwing up.

"You're going to pay," he threatened, looking down at his penis that, even in its limp state, was more than three times the length and circumference of a normal man's. "You're going to pay with all the pain and agony . . . and humiliation I can force upon you. You're going to lie beneath me and accept me—*all* of me," he emphasized, letting his hand slip down the length of his penis. "And there's not a thing you can do to stop me. Not a thing! And then, when I'm finished with you," he said, looking back at the buck's carcass, "then you *and* that green-eyed bastard brat of yours are going to die. Die! Just like the undeserving fool who sired him."


*5:11 A.M.*

Leland stepped off the elevator, walked past the nurse's station, and headed down the corridor angling off to his right. Halfway down the hall, he hesitated in front of an open door, then took a short step into the visitor's lounge. He glanced around the room and saw what he had expected.

"Hollie?" Leland walked across the room, slid a chair over in front of one of the couches, and sat down. "Hollie," he said again, placing a hand on her shoulder.

Hollie lay on the couch on her side, her knees drawn up far enough to keep her feet from hanging over the end. Her arms were crossed in front of her; her head was coiled so far forward her chin almost touched her chest. Her five-foot-eight-inch frame had been squeezed onto a three-and-a-half-foot vinyl couch. There was no way she could be comfortable, and yet, she was sound asleep.

"Hollie." Leland shook her gently. Hollie stirred, and a groan escaped her lips. "Hollie, wake up."

"What?" she asked, still half asleep. Hollie turned her head and looked up at Leland through slitted eyes. "Dr. Wagner," she said groggily as she turned to sit up, "is something wrong? Has something happened to Warren?"

"Nothing's happened that I know of," Leland answered. "Have you been in here all night?"

Hollie nodded as she shifted her legs in front of her and put her feet down on the floor. "Warren doesn't have any family," she explained, "so I thought I'd stay around for a while in case he wanted to talk to someone." She glanced at the clock on the wall above the hallway door then eyed Leland. "It is a little past five in the *morning*, isn't it?" Leland nodded. "What are you doing here so early?"

"I've been up all night studying Warren's notes," Leland said as he grasped the notebook that had been tucked up under his arm. "The boy has done some interesting things, and I was wanting to ask him a few questions."

"At *this* hour?"

"Right now, I'm running on adrenaline. If I stop before I talk to Warren, I'll probably go to sleep and won't have a chance to talk to him until sometime late tonight or even tomorrow. The questions I have to ask him are short, but the answers he can provide might help solve some of the mysteries I've had rolling around in my mind for over twenty years—"

"Help! Someone call an orderly. I need help down here. Hurry!"

Hollie and Leland looked at each other in startled surprise; then both stood and hurried toward the door. They stopped a few feet out into the hallway and looked toward the nurse's station. A man dressed in white hurried past them, and they turned to follow his movement down the hall. Instantly, they saw a nurse standing outside Warren's door, waving for someone to come help her.

Without conferring, they immediately fell into step behind the orderly. The man slowed ahead of them, turned, and went into Warren's room. Hollie pulled up short at the doorway; Leland almost bumped into her as he, too, came to a sudden stop.

"Oh, my God . . ." The words left Hollie's lips in little more than a whisper. She turned toward Leland, her face ashen, and leaned her head against his chest.

Leland wrapped an arm around Hollie as he looked past her into Warren's room. A lump came to his throat as he silently watched while the orderly and nurse untied the sheet Warren had used to hang himself.

*5:45 A.M.*

Barry sat at his desk, the phone tucked between his ear and shoulder. For the past fifteen minutes, he'd been alternating between the phone and the radio, checking with the night patrols and off-duty officers who had come in to help stake out the Patton estate. So far, no one had seen anything out of the ordinary. He was still waiting to hear from the park rangers.

"Deputy Robbins?"

Barry looked up into the face of a young man who looked barely old enough to shave. The man's bright blue eyes sparkled. His blond hair was razor cut and styled; he wore a three-piece pinstriped suit and carried a hand-tooled leather briefcase. He could have easily filled the role of a federal agent in any movie that was looking for a quick typecast. After Barry made his quick survey, he nodded to affirm his identity.

"Deputy Robbins, I'm Lanny Underwood from the Bureau of Disease Control," the young man said, taking his wallet from his jacket's inside breast pocket, opening it, and showing

Barry his credentials. "May I?" he asked, gesturing to the chair beside Barry's desk.

Barry nodded, replaced the phone in its cradle, and leaned back in his chair. "What brings somebody from the Bureau of Disease Control out here?" he asked, still eyeing the man's stylish attire.

"A variety of unusual reports from the area over the past few days," Underwood answered as he slipped his wallet back into his jacket's pocket, "and *you*, Deputy Robbins."

"Me? Why me? Do I have some kind of disease I don't know about?" he asked.

"Let's hope not." Underwood set his briefcase on the corner of Barry's desk, opened it, took out a manila folder, and laid it on top of the papers already spread out in front of Barry. "This is a copy of the report sent to our office by . . ." Underwood opened the folder and pointed to the name on the bottom of the first page, ". . . by a Dr. Stanley Calvin. I presume you know Dr. Calvin."

"I know him. Doc Calvin does the lab work for both the city police and the county sheriff's departments." Barry picked up the folder, thumbed through the pages and scanned the report that was nearly ten pages long. "What's this all about, anyway?" he asked.

"The report is in reference to the Dunn case. I believe their names were Danford and Loretta."

"I saw that much, but what does it have to do with me?"

"You were there, Deputy Robbins. We would like for you to take as much time as you need to look over the report and verify everything as it is stated. We would also like for you to add anything that might have been omitted."

"I doubt if I can be much—if any—help. I wasn't up at the Dunn place much more than five minutes. If you want somebody to check out the details, I suggest you talk to Terry Neville or Phil Burnette. They were both on the scene for most of the afternoon."

"Oh, I plan to talk with both of them and a few others as well, but since you're the only one here at the moment," Underwood said, turning his head to look over his shoulder and make a sweeping glance of the nearly vacant squad room, "I thought I'd begin with you."

Barry glanced at the first couple of pages of the report again, then a thought came to him. He looked at Underwood out of the corner of his eye. "Am I losing track of time, or if I'm not mistaken, didn't this just happen . . . yesterday?"

"Yesterday. That's correct."

"It seems to me like you got in on this one in a mighty big hurry."

"We try to do our job."

"But I've never known *any* government agency to be *this* efficient. Usually it takes two to three weeks—sometimes even months—to get any kind of action going."

"We try to do our job," Underwood said again, his voice revealing a hint of nervousness.

Barry looked at a couple more pages of the report, then closed the folder and laid it on the desk beside Underwood. "This stuff—the stuff in here," Barry said, tapping the folder with his forefinger, "it doesn't have anything to do with disease control. Does it?"

"What makes you say that?" Underwood asked defensively, shifting stiffly on his chair.

Barry leaned back in his chair and eyed the young agent, taking a few extra seconds to look him over from head to toe. "Yes, you're federal all right, but you're not here because you're interested in any disease." Barry studied Underwood for a few moments more, then he said, "You're here to try to find out if any of the strange things that have been going on around here are the products of . . . of maybe some government experiment that got set loose when the animal rights people broke into all those labs a week or so ago." Barry paused. "Aren't you?" Underwood said nothing. Barry held eye contact with him for a moment and then added, "Or maybe you're not looking for a government experiment. Maybe you're looking for one the government *doesn't* know anything about . . . but would like to. Is that it? Did I break through your cover with five easy questions?"

"Deputy Robbins, would you please verify the accuracy of the report to the best of your knowledge?" Underwood said in a neutral voice.

Barry continued to eye the young agent. "If Doc Calvin says that's the way it was, then that's the way it was. Like I said before, I was only there a few minutes, so I won't add or subtract anything from his report."

The elevator on the far side of the squad room opened. Barry saw Leland Wagner step out hesitantly and look around as if he were lost.

"Dr. Wagner," Barry called, waving for him to join them. Then, in a low voice he said to Underwood, "If you want to talk to someone about anything strange that's been going on around here, *that* is the man you want to see. Dr. Leland Wagner's the name."

"He's on my list," Underwood said sharply.

"I thought he might be." Barry smiled broadly in self-satisfaction, mentally patting himself on the back for breaking the young agent's cover story. "Funny, as far as I know, Wagner didn't have anything to do with the Dunns. I doubt if he even knows what happened up there on Haggerty Ridge. I know *I* didn't tell him anything—" Barry shifted his attention to Wagner, stood, and walked around his desk. "What can I do for you, Dr. Wagner?"

"I came by to tell you that . . . Warren's dead."

"Dead?" Barry questioned in surprise. "How did it happen?"

Leland hesitated, ran his tongue over his dry lips, and glanced down at the floor when he said, "Suicide." Then he looked up at Barry. "Warren hung himself with a bed sheet . . . right there in his hospital room."

"I'm sorry." Barry pulled a chair around from an adjacent desk and motioned for Leland to sit down. "But you didn't have to come in to the station to tell me; someone from the hospital will report it."

"There's more," Wagner said nervously. He glanced at Underwood, then looked up at Barry.

"This is Lanny Underwood. He says he's from the government," Barry said.

"From the Bureau of Disease Control," Underwood clarified crisply.

Barry looked at Underwood as if to say "You're not fooling anyone" before returning his attention to Leland. "He's going to find out about everything sooner or later," Barry said. "Hell, everybody's going to find out about everything before it's all over, so you might as well go ahead and say what you've got to say."

"This is Warren's notebook," Leland said as he slipped it out from under his arm. He laid the book on the desk beside him and placed a hand on top of it. "I was up all night reading through it"—he looked at Barry—"and by what we've seen happen during the past twenty-four hours . . . I'm afraid Warren's theories were more correct than not." Leland glanced at Underwood, then looked back at Barry. "He speculated that . . . *it* could be passed on from one person to another via body fluids," Leland hesitated, "and it appears he was correct—"

"Are you talking about some kind of communicable disease?" Underwood asked.

"Communicable, yes," Leland answered, looking at Underwood, "but a disease? I'm not sure that would be an exact classification." Leland returned his attention to Barry. "Do you remember last night when Warren cried out about being bitten?" Barry nodded. "Well, he'd been pretty badly bitten on the left forearm, and by the time he died, the . . . the wound had already healed completely with regenerative—mutant— characteristics."

"Meaning?" Barry asked.

"This morning, there was a sizable mass of scar tissue covering the wound, and there were indications that his skin was beginning to thicken and . . . and—" Leland shook his head. "No, I might be wrong. I only had a chance to take a quick look at Warren before the orderly made me leave his room."

"And what?" Barry prompted. "You said *and*. What else did you find?"

"There . . . there were a few scales mingled in with the scar tissue."

"Scales?"

"The kind of scales you find on fish."

"Fish scales?" Barry questioned in disbelief.

"I think so." Leland nodded. "At a quick glance, that's what they appeared to be."

"This is getting too bizarre to be real," Barry said as he began to pace back and forth beside a nearby desk. "First, Dan turned into this creature from a horror movie, and then you say he passed it on to Warren because he bit him." Leland nodded again. "Okay, and if he bites someone else while he's out there— Could this thing spread on and on without an end?" he asked abruptly.

"I don't know. Maybe, it's possible."

"Are you two talking about some kind of epidemic?" Underwood asked.

"If all of this stuff that Wagner here is talking about is true, I think you would consider an epidemic as being mild," Barry said. "At least with an epidemic, people will eventually die, but if this thing goes on the way it sounds like it could, infected people . . ." Barry glanced at Leland to confirm his choice of words. Leland shrugged his shoulders and nodded at the same time, relaying his lack of certainty on what terminology to use. ". . . infected people would just keep healing themselves and healing themselves and healing—" Barry abruptly stopped pacing and looked at Leland. "Wait a minute. How did you say Warren died?"

"He hung himself."

"Why would that kill him? If he broke his neck, wouldn't he just regenerate? If he—"

"Lack of oxygen." A smile came to Leland's tired face as he realized they might have just stumbled onto the answer that could put a stop to the progressive regeneration. "A lack of oxygen," he repeated. "That has to be it! Cells can only survive so long without oxygen before they begin to die. Without oxygen, they'll also lose their ability to regenerate—"

The phone rang. Barry reached across his desk to answer it. "Robbins here. Yes." Barry listened for a few moments. "Where?" He turned to the map hanging on the wall behind his desk. "But that's clear across the county. It doesn't make sense he'd go that direction—" Barry focused on the map; his breath all but caught in his throat. "He didn't head home like we thought he would." Barry concentrated on a rectangular area of the map just inside the Indiana border. "How soon can you get a car to the compound?" he asked. "Then do it. I'll call." Barry hung up and immediately began dialing. "A couple of rangers found three dismembered deer carcasses along Lynch Creek in the park," he said, looking at Leland. "Freddie said they also found what looked like a set of giant lizard tracks in the mud down by the water."

"Do you think it could be Dan?" Leland asked.

"It looks like it. Damn!" Barry said, slamming down the

phone, "It's busy."

"Who are you trying to call?"

"Jackie." Leland looked at him in question. "Lynch Creek runs out of the park through the north woods on Bruce Cameron's farm. By the way those deer carcasses were lined up along the creek, I'd say it looks like Dan may be heading straight for Jackie."

5:49 A.M.

"I just don't know about you, Little Cork," Bruce said as he set a bowl of puppy food on a mat beside the refrigerator and picked up the dog's empty water bowl. "You've sure been acting awful strange this morning." He eyed the pup for several moments, then shook his head.

For the past twenty minutes, the dog had been sitting attentively on the back porch, looking out the bottom of the screen door. Occasionally, she would growl or bark, but more often than not, she whimpered uneasily. It was almost as if she were waiting for—expecting—something to happen.

Bruce stepped beneath the open archway leading from the kitchen to the porch and talked to Little Cork as if she were human. "I open the door to let you out, and you back away from it. I close the door and come back in the kitchen and you whine. Well, I'll tell you one thing, if you're going through one of those 'pay attention to me all the time' stages, I'm not up for it. You're just a stray mutt dog I took in, and that's how you're gonna be treated as long as you stay around here."

Little Cork turned her head and looked up at Bruce over her shoulder. Her big brown eyes locked with his, and she yipped as if to disagree with his words.

"All right," Bruce conceded, "you *are* more than just a stray mutt dog I took in, but I'll be damned if I'm gonna cotton to your ever' little whim." He paused, continuing to look into Little Cork's eyes. "I can't treat you special . . . even if I wanted to. Somebody might see me sometime when I'm not looking. They might start asking questions about you—they might even find out where you came from—and I'll be damned if I'll let anybody come take you away from me and put you back in a cage. I'll be damned . . ."

Bruce turned and walked to the kitchen sink, where he rinsed out the water bowl and began to fill it. While he waited, he glanced out the window overlooking a small side yard and the tractor path leading up to the woods. Something caught his attention.

"What the heck is that?"

Bruce stretched over the sink to get as close to the window as possible. He tried to focus on a dark mound on the far side of the tractor path, some seventy-five feet away, but it was bathed in shadows not yet burnt away by the rising sun.

"Do you see that out there, Little Cork?" Bruce asked as he turned off the water and returned the bowl to the mat beside the refrigerator. "Do you see it?" he asked again as he walked out onto the porch and stood behind the dog to look out the screen door. Little Cork stood, looked up at Bruce, and barked. "Is that what you've been trying to tell me about all morning?" The dog barked again, as if to answer, then she jumped up to put her front paws on Bruce's leg. "And I suppose you want me to go out there and see what it is," he said, ruffling the dog's ears. Again, Little Cork barked and wagged her tail. "All right, if it'll make you happy."

Bruce took his straw hat off the pegboard beside the door and put it on. He pushed open the screen door and paused a moment, waiting for the dog to slip out ahead of him. When Little Cork didn't immediately scamper out into the yard, Bruce looked at her questioningly.

"What's the matter with you now?" Little Cork looked up at

him with big, round eyes and whimpered. "Oh, no, you don't. You brought it to my attention, so you're going to go out there with me to find out what it is." Bruce reached with his foot behind the dog and used his boot to scoot the puppy across the floor. "Out with you," he said as he pushed Little Cork out onto the back stoop.

"Come on," Bruce said as he descended the steps and started across the yard toward the dark mound. Little Cork watched him, whimpered, then hesitantly—cautiously—she followed a few steps behind him.

When Bruce reached the edge of the yard, he stopped short, wrinkling his nose in disgust and shaking his head. "Phew! Whatever it is, it sure stinks." He glanced up at the leaves on the old maple tree at the northernmost corner of the yard. They were motionless. "We're not downwind of it, so that thing's putting out a perty potent scent on its own for it to carry this far." Bruce looked back at the mound, which was beginning to take on a familiar shape. "But it wasn't here last night," he said as he took a few more steps toward the tractor path, "so it can't have been dead long enough to smell as bad as it does. No," he said, shaking his head, "something has to have drug it down here." He stopped a few feet from the carcass and was able to verify its identity. "But what, in heaven's name, is big enough to carry a full-grown buck deer all the way down here from the woods?"

Bruce studied the carcass for a few moments, then he looked up the tractor path toward the woods. He turned to his right to scan the pasture beyond the house and yard, then he turned back toward the open farmland to the west. After completing the quick survey of the area around him, his attention returned to the carcass. An uneasiness filtered through Bruce as he began to circle it, looking for tracks.

"I sure hope we don't have a dog pack on the loose," he mumbled to himself. He stopped opposite the deer's abdomen and concentrated on the viscera that had been pulled out onto the ground. "But that doesn't look like the work of a dog pack." Bruce picked up a stick and lifted a section of the small intestines, looking for a pattern of teeth marks. Inadvertently, he inhaled the scent of the dead animal. To his surprise, the aroma wasn't the same pungent stench that had attacked his senses at the edge of the yard. Frowning, he looked around. "Something's not right here—"

Little Cork barked in alarm.

"What is it, girl?" Bruce asked, looking up from the carcass. Little Cork stood at the far edge of the tractor path, her attention directed toward the equipment barn . . . no more than fifty feet away. "What is it?" Bruce asked again, taking a couple of steps around the carcass toward her. Little Cork looked at him, barked again, then focused on the barn and growled. Her lips pulled back from her teeth; the fur along her spine bristled. "What—"

A guttural howl echoed from the equipment barn. Bruce's eyes darted toward it; his heart thumped with unexpected fear.

For an instant, he stood as if frozen, then an inner sense told him that the worst place for him to be at that moment was standing out in the open . . . on the tractor path. "Come on, Little Cork," Bruce said as he started toward the yard. "Whatever it is, we'll leave it alone for the time being. Come on," he called again, hitting his hand against his thigh as a summons for her to follow, "let's get inside the house—"

Little Cork barked again . . . and again. With each bark, she retreated, but her eyes never wavered from the equipment barn.

Bruce quickened his pace when he reached the yard. He eyed the screen door some forty feet away and thought of the shotgun inside, mounted above it. He'd never used the gun for anything other than target practice, shooting plates and tin cans. He wondered if he could aim it at something living . . . and then pull the trigger—

Another howl escaped the confines of the equipment barn . . . followed by an unearthly scream . . . and then a cry . . .

Little Cork barked as she ran past Bruce. She stopped when she reached the steps below the screen door to turn and look back toward the equipment barn.

As Bruce ran toward the house, he watched her. She was barking viciously; her hackles were bristling. Her eyes were set on something . . . that had moved out of the barn . . . and was now moving across the yard.

Bruce wanted to look back—he wanted to see what was stalking him—but he didn't want to slow his pace, and he didn't want to take the chance he might trip and fall. He was old; his legs weren't as steady beneath him as they used to be.

Suddenly, Bruce was all but overpowered by a stagnant stench. Gasping for air, he concentrated on the three concrete steps at the base of the porch . . . on the screen door . . . on the doorknob. They were getting closer . . . closer.

A loud cry nearly deafened him.

Little Cork barked. She ran past him—away from the house—toward the attacker.

He was almost there . . . almost there—

*PAIN!*

Something—*four*—somethings sank into the top of his right shoulder and slid down his back, ripping through skin and muscle, scraping flesh from bone.

Bruce cried out in agony. He dropped his right shoulder, tried to turn away, tried to escape. He tripped; his knees buckled beneath him. Bruce fell . . . and he felt hot, stagnant breath cascade over him.

Little Cork barked and yipped and snapped and growled. Her challenge was answered by a deep, menacing cry.

Bruce sensed that, at least for the moment, he was no longer the prime focus of the attacker. Using the few precious seconds that had been given him, he crawled to the porch steps, pulled himself up to his feet, opened the screen door, and reached inside for the shotgun.

He turned, let the door close, then sat down on the steps and leaned back against the doorframe. Using his left hand, he raised the shotgun, let the barrel rest on his knee, then slid his finger against the trigger. As ready as he could be to defend himself, Bruce looked up and, for the first time, saw what had attacked him.

In all of the years he'd been a veterinarian, he'd never seen an animal that could even begin to compare to the prehistoric lizardlike creature that was no more than twenty feet from him. Anything like it would have been grotesque at any size, but this monstrosity stood well over seven feet tall . . . and Little Cork was doing her best to distract it. Relying more on bravery than common sense, the little dog was darting in and out, nipping at the creature's heels, keeping its attention diverted away from Bruce.

"Get away, Little Cork," Bruce shouted. "Come here!"

Apparently, the dog understood. She ran to Bruce, made a quick stop, and turned to sit down on the step beside him. She again concentrated on the creature and continued to bark.

It turned toward them, stared at them for a moment with green, cat-slit eyes, then opened its arms to a span of almost ten feet. As if to proclaim a victory, it tilted its head back and began to howl.

Bruce lifted his left knee, aimed the shotgun's barrel at the animal's scaly midsection, and fired. A smattering of buckshot pelted the creature's face, chest, and abdomen.

It cried out more from surprise than from pain and pawed at the air as if to fend off an attack by a swarm of savage bees.

Bruce fired the shotgun's second shell. The creature's reaction was the same, then it turned and ran off, in an awkward, three-legged gait, toward the equipment barn. For the time being, it appeared to have had enough.

Bruce released a heavy sigh as he leaned his head back against the screen door and closed his eyes. The shotgun slid off of his knee and out of his hand.

Little Cork whimpered, then nuzzled her nose beneath his hand. When he didn't respond by petting her, she pawed at his arm. But Bruce was unaware of any of it; his mind was already at work, cloaking itself against the pain. He didn't know he slumped over on the step, and he didn't feel Little Cork's warm wet tongue when she began to lick his wounds.

5:52 A.M.

"Turn it down."

Kerk looked at his mother, shrugged his shoulders, and shook his head. He couldn't understand what she was trying to say.

"I said, turn it down." Jackie reached across the counter and twisted the radio's volume control knob until it clicked. "Since you're on the phone, I would imagine it's a good idea just to turn it off until you're finished."

"I can do two things at once," Kerk protested, reaching to turn the radio back on.

"I can't," Jackie said, pulling the radio's plug out of the wall socket. "And right now, I'm working on preserving my sense of hearing."

"Oh, brother," Kerk said, rolling his eyes. "If this is going to be one of *those* kind of days for you, I'm glad I'm leaving." He directed his next statement into the mouthpiece of the phone. "I've never done it before, but today, I'm game for anything that'll get me outta the house." Kerk listened for a couple of seconds, then added, "Don't worry, I'll be ready and waiting. See you in a little while." Kerk hung up the phone and ran through the kitchen to the utility room.

"What about your breakfast?" Jackie asked as he whisked past her.

"I'll get it later if I have time," Kerk said as he pulled on a T-shirt over his head and then sat down on the floor to put on the old sneakers he'd rescued twice from the trash barrel.

"You're not wearing *those*, are you?" Jackie asked, eyeing the shoes she'd been unsuccessful at throwing away.

"They're still good," Kerk said, looking up at her, "besides, you wouldn't want me to get my good ones muddy, would you?"

"I guess not," she said, giving in to avoid a useless argument. "I just know that when I was your age, I wouldn't have been caught dead wearing something that looked that trashy."

"That was a *long* time ago," Kerk said with a grin, looking up at her with sparkling green eyes. "Times have changed since the dark ages. Today, it's in to wear holey clothes."

"What a fashion statement: the scruddier the better." Jackie chuckled to herself and shook her head. "Now, about your breakfast—"

"I said I'll get it later if I have time."

"It'll be cold later . . . and you *will* make time for breakfast," Jackie said firmly, looking at Kerk over her shoulder.

"I can heat it up in the microwave and take it with me if I have to."

"It won't be as good—"

"Mom," Kerk said in frustration, "you're making me waste time, and *you're* the one who said I had to get all my chores done before I could go fishing with Allen."

"Blaming me now, huh?" Kerk looked up at her with a frown. "And was I the one who also forgot to set your alarm clock so you could get up early enough to have plenty of time—"

A distant sound attracted Jackie's attention. She cocked her head to the side, concentrated and listened. A few seconds later, the same sound broke into the silence for a second time.

"That sounded like . . . gunshots," she said, looking at Kerk with a frown.

"It couldn't have been a gunshot. Nobody in his right mind would dare do any shooting within a hundred miles of this place," Kerk said as he got up off the floor. "It was probably just Bruce's old truck backfiring again." Kerk reached around Jackie and grabbed a piece of toast off the counter as he hurried toward the living room. "If Allen and his dad get here before I get back," he called over his shoulder, "tell them I'll be done in a few minutes."

"Don't slam—" But Kerk was already out the front door, the screen door banging closed behind him.

Jackie walked across the living room and stopped at the front window. Looking out, she watched Kerk run along the circular drive and saw him enter the feed barn. She smiled and shook her head, remembering how rambunctious she had been at his age. As she turned back toward the kitchen, something reflected in her eye, drawing her attention.

Bruce's old red truck was parked in front of his house on the far side of the drive, its glass catching the morning sun. Jackie studied it for a moment, then a questioning frown crossed her face. The truck wasn't running, and no one was anywhere near it; in fact, neither Bruce nor Fritz was anywhere to be seen. How, then, could the truck have backfired?

"Something doesn't make sense," Jackie said to herself as she walked to the phone to call Bruce.

The egg timer on the stove buzzed. Jackie hesitated, looked

at the phone, glanced out the window at the truck, then started for the kitchen. Whatever had caused the noise couldn't be that important; it could wait until after breakfast.

*5:56 A.M.*

An anxious frown consumed Barry's face as he looked from Leland to Lanny Underwood to the map on the wall behind his desk. He drummed his fingers nervously on the desktop. The phone was ringing . . . ringing . . . three . . . four . . . five times—

"Hello. You've reached the Whitewater River Valley Animal Refuge and Compound," the feminine voice on the answering machine began. "No one is available to take your call at the moment. If you will leave your name and number, someone will get back to you as soon as we can. Thank you."

Barry waited impatiently through a series of beeps and buzzes, then the line was clear, ready to record his message. "Pick up, Jackie. For God's sake, be there and pick up the phone." Without waiting for her to answer, he went directly into a message. "The instant you hear this, get Kerk and Bruce and anybody else who's out there at the compound with you and get out of there. Get out—"

"Barry?" Jackie finally answered a bit hesitantly. "Barry, is that you?"

"Jackie, get out of there," he stated bluntly.

"What's going on?"

"Don't waste time asking questions," he snapped. "Get everybody and get out of there."

"What's going on?" Jackie asked again. "You've got to tell me what's going on. I can't just pick up and leave without a good reason. I've got a responsibility—"

"Jackie, listen to me," Barry said, trying to maintain the last ounce of control he was on the verge of losing. "Dan may be on his way to the compound, and I'd just as soon you not be there until we have time to check it out."

"Dan? What makes you think—" The phone went dead.

"Jackie? Jackie!" Barry hammered the phone, and then his face paled to a ghostly white. He glanced at Leland and then at Underwood. "I think he's already there." Barry pushed the chair back from his desk and shot out of it, heading toward the elevator. "I've got to try to get out there to help her."

"How far is it?" Underwood called after him.

"A good forty to forty-five minute drive," Leland said.

"He'll never make it in time in a car," Underwood speculated. "Robbins," he called, following Barry to the elevator, "give me a minute to call the airport, and I'll have my helicopter pick us up here in the parking lot."

Barry didn't hesitate. He nodded at Underwood, then looked at Sheriff Joseph's secretary. "Joyce, make a general announcement for everyone in the building to move their car out of the back parking lot." Barry picked up a phone from a nearby desk and handed it to Underwood. "Make your call . . . and tell them to hurry."


5:58 A.M.


"Barry? Barry!" Jackie shouted into the mouthpiece. Barry didn't answer. Not a single sound came to her over the phone; it was dead. For a moment, she stared at the phone in disbelief then, almost in slow motion, she returned it to its cradle.

Was Dan on his way to the compound? . . .

Jackie turned sharply toward the front window and adjusted her seat on the sofa so she could look out. She focused on

Bruce's old red truck parked across the drive. Had it been a backfire? Or had it been gunshots?

. . . or was Dan already there?

A soundless gasp crossed Jackie's lips as she let her mind run wild in speculation. Her heart pounded savagely. An ominous shiver chilled her blood; a cold sweat oozed from her pores—

Kerk!

Her eyes snapped to the front entrance of the feed barn. Kerk! Where was he? Was he still in there? Or had he already started to go from barn to barn, scooping grain into the feeders and forking hay down from the lofts? Where was he . . . and how soon could she find him?

Jackie started for the front door, but stopped halfway across the living room. What if Dan *was* out there? If there was a confrontation between them, what could she do to protect herself and Kerk? There had to be something.

She turned back toward the heart of the room, looked at the rifle rack above the fireplace, then hurried toward it. Even if a bullet wouldn't kill Dan, maybe it could cause him enough discomfort to buy her the time to find Kerk and Bruce and find a way to get out of there.


"Don't tell Mom I'm short-changing you this morning," Kerk told the calves and ponies as he haphazardly dumped a scoop of grain in each of their feeder boxes. "I'll fork down your hay for you this afternoon when I get back, but I don't have time to do both now— Say, that's what I'll do," Kerk said to himself as he continued working his way from stall to stall, moving toward the back door. "I'll hand out the grain until this cartful runs out, and I'll just give the rest of them hay. Then, after I get back this afternoon, I can sneak out here and finish up what I didn't get done this morning." He smiled broadly, thinking his idea clever, then he contemplated the grain remaining in the cart. "It's a lot faster to toss down hay from the loft than it is to scoop out grain . . . and Mom'll never know the difference." Kerk looked over his shoulder toward the front door to make sure no one was watching him, then he pushed the feed cart into an empty stall near the back of the barn.

"Kerk?" Jackie called out in a loud whisper as she peeked around the doorframe into the feed barn. When he didn't answer her, she stepped fully into the doorway and scanned the interior. She didn't see Kerk, but she noted the lids were askew on the feed barrels and the feed cart was gone. "Kerk?" she called again, doubting if she would receive an answer and yet hoping—

A board creaked in the loft overhead.

Jackie pulled back, pressing her back hard against the inside wall, and raised the rifle. "Kerk, are you up there?" Her eyes traveled slowly along the loft's overhang, watching . . . waiting. Nothing looked over the edge at her; no one responded to her summons; all was silent.

Jackie sidestepped toward the door. When she stepped outside, she immediately turned so that her back was to the barn's exterior wall. Her eyes darted from the first livestock barn to Bruce's house to the red truck, then she made a sweeping survey of the oval drive, the ducks swimming lazily on the pond and the pasture that lay beyond.

Off in the distance, the pygmy goats were grazing nonchalantly; newborns frolicked. Arthur, the old billy, lay lazily beneath a tree, tolerating the antics of his latest offspring. Everything looked so peaceful. How could anything be wrong?

One of Bruce's mustangs whinnied.

Jackie jerked her head around; her eyes moved quickly

between the entrances to the four barns fronting the drive. "Where are you, Kerk?" she asked barely loud enough for her own ears to hear. Holding the rifle leveled in front of her, she started toward the first livestock barn.

When Jackie reached the open front door, she hesitated before leaning around the corner and peeking inside. An intermittent trail of grain, scattered along the hard-packed dirt floor, indicated Kerk had already been there.

Jackie glanced at the hay feeder on the wall of the first stall. It was empty. She turned her attention to the loft. By all rights, Kerk should be up there, breaking up bales of hay to toss down into the feeders.

"Kerk," she whispered as she walked to the loft's nearest ladder and looked up. "Kerk," she repeated in a normal tone, concentrating on the loft's edge . . . waiting. She didn't receive a reply.

A horse whinnied in the next barn, and it sounded as if the animal was kicking in its stall. But why? The mustangs had readily accepted their new home—unless something had frightened it. If the horse sensed something was going to harm it, it might try to find a way out—

Jackie stepped back outside and scanned the fronts of the remaining buildings. The equipment barn was at the far end; there was no reason for Kerk to be in there. Logic told her he had to be in one of the middle two barns. But which one? And how long was it going to take to find him?


Kerk stepped from the top rung of the ladder into the loft. He pulled a pitchfork out of a bale of hay beside the ladder and began working from the front of the barn to the back. He hurried along the edge, forking loose hay into the feeders set just beyond the overhang. When he reached the back of the barn and started down the ladder there, he hesitated and looked across the loft with a questioning frown, accepting a fact he'd been trying to ignore the whole time he'd been up there. Something didn't smell right. Something downright stunk!

"Something's died up here," he said with a curl of his lip. He looked past the broken bales of hay to the stacks piled clear to the rafters along the side wall. The loft was a perfect place for wild animals to make nests and dens, but not everything born in the barn always survived. "I'll have to tell Bruce—"

A piercing howl filled the loft. A half-dozen bales of hay suddenly flew toward the overhang; one bale hit Kerk on the right shoulder and side and knocked him from the ladder. He landed on the barn's hard dirt floor, shaken but conscious.

A primitive scream rained down over him. Kerk looked up to see a scale-covered claw reach over the edge of the overhang—

A rifle shot split through the scream.

Muscle and skin, tissue and bone . . . blood exploded from the back of the menacing hand. The scream changed to a cry of agony, and the hand retreated back into the loft.

"Mom!" Kerk called out, looking toward the front of the barn and seeing her only as a silhouette against the rising sun.

Jackie ran to him and knelt at his side. "Are you okay?" she asked, looking first at his arms and then at his legs.

"I think so."

"Can you get up?" she asked as she stood and took a hold of his upper arm.

"I think so— What . . . what was that?" Kerk asked, looking up at the loft as he worked his way to his feet.

"It's Dan."

"What?" Kerk looked at her in disbelief.

"I'll explain later. Right now, we have to get out of here—"

Another earsplitting cry filled the barn. Jackie and Kerk

looked up at the edge of the loft to see large, emerald-green cat eyes staring down at them from behind a broad, saber-toothed grin.

"Go out the back way," Jackie shouted, giving Kerk a shove toward the door. She glanced back up at the loft, then followed close behind him. "We'll circle around and go to Bruce's."

They ran out the door and along the barn's back wall. When they came to the ten-foot space between the last livestock barn and the equipment barn, they hesitated and peeked around the corner. To their dismay, the creature was looking back at them from the opposite end of the building, waving a multijointed arm that looked to have two hands.

"What are we gonna do?" Kerk asked as they pulled back behind the cover of the barn's corner.

Jackie shook her head. "I don't know. Got any ideas?"

Kerk looked around and, seeing nothing to use as a weapon, shook his head. "I can go back in the barn and get the pitchfork."

"It won't do any good," Jackie said. "You can't hurt him. You saw where I shot him in the hand. It already looks like he's started to grow another one. Our best chance is to find a way out of here—"

"J-a-a-a-c-k-e-e-e," a deep, raspy voice called.

Kerk's eyes widened, and he looked up at his mother. "Was that . . . *him?*"

Jackie nodded. "I think so."

Kerk stuck his head around the corner of the barn and shouted, "Go away and leave us alone, you ugly son of a—"

Jackie grabbed Kerk's arm and pulled him toward her. "That's not going to help us. If anything, it'll probably just make him madder." She looked past Kerk and focused on the far corner of the equipment barn. "We've got to think of a way to get around him so we can get to Bruce's."

"But he's so big. What can we do?" Kerk asked, looking

up at his mother with eyes that betrayed the fear he could no longer hide.

"I don't know—"

"J-a-a-a-c-k-e-e-e, I'-m c-o-m-i-n-g f-o-r y-o-u."

"Listen to me," Jackie said, turning Kerk toward her. "I'll try to keep him busy here, and you see if you can sneak around the equipment barn and go get Bruce. The two of you get in the truck and drive around here, and I'll—"

"I can't leave you—"

"J-a-a-a-c-k-e-e-e, I'-m h-e-r-e."

Jackie turned toward the barn door behind her and raised the rifle. As if cued, the creature stepped out into the open and slowly rotated toward her with opened arms. An ominous grin enveloped his scale-covered face and sparkled in his emerald eyes.

"Kerk, run!" she shouted.

"But, Mom—"

"I said, run!"

Kerk hesitated for only a moment, then he took off on a dead run toward the equipment barn. He stumbled once—twice—over sun-hardened tractor ruts and almost fell, but he managed to keep his balance and clear the back of the barn.

As he rounded the building's far corner, he heard three consecutive gunshots and stopped to look back. Even though the .22 caliber bullets had hit the creature point-blank in the chest, they didn't stop him—he didn't even appear to be fazed by them—he continued moving toward Jackie, walking almost leisurely.

"I've got to get help," Kerk said to himself. As he turned to run along the equipment barn to Bruce's, he bumped squarely into the end of the ammonia tank. He sidestepped and started to go around it, but he stopped to contemplate the tank. The gauge indicated the pressure was still partially up, and Kerk knew from past experience that there was always a residue of ammonia in the bottom of the tank even when it showed empty. Maybe . . . maybe there was enough. He reached for the hose.

Jackie shot three . . . four . . . five more times. In desperation—possibly lulled by shock—she continued to pull the trigger even after the rifle was empty. The creature laughed in response to each futile click.

"N-o-w y-o-u a-r-e m-i-n-e," Dan bellowed, the words barely able to escape his cavernous mouth. They were distorted by rows and rows of spiky-needle teeth and layer upon layer of knobby scar tissue that had totally consumed his lips.

With nothing else left for her defense, Jackie threw the rifle at him. It bounced off his shoulder with little notice. The creature laughed and laughed and laughed—

"Laugh at this, you ugly bastard," Kerk shouted as he stepped out from behind the corner of the equipment barn and aimed the ammonia tank's access hose at the creature.

Jackie turned toward Kerk, glanced at the hose in his hands, and immediately knew what he planned to do. She made brief eye contact with her son, then ran behind him. Once Jackie was safe, Kerk opened the valve.

A milky-white liquid dripped and sputtered from the end of the nozzle, then, as air cleared the line, it began to sprinkle . . . to spray . . . and, even though the pressure was low, it finally began to stream. Kerk took a couple of calculated steps forward and aimed the liquid ammonia so it hit high on the creature's chest.

A cry of pain escaped the creature's contorted mouth. He lifted his arms in front of him to protect himself from the cold—from the ammonia's *burning* cold—then he immediately turned his back against the spray. Still, he found no relief.

The ammonia continued to shower over him. Everywhere it touched, it burned . . . and burned, seeping deep down between the scales on his skin—down *into* his skin.

Almost instantly, the area bordering the ammonia-burn wounds began to regenerate. New skin formed to replace the old... to cover the wounds... sealing the ammonia in beneath his skin so that it burned—continued to burn on the inside as well as out.

Enraged by his agony, the creature turned on Kerk. Bellowing, it started toward him.

Kerk's heart bolted, and he wanted to run, but he stood his ground. He aimed the hose high... and well. Ammonia splattered the creature's face... entered its mouth... and its nose.

Flesh was immediately burned and destroyed; flesh was immediately renewed and regenerated. Burned... destroyed. Renewed... regenerated. The process repeated itself over and over; it was multiplied tenfold... a hundred... a thousand.

Writhing in pain, the creature stumbled, grabbing for its throat. It began clawing at the leathery flesh on its face and neck. Suffering, it threw back its head and tried to scream... to howl... to cry out, but a thin wisp of pungent air was all that passed over its scarred lips.

Rocking unstably and staggering on its three legs, it turned back toward Jackie and Kerk. They immediately saw the reason for its distress. In the process of regeneration, its mouth and nose had sealed over. There was no way for the creature to breathe.

Bruce and Little Cork rounded the corner of the barn behind them. "Get back. I'll kill it," Bruce said, stopping beside Jackie and leveling his shotgun to take aim.

"No," Jackie said in a soft voice, "let him be," she added, laying her hand on top of the double barrels and directing the gun toward the ground. "He's suffered enough."

The creature dropped to its knees and toppled over onto the ground in front of them. Scraping its hands over its throat, a long claw finally ripped through the leathery skin and punctured its windpipe. For a matter of moments, it found relief, gulping in deep breaths through the makeshift airway, then the flesh around the wound began to regenerate . . . and the opening began to close.

"N-o-o-o . . ." the creature cried out. Clawing frantically at its throat, it managed to gouge out another makeshift airway . . . only to have it close again.

Another airway open . . . closed.

Another airway open . . . closed.

The creature continued to rip into its throat until the regenerated scar tissue was layered far too deeply even for its talonlike claws to penetrate. It had taken its last breath.

Succumbing to its fate, the creature rolled over onto its back and looked up at Jackie. A pathetic longing came to its emerald-green eyes as it lifted a clawed hand out to her.

Jackie looked at the hand, held palm up, wavering, its claws and scaly skin glistening with its own blood. She hesitated, then crossed the short distance between them and knelt beside the creature, taking its clawed hand into her own.

Their eyes met; tears shimmered in both. Jackie forced a smile. The creature squeezed her hand gently. Without a word passing between them, both sensed a peace—

The creature suddenly jerked violently and began to convulse. Its muscles went into spasms, and the grip it held on Jackie's right hand suddenly felt like a vise. Overwhelmed by the pain, she hardly noticed the claws pierced the skin on the back of her hand.

"Get away from it!" Bruce shouted. Little Cork barked frantically in reinforcement.

"I can't," Jackie said, grasping her wrist with her free hand and trying to pull herself free.

"Maybe the two of us . . ." Bruce reached around Jackie and took hold of her lower arm as well. Together they pulled . . .

and slowly, her hand slipped free from the death grip.

"I think it was just a muscle reflex," Bruce said as he helped Jackie to her feet.

"I know. Even after everything that happened, I'd like to think Dan never really intended to hurt me," she said, looking down at the lifeless body.

She focused on him for a few moments . . . on his arms and legs . . . on his scaly, leathery skin. She looked at his eyes . . . at his haunted, emerald-green eyes . . . that now stared vacantly, no longer transmitting the essence of life. She looked at the fresh scar tissue bulging along his throat, and she looked at the blood-covered hand that had held onto her tightly until the end. The end. At last, the nightmare was over.

"Rest in peace, Dan," she whispered.

A car horn broke into the silence surrounding them.

"That's gotta be Allen," Kerk said excitedly. "He'll never believe what's happened." He took off running between the barns toward the drive.

"Did you say . . . Dan?" Bruce asked, stepping in closer to focus his attention on the body.

"It's a long story," Jackie said. She looked at Bruce and noticed the rips on the shoulder of his shirt . . . and the section of plaid pattern on his back that had been obliterated by blood. "What happened to you?" she asked with a start, carefully lifting an edge of the torn fabric so as not to hurt him. She looked at the skin on his shoulder and upper back and saw only minor scratches. There were no wounds that would indicate the amount of blood he'd apparently lost.

Bruce chuckled and glanced down at Little Cork. "I guess you could say that's a long story too—"

"Oh, no," Jackie gasped.

"What's the matter?" Bruce asked.

As Bruce turned toward her, Jackie's right hand trailed down from his shoulder. She watched it in silence; she stood motionless, staring at the skin on the back of her hand.

"What is it?" Bruce asked again, looking at Jackie's hand but not knowing what he was seeing.

"Dan . . . Dan scratched me." Her voice trembled. Fear played through her as she focused on the four parallel scratches running from her wrist to her knuckles.

"It doesn't look too bad. We'll get you inside and put some antiseptic on it, and it'll be right as rain."

"But the blood—Dan's blood." Jackie looked up at Bruce, her eyes cloaked in sheer terror. "It was on his hands—on his claws—when he scratched me!"

"A little antiseptic will—"

"No! No, it won't!" Jackie felt an unusual tingling vibrate along the edge of the scratches. "I can feel it. It's already started. Look!"

Jackie pointed at one of the scratches on the back of her hand. It was beginning to heal, and a noticeable line of scar tissue was building along its edge.

"Nooo." Tears welled in Jackie's eyes. Her knees grew weak, and she leaned against Bruce for support. "I don't want to end up like Dan." Her legs folded beneath her, and Bruce eased her onto the ground. He sat down beside her and slipped an arm around her shoulders.

"We'll figure out something," Bruce said.

"There's nothing to figure out," Jackie countered. "There's no way to stop it." She continued to watch the scratch on her hand heal . . . and the ridge of scar tissue grow.

Bruce hugged Jackie close to him and bit at his lower lip in an attempt to hold back his own tears. He felt helpless.

"Dear God in Heaven," he whispered, looking up at the rays streaking across the morning sky, "there must be something—"

Little Cork barked.

Bruce looked at the dog, sitting a few feet away, its tail

343

wagging and tongue hanging out. After a moment, Bruce glanced at the leg he'd cut with the chain saw, then lifted a hand to touch the shoulder where the creature had grabbed him. "Can you really work miracles?" he questioned softly, looking into the dog's dark eyes. "Come here, Little Cork," Bruce called. The puppy immediately bounded toward him. "Here." Bruce picked up Jackie's hand and opened it across his leg. "Here, girl—"

"What are you doing?" Jackie asked, withdrawing her hand.

"Give her a chance." Bruce took Jackie's hand in his and extended it toward the puppy. "Here, girl, like you did for me." Little Cork nosed Jackie's hand. "Go on, girl. Lick it."

The dog sniffed Jackie's scent, wagged its tail, then began to gently lick the scratches on the back of Jackie's hand. Jackie and Bruce watched Little Cork in silence, Jackie not understanding, Bruce hoping—

A helicopter barely cleared the barn roof, then circled before setting down in the pasture to the west of them. As soon as the runners touched the ground, the doors opened and three men jumped out. Jackie recognized Barry and Leland as they ran toward her; the third man was a stranger.

Startled by the commotion, Little Cork ran behind Bruce and nosed her way under Jackie's arm. "Afraid of helicopters?" Jackie asked, ruffling Little Cork's ears, then she saw the back of her hand . . . and the scratches that had all but disappeared. A gasp crossed her lips, then she looked at Bruce. "How?"

"I don't know," he answered, "but for the time being, I think it's something we should keep to ourselves."


*8:45 A.M.*

"I tried to stop him," Rusty Snider said regretfully. He

stood with Jackie, Barry, and Bruce, watching as two ambulance attendants and four policemen strained to lift Dan's cumbersome, sheet-draped body onto a stretcher.

"I doubt if there was anything anyone could have done to stop him," Jackie said. "For as long as I've known Dan, he's always had a mind of his own. Once he got it set on something, there was no changing it."

"You should know," Rusty said, looking at her. "I'm sorry for everything he put you through over the years." He glanced at Barry and Bruce. "For everything," he emphasized.

"At least it's all over now," Jackie said softly.

Rusty looked at Jackie, hesitated, then nodded and turned away. He took a couple of steps and started to follow the stretcher to the ambulance, but he hesitated again and turned back around.

"I could leave now and never see you again," he said, his green eyes searching out Jackie's, "but if I did that, then I wouldn't be any more of a human being than Dan was." Puzzled by Rusty's statement, Jackie looked at him in silence and waited patiently for him to continue. "There's something you need to know." He hesitated. "There's . . . something I *have* to tell you."

Rusty reached into the inside pocket of his jacket and pulled out a business-size envelope. He held the envelope in front of him with both hands and stared at it for a few moments before looking at Jackie.

"Dan's father was a good man," Rusty began slowly, "but he wasn't always up front about everything he did. Like anyone, he *did* have his secrets." Rusty glanced at the envelope. "He was awful good to me—and to your Richard—when we were both boys."

"Richard told me," Jackie said.

"Well, he didn't take a liking to Richard and me just because . . . because we . . . well, just because we were . . . illegitimate kids off the street he felt sorry for." Rusty took in a deep breath and swallowed hard. "We . . . we were . . . we were *his* illegitimate kids."

Jackie felt a sudden rush course through her—as if someone's wandering soul might have actually passed *through* her body on its journey to the afterlife. She felt dizzy . . . lightheaded, and if she'd not been focusing so intently on Rusty's eyes . . . Dan's eyes . . . Richard's eyes . . . Kerk's eyes—*green eyes* . . . Everything began to fall into place.

"You should read this." Rusty's fingers tightened on the envelope—almost as if he didn't want to give it up—then he handed it to Jackie. "Look it over when you have the time," he said. "It might be a little hard to read in places. I had to tape it back together after Dan tore it up."

Jackie glanced at the envelope as she took it in her hand, then she looked up at Rusty. "How long have you known?" she asked.

"Sometimes, it seems like forever."

Rusty turned and looked toward the ambulance. Silently, he watched as the attendants loaded Dan's body. "I guess I'd better go with him. I've looked out for him all of these years, and I guess I need to look out for him a little while longer yet." He glanced at Jackie. A frown was etched on her face; she didn't understand what he meant by his last statement.

"Why, just look at those two," Rusty explained, nodding at Wagner and Underwood. Neither had let more than a few feet come between them and the body since they'd arrived. "They'd both probably sign over their souls for the chance to do an autopsy on him and run a thousand tests, but they're both going to be out of luck. Nobody's going to cut into Dan. I'm going to have him cremated as soon as possible."

"I imagine Underwood will fight you on that," Barry said.

"The fight won't last long," Rusty countered. "I've got all the money I need to do whatever I want." He glanced at Jackie. "And now, so do you." Rusty turned and walked away.

Jackie watched Rusty until he stopped beside the ambulance, then she turned toward Bruce. "You knew," she said. "You knew the three of them were brothers. That was the secret you kept for Dan's father all these years."

Bruce pretended to direct his attention to Leland Wagner, watching him walk toward them, but he slyly looked at Jackie out of the corner of his eye and grinned. "I'm good at keeping a secret," he whispered. "How about you—"

"Mrs. Mitchell," Leland said as he stopped in front of her. "I was wanting to talk to you about the dog you had with you when we first arrived." Jackie stiffened, and she shot a glance toward Bruce. "I only caught a glimpse of it before I became involved looking at Dan and talking to Lanny Underwood. Where is the dog now? I'd like to have a closer look at it—"

"The pup's mine," Bruce intervened. "Barry," he said, "Jackie's had a pretty long morning. Why don't you take her on into the house and get a pot of coffee going while I finish up with things out here."

Barry looked from Bruce to Jackie . . . and saw a hint of panic in her eyes. He sensed something was going on—something of which he was totally unaware—something he was sure he would learn about later. He decided to play along.

"That sounds like a good idea to me," Barry said as he slipped an arm around Jackie's shoulders and guided her toward the house.

Jackie took a couple of steps, then hesitated in front of Bruce and touched him lightly on the arm. Her eyes momentarily locked with his.

"Go on," Bruce said, taking Jackie's hand in his. He looked down at the healed scratches on the back of her hand long enough for her to notice, then he placed his free hand over hers and squeezed it gently. "Go on in the house, and I'll take care of all the loose ends out here." Jackie glanced from Bruce to Leland and back at Bruce, then she gave in to Barry's persuasion and started walking toward the house.

"About your dog," Leland repeated, scanning the immediate area.

"What about her?" Bruce asked somewhat aggressively, crossing his arms over his chest.

"Where is she? I'd like to take a closer look at her. She looks an awful lot like one of the dogs that was stolen from my lab last week."

"She's not your dog, so there's no use wasting your time looking at her."

"How can you be so sure she's not mine—"

"I know the dog," Bruce said bluntly, "and I know she's not yours." Bruce stood his ground, his eyes momentarily locked with Leland's, then he turned and walked to the far corner of the equipment barn.

While he stalled for time—to think up a background story for Little Cork—he picked up the nozzled end of the hose off the ground and carefully returned it to the rack on the ammonia tank. When the hose was secured in place, he took a few more moments to see that the valves were tight and to recheck the gauges.

"She's just a mutt dog," Bruce finally said. He hesitated, then looked at Leland. "She was born on the compound and . . . and named after her mother who's buried up yonder on the hill. She's just a mutt dog," he repeated. "There's nothing special about her."

As if cued, at that moment, Little Cork stuck her head around the barn door and whined. Bruce looked at her and felt his heart skip a beat. He knew it would have been easier to convince Wagner that the dog was his if she were not around to be scrutinized. Now that she had come on the scene, Bruce knew the only thing he could do was to play up their relationship and hope Wagner would accept it as genuine.

"Little Cork, come here." Bruce whistled for her, then patted his thigh as an additional indication for her to come to him. The puppy barked in response and pranced up to his side, her head held high and her tail wagging briskly.

Looking down into Little Cork's big brown eyes, Bruce again thought of Corky. He remembered a seemingly insignificant trick they had shared many times, when his old dog had been young.

Was there even the slightest hope that Little Cork trusted him enough to do the trick? If she didn't, it would be an all-but-certain indication she, indeed, wasn't his. Should he chance it?

"Little Cork," Bruce said, turning to face her squarely. "Little Cork"—he held out a finger as if he were pointing at her—"pay attention." To his surprise, the dog sat down on her haunches, looked up at him, and barked.

A tingle raced through Bruce, and he smiled. So far, so good.

"Little Cork"—Bruce patted his chest with both hands, then opened his arms wide—"up."

The dog just sat there, looking up at him.

"Up, Little Cork," Bruce repeated, again patting his chest and opening his arms. "Up. Come up."

Little Cork stood and barked.

"Come on, girl. Up. Up here."

Little Cork barked again, and then she began to turn around in tight circles.

"Up. Up." Bruce patted his chest. "Little Cork, up—"

Little Cork pushed off the ground and jumped straight up in the air. Bruce reacted quickly; he reached out for her, caught her and pulled her into his arms.

"Good girl, Little Cork. Good girl." The dog barked,

squirmed in his arms, wagged her tail, and stretched up over his shoulder to lick his ear. "Good girl," Bruce whispered, rubbing her briskly on the scruff of her neck, "you did it.

"There's proof enough she's my dog," Bruce said, looking at Wagner. "Not a whole lot of dogs will trust you to catch them without a lot of training. I can't think of too many that would do it in less than a month . . . and your dog's only been gone what . . . a week? Yes sir, as you can see, she's *my* dog," Bruce repeated. He smiled broadly, ruffled Little Cork's ears, then set her on the ground.

"Good day, Dr. Wagner. I think Little Cork and I are both past due for our breakfast."

Leland watched as Bruce walked away, Little Cork staying close to his side. He knew he'd been lied to; he knew the dog was his. But what good would it do to protest? He had no proof to counter Bruce's claim.

Leland shook his head. Bruce was probably right anyway; the dog was just a mutt. More than likely, there was nothing special about her—just as there had been nothing special to come out of the experiments he'd been conducting for the past twenty years. Maybe this was a sign that it was time to let it be.

Leland glanced at the ambulance . . . glanced at Bruce and the brown and beige dog, then he turned toward the helicopter. As he walked across the pasture, he thought about the long night and morning behind him. He was exhausted; he was looking forward to a peaceful ride home.

A large shadow glided over the ground ahead of him. Leland stopped and looked skyward and had to shade his eyes against the sun as he turned to watch a hawk soar overhead. The bird was beautiful—majestic.

It must have been returning to its nest after a morning hunt. It held a lifeless gray rabbit beneath it, clutched in its talons— in the talons of its . . . *three* . . . feet.

Leland blinked several times, then tried to refocus on the

hawk, but it was already beyond his range of vision. Had he actually seen the hawk as he'd imagined . . . or had the angle of the sun and the shadows cast by the dangling rabbit merely played a trick on him?

Leland looked off toward the woods . . . and wondered, but he wasn't sure if he really wanted to know. . . .

## *YOU'D BETTER SLEEP WITH THE LIGHTS TURNED ON!*
## *BONE CHILLING HORROR BY*

## **RUBY JEAN JENSEN**

| | |
|---|---|
| ANNABELLE | (2011-2, $3.95/$4.95) |
| BABY DOLLY | (3598-5, $4.99/$5.99) |
| CELIA | (3446-6, $4.50/$5.50) |
| CHAIN LETTER | (2162-3, $3.95/$4.95) |
| DEATH STONE | (2785-0, $3.95/$4.95) |
| HOUSE OF ILLUSIONS | (2324-3, $4.95/$5.95) |
| LOST AND FOUND | (3040-1, $3.95/$4.95) |
| MAMA | (2950-0, $3.95/$4.95) |
| PENDULUM | (2621-8, $3.95/$4.95) |
| VAMPIRE CHILD | (2867-9, $3.95/$4.95) |
| VICTORIA | (3235-8, $4.50/$5.50) |

*Available wherever paperbacks are sold, or order direct from the Publisher. Send cover price plus 50¢ per copy for mailing and handling to Zebra Books, Dept. 4034, 475 Park Avenue South, New York, N.Y. 10016. Residents of New York and Tennessee must include sales tax. DO NOT SEND CASH. For a free Zebra/Pinnacle catalog please write to the above address.*